John Sherlock was born and raised in Lancashire. He wrote *The Ordeal of Major Grigsby* (Book Society Choice) which was made into the film *The Last Grenade*. Mr Sherlock currently maintains homes both in Europe and in America.

David Westheimer is the author of *Von Ryan's Express* which was produced as a film starring Frank Sinatra. He lives in Los Angeles.

D1419170

Also by John Sherlock

The Ordeal of Major Grigsby (*The Last Grenade*)

Also by David Westheimer

JOHN SHERLOCK AND
DAVID WESTHEIMER

The Most Dangerous
Gamble

GRANADA
London Toronto Sydney New York

Published in paperback by Granada Publishing Limited 1983

ISBN 0 586 05423 5

First published in Great Britain by
Granada Publishing in 1982
Copyright © John Sherlock and David Westheimer 1982

Granada Publishing Limited
Frogmore, St Albans, Herts AL2 2NF
and
36 Golden Square, London W1R 4AH
515 Madison Avenue, New York, NY 10022, USA
117 York Street, Sydney, NSW 2000, Australia
60 International Blvd, Rexdale, Ontario, R9W 6J2, Canada
61 Beach Road, Auckland, New Zealand

Printed and bound in Great Britain by
Cox & Wyman Ltd, Reading
Set in Times

Granada ®
Granada Publishing ®

For Peter Sherlock with fondest love
and
Dody

Authors' Note

The central theme of this story was inspired by events which actually took place in the summer of 1940. When the fall of France suddenly threatened Great Britain with imminent invasion, the Prime Minister, Winston Churchill, initiated a course of action which, if only for the incredible risk involved, must rank as one of history's greatest gambles. The exploit, originated and successfully executed without the issuance of a single written order, was one of the highest-priority secrets of the Second World War. It involved no less than gathering up and shipping to Canada Britain's gold reserves.

Those of you who are students of that period will be aware of these events in the sequence in which they really happened and will therefore be able to testify that the novel you are about to read is purely fiction. The authors wish to go a step further by stating that even where characters are named by rank, such as the Director of Naval Intelligence, or where members of various military and civilian groups are named, absolutely no connection is intended with the distinguished gentlemen who actually held those positions at the time of which we write. None of the people or situations in this story is based on facts or on the personalities and experience of anybody, alive or dead.

Chapter One

The horror began at ten minutes past eight on the night of
7 September 1940, when two hundred and fifty German
bombers, guided to their targets by huge riverside fires
from an earlier daylight attack, rained a near solid sheet of
high explosives and incendiary bombs on the heart of an
already agonized London. During the torturous hours that
followed, the menacing throb of Heinkels and JU 86s filled
a night sky pierced by the nervous beams of searchlights,
while the echo of exploding bomb-loads blended with the
sharper crack of ack-ack guns to form a weird cacophony
of sound which those who heard it would never forget.

Just before ten o'clock the air raid eased up as the planes
that had carried out the initial attack turned for home. No
all-clear sounded because another wave of German planes
had already been reported coming in from the east, but
there was a lull. Kensington Road, so chaotic earlier in the
evening as Londoners scrambled to find sanctuary in the
labyrinth of subway tunnels deep under the city, was
empty except for bell-ringing ambulances and fire engines
and an occasional straggler stubbornly determined to get
home to his family despite the patter of hot shrapnel still
falling from flak bursting in angry red blotches high above
the blacked-out city.

The solitary figure at the kerb before the Kensington
Palace Hotel seemed oblivious both to the eerie emptiness
and the fury of unequal battle between earth and sky. His
cap, with its garlanded visor, sat squarely on his greying
head. The carefully tended hands clasped loosely behind
his straight back did not even tighten as a delayed-action
bomb exploded further up the street, sending out a hot,

acrid blast. The cuffs of his superbly tailored uniform bore the four undulating stripes of a captain in the 'Wavy Navy', the Royal Naval Volunteer Reserve.

When a black Humber staff car crept towards him from Kensington Road, its dimmed-out headlamps tentative slits in the night, he picked up the attaché case at his feet with an unhurried motion and stepped forward. The driver, an attractive blonde-haired girl wearing the uniform of the Women's Royal Naval Service, got out quickly and left the engine running.

'Captain Penrose?' she asked.

When he nodded she saluted and reached for the attaché case. Her hand was trembling slightly.

'I can manage,' he said, his voice calm and reassuring. 'Thank you,' he added as she held the door open.

He settled comfortably into the back seat as the Wren turned the staff car east on Kensington Road, the direction from which it had come.

'Jerry's busy tonight, isn't he, sir?' she said, trying to hide her nervousness in conversation. 'They say mobs have broken into the Savoy looking for shelter.'

Before he could answer, a policeman at the junction of Brompton Road and Sloane Street waved them to a stop and checked their papers. Satisfied, he touched his helmet and motioned them on. Ambulances and private cars were unloading casualties at St George's Hospital. The sight of them made Penrose grateful that his wife Nellie and daughter Meg were at home in Epsom, far enough from the centre of London to be out of the worst of the bombing. The daylight bombing had been still under way when the message in his attaché case was delivered to him by hand but the holocaust had been remote enough for him to give his roses a final inspection before departing for the meeting to which he had been summoned in the city.

*   *   *

Instead of waiting for the evening train to Glasgow he
had taken a room at the Kensington Palace. It was his
custom not to make reservations at one of the more
fashionable hotels because he knew they were favoured by
those who sailed with him as first-class passengers when he
was the master of luxury liners plying between
Southampton and New York. He preferred that they
remember him as captain of the *Empress*, the finest vessel
of its kind afloat. At Brown's or Claridge's, both of which
he could well afford, he was merely another guest.

The message from the DNI still puzzled him. Preparations
for the departure of the *Amindra*, his wartime command,
had already been completed. All that remained to be done
was to finish loading passengers and cargo. There would
be the customary briefing from the Naval Control Service
Officer, of course, but that was scheduled to take place at
Greenock. What need was there for a meeting with the
Director of Naval Intelligence in London? At such an
hour, at the Office of Public Works, and one listed as
'top secret'?

'Enough to make the old girl turn in her grave, isn't it,
sir?' the Wren said, breaking into his musings as she
guided the Humber past the monument to Queen Victoria,
rose-tinted by the reflected glow of fires burning
throughout the city.

He saw her glance in the rear-view mirror and gave her
the expected smile.

She stopped the car in front of the desolate, grimy old
Office of Public Works across from St James's Park. It

seemed a strange site for a midnight briefing.

'Shall I wait, sir?' she asked, holding the door open for him.

He shook his head. 'Better find yourself a safe place to shelter from this lot,' he said, looking up at a night sky still laced with searchlights. 'My guess is we're in for a long night.'

'Thank you, sir,' she said gratefully, bringing her arm up in a smart salute.

Not much older than Meg, Penrose thought, to whom he had said goodbye just a few hours earlier and who was now no doubt safely in bed. And younger than his daughter Alice, who had already made him a grandfather long before he was prepared to accept that symbol of advancing years.

He returned the salute and watched her drive off into the darkness. A child playing at war. But he felt he was only playing at war himself. After years of commanding the most luxurious passenger liner afloat he had been assigned a new and lesser role: master of a plodding cargo vessel designed to carry butter and lambs' carcasses.

He put on his glasses and flicked on his cigarette lighter to see the time. Ten-fifty P.M. Ten minutes early. He looked into the thundering sky, still speckled with the flashes of bursting flak. Towards Westminster Abbey and the Thames a barrage balloon turned silver in the cold, hard beam of a probing searchlight. He went slowly up the stone steps of the seemingly deserted building. It was, as far as he knew, only a depository for outdated government documents. His footsteps echoed in the empty foyer. He was looking at his watch again when a slit in the wall, scarcely larger than a letter drop, abruptly spilled a narrow band of light. Moments later a door swung open and two Royal Marine guards motioned him forward with their tommy-guns.

'Tally, please sir,' said the taller of the two.

Penrose produced his identity card and the flimsy from the DNI. The second Marine inspected both him and his papers intently before admitting him to the presence of an armed Grenadier Guard stationed on a small landing. Reading directly from Penrose's identity card and flimsy, the guardsman spoke briefly in low tones into a wall phone and, satisfied the captain was expected, returned the documents. He opened a green-painted metal door, thick as armour plate.

'If you'll follow me, sir,' he said, and without a backward glance led Penrose down a steep spiral staircase.

As far as Penrose could estimate it corkscrewed down at least two hundred feet. 'The Hole in the Ground,' he thought. So it wasn't just a rumour. He'd heard there was a subterranean headquarters hidden deep beneath the streets of London but had never expected to see it for himself. He was more perplexed than ever. What was there about either himself or his pending voyage that warranted a summons to this most secret of hideaways?

His escort left him in a small waiting-room, saying, 'The DNI's in a meeting at the moment, sir. But he knows you're here and shouldn't be too long.'

Penrose looked at his watch. It was a gift he had received from a grateful passenger on the last transatlantic crossing the *Empress* had made before the outbreak of war. Solid gold, but small. He squinted as he read the numbers. Had the guardsman not still been watching him from outside the open door he would have put on his glasses. Twenty-three hundred precisely. He did not like being kept waiting, even by a Director of Naval Intelligence. And this little room was far from comfortable. It seemed inappropriate for what was reputed to be the nerve centre of Britain's war effort. More like the waiting-room of a slum doctor's surgery. No one piece of furniture matched another and all showed signs of hard use. A metal medicine cabinet painted dark green contained not drugs but an assortment of partially filled liquor bottles. A shallow sink was streaked yellow where the single brass tap dripped. Cheap prints of the English countryside were dominated by an enormous photograph of a Royal house party at Balmoral in the reign of Edward VII. A discarded copy of the *Daily Express* lay with another of the *Listener*. Definitely a curious place for a top-secret briefing of any kind, let alone one by the DNI himself.

He looked at the attaché case he had deposited on the table as if searching for a clue to the meaning of his presence in this subterranean cubicle. The case, like its owner, was elegant in a sturdy way, well-made, well-kept and well-used. Its brass fittings gleamed and the leather, although cold, was lustrous from many polishings.

In it were copies of the *Amindra*'s passenger and cargo manifests as well as other papers which accompanied him on every voyage. What, he wondered, could there possibly be among them to justify this mysterious summons on the eve of his departure for Scotland? Andrew Donahue, perhaps. As Special Envoy of President Roosevelt it was possible he warranted the attention of the DNI. The rest of the list was undistinguished except for Lady Anne Saville-Fletcher, whom he knew as a first-class passenger who had frequently travelled aboard the *Empress*. Thirty-seven schoolboys and their escort. The youngsters, between eight and thirteen years of age, were part of a scheme to evacuate children from the London area to the safety of homes in the United States for the duration of the war. Their escort was an American woman, Shirley Hunt, who had held a post teaching Embassy children in Paris prior to the Nazi occupation. The man chosen by the Children's Overseas Reception Board to assist her was a professional entertainer, Joseph Millis. Apparently medically unfit for any of the military services, he was seizing the opportunity to escape the war. This fact alone had prompted an instinctive dislike when Penrose read it but he'd decided it wasn't

14

his duty to make judgements. So long as Millis did his job efficiently aboard the *Amindra*, and kept out of the way, there wouldn't be much chance of them spending too much time together.

If the passengers did not warrant this meeting, what of the cargo? Unless the Admiralty was trying to curry favour with the United States, still a neutral country in this war, it certainly didn't seem worthy of such attention. Documents, records, office equipment and furniture, all belonging to American companies prevented by the war from continuing to do business in the British Isles. When he first read the manifest he'd wondered why, when Britain needed every available ship to serve its own ends, a vessel had been assigned to make such a crossing. It seemed an odd lapse of reason on the part of the Admiralty. But because he'd spent his life obeying the orders of whatever company he worked for, Penrose had put the question out of his mind and simply went about making the appropriate arrangements for a safe crossing from Greenock to New York.

Once again he looked around the small, undistinguished room, and suddenly had the odd sensation that he was at sea. The furnishings most certainly did not suggest shipboard, nor did the stillness and utter lack of motion. Then he realized it was the air he was breathing. The square, cream-painted ducts from which it came were not unlike those of the *Amindra*. Because she was built as a refrigerator ship they were larger than in those carrying less perishable cargo.

He put on his gold-framed glasses to see the time. The DNI had already kept him waiting more than ten minutes. He shrugged off his irritation. There was a war on and the DNI no doubt had more important matters in hand than a meeting with the master of a 10,000-ton cargo vessel, even if that master had once been captain of the *Empress*. The difference between the two took some getting used to. The door opened and a tall, gaunt-faced man in Navy uniform entered.

'Sorry to keep you waiting, Captain,' the DNI said, extending his hand. 'A meeting went on longer than it should.'

'I understand, sir.'

It still was not easy for him to 'sir' a superior officer. It had not been too many months since he had had no superior.

The DNI led him along a corridor. Hung among the electric lights were storm lanterns holding candles for emergency illumination should there be a power failure. A wooden holder on a wall displayed a board on which a single word, WINDY, was painted in block letters. Noting Penrose's glance at it, the DNI's weary face was brightened by a brief smile.

'It's meant to tell us what the weather's like top-side,' he said. 'Working down here, we never know. Windy is Mr Rance's way of letting us know London's taking a bashing. Did you have any trouble getting through?'

'Not at all,' he said, wondering who Mr Rance might be. 'I had a very capable driver.'

An armed sentry stood before a black metal door on which were painted the initials 'C.W.R.', beneath which was 'Keep Shut'. The door was fitted with dogs, fastening devices which could be screwed shut, like the watertight doors of a naval vessel. The sentry saluted and opened the door.

'Cabinet War Room,' the DNI explained. Noting Penrose's expression he added, 'You'll not be facing that lot. We have the loan of it for a while.'

Beyond the heavy door another armed sentry waited before another door. It afforded a view of the interior through a small glass window protected by wire mesh. Inside the Cabinet War Room a sallow man in a sober civilian suit started to rise from the chair in which he was sitting but did not complete the motion. He did not look to Penrose as if he belonged here.

'Captain Penrose, Mr Rosten.' the DNI said.

The sallow man got up then and offered his hand. It was bony, dry and tense but the grip was surprisingly firm.

The DNI sat down and motioned for them to do the same. Instead of getting down to whatever business had prompted him to summon Penrose he looked at one of the two wall clocks and frowned. They were obviously waiting for someone. Rosten fidgeted in his hard chair. Penrose, despite his mounting curiosity, sat without moving, his face composed. He studied the room without outward signs that he was doing so. He might never have another chance to inspect this holy of holies.

The Cabinet War Room was large and square, with thick girders, painted red, criss-crossing the ceiling. Small electric fans set high up in each corner stirred the metal-scented air coming from the ventilating ducts. Above the door were two naked light bulbs, one green, one red. The red one was on. Metal chairs, upholstered in green, were ranged around a vast table, open in the middle. The table was covered with black baize, bare except for metal tins of paper clips and a paper punch set before each chair. One chair, facing a Navy League map of the British Empire, was different from the others. It was the sort known as a 'Captain's' chair – heavy dark-brown wood with curving arms. The cushion on it was not new. On the desk in front of it lay a large rectangle of cardboard with an inscription which Penrose was unable to read. In the wall behind the chair was a fireplace, empty except for a fire bucket. Two small desks with chairs were ranged near the map of the British Empire.

There was a bustle at the door and the three men looked towards it. They rose quickly, Penrose feeling awkward for the first time since his arrival, when Winston Churchill lumbered towards them trailing a plume of cigar smoke.

He waved them down with an impatient gesture and lowered his plump body into the captain's chair. He was wearing a siren suit and slippers, the latter embroidered with dragons.

The Prime Minister studied Penrose for a moment without speaking, his head thrust forward in a manner which might indicate truculence in other men but which was his normal posture. It made Penrose uneasy. It was an unfamiliar sensation. He had always been the one to study and scrutinize.

'Captain Penrose,' the Prime Minister said at last. 'Do you have any foreign shares?'

'Sir?' Penrose said, taken completely by surprise.

Rosten was also startled by the question but the DNI seemed not to find it unusual. He was no doubt accustomed to the Prime Minister's ways.

'Foreign shares. Do you have any?'

'Yes, sir.'

Over the years he had invested modestly in American corporations on the advice of American first-class passengers with insiders' knowledge, and had done well. But what had that to do with the Prime Minister and secret midnight meetings two hundred feet beneath the streets of a city reeling under the mass attack of the Luftwaffe?

The Prime Minister smiled then, looking both sly and jolly and radiating a warmth that put Penrose at ease without lessening his bewilderment.

'Then I suggest you take particular pains in seeing your cargo safely to its destination,' the Prime Minister said. 'Those shares of yours may be aboard the *Amindra*. In the company of two hundred and fifty million pounds sterling in gold bullion and other trifles.'

Chapter Two

Neither Rosten nor the DNI, who had been watching Penrose closely, turned a hair. Penrose sat immobile for a moment, transfixed by the revelation. To be brought to such a place at such an hour, to find himself face to face with Winston Churchill, and now this.

'I see, Prime Minister,' he said at last.

He did not, really, and it was obvious the Prime Minister was aware of the fact.

'War is an expensive business,' the Prime Minister said. 'We have for some months been carrying forward a scheme to ensure that, whatever our fortunes in the coming months, Britain will not be left without the means to finance its most vigorous prosecution. Already four-fifths of Britain's negotiable wealth has been safely transferred to Canada. You and the *Amindra* have been selected to transport the balance.'

A long breath, almost a sigh, escaped the captain. Penrose could not suppress it. It was almost too much to grasp. Particularly the realization that, despite everything to the contrary which had been said and written in these past desperate months, Britain's leaders felt the need to spirit the nation's wealth out of England. And of all the ship's masters available and all Britain's naval forces, he had been chosen to do it. He supposed that once he had overcome the initial impact of the revelation he would appreciate the great honour of being selected, but for the moment he could only try to grapple with the awesome significance of what he had just heard.

'Yes,' said the Prime Minister, nodding. 'It is a responsibility of the greatest magnitude. Greater, perhaps, than you may immediately comprehend. And important as this vast sum may be to our nation's future, it is of even greater urgency that our enemies and, indeed, our friends, have not the slightest inkling of this undertaking.'

Despite the impact of the Prime Minister's announcement, Penrose could not fail to notice that even in this private conversation the Prime Minister spoke with the compelling eloquence of a speechmaker who relished words.

The DNI, who was leaning forward closely observing Penrose, nodded reflexively. Rosten from the outset had been regarding Churchill with undisguised awe. It was obvious from the other man's expression that this was also his first meeting with the man guiding Britain's fortunes.

'Were it known that we have sent the nation's wealth out of Britain in the face of threatened invasion,' the Prime Minister continued, 'it would have a devastating effect on both world opinion and the morale of the ordinary people of this country – men and women who are preparing to fight the enemy on the beaches and in the hills. Until the bitter end, if necessary.'

Penrose remembered the words of the famous speech Churchill had made in the House of Commons in the early part of June. It had been repeated on the BBC news and his words had stirred the imagination of everybody who had heard them.

'It would be a propaganda victory for the Nazis, of greater significance than anything they have yet achieved,' the Prime Minister said gravely. 'And enough, I fear, to end any hope of assistance we might otherwise expect from the United States. President Roosevelt is a staunch friend of Britain but many of his countrymen are less so. Notable among them is Ambassador Kennedy. And we have reason to believe that one of your passengers, Andrew Donahue, is taking a report back to President Roosevelt which supports Ambassador Kennedy's misguided belief that Britain will lose this war. Should we give the Americans even the slightest cause to doubt our firm resolve to survive, I fear the President will find his hands tied.' He paused. His chin sank to his chest and for a long time he seemed lost in his own retrospection. 'It may well be,' he said, finally breaking the silence, 'that this mission will prove to be the most desperate gamble of the war.'

He plucked the stub of his cigar from his lips and, without a backward glance, flung it over his shoulder. Penrose watched, fascinated, as it arched neatly into the fire bucket standing in the fireplace.

'In short,' the Prime Minister continued, 'should the situation arise, though we have made every effort to ensure the successful completion of your mission, it is better that the *Amindra* and her cargo be lost at sea with all hands than to risk the nature of its errand becoming known.'

He produced a fresh cigar from a drawer inside the desk and lit it carefully.

'To that end,' he said, exhaling a dense cloud of blue smoke, 'the *Amindra* has been fitted with scuttling charges. Should the security of your cargo be threatened, you must activate them without hesitation. Is that clear?'

'Yes, sir,' Penrose answered.

'May I, Prime Minister?' the DNI said.

Churchill nodded.

'The master switch activates all the charges simultaneously,' the DNI said. 'But once activated they may be deactivated only individually, *in situ*.'

'Only you and Mr . . . ,' Churchill said, looking at Rosten and then the DNI.

'Rosten,' the DNI murmured.

'Only you and Mr Rosten will know the location and

purpose of the master switch and have keys to get at it.'

'Yes, sir,' Penrose said, surprised that the drab, sober man was coming along. He was not on the passenger list.

There was a question he felt compelled to ask.

'What of the children, sir? There will be thirty-seven evacuee youngsters aboard.'

The Prime Minister regarded him quizzically.

'Do you have children, Captain Penrose?' he asked.

'Yes, sir.'

'So do I. I would not wish them or their children to endure the consequences of a Nazi victory. Would you?'

'No, sir.'

'Does that answer your question, then?'

'Yes, sir.'

'And the presence of the children aboard the *Amindra* is not without purpose,' Churchill added, less grimly. 'You doubtless recall the *Athenia*?'

'Of course, sir.'

The Donaldson liner *Athenia*, bound for Montreal, had been sunk by a German U-boat on the first day of the war, 3 September 1939, with the loss of 112 of the more than one thousand passengers and crew. Many of the passengers, including 311 Americans, were women and children. The public outcry in America against the Germans had been tremendous. Hitler attempted to counter it by claiming the British themselves had sunk the ship at Churchill's direction in a bid for American sympathy.

'Oddly enough,' the Prime Minister said puckishly, 'Herr Goebbels also claimed the *Athenia* was carrying fifteen million pounds in gold bullion. I assure you we're making no attempt to hide the fact from the Nazis that the *Amindra* will be carrying both innocent children *and* an American Presidential Adviser. I doubt they'll want to repeat the error of the *Athenia*.'

His smile vanished and he fixed Penrose with a stern

glance.

'Now I'd like to know your feelings about this transfer of assets,' he said. 'Does it create any doubts in your mind about Britain's ability to win the war?'

'None at all, sir,' Penrose answered firmly.

Churchill studied him a moment or two longer, then, apparently satisfied, turned the piece of cardboard Penrose had noticed earlier. On it, hand-printed, was 'Please understand there is no pessimism in the house and we are not interested in the possibilities of defeat: they do not exist.'

'A maxim I hold dear,' the Prime Minister said, heaving himself from his chair. The others rose quickly. 'You have been given a grave task,' he said, addressing himself to Penrose. 'I have no doubt you will carry it out no less ably than you performed your duties aboard the *Empress*.'

Penrose felt gratified even though he suspected the compliment was calculated.

Churchill held the other man's eyes with his own for a long moment. 'During the next seven days the outcome of the war as well as the future of the British Empire may well be in your hands, Captain. I wish you Godspeed and good luck.'

He shook Penrose's hand and, with a nod for Rosten, left the Cabinet War Room, leaving only the aroma of his cigar to confirm that Penrose had been in the presence of Britain's most powerful man.

The long moment of silence following the Prime Minister's departure was broken by the DNI.

'You've heard the highlights,' he said. 'Now I'll fill in the squares.'

Every bank in the United Kingdom had been stripped of its gold bullion, gold coins and negotiable securities. This vast scooping-up of wealth, the accumulation of decades of trade and investment, was done with unprecedented secrecy. Few of Britain's most highly placed officials were aware of the undertaking, which was accomplished without issuing a single written document. Had they known, many would have objected, not only because of its questionable legality but also because of its implications. One man, Winston Churchill, had taken it upon himself to commandeer the wealth of the nation and put it to the use he considered best for the country.

And commandeer it he had. The securities already overseas were even now being sold for American dollars without the knowledge or permission of their owners, who were to be reimbursed in pounds sterling. Britain was on a cash-and-carry basis and desperately needed the dollars for war material, food and medical supplies.

The first shipment of Britain's assets had left Greenock, Scotland, for Halifax, Nova Scotia, aboard the cruiser, HMS *Emerald*, on 24 June. Its cargo comprised 2,229 bullion boxes, each containing four 27-pound bars, and 488 boxes of negotiable securities valued at upwards of eighty million pounds sterling.

The second shipment followed on 8 July aboard three former ocean liners escorted by the battleship *Revenge*, the cruiser *Bonaventure* and four destroyers. The gold bullion transported in that convoy was valued at more than one and a half billion American dollars.

The *Amindra* alone was carrying a cargo worth almost half that of the 8 July convoy.

'I'm afraid we can't give you an escort,' the DNI said. 'We need every available ship to defend our coastal waters. And the Germans know it. An escort of any kind would only arouse their suspicions.'

There was a long silence. It was broken by Rosten, who had grown increasingly distracted.

'I wonder if I might telephone my wife?' he asked. 'She's alone, and what with this bombing . . .'

'We're almost finished.' The DNI turned to Penrose. 'Mr Rosten will be responsible for supervising the transportation of your cargo by train from Halifax to Ottawa.'

'Halifax?' Penrose said. 'It's manifested to New York.'

'More cloak and dagger. Only you and Rosten are to know it's Halifax until it becomes obvious to the crew.'

Rosten, the DNI explained, was a Bank of England 'gilt-edged specialist' who had been a key figure in assembling and cataloguing the foreign securities. He would be aboard the *Amindra* as an official of the Children's Overseas Reception Board on his way to Washington for a conference. He would be inspecting the cargo periodically throughout the voyage. Penrose was to ensure that he could do so inconspicuously.

'And should you be incapacitated by enemy action before you can activate the scuttling charges, it becomes Mr Rosten's duty to do so should his estimate of the situation dictate such action,' the DNI said.

'A decision of that nature is solely the responsibility of the ship's master,' Penrose said stiffly. 'If the *Amindra* is threatened I'm confident I'll know what to do in ample time to take the necessary measures.'

'Of course,' the DNI said. 'But we can't leave anything to chance, can we? By the by, I'm afraid we've had to take a few liberties with your ship. We've had a crew working around the clock reinforcing the hold stays and stanchions. All very hush-hush, of course. Gold's a good bit heavier for the space it occupies than anything the *Amindra* was designed for.'

'Not a sea-kindly cargo,' Penrose said.

'Sea-kindly?' Rosten said.

'Cargo that fills a lot of space in the holds,' Penrose explained. 'When it doesn't, it leaves all that much more room for the sea. The faster your holds flood when you're hit, the faster your ship sinks.'

25

Rosten was less dismayed by this information than Penrose had expected.

'All the better,' the 'gilt-edged specialist' replied. 'That's what we want if we're attacked, isn't it?'

'Actually, the weight won't be as concentrated as it was in the *Emerald*,' the DNI said.

On the cruiser, he explained, the bars in their bullion boxes had bent the angle irons supporting the ship's magazines, where they were stored. On the *Amindra*, the four-bar boxes were being packed ten to a crate, stencilled appropriately for its consignee and destination in America. The extra space was filled with lighter material which served to keep the bullion boxes from shifting and made the weight of the crate seem normal for its proportions.

There were more than twelve hundred such crates now being loaded aboard the *Amindra* under the supervision of an Admiralty specialist.

'Loading cargo's a job for my First Officer,' Penrose said. 'And you won't find a better man than Campbell for it.'

'I thought you'd been informed,' the DNI said. 'Campbell was in an accident, run down by a cab in Glasgow this morning. Only a broken leg, fortunately, but . . .'

'How am I expected to find a replacement?' Penrose demanded. 'We sail in less than forty-eight hours.'

'Twenty-four, I'm afraid,' the DNI said. 'And we've found you a First Officer every bit as capable as Campbell. You'll get on well with him, I'm sure.'

'Whether he'll get on well with me is more to the point,' Penrose said.

'I have no doubt he will,' the DNI said with a faint smile. 'First Officer Barrett knows your reputation as well as the next. I'm sure you'll find him more than adequate for the job. He's a seasoned veteran of the Happy Time.'

'The Happy Time?' Rosten said.

'That's what Jerry's taken to calling the past months,' the DNI explained. 'His U-boats have been enjoying good hunting. Nearly 250,000 tons in May, over twice that in June, a bit less than the June bag in July and not too badly in August, thank you very much.'

He paused to let that disquieting information sink in before returning to the nature of the *Amindra*'s burden. Each of the 1,200 crates contained forty 27-pound bars of pure gold, some 48,000 ingots all told, weighing in excess of a million and a quarter pounds. Nearly six hundred metric tons of solid gold. In addition to the bullion there were, in similar crates, 138 large canvas sacks of the gold coinage of many nations, a considerable number of the coins old and rare and of great value on the numismatic market. There were, as well, 187 boxes of negotiable foreign securities with an estimated value of forty million pounds sterling.

'Altogether a tidy little sum,' the DNI said.

Rosten's pained expression showed plainly he was not amused by the DNI's comment that the cargo he was seeing to Canada was a 'tidy little sum'.

'You've been equipped with new, experimental Asdic which greatly increases the range of detection,' the DNI continued, adding, for Rosten's benefit, 'picks up underwater sounds. Very useful against U-boats.' Turning back to Penrose, 'You'll have a six-incher at the stern and a crack gun crew,' the DNI continued. 'Disguised as a deck load. As you well know, U-boats often surface to attack lone, unarmed vessels. So you might get a crack at one of them. But in no event are you to risk being boarded.

'You have two options: escape unharmed, or scuttle. There are no other choices.'

Chapter Three

Shirley Hunt sat in a hard folding chair and tried not to wince each time the cavernous basement responded with small shiftings and muted creaking noises to the bombs which were still falling with random malevolence across London. She knew she must set an example for the thirty-seven boys sharing the cellars of the Grosvenor House Hotel with her and several dozen guests and employees. Apart from the children she was by far the youngest person in the basement and, she was sure, the most apprehensive except, perhaps, for Peter Barlow. The thin little boy was one of the few children travelling at government expense because his parents were unable to afford the normal peace-time fare which the other boys' parents had been obliged to pay. She had noticed how uncomfortable he had seemed among the luxurious surroundings of the hotel lobby and how the other youngsters had shown little friendliness towards him.

At twenty-six Shirley looked barely out of her teens. With light brown softly waving hair, large, serious brown eyes and finely wrought features just short of being sharp, she had a face that gave promise of real beauty once it matured.

She had been in the basement for more than two hours now, getting up only to circulate among the boys to offer the comfort and reassurance she believed was expected of her. None of them seemed to welcome her attention, though they were polite about it, like little gentlemen, which was exactly what she had expected of English schoolboys. As the hours dragged by they had become restless and made endless trips to the bathroom at the bottom of the stairs. They went in groups of two or three, whispering and frisky. It was hard for Shirley to believe that less than twelve hours ago they had all been complete strangers. Now names had been exchanged, secrets shared, prize possessions displayed, such as vinegar-hardened chestnuts or marbles.

Of them all, only Peter Barlow seemed an outsider and in need of comforting. But when she had knelt beside him, concealing her own nervousness, and put her arm around his shoulder, he had ducked his head and shrunk deeper within himself. She had heard some of the boys snicker and understood at once that she had only embarrassed the child.

The crash of explosives reached a new peak, echoing down the elevator shaft and filling the basement with waves of sound. Shirley was gripped by the obsession that somewhere up there in the darkness a German bomber pilot was circling, looking just for her.

Barlow lifted his head and said in a strained but oddly didactic tone, 'Junkers 88s.'

'Heinkels,' said a sturdy, handsome boy who seemed unruffled by the tumult. He wore a blue blazer bearing the crest of a well-known public school. Shirley remembered his name because of his manner. Self-assured, beautiful manners, a natural leader. Oaks. Gregory Oaks. He had arrived at the hotel in a chauffeur-driven Rolls-Royce, unaccompanied by either of his parents.

'Junkers 88s,' Barlow insisted doggedly, fumbling at his suitcase. Just because he was grant-aided they thought he didn't know anything. He'd show them who was right.

His suitcase was made of pressed cardboard held together at the corners with brown metal triangles. When he opened it Shirley saw that it held much less clothing than parents had been instructed to supply for the bitterly cold weather of a North Atlantic crossing.

Removing a stack of tattered comic books, he leafed through them lovingly until he found the one he wanted and deposited the others carefully on his suitcase.

'Here,' he said triumphantly, holding up the open comic for Oaks to see a page showing aircraft silhouettes. ' "The Junkers 88 may be most easily distinguished by the sound of its engines",' he read aloud, ' "because they are desynchronized and appear to throb . . ." '

'Let me see that,' Oaks interrupted, reaching for the comic.

Barlow jerked it out of reach. His elbow knocked the suitcase over, scattering his precious comics on the damp cellar floor. Several boys quickly swooped in to snatch them up while another pinioned Barlow's arms.

'Stop that!' Shirley cried, more shrilly than she had intended.

Her strident tone startled the boys for a moment. Then, grinning, they released Barlow and returned his comics.

They were laughing at her because they knew she was frightened, Shirley thought. The first test of her authority and she had failed it miserably.

She wondered if Joe Millis would have handled it any better. She doubted it. Anyone who was willing to flee his own country when it was so desperately threatened couldn't have much backbone. She had met him briefly that afternoon when the children and their parents gathered in the Grosvenor House ballroom for leave-taking and had been singularly unimpressed. She had wondered why the American Committee had agreed to accept him as her assistant. It seemed such an odd choice. She had been told he was a professional entertainer whose job it was to keep up the boys' spirits during the long, dangerous voyage.

He was large and she supposed he might be clumsy. His

30

face had been pleasant enough, with that ruddy English complexion and nice hazel eyes, but she thought there was something unsure about his manner, as if he were courting acceptance with his steady barrage of bad jokes. His fair hair was thick and untidy. He looked perfectly healthy to Shirley, making her wonder if the unidentified disability which rendered him unfit for active military service was mental rather than physical.

Now, as she looked around the basement where Barlow huddled against a wall and the other boys jostled one another around Oaks, she was deeply aware of the crushing burden of responsibility which had haunted her since the last parent had departed, leaving her in charge of a throng of young children.

One of the questions asked prospective escorts by the Children's Overseas Reception Board had been, 'Will you help plan this hazardous voyage in the spirit of gay adventure?' Until the moment the parents left, the enterprise had seemed, indeed, a gay adventure which she imagined would not be too different from the position she had been obliged to abandon by the fall of France.

But then her pupils had gone home to their parents at night. Now she was the parent, as well as teacher, counsellor, nursemaid. As much as the awesome responsibility filled her with unease and self-doubt she still did not regret seeking it. She was doing her bit. Since early childhood her father had impressed on her that one must make one's contribution to the common good. It was this sense of duty which had led her to war-torn France where, not considered suitable to drive an ambulance or minister to wounded soldiers, she had taken the first available job that would keep her there. It had not been entirely a sense of duty, she had admitted to herself later. It was also to get out of an embarrassing situation with a man. He had kept after her to marry him until she finally agreed, only to discover it was just a ruse to get her into bed with him. It hadn't succeeded, of course, but she had felt such a fool, as if everyone had known what he was up to except herself.

Shirley knew she had not behaved particularly well after the fall of France, eagerly accepting evacuation with the first group of dependants, but she had tried to make up for it by remaining in England looking for a way to help. That opportunity had presented itself through the American Committee.

The cellar quivered with the concussion of a string of bombs in the near distance. Shirley stiffened and clutched the sides of her chair. This won't do, she thought. It was not the way her father would like to see her behave. She forced herself to her feet, pulled Barlow from his place against the wall and led him to join the other boys.

'Well, now,' she said brightly. 'Are we down-hearted?'

And led the children in a chorus of 'Noes.'

Despite the air raid, a third of the small tables jamming the narrow darkness of the Blue Onion were occupied. All but a few of the occupants were in uniform, including several of the vastly outnumbered women. On-stage, Joe Millis was shambling back and forth peering out into the house and shading his eyes against the spotlight which pretended to have trouble keeping him in it.

'I know you're out there,' he said. 'I can hear the snores.' He cupped an ear and said, 'Did I hear a laugh? No laughing here. This is serious business. Just a young chap trying to make a living. Anyway, that's my excuse for bein' here. What's yours? You, there, eating the toffee apple. Oh, it's not a toffee apple? It's your nose?'

The room shook and the spotlight wavered. Chairs scraped as the audience shifted uneasily and several moved quickly towards the exit.

'I know it's my closing night but I didn't expect such a

send-off,' Millis said. 'Fireworks and all. I'm touched, really I am. As I was telling the owner – you know, Harry, the one whose heart don't go thump, thump like mine and yours but more like a cash drawer opening and shutting – nothing special, just a quick turn, get my lolly and a kiss on the cheek and I'm off. No tears, no bubbly. But not Harry. He has to arrange this smashing celebration. Bit much, though, isn't it?'

He hadn't wanted to go on tonight. He was leaving for America first thing in the morning and had loads to do.

But he must say he was going over well. The laughter out front wasn't all nervous. He didn't mind the bombs all that much as long as he was getting laughs. It was a silent audience that killed you, not Jerry's crackers.

'Met a nice bit of Yank fluff today, you know. Oh, you didn't know? Just told you, d'int I? She says to me, she says, "What's a fine figure of a man like yourself doing in mufti when his country calls?"'

He expanded his chest, put a hand on a hip and did a nancy-boy turn.

'Oh, you were wondering, too, were you? It's me poor insides, that's what it is. Got no stomach for fighting.'

There were boos amid the laughter.

'Thank you,' he said, curtseying. 'Thank you very much, I'm sure. And then there's my skin. You might not think much of it but I've been in it thirty-two years and grown proper attached to it, you might say.'

A huge explosion interrupted him and plaster drifted down from the ceiling. The audience began leaving in droves.

'Is it something I said?' he demanded plaintively.

Someone hissed in the wings. He turned towards the sound. It was the owner, waving him off with a hand on which a stone too large to be a genuine diamond caught the light.

Millis hurried after the owner, who moved quickly for a fat man, and caught his sleeve just as Harry reached for the switch to darken the house.

'Forgetting something, ain't we?' he said.

'Oh, that,' Harry said, unabashed, taking an envelope from his coat.

Millis tore off the top and shook coins and a few notes into his hand. He began counting them.

'Don't you trust me?' Harry demanded.

'Like my own dear mum. Served up my pet bunny for Christmas dinner and said it was goose.'

Shaftesbury Avenue was empty when he reached it, the theatres dark and the shops tightly shuttered. The windows of those without shutters were banded with heavy tape. The last wave of bombers had departed and the next had not yet arrived, leaving the city waiting in a breathless silence broken only by the distant clamour of bell and siren. Millis hurried towards his flat off Charing Cross, keeping to the centre of the road until the shriek of an approaching emergency van sent him scurrying for the kerb.

'Everybody's in a bloody hurry these days,' he shouted after it. 'Worth an honest man's life to take a bit of a stroll.'

His flat was among the topmost of a forlorn building, eerily silent now that the occupants had fled to basements and tube stations. The halls reeked with the dead, pervasive smell of ancient tobacco smoke and countless pots of Brussels sprouts and cabbage. There was little in Millis's flat that was his own – a music-hall poster on the wall with his billing well down in the ruck, a few bits of clothing on nails, half a dozen old books, a holiday cushion from Brighton and a scarred travelling case, now open on the narrow bed. It was remarkably tidy for a rootless bachelor's digs and even more so for such a rumpled man as Joe Millis.

Standing at the wreck of a bureau, he pencilled a scribbled message, folded a pound note in it, and went out into the hall to shove it beneath the door of a nearby room. Walking quietly, as if there were sleepers in the empty rooms, he climbed the stairs to the roof. His pigeons greeted him with coos and sharp movements of their reptilian heads. He reached into a case and took one out. Nestling it in his palm, he stroked its neck with the back of his nicotined index finger.

'There,' he murmured. 'It's all right . . .'

'That you, Millis?' a voice called across the roof.

'Who else talks fluent pigeon?'

The speaker laughed. 'You're a caution and no mistake . . .'

Millis joined the other man and they stood side by side for a moment looking out over the city. The blacked-out sprawl of buildings was lit by a score of fires, the nearer ones an angry crimson, those farther away embroidered with purple. The air carried an acrid smell of cordite and burning rubber and flakes of white ash drifted down from the night sky like sparse snow. Millis's companion wore the black metal ARP helmet of an air-raid warden. Binoculars swung from his neck on a leather strap. He was a man in his sixties who had been invalided out of the army after the First World War.

'They hit the docks at Limehouse,' he said. 'A whole warehouse of rum went up in flames.'

'Criminal!' Millis said.

'Impressive sight, though, isn't it?'

'Makes the Blackpool illuminations look like a lot of bloody sparklers.'

'We should sell seats.'

'Rich overnight. That's what we'd be.'

'Left a note under your door,' Millis said, breaking a

35

short silence. 'Off to Blackpool first thing in the morning. Top of the bill at the Winter Gardens. A full week guaranteed. Longer, if they like me.'

'They'll like you, Joe.'

There was another pause. Somewhere in the direction of Regent's Park an anti-aircraft gun opened up. Its sharp bark sounded like a whip cracking.

'Look after 'em, will you?' Millis said. 'The birds, I mean. They get lonely without their old mum. That's what I am to them, you know. Their mum. They don't want me in uniform.'

'Don't be too hard on yourself not getting in this lot,' the other man said. 'I was in the first go-around. Verdun. Bloody horrible it was.'

'Bonkers. The whole thing.'

'And you're doing your bit entertaining the boys in uniform.'

Millis had a quick answer ready but didn't use it. Instead, he leaned on the balustrade and looked out over the burning city as if at a performance.

Andrew Donahue stood at the window of his Dorchester Hotel suite with his hands thrust deep into the pockets of his silk dressing-gown. He had spent most of the evening there, not enjoying it exactly – people were dying, he knew – but with a certain satisfaction. If he had needed confirmation of the conclusions he had drawn after three weeks of study, questioning English people in every walk of life, conferring with top government officials, reading every newspaper he could get his hands on, listening to daily radio broadcasts, interviewing the top echelon of the US Embassy staff and, most telling of all, studying the top-secret material Ambassador Joseph Kennedy had obtained, tonight's show did the trick.

Churchill could say what he wanted about the Germans,

36

but there was no denying they had both the men and weapons to win the war. They also had the spirit necessary for triumph, an almost fanatical belief that Hitler was invincible. It had impressed Charles Lindbergh enough for him to warn Americans to stay out of the conflict. And in a week or so when Donahue delivered his report, President Roosevelt would have the truth confirmed. There was no way Britain could win the war, and it would be suicide for the still neutral United States to get involved by coming to its aid.

Across Park Lane, deep inside the darkness that was Hyde Park, the Serpentine was tinged with reflected fire-glow. The sirens continued wailing, searchlights stabbed the sky and the murmur of aircraft engines slowly grew to a roar. Rather than fear, Donahue felt a strange sense of detachment. The Germans weren't after him. He was an American.

At the Connaught Hotel Lady Anne Saville-Fletcher was repacking her suitcases for the fourth or fifth time. She had come in from Surrey that afternoon, bringing with her far more than she could possibly take on the voyage to America aboard the *Amindra*. The blackout curtains were tightly drawn and if she noticed the sounds of the attacking German bombers at all it was with anger, not fear. In a proper war soldiers fought each other, not innocent women and children. She had refused the manager's plea to take shelter with the other guests. If the Hun had nothing better to do than murder an old woman let him try. If only Tony could have had his go at them.

She glanced at Tony's photograph on the mantel in its folding leather frame. How young he had looked in his RAF uniform, this child of her middle years when she had long since given up hope of ever having one. She felt an overwhelming sadness but did not cry. She had shed tears only once since she was notified of his death a week ago, and those when she was alone in the privacy of her own bedroom. The Air Ministry had said in the telegram that he died in the service of his country, even though the accident which killed him had happened while he was still undergoing flight training in Canada. A fine distinction, perhaps, yet one that still triggered deep resentment in her. Fate should at least have permitted him to die in battle against the enemy.

His body was being kept at a mortuary in Toronto until she could attend the burial service. Friends had promised to meet her when the *Amindra* reached New York and drive her north across the Canadian border. The Air Ministry had arranged her passage on the ship transporting a group of refugee children. She had mixed feelings about the scheme under which these youngsters were being sent to spend the duration of the war in the safety of American homes. The concern of their parents was understandable, but sending them so far away seemed to indicate a certain acceptance on the part of the adults that Britain was no longer a safe place. And this she deplored. If Hitler did send his legions across the Channel he would find the British were made of far sterner stuff than the French. Her only regret was that she would not be there to witness his defeat.

She held a long gown against her tall, almost gaunt frame and studied the effect in the mirror, wondering if one should dress for dinner on a cargo boat in war-perilled seas. She folded it carefully and put it with the rest of the clothing she intended taking with her. She should and would keep up established standards. That's what this war was all about. And she could do no less for a man like Captain Penrose, an utterly charming man, and one who believed a great deal in the importance of keeping up appearances. She had come to know him well from the times she had crossed the Atlantic aboard the *Empress* and the one bright spot in this otherwise sad journey was that she would be in the hands of such a delightful and capable person.

Benjamin Rosten slumped in the back seat of the staff car, exhausted from twenty hours without sleep but quietly exultant. At last he had been given the opportunity to do something important for the war effort, far more important than, and quite as dangerous as, anything a man in uniform might be called upon to do. His only regret was that he could tell Marjorie nothing about it. She thought he was being called away to northern England on Bank of England business. He had already written the letters which were to be mailed to her from Newcastle every day. He'd wanted to enlist the day war was declared but had been informed that his position with the Bank of England was a 'reserved occupation'. To make it worse, everyone thought he had wangled it. Rifle instruction two evenings a week with the Auxiliary Military Pioneer Corps had done little to still the nasty little jokes he knew had been made behind his back or to temper his bottomless desire to strike back personally at the filthy swine tormenting his people. Strange, he had not thought of Jews as his people until Hitler came along. His fellow Englishmen were his people. They still were, but he had more reason to hate the Nazis than had ordinary Englishmen.

More than Penrose, for one. The captain had spoken scarcely a word to him from the time they left Great George Street until he stepped out of the car at the Kensington Palace Hotel. A cold, vain man. But he must be the best at what he did or he would not have been chosen for such an awesome responsibility. Be that as it may, Benjamin Rosten had been chosen, too. And why

39

not, he thought, smiling grimly. Wasn't he one of the Chosen People?

The smell of explosives, plaster, escaping coal gas and blue London clay filled his nostrils. He opened his eyes to a vista of gutted walls and mounds of smoking rubble among which dazed survivors were picking through the remnants of what had once been their homes. The tyres of the staff car crunched over broken glass with a sound that set his teeth on edge. He felt a surge of panic. His home was only two squares away from Kensington High Street.

'Could you please hurry?' he asked, leaning forward so the WREN driver could hear him over the sound of explosions, crackling fires, and strident ambulances and fire engines.

'I'll try, sir,' she said, looking at him in the rear-view mirror.

Shattered road surface and rescue workers who ignored the constant honking of the horn held them to a crawl. Unable to endure the tortuous pace any longer, Rosten threw open the door and ran the rest of the way. He stopped short, frozen, when he saw his home. The entire row of houses was lit by a reddish glow, with rubble and debris everywhere. Down the street a car burned. The heat was so intense that lamp-posts had wilted grotesquely and the wooden paving blocks of the road had begun to burn, sending up showers of sparks that drifted like flaming snowflakes in the brisk eddies of hot air.

A man sat with his back against a wall. One leg was gone. To Rosten's numbed brain that did not seem nearly as remarkable as the fact that he was wearing only long, old-fashioned woollen underwear. A cluster of survivors reeled past Rosten like sleepwalkers, covered in a yellow patina of dust that gave them an oddly clown-like appearance. Others milled nearby, shouting helplessly.

Rosten could hear the screams of those still trapped in

the burning houses. Was that Majorie's he heard among them? Someone tried to hold him back as he ran towards the inferno. Before he could pull free the block of buildings gave out a stealthy rustle, like the first warning of an avalanche, followed by a smothered roar and a burst of sharp, crackling reports. As he watched in horror, the whole row of houses collapsed in a gush of plaster as the walls fell inward to bury anyone who had not already escaped under tons of rubble.

The shouting mob was suddenly quiet. Hair matted grey with dust, some of the faces masked with blood, they looked with blank eyes at the pall hanging over the shattered buildings and drifting down to veil the upturned faces of the dead.

The man who had tried to stop Rosten gripped his shoulder and said, 'Ben . . .' He did not have to finish the sentence. His face revealed it all. Marjorie was dead. Tears burst from Rosten's eyes and he gritted his teeth until his jaws ached.

The bastards! The bloody, bloody bastards!

Slow rolling columns of yellow-grey smoke drifted over the still burning ruins. And above the smoke a flock of pigeons wheeled aimlessly, searching for vanished reference points, lost and confused in the unnatural dawn.

The Swedish freighter *Vetlanda* plunged northwards in the grey morning light at a surging sixteen knots. On the bridge, the master and his chief officer scanned the horizon through heavy binoculars. A lookout dangling from the forward mast in a bosun's chair turned his face from the eyepiece of the periscope the mast concealed and bellowed, 'Masthead off the port bow!'

The language was German, not Swedish.

'Congratulations to the navigation officer,' the chief

officer murmured without removing the binoculars from his eyes. 'You were right.'

He also spoke German.

'Let's not congratulate ourselves yet,' the master said. 'It might not be the *Nordmark*. Order action-stations.'

Alarm bells rang, whistles blew and seamen ran on to the deck to take positions along the *Vetlanda*'s length, one group assembling aft near a huge crate marked with the name of a Swedish consignee. Once in place, they busied themselves coiling lines, chipping paint and polishing brightwork.

'Funnel in sight!' the lookout called. 'Two points to port.'

The officers on the bridge kept their binoculars trained on the other vessel as they closed.

'It's the *Nordmark*, all right,' said Kapitän zur See Manfred Freiburg, returning his binoculars to their case.

'What was the rush, I wonder?' Senior Lieutenant Schramm asked.

'We'll know soon enough.'

The Swedish flag, markings, altered masts and funnel, false decking and upper hull plates of the *Vetlanda* were only one of several disguises for the HK *Adler*. HK. *Hilfskreuzer*. Auxiliary cruiser. Armed merchant raider.

The false decking and upper portion of the hull concealed four 5.9-inch guns. A system of counterweights could drop the hull plates in two seconds, unmasking the guns and allowing superbly trained crews to fire with deadly accuracy. The aft deck-load was a dummy, concealing another 5.9-incher. Heavy machine- and anti-aircraft guns were similarly well concealed, as were the torpedo launchers. Special winches could raise or lower the funnel swiftly, and prefabricated metal sheets change its circumference. The masts, set in wells, could also be raised or lowered by special winches. Guard rails could appear or disappear in a flash and the deck configuration could quickly be altered. An Arado seaplane, wings folded, sat concealed in a forward hold from which it could be raised by electric winch and lowered over the side to patrol for victims.

Five days earlier the *Adler* had been prowling shipping lanes in the South Atlantic between the tip of Africa and the Americas. An urgent message from SKL, *Seekriegsleitung*, the German Naval Staff, at Norddeich on Germany's North Sea coast, had ordered her to proceed immediately and with all possible dispatch to rendezvous with the supply ship *Nordmark* midway between the bulge of Africa and northernmost South America. There its captain was to receive detailed orders too sensitive to be transmitted by radio.

The crews of both vessels lined the rails as the two ships drew within hailing distance. Captain Freiburg, who had gone to his quarters to change into navy uniform, ordered his launch to be lowered and the two ships circled at quarter speed to make a lee while it took him the hundred yards or so between them. Some minutes later, at a signal-lamp message from the *Nordmark*, Lieutenant Schramm ordered the *Adler*'s prisoners to be brought on deck and readied for transfer to the supply ship. The prisoners were a mixed lot, British, Norwegian and Lascar seamen. Some of them were still suffering from wounds they had received when they were taken, and had to be assisted down the Jacob's ladder hung over the side to the lifeboats lowered to carry them.

Aboard the *Nordmark*, Captain Freiburg waited to see the prisoners come on board. There was little in their manner, or his, to indicate that Freiburg was the man who had sunk their ships or taken them as prizes. His smile was genuinely friendly and, when shaking hands with several of the British and Norwegian officers, he seemed almost to regret that they must part.

Freiburg was a strongly built man of average height, but because of the breadth of his shoulders and the thickness of his chest he appeared almost squat. He was not the classic Nordic blond so admired by Hitler. Most of the Norwegian prisoners and many of the fair-haired British were far closer to that mould. With his dark, curly hair, dark eyes and miner's physique he might easily have been taken for a Welshman. His face was deeply tanned from years of exposure to wind and sun, weather-aged far beyond his forty-seven years.

The master of a British freighter who had been taken prisoner weeks earlier asked Freiburg to pose for a snapshot with him. The English officer owned a camera which had been confiscated when he was captured but temporarily returned to him for the transfer from the *Adler* to the *Nordmark*. He handed the camera to a fellow officer and guided Freiburg to a position by the rail. The *Adler* lay motionless in the background. Freiburg smiled and led the other man to a place where neither the *Adler* nor any detail of the *Nordmark* would appear. In the days since the *Adler* had sunk the other man's freighter, Freiburg had come to know him well. Should the *Nordmark* fall victim to a British warship and the officer and his camera be rescued, Freiburg had not the slightest doubt the photograph would quickly find its way into the hands of Intelligence experts at the British Admiralty.

'Well,' the British captain said with a sheepish grin, 'it was worth a try, wasn't it?'

'In your place I would have attempted exactly the same thing,' Freiburg assured him.

An hour later, when sacks of personal mail had been delivered to the *Adler* and diesel fuel was being pumped to the raider through a long oil line snaking between the two vessels, Freiburg returned to his ship to find his officers congregated near the rail, some with studied nonchalance but others, including Schramm, with open curiosity.

Freiburg carried a locked dispatch case to which lead weights were attached. He studied his assembled officers as if puzzled by their presence. Otherwise his face betrayed nothing except, or so Schramm thought, a gleam of excitement in the dark, narrowed eyes. Without a word, Freiburg motioned Schramm to follow and led the way to his quarters. Shutting the door behind them, the captain tossed the dispatch case on his bunk, took off his tunic and began rummaging in a locker.

Schramm, bursting with curiosity, watched him intently as he brought out a bottle of old brandy taken from a captured Norwegian freighter, selected two water glasses that had been fitted into metal holders over the sink and poured a generous measure into each. He handed one to Schramm and stood gazing thoughtfully into his own.

'Well?' Schramm could no longer contain his curiosity.

'We have orders to take a prize,' Freiburg said.

'That's standing orders,' Schramm said, disappointed.

'This one is special. It's called the *Amindra*.'

Chapter Four

The chartered bus turned into Drummond Street and pulled up at Euston Station. It had arrived to pick up Shirley Hunt and her charges shortly after five in the morning, barely half an hour after all-clear. Giddy from lack of sleep and a little nauseated from a hasty breakfast of powdered egg and glutinous sausages, Shirley did not know how she would have managed to see them and their belongings into it were it not for the help of two unruffled Englishwomen from the Children's Overseas Reception Board and the gentlemanly Oaks boy. He had quieted the unruly children, prodded the sleepy ones and helped the little ones with their luggage.

A direct hit early in the night raid had smashed the towering glass roof of the station. The asphalt of the platform, which had caught fire and melted, was littered with its shards. Women from the Children's Overseas Reception Board had set up a booth on the platform and stood ready to dispense biscuits and milk, hard to come by in wartime England, to the children. Joe Millis, dishevelled and needing a shave, was already there, drinking milk, eating biscuits and entertaining the ladies with his jokes. When he saw Shirley, he hurried over to assist her.

He gestured towards a sign, prominently displayed and asking 'Is Your Journey Really Necessary?' and said, 'Madam, you will please read and make your decision. Absolutely your last and final opportunity.'

She forced a smile. It was not at all funny.

He knelt beside one of the smaller boys, who was burdened like many others with more than the single suitcase parents has been specifically instructed to send with their children, and said, 'Been doing a bit of looting, have we? I'll help you with it for halvers.'

The other boys thought it much funnier than Shirley did.

Millis went among the small ones collecting luggage, looping satchel straps over his shoulders and clutching suitcases to his sides until he was almost hidden.

'Thank you for your kind donations, I'm sure,' he said, trotting towards the exit.

The boys hooted with delight when one of their number ran after Millis, shouting, to stop him.

'Mr Millis!' Shirley said curtly. 'You're supposed to be helping me, not disrupting things.'

He might as well know right now who was in charge.

Millis gave the boys a droll look, pretended to cringe, and carried his burden of luggage to a carriage whose windows were marked with Children's Overseas Reception Board stickers.

'Quiet down, please, everyone,' she ordered. It was time she showed the boys a firm hand, as well. 'Gregory . . . Oaks, please see that the boys keep in line.'

'All right, chaps,' Oaks said. 'Queue up now. Barlow, stop that snivelling. You're setting a bad example.'

Shirley did not think that was fair. Barlow looked mournful and bewildered but he certainly was not snivelling. She went to the head of the line and brought him milk and biscuits. She could tell from his reluctance to accept them and the resentful faces of the boys not so favoured that it was a mistake.

Millis made more trips to the reserved carriage with luggage while the boys had their milk and biscuits. At least he had a strong back and was willing to work, Shirley thought. If only he wasn't always trying so desperately hard to be funny.

The most distinguished-looking man Shirley had ever seen came across the platform towards her. He was very trim for his age, which she thought must be the early fifties like her father, silver at the temples, his expression and carriage radiating authority and self-confidence. His visored cap was set just so and his tunic with four wavy stripes at the cuffs fitted him perfectly. He was carrying a beautifully aged leather suitcase and matching attaché case. He started to put them down when he reached her but, noting the condition of the platform, thrust them towards two of the larger boys as if he expected the boys to take them without question. The boys did so, sensing exactly that.

He swept off his cap in a courtly, old-fashioned gesture and said, 'Miss Hunt? Miss Shirley Hunt?'

'Yes?' she replied, wondering how this unusual man knew her name.

'I thought you must be,' he said, holding out his hand. 'I'm Captain Penrose, master of the *Amindra*. You'll be making the voyage with me.'

His grip was strong and reassuring but somehow gentle. She was unexpectedly stirred by the contact and withdrew her hand guiltily from his. This was not the way to react to a man who reminded her of her father. She sought for proper words to break what was to her an uncomfortable silence.

'It's very decent, what you're doing, ma'am,' he said. 'And plucky. When it's not even your war.'

'I think it is my war,' she said.

If only he were a little younger, she thought. But if he were, he would not inspire such – what was the word she was looking for? – trust. No, she preferred Captain Penrose exactly the age he was.

Millis came walking up with milk, a grin on his face. He offered it to Penrose, saying, 'Have a drink, sailor? Nothing's too good for our lads in the fighting forces.'

Shirley wanted to kill him.

'Who might you be?' Penrose demanded icily, ignoring

48

the milk.

'Joe Millis, at your service.'

'So you're Millis,' Penrose said. 'You do what you signed on to do and we may just get along. You must have something better to do here. I suggest you hop to it.'

'Aye, aye, sir,' Millis said, undaunted, leaving them.

'My dear Captain,' a woman's voice called. 'There you are.'

A bony, grey-haired woman approached them, followed by a porter carrying two obviously very heavy suitcases.

'Lady Anne,' Penrose said, hurrying to meet her. 'I was so pleased to find you were crossing with me once again. So dreadfully sorry it must be on such a sad errand.'

He beckoned Shirley to join them.

'Lady Anne, this charming girl is Miss Hunt,' he said. 'She's escorting the boys to America. American, you know.'

Lady Anne held Shirley's soft hand in her own thin one.

'You're so young,' she said. 'Hardly older . . .'

She did not finish the sentence and her faded blue eyes softened for an instant. The girl was almost as young as Tony, she thought. Tony would have liked her. He was keen on Americans.

Despite the momentary softening, Shirley felt intimidated by the woman. Lady Anne was, in her own way, as imposing as Captain Penrose. Erect, confident, accustomed to privilege.

'I expect we will be seeing a good deal of one another over the next few days,' Lady Anne said, releasing her hand.

'That would be nice,' Shirley said, knowing how banal it sounded.

A slender, hollow-eyed man with the beginning of a paunch came slowly along the platform as if in a daze and stopped to regard the carriage with the Children's Overseas Reception Board markings. He wore a dark suit and a bowler, both lightly flecked with ash, as if he had been out in the bombing the night before and neglected to brush it off.

The jumped-up little clerk has the wind up already and we haven't even left Euston Station, Penrose thought. What could the DNI have been thinking of, lumbering him with a man like that?

Rosten looked his way but did not respond to Penrose's curt nod. He continued on to the carriage steps.

'You can't go in there, sir,' Shirley called. 'It's reserved for the children.'

Rosten looked at her as if he did not understand English.

'It's all right,' Penrose told her. 'He's with the Board. He's meant to go along.'

'No one told me,' Shirley said.

No one told you a lot of things about this voyage, Penrose thought.

Rosten disappeared into the carriage.

Penrose motioned for the boys to give his cases to Lady Anne's porter, who tucked them under his burdened arms.

'Until Glasgow, then,' Penrose said to Shirley, conducting Lady Anne towards a first-class carriage.

Exasperated with Millis for not coming back out to help, Shirley urged the boys towards their reserved carriage. Their shoes left prints in the crusted platform and bits of burned asphalt clung to the soles. They were going to be hard to clean, she thought, remembering a question on the Children's Overseas Reception Board's list. 'Will you be willing to wash clothes, go on straight twenty-four-hour duty, care for fifteen seasick children . . . ?' Shoes had not been covered but she had no doubt they were included. And she had thirty-seven to look after, not fifteen, unless Millis really pitched in. Cleaning shoes was something he should be able to manage. Where was he, anyhow?

Rosten was sitting in a compartment gazing out of the

50

window as vacantly as he had regarded Captain Penrose. Though he did not look like a drinking man she wondered if he were drunk. He was hardly an impressive representative of the Board. She wondered if he was supposed to help with the children or was going along to see to arrangements in the United States.

The line of boys stopped moving. A knot of them were jammed together at a compartment in the middle of the carriage. Oaks went in briefly and pushed his way back to her.

'Someone's in there,' he said. 'I ordered him out but he told me to bugger off. If you like, I'll take some of the other chaps and put him out.'

'I'll handle this, thank you,' she said.

Where was that clownish Millis? If this was the way he was going to be, never around when needed, Captain Penrose would put him straight. But she wasn't going to Captain Penrose with her problems. She was a grown woman and would take care of them herself. As was expected of her.

Before she could follow Oaks, a long, ragged sigh arrested her. It had come from Rosten. He looked ill. She went to him quickly.

'Are you all right, Mr . . . ?'

'Rosten,' he said, rising. 'Benjamin Rosten.'

'Sit down, please. Are you ill? Can I get you anything?'

He shook his head and smiled wanly.

'Thank you, no. My wife . . .'

'Your wife?'

'She was killed last night in the bombing.'

'Oh. I'm terribly sorry. If there's anything . . .'

He shook his head again and went back to staring out of the window. Embarrassed at her earlier thoughts about the man and desperately sorry for him, she let Oaks lead her back to the occupied compartment. A man in the uniform of a merchant-navy officer lay sprawled on one of the

51

seats. An arm covered his face and she could not see if he was young or old.

'Excuse me,' she said hesitantly, and then with greater firmness, 'you'll have to find another car. This one is reserved for the children.'

The arm slid from his face and one unblinking eye regarded her. He sat up slowly, continuing to stare. There was something nakedly appraising in his look. She felt herself flush. It was partly because of his insolence but also because he was arrestingly handsome. And he obviously knew it. And its effect on her. First Captain Penrose and now this . . . this person. Why was she so vulnerable? She hadn't been like that since college. It was all this excitement and responsibility.

'Didn't you hear what I said?' she demanded.

'What are you doing here, then?' he said. 'You're no child. And certainly not their mother. Much too young and sexy.'

'I'll call the guard,' she threatened.

'Don't do that, love,' he said easily. 'Isn't this the lot for the *Amindra*?'

'What's that to do with you?'

'I'm for the old tub, too. First Officer Robert Barrett. My friends call me Robbie.'

So he could turn on the charm when he wanted to, but she wasn't going to fall for that. She knew how to handle his type. She'd had to do it since she first developed breasts at thirteen.

'And what do they call you?' he continued.

'Miss Hunt. And you'll have to find yourself another car.'

'If you insist, love,' he said, getting to his feet and taking down a seabag from the rack. 'Will you be escorting the little monsters?'

'Yes, I will, and I'll thank you not to call them that.'

'I expect I'll be seeing a good deal more of you, then,' he

52

said, touching the visor of his cap in a parting salute.

Not bloody likely, you conceited ass, she thought grimly as he shouldered his way through the boys standing at the entrance enjoying the spectacle. Even if you do look like Robert Taylor, a crude, more rugged Robert Taylor. Why did they all think they were God's gift to the ladies? And not recognize a lady when they saw one? If only young men behaved like Captain Penrose.

The *Amindra*, 10,000 tons, 400 feet long and bristling with masts, spars and cranes, lay heavily in her River Clyde berth at Greenock, dripping with the chilly, mid-afternoon drizzle. Captain Penrose had not come aboard with his passengers. He had got off the train ahead of the others in Glasgow and taken a taxi to Castle Street to visit his injured First Officer in Glasgow Royal Infirmary before going on to Greenock to report to the Naval Control Service Officer.

First Officer Campbell, his head bandaged and one plaster-encased leg suspended in traction, had shaken his head in frustration as he described the accident that had incapacitated him.

'There I was, sober as a priest and minding my own business, when the bastard comes right at me over the kerb. Been a dead man, I would, if I hadn't had my wits about me. Bloody bastard says his brakes failed.'

First Officer Campbell did not normally sprinkle his conversation with obscenities when addressing Penrose – none of his officers did if they hoped to continue serving under him – but in the circumstances the captain thought his First Officer's salty language was justified. He would have not been so tolerant had they been aboard ship. He patted Campbell's shoulder, awkwardly because he did not ordinarily indulge in such familiarities with anybody, let alone his officers, and left him a scarce bottle of Laphroaig for solace. Aboard ship he permitted only an occasional social drink and no officer or seaman dared come on watch with the hint of liquor on his breath. But a skinful of the strong, peaty whisky was little enough consolation for missing a voyage which one day would be in the history books.

In Greenock, it was obvious from the Naval Control Service Officer's instructions that the NCSO was not privy to the nature of the *Amindra*'s cargo or to her true destination. In addition to the usual orders, minefield charts and other documents, he gave Penrose two sealed green canvas pouches fitted with brassbound eyelets and lead weights. The holes and weights, Penrose did not have to be told, were to facilitate sinking should it be necessary to jettison the pouches.

One of the pouches, the NCSO told him, contained orders meant to be opened when the *Amindra* was well at sea. Penrose guessed they were orders directing him to Halifax along with instructions for approaching the harbour there – the course to be steered, the identification flags to be hoisted, special coded signals and regulations to be followed. There would be, he knew, nothing in writing about the true nature of his cargo or its disposal. The second pouch was to be delivered by hand to 'appropriate authorities' at destination. Its contents, Penrose speculated, would be for Rosten to present to the bank officials from Montreal.

Rosten, too, had stopped over in Glasgow. Having nothing but the clothes on his back he had been obliged to shop for a wardrobe and other necessities to see him through the voyage. There was little choice in wartime Glasgow but, though normally a fastidious, albeit conservative, dresser, he did not care, taking whatever was available. He paid a hall porter at the Glendower Arms, a small hotel off Princess Street, for pressing and brushing his suit.

Still numb from his loss but refreshed by a hot bath, he

reached the *Amindra* well after the other passengers, carrying everything he owned in a glaringly new tin suitcase he had purchased at Woolworth's and wearing an out-of-character cloth cap instead of the bowler with which he had begun his journey. Feeling naked without his umbrella, which he had forgotten to replace, he regretted now that he had left his bowler in the shop where he purchased the cap. With everything in such short supply, a good hat would be hard to come by when he returned to England.

The regret was fleeting. Why should he be concerned about a hat when it hardly mattered if he returned at all? There was nothing there for him now.

Shirley and Millis were helping the boys settle in. The *Amindra* had peace-time accommodation for only fourteen passengers, two to a stateroom, and even with the most extreme crowding the youngsters could not have been jammed into cabins for a whole week. The Number 4 'tween-deck, just aft of the bridge, had been hastily fitted out as a dormitory, with double-decker bunks made of iron piping set end to end and held fast against the bulkheads. Each bunk had a straw-filled palliasse and two blankets, and between each set of two were battens intended to keep the boys' suitcases from sliding around the deck in heavy weather. There being no room for so many extra in the captain's, engineers' or crew's messes, the boys' dining facilities were also in Number 4 'tween-deck – long, metal-legged tables and benches screwed to the deck, with fiddles around the outer edges of the tables to keep plates and cutlery from skidding off in heavy seas.

Shirley approved of the arrangement. It was good to have all the boys together and the benches and tables afforded an excellent play- and study-area when not in use for meals. Millis was proving to be unexpectedly helpful, getting the children sorted out into their bunks and showing the younger ones how to stow their suitcases, though his antics did make them more unruly than she would have liked. She decided to talk to him about that privately. Her father, once a teacher himself, had advised her, after she got her job in Paris, that if she must scold a pupil she should do so by taking him aside so humiliation wouldn't be added to his punishment. Captain Penrose hadn't done that with Millis at Euston but she could hardly blame him.

Barlow had stood back, clutching his cardboard suitcase, while the other boys had scrambled for what they imagined to be the most desirable bunks. A number of them had already formed friendships and wanted to be close together. No one had shown enthusiasm about bunking with Barlow until Oaks, that manly youngster, led him to a tier under a ventilator duct and said, 'You take the top one, where you'll have plenty of fresh air. I'll kip below.' Poor little Barlow had accepted the proposal with obvious suspicion. During the coming days she intended teaching him how to accept kindnesses graciously.

Millis was quartered with the boys. He had a separate single bunk against the bulkhead near the entrance, with a curtain which could be drawn for privacy along a semi-circular metal track fixed to the overhead. He also had a metal locker for his personal effects fastened to the bulkhead above his bunk.

She was pleased with that arrangement, too. The boys would always have an adult, if you could call Millis an adult, near at hand.

'If you have any problems, any problems at all,' she instructed Millis, 'you'll come to me. Any hour of the day or night.'

'I'm that relieved,' Millis said. 'I was wondering who'd look after me. My mum always did before, you know. Saw I said my prayers and tucked me in every night. Will you be tucking me in?'

The boys laughed and nudged each other. Shirley

flushed and started to make an angry retort. But that was not the way to handle this oaf.

'I couldn't compete with a mother like that,' she said sweetly. 'You'll just have to make do with your teddy bear.'

The boys were now laughing with her instead of at her. She wondered how she had let herself be so helpless and discouraged at the prospect of the journey.

Even the anticipated problem with the boys' filthy shoes had taken care of itself. All their running up and down the aisle on the train ride and the walk along the puddled wharf had cleaned the soles nicely.

Except for the incident with Barrett when they boarded the *Amindra* this was a most auspicious beginning. With his seabag on one broad shoulder, he had taken her arm to help her up the gangplank and only tightened his grip when she tried to pull away. He had held her arm high up, with the back of his hand against her breast.

'I'll see you to your cabin,' he'd said. 'I'll need to know where to find you if you get lonesome.'

Fortunately, the ship's steward, a roundish, balding middle-aged man called Harry Dutton, had seen what was happening. He stepped forward and took her suitcase.

'The lads have been asking for you, miss,' he said diplomatically. 'Why don't you go and check on them while I take these bags to your quarters?'

The steward was back in his customary position at the top of the gangplank when Captain Penrose came aboard late in the afternoon. This time he was accompanied by the chief engineer, the bosun, and the Second and Third Officers. They had all been on the lookout for the captain and assembled quickly when they heard he was arriving. They greeted him formally, as they knew was expected of them. Penrose was notorious for running a tight ship. His reputation for discipline was legendary when he was master of the *Empress* and had in no way diminished now he was commanding a cargo–passenger vessel. All of them had sailed with him before except the Third Officer, a pink-cheeked youngster from Cornwall named Nutley.

'Where's the new Number One?' Penrose asked.

'Came aboard with the young lady escorting the evacuee children, sir,' Dutton said.

The captain nodded. 'Mr Nutley,' he said, addressing himself to the young Third Officer. 'It is Nutley, isn't it?'

'Yes, sir.'

'Please find Mr Barrett and tell him to report to my quarters immediately.'

Nutley saluted smartly and disappeared up a companion-way. Penrose watched him go, then gave his suitcase to Dutton and followed the steward to the master's cabin. There, after carefully stowing the green canvas pouches in a locked drawer, he questioned Dutton about the way the passengers were settling in.

'Like ducks to water, most of 'em, sir,' the steward replied. 'Except that Mr Rosten.' He shook his head. 'A rum lot he is, and no mistake.'

Penrose fixed the other man with a look that implied it was not the crew's job to make personal observations about passengers unless asked for them. Chastened, Dutton turned back to unpacking the captain's bags.

'What about Mr Donahue?'

'Not aboard yet, sir.'

Penrose glanced at his watch. It was a gesture designed to hide his irritation. He had long ago learned not to display emotion of any kind in front of the crew.

'I want to be informed the moment he arrives,' he said. 'And see what's keeping First Officer Barrett. Mr Nutley seems to have got lost.'

He never referred to ship's officers or first-class passengers by their bare last names when talking to subordinates.

Dutton had been gone less than five minutes when there

was a sharp rap at his door. He sensed it was Barrett and decided to let him cool his heels. He finished fitting his framed photographs into their brackets on the bulkhead – his wife Nellie with Meg, their younger daughter, and Alice with her husband and young Edward – and was putting up a framed motto Nellie had needlepointed for him years ago, 'Keep then the Sea, which is the Wall of England, And then is England kept in God's own hands', when the door opened.

'You will wait to be invited before entering my quarters,' he announced without looking round.

He heard the door close. When he turned, there was no one there. The knock came again. Penrose took a seat in the heavy chair at his ornate desk. Both were too large for the cabin. He had been permitted to take them from his quarters aboard the *Empress* when the Admiralty converted the former luxury passenger liner into a troop carrier. The furniture gave him a sense of continuity. One day, God willing, they and he would be back aboard her.

'Enter,' he called finally.

Barrett was younger than he expected, and very different-looking. He came in carrying a manila envelope in his hand and wearing his cap at a jaunty angle. Penrose took an immediate dislike to the man. Too cocksure. It was an attitude he'd seen in other handsome men. They seemed to feel their good looks gave them special privileges. Penrose decided the other man needed taking down a peg or two and let him stand for almost a full minute before speaking to him.

'Cap,' he said, breaking the silence.

'Sir?'

'You will remove your cap in the master's quarters.'

'Aye, aye, sir.' Barrett removed his cap and tucked it under his arm. 'First Officer Barrett reporting as requested, sir.' He came to attention and offered the other man the envelope he was holding.

Instead of taking it, Penrose nodded his head to indicate Barrett was to put it on the desk. Then, instead of telling him to stand at ease or inviting him to sit down, the captain let him remain where he stood.

'You weren't here when I came aboard,' he said.

'Nature called, sir.'

'Nature – ?'

'I was in the head –'

'You're not British, I take it.' Penrose made the observation sound like an accusation.

'Close enough, sir. I'm Canadian.'

The sound of motor-cycle engines filtered through the rain-streaked portholes.

'I'm informed you know your job, Mr Barrett, but you've got a great deal to learn about the way I expect officers aboard my ship to . . .'

A polite knock at the door interrupted him and Dutton called, 'Mr Donahue's arriving, sir.'

'That will be all for now, Mr Barrett,' the captain said curtly. 'I'll finish with you later.'

He waited until the door closed behind Barrett before putting his cap on and going out on deck. A Rolls-Royce flanked by two motor cycles with red-capped Military Police drivers was drawn up alongside the *Amindra* and a big, well-fed civilian carrying a large briefcase was climbing the gangplank, sheltered by a streaming umbrella in the hands of a liveried chauffeur. The lid of the boot was open and a man in a raincoat was lifting out luggage. Two leather suitcases were already on the wharf beside the car. When Donahue drew closer, Penrose saw the briefcase he was carrying was chained to his wrist.

Penrose welcomed him aboard and instructed Dutton to take a couple of seamen and fetch his luggage. Donahue refused the captain's offer to put his briefcase in the ship's strongroom.

'I hope your boys'll be careful with my car when they

60

bring it aboard,' Donahue said jovially.

'I beg your pardon?' Penrose said.

'My Rolls-Royce,' the other man said. 'Weren't you informed? I've got Admiralty clearance to take it back to the States.'

On the wharf, the man in the raincoat was already siphoning the petrol tank and draining the oil.

Penrose had not noticed a motor car on the bill of lading but this was hardly a great surprise in view of all else that had not been on it. He was nevertheless annoyed at Donahue's calling his men 'boys'. He hid his annoyance. Donahue had diplomatic status and, more important, he was a first-class passenger.

Late on Sunday night the *Amindra* slipped past the Tail-of-the-Bank naval anchorage on the ebb tide and crept through the opening in the anti-submarine boom, in total darkness except for the wink of beacons. She moved through a world of complete silence, the only sounds those she made herself – thump of diesels, creaking of plates and masts.

Shirley Hunt lay sleepless in her bunk, her door securely locked against any nocturnal visit from Barrett. She didn't think he would dare but was taking no chances. She wondered how she could even let herself think about him after the way he'd behaved. Thank God for Captain Penrose. He had been marvellous, taking time from his duties to come down and look in on the children and tell her that if there was anything at all she needed to go directly to him. Such a thoughtful man. And he emanated a strength, a solidity that made her feel, well, safe somehow. She sensed he'd been impressed by her, too. It was this thought which, despite the obvious difference in their ages, still exhilarated her. Enough to make sleep impossible. She considered getting dressed and going below to check on the boys. She was, after all, on twenty-

61

four-hour duty. But it was bitterly cold outside – Captain Penrose had told her Greenock was almost the same latitude as Goose Bay, Labrador – and she'd given Millis explicit instructions to fetch her if any of the lads needed attention.

Below, Millis slept peacefully despite the piercing cold penetrating the Number 4 'tween-deck through the hull plates and sweeping in through the ventilator duct above Peter Barlow. He had sent the boys to bed giggling with clever routines, some of the best he had stolen from Max Miller, Arthur Askey and others. Seeing immediately that Barlow was on his way to becoming an outcast and the special butt of the Oaks boy – he was certain Oaks had known what it would be like under the ventilator duct – he had worked Barlow into one of them. He gave Barlow a lemon cadged from the galley and after a whispered conference persuaded him to participate despite Barlow's shyness and mistrust. He sent the boy strolling between the mess tables holding the lemon screwed in his ear.

'I say, I say, I say, do you know you've a lemon in your ear?'

'I can't hear you,' Barlow replied nervously. 'I've got a lemon in my ear.'

'What are you doing with a lemon in your ear?'

Emboldened by the laughter, Barlow said more confidently, 'You've heard of a hearing aid?'

'Of course I've heard of a hearing aid.'

'Well, then, this is a lemon aid.'

Barlow had gone to bed swollen with success.

Soon afterwards Millis tucked the smaller, more homesick boys in their bunks, saying, 'Just call me mum,' and went to bed himself.

Now he was awakened by a startled cry and a heavy thud, accompanied by a gasp. He took the flashlight clipped to the bulkhead beside his bunk and played its beam across the deck. Barlow was picking himself up, clutching an elbow to his side, and Oaks was snickering in his bunk. Millis had no doubt Oaks had reached up with his feet and prodded the smaller boy out of the upper bunk.

'You all right, lad?' Millis said, hurrying to him.

Oaks had his eyes closed, pretending to sleep.

Barlow nodded that he was and climbed back into his bunk, favouring the elbow. I've been hurt worse by bigger boys than you, Oaks, he thought, and if you think I'm going to cry or snitch you don't know Peter Barlow.

The lad was spunkier than he looked, Millis thought, and not one to tell tales. Oaks might find he had his hands full if he didn't watch out. He moved Barlow's suitcase to the tier with the vacant bunk and carried him, blankets and all, to it.

'Thank you, Mr Millis,' Barlow whispered, too low for any but Millis to hear.

'Call me mum,' Millis said.

Andrew Donahue's stateroom was brightly lit behind its blacked-out portholes. He sat at the dressing-table, which also served as a desk, making notes for the report he intended delivering to President Roosevelt. Writing down his thoughts was difficult for him. He had long been accustomed to dictating everything to a secretary. He was smoking a cigar of the type he'd heard Winston Churchill favoured and sipping brandy from the small silver cup that formed the cap for his silver hip flask. He smiled to himself as he worked. It was not that he particularly enjoyed writing a coroner's report on Britain's coming demise, it was just that he could not help thinking about that stuffed shirt, Penrose, who had no idea the briefcase he'd brought aboard chained to his wrist was full of secret memos about British production capacities and lack of raw materials and reports of casualties far higher than had been released to the British public.

There was a lot Penrose didn't know. Too full of his own importance to see past his nose. Like the Rolls-Royce. The Admiralty hadn't approved its being loaded aboard. But the captain had fallen for that innocent, 'Weren't you informed?' The car was one reason he was aboard this slow-moving tub instead of flying back to Washington. That and all the other great stuff he'd picked up at bargain prices in London antique shops. They were almost giving away Georgian silverware. Growing up, he'd never even heard of Georgian silverware. And if he had, he wouldn't have been interested. But he'd learned a lot since those lean days.

The Rolls wasn't the main reason for returning by sea, of course. Aboard ship he could work on his report without distractions and have it in shape to give to the President in time to head off the lend-lease programme. Giving aid to Britain would be a total waste.

Donahue had dined with Ambassador Kennedy the first evening he'd spent in London. They had known each other for over twenty years and Kennedy had felt free to confide in him.

'Listen, Andy,' the Ambassador had said, 'the root problem in Europe today isn't Hitler or Fascism, but simple unemployment. When a man's hungry he doesn't give a damn who's in command so long as he, and his family, get the promise of a decent meal. That's why this war is such a mistake. All it's ever going to achieve is a foundation for Communism, and I hate to think of a single American dying for that.' As they walked to the taxi together Kennedy had put his hand on Donahue's shoulder and said, 'I've got four boys, Andy, and they've got their whole lives ahead of them. Every one of them is going to outlive me and I don't want to see them killed off in a war that's only going to benefit Russia. You understand that, don't you?'

Donahue did understand the hopelessness of Britain's

chances against Hitler. The Germans had troops that were better equipped and far better trained. The English hadn't even begun to gear up for the production of war material. And, as an island, Britain was dependent on shipping for importing almost all its raw materials as well as its food. Churchill might make great speeches but he was fooling himself and his people if he thought words were going to bring him the victory he so loudly proclaimed was only a matter of time.

Lady Anne lay awake in her stateroom. She had not slept at all well since receiving the news of her son's death. It was much more difficult alone in the dark than among friends during the day. It was especially difficult tonight. The motion of the ship brought back poignant memories of another voyage with Captain Penrose when Tony was alive, and her husband as well. Tony had been only twelve then, on his first Atlantic crossing. Now he would never make another unless after the war she brought him back to England to lie beside his father. Though the other passengers had thought Captain Penrose a formal man, he had invited Tony to the bridge and let him wear his braided cap. It had come down over Tony's ears in the most ridiculous manner but Captain Penrose had not embarrassed the lad by so much as a smile.

Dear Captain Penrose. It was such a comfort to be on a ship commanded by him. Despite his stern appearance he could be utterly charming to those he liked. He'd quite turned the head of that little American girl without at all intending to. Lady Anne did not, generally speaking, care much for Americans, particularly the vulgarly rich, self-satisfied ones like that fellow Donahue, but Shirley Hunt seemed cut from a very different cloth and one couldn't help but admire the way she was risking her life to help get British children out of the bombing.

Tomorrow night Captain Penrose had promised a

special dinner in the saloon. Perhaps it would stretch out into the late evening and she would be tired enough to sleep.

Rosten slept heavily. Tormented by the memory of his house collapsing in flames and the wife he'd never see again, he had taken a five-grain Medinal immediately after returning from a surreptitious visit with Penrose to the hold containing the secret cargo. Everything had looked well enough to him, with the crates innocently stencilled and neatly stacked among those actually containing what their markings said they did. Except that he had wondered why they weren't put underneath the genuine cargo and had raised the question with Penrose. Penrose had explained brusquely that what came off first at destination went on last at the port of embarkation. But Penrose had not been too pleased with their location, either. The way some of them had been stacked there was the possibility of their shifting in really foul weather.

On the bridge, Captain Penrose stood with his feet planted, sipping sweet, hot cocoa from a white mug and staring through the Kent screen for the Ailsa Craig beacon. The Kent screen was a swiftly rotating circular glass pane meant to spin off the rain that obscured flat surfaces. His presence on the bridge was unnecessary – the Officer of the Watch was eminently capable – but despite his seeming impassivity he was exultant and surging with energy. He had not felt so since the maiden voyage of the *Empress*. This voyage would be the capstone of a long and brilliant career. He would continue sailing as long as he was needed, of course, but never again would he be given another opportunity to render such a tremendous service. And he was pleased with the crew they had given him. Except for Barrett and possibly young Nutley, who was green but willing enough to learn, there was not a man among them he would not have chosen himself. A war-time mix of seasoned veterans, including some, like Second Officer Briscoe, who had returned to sea after a long stay ashore, and willing young men who had turned to it because of their country's need. Not one among them, barring Barrett again, did he expect to do anything but measure up under even the most adverse circumstances. Of the ninety-five men serving aboard the *Amindra*, the only really unknown quantity was the gun crew. Defensively Equipped Merchant Ship 'hostilities only' Naval Reserve types, they lacked sea-going experience, but appeared keen enough. And for icing on the cake, there was Lady Anne Saville-Fletcher, one of the most gracious women it had been his good fortune to skipper across the Atlantic aboard the *Empress* in pre-war days. He no longer resented even Rosten so strongly. The other man had explained what had happened to his wife. His was a tragic story and Penrose felt genuinely sorry for him. The fact that Rosten could carry on after such a loss was admirable.

In mid-Atlantic a thousand miles off Dakar, Captain Freiburg leaned over a map table in the pitching chart room of the *Adler*. Schramm and the Navigation Officer, Lieutenant Sperling, looked on as he studied the position Sperling had entered for him from co-ordinates pencilled on a slip of paper. Four small chamois pouches filled with sand and placed at four corners of the chart on the table kept it from rolling closed.

'This is where we take the *Amindra*,' Freiburg said, planting his broad thumb on a neatly marked X.

It was roughly two-thirds of the distance between the southern tip of Ireland and St John's, Newfoundland.

Looking dubious, Sperling laid down a long straight-edge and with the dividers stepped off the distance to the point of interception, first from the *Adler*'s present position and then from the Irish Sea's North Channel exit.

Freiburg could almost see the wheels turning in the other man's head as he made mental calculations. The stork-thin, bespectacled Sperling had been a *realschule* mathematics instructor in civilian life and was considered something of a genius with figures.

'If we were able to maintain a steady sixteen knots,' Sperling said, 'we will be there in five days. If the *Amindra* can do only as well as fourteen knots, she will be there in four. We'll never manage it.'

Freiburg smiled and filled his pipe with Player's tobacco which he had appropriated from an English ship he had taken prize some weeks earlier.

'She'll be delayed,' he said. 'We have a friend aboard the *Amindra*.'

Chapter Five

The 7,680-ton *Adler*, 'Eagle', had been converted from an ordinary freighter to a deadly merchant raider at Kiel soon after the outbreak of war. She had broken out of the British air–sea blockade in May, nearly four months before her present mission. She was one of the 'first wave' of such raiders, those running the gauntlet between late March and early June. With the others, the *Atlantis, Orion, Widder, Thor, Pinguin* and *Komet*, she had ravaged shipping in the South Atlantic and the Indian Ocean, laying mines, sinking freighters and tankers, seizing vital cargoes and sending vessels back to the homeland with prize crews.

She was manned by fifteen officers and 326 petty officers and sailors. Captain Freiburg and the ship's surgeon, Dr Teuer, were the only officers who had seen service aboard warships in the First Word War – Teuer had not been a doctor then – but a number of the older petty officers had seen action in that conflict. As in the case of the *Amindra*, the crew comprised a mix of old-timers and new men, though in the case of the *Adler*'s complement the men had been welded into a superb fighting instrument by rigorous training and fifteen weeks of attacking enemy shipping and evading roving enemy naval forces. Fewer than half the *Amindra*'s crew had ever sailed together before.

Since the rendezvous with the *Nordmark*, while the *Adler* continued to plough northward at her top cruising speed of sixteen knots, the crew had been industriously converting the Swedish *Vetlanda* to the Norwegian *Ole Lavrans.* Freiburg had selected the new identity with great care, consulting Lloyd's Register for a vessel approximating to the *Adler*'s dimensions and studying the most recent Intelligence reports of Allied shipping activity. Not only must the *Adler* look like an existing Norwegian vessel but it must also look like one known to be plying that part of the world.

The Cross of St Olaf flag was already flying from the masthead. A leading seaman who had been a sign-painter in civilian life dangled in a bosun's chair at the bow, lettering the *Adler*'s new name and cursing the seas that made his job more difficult. A crew-mate working on the deck above him paused long enough to shout down, 'I'll ask the captain to find a nice level stretch for you.' The sign-painter cursed him, too.

Other seamen in bosun's chairs were painting the hull and the newly recontoured funnel, adding the markings of the *Ole Lavrans'* shipping line to the latter. Aft, a seaman was stencilling a Norwegian consignee and port on the deckload concealing a 5.9-incher, while all about him carpenters and welders were converting the flush-deck *Vetlanda* into the well-deck *Ole Lavrans*. Different gangs, working from diagrams, altered the masts and cranes to match the silhouette of the Norwegian vessel. Everyone except the men dangling in the bosun's chairs at the mercy of the waves worked cheerfully, with the ease and competence born of much practice.

They all wore ordinary seamen's clothing. Their officers wore the peaked uniform caps of Norwegian ship's officers and uniform tunics with appropriate sleeve markings.

Captain Freiburg, hands clasped loosely behind his back, strolled the deck observing the progress of the transformation. He went at a leisurely pace, pausing for consultations with petty officers supervising the work or to address a deck-rating by name. More often than not his remarks were greeted with laughter.

'Masthead in sight!' the periscope lookout shouted.

From periscope height, a ship's masts could be seen as far away as twenty miles when visibility was good, a far greater distance than that from which the *Adler* could be sighted from a navigation bridge.

The men straightened eagerly, in anticipation of 'Action Stations!'

Freiburg cupped his hands around his mouth and shouted, 'Details?'

'Bearing port five degrees, sir. Closing course.'

The other ship, still invisible from the deck of the *Adler*, was angling towards it.

The men put down their tools and turned to haul up the hull painters. The mast painters began letting down their chairs.

'Carry on,' Freiburg ordered.

The petty officers relayed the captain's orders to get back to work to the disappointed ratings in far more colourful language. Freiburg walked unhurriedly to the foot of the bridge and blew the windpipe to activate the whistle on the bridge. There was a similar whistle over the captain's bunk, by which he could be alerted from many parts of the ship.

'Bridge,' the Officer of the Watch answered over the speaking tube.

Freiburg barked instructions to order full speed and alter the course ten degrees to starboard. That would take the *Adler* well out of the path of the oncoming vessel.

Acetylene tanks slid across the deck, men scrambled to keep their footing, the mast painters swung in their chairs and the bow sign-painter banged against the hull and dropped his brush into the sea as a swell broadsided the veering *Adler*. Freiburg, feet firmly planted, did not even sway.

'And tell the radio operator to monitor British frequencies for any transmissions about a sighting in this area,' he added.

The other vessel could not have seen the *Adler* at this distance, but where caution was advocated the quick-acting captain of the *Adler* could be cautious. He was already composing an innocuous signal to be sent in Norwegian – he did not know the language, but two of his signals men did – to be transmitted to an imaginary recipient in the event that his ship had been sighted. Whatever the nationality of the other vessel and whatever its cargo, it was not a prize remotely approaching the importance of his intended prey. His orders were clear: take the *Amindra* at any cost.

He sent a rating swarming up the mast to the periscope lookout with orders to report back to him immediately the intruding masthead dropped below the horizon. The man was back in minutes. Freiburg ordered the *Adler* back on course at cruising speed and went to his quarters for a nap. Such was the nature of the *Adler*'s work that often Freiburg could not sleep for very long periods at a time, so he had learned to nap when he could.

His cabin was cramped and much more austere than Captain Penrose's on the *Amindra*. Like Penrose, Captain Freiburg's family photographs were fitted into battens on the bulkhead over his bunk. His wife of fourteen years, Hilde – among friends he called her Brünnhilde because she was fair, sturdily blonde and as tall as he – with Friedrich and Hermine when young, Friedrich in a little sailor suit. There were separate, more recent, photographs of the two children alone. Hermine twelve now and Friedrich nine. She resembled her father, he his mother, 'unfortunately', Freiburg always commented wryly, 'for Hermine'.

Few other personal possessions were in evidence. A rack of well-caked pipes, a gramophone on which he sometimes listened to his small collection of recordings by Hans Alber and the actress Marika Rökk – he favoured the more sentimental ones – and an ornate beer mug with a hinged

72

pewter lid and the inscription, *Ofen Warm, Bier Kalt, Frau Jung, Wein Alt.* 'Oven Warm, Beer Cold, Wife Young, Wine Old.' The mug had accompanied him on every ship in which he had served since he was a sub-lieutenant aboard the cruiser *Breslau* in the First World War. To the crew of the *Adler*, who knew its history, it was the Old Man's *Glückskrug*, 'Lucky Mug'.

It was full dawn when the *Amindra* drew past the rain-washed hills of the Mull of Kintyre and altered course to go between the tip of Scotland and Fair Head on the Irish coast to leave the North Channel for the open Atlantic.

Shirley Hunt, wearing all the heavy clothes she possessed, stood at a porthole looking out at what would be her last glimpse of land for a week. She thought the bracken-covered, mist-veiled hills quite the loveliest view she had ever seen, conscious that the perilous, difficult journey she was beginning had heightened her awareness and therefore her appreciation.

Though it had taken hours for her to fall asleep she had awakened early, eager to begin working with the boys and wondering if Millis had taken proper care of them during the night. She wished she had reminded him to keep a special eye on Peter Barlow; the boy seemed so lost and vulnerable. It was still too early to join them now. They would be washing in the shower-room near their dormitory and getting dressed and certainly would not want a female around during all that. Millis would just have to handle them by himself for a little while longer.

She heard footsteps and saw Barrett coming along the deck outside her cabin. He saw her standing at the porthole before she could pull away. He smiled at her – he had very white, even teeth – and held his thumb up in a friendly salute. She smiled back at him, but not too broadly. The last thing she wanted was to give him any encouragement.

In the dormitory most of the boys were up, shivering,

though a few of the younger ones were still curled up in their bunks. Except for Oaks they seemed a bit uneasy but did their best to hide their apprehension with loud shouting and exaggerated horseplay. Millis woke the still sleeping youngsters, taking time to chat to each of them until the child was fully aware of where he was and, on the surface at least, became reconciled to it. Then he set them all to making their bunks. Many of them had been in boarding schools and did not have to be shown how. They were boys from families well off enough to pay full price for their passage aboard the *Amindra*. A few, however, like Barlow, who were from the slums of East London, their fares paid by a government grant, needed to be taught how to make a tight bunk. Oaks volunteered to help.

Millis left him in charge of the others and went off on his own. After making sure he was not observed, he threaded his way along bulkheads and down companionways until he finally reached the holds. Groping through inky darkness for a switch-box, he encountered a lever, pulled it down and light suddenly flooded the area where he stood. Wooden crates were piled tier after tier like huge building blocks with narrow aisles between them. What little could be seen of bulkheads and hull was covered with the wooden frames of insulation and laced with pipes which normally carried refrigerant. Ventilation louvres, set high in the bulkhead, five feet or more above the topmost tier of unpainted crates, poured in outside air in a low, unending hiss. There was a smell of mildew in the air, and a metallic taste like copper.

Millis prowled among the stacks, reading the markings on the crates. 'International Harvester, Indianapolis, Indiana,' 'International Business Machines, New York, N.Y.' 'General Motors Corporation, Detroit, Michigan.'

'You!' an angry voice shouted. 'What the hell are you doing down here?'

Millis whirled to face a scowling man of about his own

age and size, though muscular instead of pudgy. He wore the tunic of a ship's officer.

'Well, now,' Millis said. 'Everybody's got to be somewhere, don't they?'

'Don't get smart with me, you stupid bastard,' Barrett said, moving towards him with his fists clenched.

Millis pretended to cower.

'I was only looking for Leicester Square station and lost my way,' he said. 'If you could direct me I'd be ever so grateful, I'm sure.'

'Who the hell are you, anyhow?'

'Millis is the name, sir. Little Joe Millis, Mrs Millis' favourite and only child.'

'What's your job?'

'I'm a mum, sir.'

Barrett grabbed a handful of Millis's sweater and cocked his other fist.

'I am, really. To the evacuees.'

'Shirley Hunt's lot?' Barrett said, lowering his fist but not releasing his grip on Millis's sweater. 'How'd you manage to get in with a lovely piece like that?'

'My mum always said I'd go far, she did.'

'You'll go over the flipping side if I catch you down here again.'

'Right, sir. And who might you be?'

'First Officer Barrett, and don't you forget it. Now get back where you belong.'

He herded Millis out of the hold, treading on his heels to hurry him along.

'How'd you happen to know I was down there?' Millis asked over his shoulder.

'I saw you skulking along 'tween decks and knew you were up to no good.'

Dutton, the steward, knocked on Shirley's door to announce breakfast in the captain's saloon. She removed the bulky cable-knit sweater she was wearing over her cashmere cardigan and did what she could with her hair. She wanted to look her best for Captain Penrose. He was not in the saloon, however. Seeing her disappointment, and sensing its cause, Lady Anne explained that the captain did not customarily take his meals with the passengers except at dinner.

'However, he did ask me to tell you he was looking forward to your company this evening and to assure you you must feel free to confer with him whenever you wish,' she added.

It was not exactly what Captain Penrose had told her but the child had been so disappointed at not finding him in the saloon Lady Anne thought she needed a bit of bucking up. What the captain had actually said was that with that clod Millis and thirty-seven children to contend with Miss Hunt might have more on her plate than she could handle. Since she did not seem the sort to complain, he would be grateful if Lady Anne would keep an eye on her and inform him if she appeared in need of his intervention.

The dining-room was hardly what 'captain's saloon' suggested, though attempts had been made to enhance its appearance. It was carpeted, and the bottom half of the bulkheads wood-panelled. Both long tables, which filled most of the space, were of teak and the chairs were heavy and comfortable.

Two stewards, one of them not much older-looking than the eldest of the evacuee youngsters, served breakfast from a pantry connecting the saloon with the galley. Because of Donahue's presence aboard, the *Amindra* had been exceptionally well provisioned, and for the passengers there was porridge, real eggs and tinned ham and butter.

Shirley did not join the others – Lady Anne, Donahue, Rosten and two men she had not met before whom Donahue, acting as host, introduced as Chief Engineer Richardson and Dr Grimes, the ship's surgeon. The *Amindra* did not ordinarily carry a ship's surgeon but

76

because of the children and the distinguished passenger one had been added to the complement.

She had come to the captain's saloon with some hesitancy, feeling her place was with the children. When she learned Penrose would not be there it solidified that feeling. When she started to excuse herself Donahue urged her to change her mind and have breakfast with them. Only when she proved adamant did he abandon his efforts to persuade her and even then he insisted on escorting her to the door.

'I admire your dedication, Miss Hunt,' he said. 'But I'll admit I'm just a little bit jealous of those kids for monopolizing you.'

A pity she was so tied up with the kids, he thought. Though she seemed a touch man-shy, if she weren't so busy he was sure a few days of the usual shipboard intimacy would reassure her and even thaw her out. After all, a man did need some relief from production figures, casualty reports and shipping losses. He'd give it a try, anyhow. Even if nothing came of it it would be a relief from such dull company. Stiff-necked limeys.

Shirley was flattered by his obviously sincere compliments. Though he was much older than she, in his late forties – how surprising it was, she thought, that though Donahue was younger than Captain Penrose she did not consider the captain so much older than she – he was an impressive-looking man. Strongly built, though a trifle overfed – how did he manage that in wartime London? – perfectly barbered, recently manicured, shoes hand-made, suit perfectly cut, silk tie perfectly knotted. His face did not quite fit the carefully correct trappings, having more than a hint of Irish toughness and grey-green eyes that could probably bore through you when they were not smiling, as they were now.

And Andrew Donahue was a very important man. Like most Americans, Shirley knew something of him, and not just that he had been in London on a special mission for President Roosevelt. He had first come to national attention as a tireless campaigner for Roosevelt in the 1932 election. She'd been eighteen then. Though of immigrant Irish stock, which he liked to point out in interviews, he had been by then already a wealthy man, and a widower. His oldest child must be around her age now, Shirley thought. She seemed to recall reading he had begun his now great fortune as an associate of Joseph Kennedy importing Scotch whisky after prohibition. She had seen a photo of the two of them together in the London *Times* only a few days before.

And now he was only a foot away, paying her compliments. Something else to tell her father when she was back in California. Yet she left the saloon without reluctance. Her boys came first.

Rosten ate mechanically, his eyes fixed on his plate, not really noticing or enjoying what he was eating. Donahue was overly attentive to Lady Anne, snapping his fingers for a steward's attention whenever she appeared to have a need for anything.

'I read about your tragic loss, Lady Anne,' he said. 'Such a waste.'

'Yes,' she said. 'Poor Tony never got his turn at the Hun.'

Donahue looked at her in surprise.

'A waste any way you look at it,' he said. 'It doesn't really matter how it happened. One more pilot isn't going to change the outcome.'

'I suppose an American would think that,' Lady Anne said coldly. What could he know about losing a son, and at such a time and in such a manner when England needed every pilot?

'My apologies,' he said. 'I shouldn't have said that.'

In the children's mess Shirley found her boys were not faring nearly as well as the other passengers. They

78

appeared to be getting the same sort of breakfast she supposed the crew was getting. She would have to mention that to Captain Penrose and see if he could do something about it.

Some of the children were not eating their breakfast and she neglected her own to go from one to the other encouraging them to do so. Barlow, looking pale, could not be persuaded to take a single bite.

'I'll see Captain Penrose about getting them better food,' she told Millis, who was busy entertaining the children with tricks involving cutlery and mugs.

'It's not the victuals,' he said, 'it's the waves. Stomachs weren't meant to be turned every old way, except on hula girls.'

'Why do you have to make a bad joke out of everything?' she demanded.

'Don't you be jealous,' he said. 'We can't all have my gift for it.'

The loudspeaker on a bulkhead crackled and a voice whispered, 'Ready, sir.'

'Good morning, passengers and crew,' said Captain Penrose's calm, dignified voice.

'Sssh, everyone!' Shirley cried.

The boys ignored her. Those who were not seasick continued their shouting and horseplay.

'This is your captain . . .'

'Quiet, you lot!' Millis roared.

Startled by the sheer volume of his voice, they immediately fell silent.

'I'd appreciate your staying out of this,' Shirley said in a low, icy voice. 'It's high time they learned to obey me.'

'Sorry,' Millis said, thinking, such a pretty thing but touchy as a boil.

'We will shortly be entering the open Atlantic,' Penrose continued. 'By tomorrow afternoon we will be outside the range of friendly patrols. German U-boats have been

79

active all along our route and I would be less than candid if I did not tell you that they represent a continuing danger. However, we have the means to detect their presence at a considerable distance. For those passengers who are unfamiliar with this device, it is called Asdic and is capable of detecting underwater sounds. Our Asdic is already in operation and will be manned twenty-four hours a day. Should we detect the presence of a German submarine we will immediately take the necessary evasive action. You will know this by the ship's frequent changes of course. However, we must all remain constantly alert to the possibility of attack and be prepared to act in an orderly manner. Beginning immediately, all passengers and crew will wear the life-jackets now being distributed at all times whilst awake and keep them immediately at hand when sleeping.'

'Hard to bath in, though,' Millis announced in a stage-whisper. 'Unless you like to float in the tub.'

'There aren't any tubs,' Barlow said earnestly. 'Only showers.'

'What an idiot,' someone cried as the older boys hooted.

'You just don't appreciate his wit,' Oaks said, winking at his companions.

Barlow flushed and bit his lip. Why was Oaks always at him? Because he'd stood up to him about the JU 88s, that's why.

'Quiet, all of you!' Shirley ordered.

'. . . seven short blasts followed by another long one is the signal for lifeboat drill.' Captain Penrose was still speaking. 'A single blast accompanied by police whistles means attack is imminent. The first drill will be conducted shortly. At the warning you will assemble on deck, where you will be assigned the stations to which you will report in all subsequent drills. Miss Hunt, please join your youngsters at the warning and take them directly to the nearest station, which is starboard amidships.' Changing to a conversational tone, he added, 'That's in the middle of the right-hand side of the ship, just up the companion-way from their quarters.'

Shirley was pleased to be singled out and impressed by the captain's thoughtfulness even though she knew what amidships meant. And he'd told Lady Anne he was looking forward to her company at dinner.

'That is all,' the captain concluded. 'Thank you for your attention.'

Millis applauded. The boys followed his lead. Shirley looked at him sharply. If he was encouraging the boys to make fun of the captain she intended putting a quick stop to it. But she couldn't be sure. The boys' enthusiasm seemed genuine. Maybe she'd misjudged Millis.

Some of the boys needed assistance in getting into their life-jackets. Millis pitched in and helped her with them. He did have his uses, she was forced to admit.

She assembled the boys in alphabetical order, checking names off the list she carried – she resolved that as quickly as she could she would learn to match faces with names – and divided them into two parallel lines.

'We will use what we call the "buddy" system in America,' she said. 'I want each boy to look at whoever is across from him.'

They did so with much chatter and shoving.

'That's enough larking around,' Millis cautioned. 'This buddy system is serious business, as the barmaid said to the . . .'

'Stop it!' Shirley whispered through clenched teeth. And in a louder voice, 'In future drills, you are to be sure your buddy is with you before going on deck. And when you get there, be sure he is still with you.'

As chance would have it, Barlow was near the head of the first file and Oaks across from him in the second. The younger boy eyed his opposite number warily.

'Barlow the Witty's my buddy,' Oaks said. 'What great luck.'

Why don't you just shut up, you sod? Barlow thought. If it wouldn't seem I minded all that much I'd ask Mr Millis to change us.

Klaxons and sirens joined in a staccato chorus.

'Follow me,' Shirley ordered, hurrying to the exit. 'Millis, you stay behind until you're sure all the boys are out.'

'Aye, aye!' Millis snapped to attention. He knew she wouldn't like that but he could not resist. She seemed such a drill sergeant at times. She might be different if she weren't so caught up in her responsibilities.

Captain Penrose was waiting on deck when she emerged from the companionway. He smiled at her – he always had a special smile for her, she thought – and said, 'Any problems with your brood?' When she smiled back and shook her head he turned to the boys. 'Look smart there, lads.' What easy authority he had. Getting things done without bluster and without trying to ingratiate himself.

Barrett was there, too, slouched against the side of the bridge, a cigarette in his hand. He leaned forward and whispered, 'If we're torpedoed I'll make room for you in my boat.'

She did not answer.

'Mr Barrett!' Penrose snapped.

Shirley thought the captain had overheard Barrett's remark and felt both vindictive satisfaction and reluctant sympathy for the First Officer. It was a silly thing to say, but he had meant it as a compliment.

'Sir,' Barrett replied.

'I do not permit smoking on duty aboard my ship.'

'Sir,' Barrett said again, dropping the cigarette without haste and grinding it under his heel.

'Nor do I allow my decks to be littered,' Penrose added curtly.

Barrett motioned to a nearby seaman to pick up the butt. Penrose stopped the man with a gesture.

'You dropped it, Mr Barrett,' he said. 'You pick it up.'

His neck red above his pea-jacket, Barrett reached down for the butt, swept the crumpled paper and shreds of tobacco into his cupped palm with exaggerated care and let the wind carry them over the rail.

'Mind you never do that with anything large enough to float,' Penrose snapped. 'I have no intention of leaving a signpost for the enemy.'

'Aye, aye, sir,' Barrett said stiffly.

Shirley was impressed. Penrose was the kind of man she could feel utterly safe with even though they would soon be in waters infested with U-boats. She wondered if he was married. He must be. Or maybe he was a widower. Vaguely embarrassed at her own thoughts, she turned quickly and said, 'Boys, do you each have your buddy?'

All along the deck the crew and passengers were being sorted into lifeboat-sized groups by ship's officers and the bosun. The boys appeared to regard it as a game except for those on whom the yawing of the deck was still taking its toll. Two boys vomited without warning and several others ran to the rail.

'Spirits of ammonia in water helps a bit sometimes,' Barrett said at Shirley's elbow. 'I'll see if I can find some and have it sent down to you when this idiot drill's over.'

She smiled at him in grateful surprise. It was nice to discover he had some sensitivity after the crude way he had behaved towards her until now.

'Thank you,' she said. 'It looks like I'm going to need all the help I can get.'

'Count on me,' Barrett said.

He continued watching Shirley as she went among the sick boys with Millis, wiping chins and murmuring words of encouragement. Barlow was at the rail on tiptoe, too short to get his head over it flat-footed, retching threads of stringy green bile. She put her arm around his shoulders in an effort to steady him, but he quickly pulled away.

'I want my mum,' he said miserably.

'Your mother's at home,' she said gently. 'But I'm here.'

'Mum,' he repeated angrily. 'Mr Millis.'

Hurt, she beckoned Millis over to take her place.

Aft, the DEMS gun crew lounged around the huge crate masking the *Amindra*'s stern gun. That was their station during an attack. They would go to lifeboat stations only when ordered to do so by the ship's master.

Lady Anne was at a forward lifeboat station with Donahue and Rosten, remembering another drill. Tony had forgotten his life-jacket and his father scolded him. A ship's officer said he would send a man to fetch it but Tony had said it was he who had forgotten it and he who must fetch it. 'Even if the ship were really sinking,' he had said gravely. Tony had not often been grave. He was such a merry child, and such a carefree young man. He had gone off cheerfully to Canada. When the image of him lifeless in a box did not intrude, she remembered him laughing.

Rosten appeared bemused, as if he had no part in the bustle and clatter. Were it not for the cargo the *Amindra* carried, he thought, it would matter little to him if the emergency were real.

Donahue surveyed the milling groups on deck, thinking, 'If this is the best they can do in a drill, Lord help us if we run into the real thing. No wonder Britain's losing the war.'

The crew of the *Adler* worked steadily at its transformation. The new name had already been lettered at stern and bow, the funnel sections were in place and the masts and other projections were nearly in their new positions and alignments. Captain Freiburg made a circuit of inspection around the deck then climbed to the bridge.

Klaxons sounded and the loudspeaker bellowed, 'Action Stations!'

The men working on deck stopped immediately and went quickly to their stations, some topside and some below, while others came boiling up from the companion-ways. The men going below and those coming topside did not get in one another's way. Half the *Adler*'s crew were already at action stations. Below the false deck, gun crews were quickly poised at the four 5.9-inchers, as was the gun crew at the stern at its weapon and the crews which manned the smaller deck guns, all of which were concealed.

Reports crackled on the bridge.

'Number one gun ready!'

'Number two gun ready!'

'Torpedo tubes ready!'

When all stations had reported, Captain Freiburg said, 'Prepare to fire,' and started his stopwatch.

The hull and rail sections masking the guns clanged down, a sound carrying easily to the bridge.

'Three seconds,' Freiburg said to Schramm. 'Not fast enough.'

'*Feuererlaubnis,*' he said into the speaker, resetting his stopwatch. Permission to fire.

The gun crews sprang quickly into action, loading and 'firing' dummy shells. As they dropped into wire baskets placed to catch them the crews were ready loading new rounds. Freiburg counted off twenty seconds and nodded at Schramm, who spoke into the phone to a petty officer stationed at the first gun position.

'How many?' Freiburg asked.

'Three,' Schramm replied.

'Not bad,' Freiburg said. 'But for the *Amindra* we'll do better.'

Chapter Six

Andrew Donahue, as guest of honour, sat at Captain Penrose's right, Lady Anne at the captain's left. Shirley was next to Donahue, with Rosten to her right, and across the table with Lady Anne were Chief Engineer Richardson and Dr Grimes.

The seating arrangement was not at all what Shirley had anticipated. She had hoped Captain Penrose would want her closer to him. She could not have been mistaken, she thought, about his attentiveness at every chance encounter, reserved though it might be. She comforted herself with the thought that shipboard protocol demanded that a title and diplomatic status receive the places of honour. Captain Penrose himself confirmed that when Dutton seated her.

'I'm afraid we're rather slaves to custom, Miss Hunt.' he said gallantly, 'even though the *Amindra* is hardly my old *Empress*. But my loss is Mr Rosten's gain.'

Penrose and Donahue were in black ties. Lady Anne wore the long dress she'd debated taking in her room at the Connaught. Her only adornment was a single string of exquisitely matched pearls, the sort called a choker, and an old-fashioned brooch at her flat bosom.

She was quiet at first, remembering happier dinners on other crossings. She and her husband – the one time Tony was aboard with them he dined at the early sitting – Captain Penrose, all younger then, everyone at the table fitting in beautifully, the silent, white-gloved waiters, the murmur of voices and laughter mingling with the music of the ship's orchestra. But that was another age, so utterly different from now, and it served no useful purpose to dredge up old memories. This was the nearest thing to jolly company she'd known since Tony's death and she was not going to spoil it for the others. And in any case, it was so much better than being alone with her sorrow.

Shirley thought Lady Anne looked positively regal and initially, as the only other female present, felt out of place. However, she knew she was looking her best tonight in the one good dress she had brought along. Blue, silky and low-cut exactly to the point of good taste, it attracted admiring glances from all the men except Rosten, who was deep in his private world. Captain Penrose looked her way often and Donahue was particularly attentive. Almost overly so.

A life-jacket hung from the back of each chair. Donahue had arrived without his and when Penrose diplomatically offered to send Dutton for it refused and fetched it himself. Donahue had done so graciously, and with a haste that puzzled Shirley until Penrose explained, while Donahue was gone, 'Doesn't want anyone in his cabin, I imagine. He came aboard with a briefcase chained to his wrist.'

There was Scotch smoked salmon served with freshly-baked brown bread and tinned New Zealand butter, a beautifully browned saddle of lamb with peas with pearl onions and roast potatoes, and, for dessert, a huge trifle laced with the same excellent sherry that was served as an aperitif, heaped with whipped cream and offered in an enormous silver-plate bowl from the *Empress*. All served on immaculate white linen with fine crystal and china and an imposing array of cutlery. Shirley surreptitiously watched Lady Anne and used the same implements she did.

Penrose carved the lamb ceremoniously at table, giving the gleaming knife a few swift, practised whisks along the steel before carving perfect slices, which he deposited on plates passed to the head of the table. It was a performance as much enjoyed by the passengers as by the captain himself. It was so typical of Captain Penrose, Shirley thought, to be as competent at carving a roast as he was at running a ship.

Donahue commented knowingly and with appreciation on the wines, a white burgundy with the salmon and a claret with the meat, both, he said, impressive vintages. Shirley thought he was showing off just a little, but in a way she found agreeable because he did so with an ingenuousness unexpected in a man of his attainments.

During dinner Shirley devoted herself to drawing out Rosten. Though she felt great sympathy for him and genuinely wished to take his mind off his grief, she wondered if she would have been so solicitous if she were sitting close enough to Captain Penrose to capture and hold his attention without being too obvious. Though Donahue and Lady Anne had his elbow and his ear, he looked her way often enough for her to understand that he was not ignoring her. Donahue was more than willing to draw her into the conversation at the head of the table but in a manner she found too smoothly calculated.

She was not entirely comfortable with him or with Lady Anne, being acutely aware that under normal circumstances she would not be in such company. A twenty-six-year-old of no particular background dining with a wealthy, famous fellow-American, a titled Englishwoman and a ship's captain accustomed to entertaining the cream of British and American society at his table, and all of them years older than she. Though in the case of Captain Penrose she did not consider the age difference important.

Conversing with Rosten was not easy. Wrapped in his own thoughts, he seemed oblivious to his surroundings and ate mechanically, as if unaware of what was on his plate, almost like a blind man, Shirley thought. But he was not as unaware as she believed. Though the conversation at the head of the table and even the words of the young woman next to him were but an incomprehensible blur, he was conscious of the air of jollity and was thinking how Marjorie would have enjoyed this. She liked people and did so fancy her bit of smoked salmon and really good lamb, neither of which were to be found in the shops these days.

Something Shirley was saying managed to get through to him.

'I hope you'll find time to come down and visit my boys.'

Her boys? Whatever did she mean?

'Yes. Of course,' he said absently.

'They're a wonderful group of youngsters. You can tell the Board they've behaved like perfect little gentlemen.'

'The Board?' Rosten looked puzzled.

'The Children's Overseas Reception Board.'

'Oh, yes,' Rosten said with a hint of sheepishness. 'Quite.' How careless of him. He must remember he was meant to be an official of that organization. Though he understood the necessity of the pretence he was not comfortable with it. He did not like pretending to be what he was not.

'How long will you be staying in New York?'

'New York? Yes, yes. New York.'

Shirley realized how difficult it must be for him to keep his mind on his mission under the burden of his bereavement.

'I suppose you'll have a lot of people to see and all kinds of meetings,' she continued. 'It's just great what the Board is doing for your country's children.'

'Yes,' he said, staring at his plate. 'Thank you.' It was most unpleasant accepting credit he did not merit.

'I don't like to complain,' she said, 'but I noticed this

morning that the children were not getting the same food we are. I wonder if you'd mention it to Captain Penrose?'

It was better coming from Mr Rosten than from her. He was an executive and she was only a chaperon.

'I'd be glad to,' he said. 'It's very kind of you to take such an interest.' He could try to help her even if he were not actually what she thought he was, though he was not at all sure of Penrose's response. The captain did not seem overly fond of him. The feeling was mutual.

He smiled at her with bright, sad eyes. For a moment he permitted her to see beyond his veil of grief and she realized for the first time the sort of man Rosten must be when not labouring under such a crushing weight of tragedy. Mild, gentle and what the British called terribly decent.

'And how do you feel about it, Shirley?' Donahue asked.

Midway through dinner he had begun calling her by her first name. Though he had urged her to call him Andy she could not bring herself to do so. She was too conscious of his position and the difference in their ages.

'Sorry,' she said, 'I wasn't listening.'

'I was just telling Captain Penrose and Lady Anne that despite the fact we Americans feel a great bond with England, most of us believe we should not get involved in a war that does not concern us.'

Captain Penrose and Lady Anne were regarding her intently.

'But I don't agree,' Shirley replied quickly. 'I think it does concern all Americans.'

Captain Penrose smiled at her like a proud parent or a fond admirer. Shirley preferred to interpret it as the latter.

'Hear, hear,' said Lady Anne, miming applause. 'I like you, young woman. I like you very much.'

'As do we all,' Donahue added smoothly. 'A beautiful

woman who has brains and the courage of her convictions. That's a rare combination.'

'It concerns us all very much,' Rosten said, surprising everyone. Except for Shirley, they seemed to have forgotten he was there.

He seemed to have undergone a sudden transformation. His voice was firm, his gaze direct, with no hint in his expression of the sorrow consuming him.

The eyes of everyone at the table were fixed on him.

'If England falls,' he said quietly, 'America will be next.'

'I doubt that,' Donahue replied.

'Hitler is a madman,' Rosten said. 'He intends to conquer the world.'

'Only Europe. He's repeated that constantly in his speeches.'

'If you believe that, you're a fool,' Rosten said.

The insult shocked the others at the table but Donahue's smile did not waver.

'I think you owe Mr Donahue an apology,' Captain Penrose told Rosten frostily.

'Please.' Donahue held up a placating hand. 'Mr Rosten is entitled to his opinion. Speaking your mind is a fundamental right in my own country. Isn't it, Shirley?'

She nodded. It was easy to see why President Roosevelt had chosen Donahue to serve as his Special Envoy.

'I can understand your feelings about Hitler, Mr Rosten,' he continued.

Can you now, Mr Special Envoy? Rosten thought. Was your wife murdered by Nazis and your house destroyed. Are you a Jew? He wondered if Donahue even knew he was Jewish.

'I doubt that,' he replied quietly. 'But the captain is right. You are his guest. I apologize.'

He spoke with simple dignity. Then he rose, took his

life-jacket from the back of his chair and said, 'If you'll excuse me, I'm feeling rather tired.' He knew he had behaved discourteously but somehow he felt the better for it.

A strained silence followed his departure. It was Shirley who finally ended it, saying, 'You know his wife was killed by a German bomb just before we left, Mr Donahue.'

'His grief is understandable,' Penrose said, 'but no excuse for such execrable manners.'

Lady Anne reached over and lightly patted the captain's hand.

'You must make allowances,' she said. 'We are living in a time when anger may be all we've got left . . .'

'You're quite right, ma'am,' Donahue said. 'Though I'm afraid it's going to take more than that to stop the Germans.'

'Then, sir, you underestimate British anger.'

'I don't think so,' he countered, 'if the débâcle at Dunkirk is any example.' ·

'The French let us down,' Lady Anne said. 'If they had put up a fight the thousands of brave men we lost at Dunkirk would still be alive.'

'That might be your view, ma'am,' the American replied, 'but it isn't necessarily the right one. I've seen dispatches from William Bullitt, our Ambassador in Paris during late May and June, which endorse the view that Britain betrayed France by withholding the full strength of the Royal Air Force . . .'

'Absurd!' Lady Anne snapped.

Donahue shrugged. 'Our State Department isn't so sure. They think there's some merit in Pétain's contention that Britain was conserving its air force and fleet in order to use them as inducements in bargaining a negotiated surrender . . .'

'Surrender?' Lady Anne's anger showed in her rigid

face. 'Are you suggesting a man like Winston Churchill would even consider the possibility of Hitler's threatened invasion of the British Isles succeeding?'

Penrose wondered what Lady Anne would make of the *Amindra*'s secret cargo.

'Even he can't blind himself to the facts, ma'am.'

'Which you seem to feel you know.'

'That's why President Roosevelt sent me to London,' Donahue said, his tone still as quiet and even as it had been from the beginning.

'I would have thought Ambassador Kennedy has already told your President all he needs to know to justify America's continued neutrality,' Lady Anne said brusquely. 'He makes little secret of his conviction that Britain is going to lose. I gather he even had the gall to voice this opinion to the King.'

'My conclusions aren't based solely on what Ambassador Kennedy told me,' Donahue said. 'I took a very hard look at every aspect of the problem. Britain might have the spirit to win, but she simply doesn't have the tools.'

'She would have if America provided them,' Lady Anne said. 'And what you put in that report of yours could tip the balance in our favour.'

Donahue did not answer immediately. He was privy to facts which Lady Anne clearly did not know. One was that America's Atlantic Fleet consisted of four elderly battle-ships, four heavy cruisers, one aircraft carrier and a single destroyer squadron. President Roosevelt was depending very desperately on British naval protection in the Atlantic. Nor was the American economy geared for the production of war *matériel*. If anything, the United States was militarily weaker than Britain and, according to Louis Johnson, the Assistant Secretary for War, American industry could not be converted to a 'full defence' capacity for at least two years.

'I doubt the average American would support such a move,' he said, finally breaking his silence. 'When war broke out, eighty-two per cent of the public expected a British victory. After the fall of Norway that went down to fifty-five per cent. Now the French have capitulated fewer than thirty-two per cent feel Britain can win.'

'We are talking about human lives, not statistics,' Lady Anne said.

'I know,' Donahue replied. 'And that's why I'm convinced the American people want no entanglement in a war taking place half-way across the world. What's happening in Europe has nothing to do with the lives of the average American.'

'Is that what you think, Shirley?' Lady Anne asked.

Her question took Shirley by surprise. She thought she'd already made her position more than clear.

'No,' she said. 'And I don't think President Roosevelt does, either. He has a reputation for making his own decisions. My father always used to tell me, "FDR has the heart of a lion, the mind of a fox and the soul of a mule." '

Disarmed, Lady Anne smiled.

Penrose gave Shirley a salute of approval.

'Very well put, Miss Hunt,' he said.

'That's good,' Donahue said. 'May I steal it?'

'I'm sure you will,' said Lady Anne.

Donahue broke into hearty, infectious laughter. Even the silent Chief Engineer and the slightly seasick Dr Grimes joined in. And Dutton, who had been hovering nervously throughout the meal, smiled broadly.

'For a vulgarly rich American, and one with whose philosophy I thoroughly disagree,' Lady Anne said, 'you're a reasonably amusing man, Mr Donahue.' It was really turning into a most agreeable evening. She hoped it would go on and on. Then perhaps she could sleep.

94

The mood of the evening changed as the stewards cleared the table and brought the trifle from the pantry.

'Do we still have any of my special port left, Dutton?' Penrose asked.

'Yes, sir,' the steward said. 'And I've already taken the liberty of decanting a bottle.'

'Excellent. Serve it around, will you? I'm not sure you know port, Miss Hunt, but I'm confident you'll find this most pleasant.'

When the *Empress* was removed from civilian service Penrose had been permitted to buy what he wished from its wine store at very reasonable prices. As a result, he had quite a good cellar at home and even kept a few bottles aboard for his private use. He drank sparingly at sea, of course, but when he did have a drop he liked it to be the best.

Donahue took a sip of the port and savoured it a moment with his eyes closed.

'Good,' he said. 'Damned good.'

'Almost like the old days, isn't it, Captain?' Lady Anne observed.

Penrose nodded.

'When you sailed with Captain Penrose,' she explained to the others, 'you could be as sure of the wines as of splendid service and a swift passage.'

'To the old days, then,' Donahue said, raising his glass.

'No,' said Lady Anne. 'To England.'

Without waiting for Donahue's approval, she raised her glass. The others immediately joined in the toast. Shirley was deeply moved. Lady Anne, Captain Penrose, the children below decks, they *were* England, and she was part of it. 'To England,' she said, eyes glistening and tone as fervent as anyone's present.

Donahue smiled at her and touched her arm.

'I'll be damned,' he said. 'You've got goosebumps. I

wish I could feel as strongly . . .' He did not finish, but instead said, 'Good wine calls for good cigars.'

'I'm afraid we haven't any,' Captain Penrose said apologetically. In the old days there was never anything a passenger might desire which could not be provided for him.

'I've come prepared,' Donahue said, reaching inside his dinner jacket and bringing out a mahogany-coloured cigar case. 'Allow me to make my own small contribution to a grand dinner.' Before passing it around he looked at Lady Anne and asked, 'May we?'

'Please do. I'd have one myself if I weren't so terribly conventional.'

'We'll never tell, will we, Penrose?'

The captain stiffened at being addressed without his rank. Shirley wondered if any of the others had noticed. She doubted it. They were too busy looking at Donahue's cigar case.

'But I will have a cigarette,' Lady Anne said.

Shirley was glad to hear that. She had been dying for one herself but did not know if ladies were expected to smoke on such occasions and in such company. She offered Lady Anne one of hers – someone on the American Committee had given her two packs of Chesterfields as a parting gift – as the older woman was taking a box of Players from her small silver-mesh evening bag.

'Thank you, but I prefer my own,' Lady Anne said. 'I'm used to a stronger tobacco, my dear.'

Donahue's gold lighter was poised by the time Shirley's cigarette reached her lips. He held her hand to steady it against the motion of the ship as she leaned towards its flame. She saw his eyes drop briefly to her neckline and resisted an impulse to cover herself with her free hand. It would have been obvious and insulting. And perhaps she was imagining an interest that wasn't there. It must be the excitement of the voyage that had made her feel so unusually vulnerable – how else could she account for her response to such exact opposites as Captain Penrose and First Officer Barrett? Donahue's touch was impersonal, she decided.

'Penny for your thoughts,' Donahue said.

'Oh. I was just wondering about the boys.'

'I'll look in on them before I turn in, if you like.'

'That's kind of you, but it's really my job.'

'And you're darn good at it, too, from what I hear.' He glanced at Penrose. Shirley sensed the captain must have said something complimentary about her. 'Will you be looking for a job when we get back to the States?'

'I'm not sure,' Shirley said, aware that her cheeks were glowing. 'I suppose I will have to find some kind of work.'

'Well, if you stay in New York come and see me. I'm sure I can find something interesting in one of my . . .'

He broke off abruptly when the *Amindra* lurched wildly and coffee cups, wine glasses and ashtrays levitated without warning and hung in the air an instant. There was a loud crash from the pantry, the sound of someone falling, and angry curses. Dutton staggered and clutched the edge of the table to stop himself falling. It was not until the crockery and glasses plummeted to the table that Shirley had any sensation of dropping. And then it seemed the bottom had fallen out of her stomach. For the first time she was conscious that throughout dinner the ship's motion had been becoming steadily more violent. Clearly the wind was rising sharply.

The *Amindra* struck the bottom of the trough with a force that sent tremors along her entire length. Donahue held Shirley in her chair with a hand on her shoulder and with the other snatched the handkerchief from his breast pocket and held back the spilled coffee threatening to slop over the fiddles into her lap. Lady Anne sprang to her feet, the front of her dress spattered with wine. The Chief Engineer had caught his plate in mid-air and sat looking at it in dismay. Dr Grimes ran for the pantry, a hand covering his mouth. Penrose had gripped the arms of his chair and remained totally unruffled.

'Everyone all right?' he asked calmly.

Donahue let out a long breath. 'Jesus and Mary,' he said, 'what the hell was that?'

'We're getting into weather,' Penrose said. 'I'd thought it would be a bit later, but it's been getting steadily worse as we've been sitting here. Nothing to worry about, but you'd probably all be more comfortable in your staterooms.'

The ship lifted again but this time everyone was expecting the sudden movement and when she dropped they held firmly to the edge of the table.

'But the evening's hardly begun,' Lady Anne protested. She did not want it to end so soon. Please God let it go on a bit longer.

'I'm afraid it's going to get a lot worse rather soon,' Captain Penrose said, getting to his feet. 'I'll see you to your cabin, Lady Anne.'

'It's quite all right,' Lady Anne said. 'There's absolutely no need . . .' If she remained, perhaps Mr Donahue and Miss Hunt would keep her company.

'Dutton,' the captain said, turning to the steward, 'you look after Miss Hunt.'

'I'll take care of her,' Donahue said. 'I'm sure Dutton'll have his hands full cleaning up this mess.'

On deck, a frigid wind was blowing strongly. Shirley had only a light shawl thrown over her shoulders and Donahue offered her his jacket for the short walk to her cabin. She refused with thanks. He helped her across the heaving deck and along the passageway to her stateroom. He stepped into the dark cabin behind her and closed the door. Before

98

she could protest the light came on. He stood there with his hand still at the switch inspecting the room. Her possessions were strewn across the bed and over the floor.

'Not as bad as I expected,' he said. 'I can imagine what my cabin's like. I'll help you straighten things up.'

'It's all right. Really. I can manage.'

'Then maybe you'll help me straighten up mine,' he said.

You old devil, she thought. You're no different from First Officer Barrett. Smoother, perhaps. Much, much smoother. But that was something she thought she could handle.

'Thank you, Mr Donahue, but . . .'

'Andy,' he said.

'All right, Andy,' she said. 'But I'd better get into warmer clothes and look in on the boys.'

'I'll take a rain-check,' he said. 'And be careful,' he cautioned. 'I know these Atlantic storms. It's going to get a lot rougher.'

As soon as he left she turned the lock and got out of her thin dress and into warmer clothing. She was flung from side to side as she made her way below, and could not hold the beam of her flashlight steady. She dropped it once and had to crawl on her hands and knees chasing after it as it rolled erratically as if deliberately trying to escape.

Millis had the lights on in the dormitory. The boys lay in their bunks wide-eyed, wearing life-jackets, clutching the sides with both hands and bracing their feet against the pipes. Suitcases freed from their restraints under the bunks skated across the pitching deck. Some of them had burst open, strewing their contents everywhere. Millis sat on the vacant bunk above Barlow, feet dangling, palms braced against the overhead.

Shirley's entrance went unobserved. Everyone was too preoccupied with hanging on. None of the boys except

99

Barlow appeared to be seasick. She could thank First Officer Barrett for that, she thought. The spirits of ammonia he'd had sent down appeared to be working. Of all the boys, only Barlow and Oaks appeared to be in no way frightened, Barlow because he was too ill to care if he lived or died, Oaks because he relished Barlow's discomfort.

'What a lovely groan, Barlow,' he said. 'And so witty. Hasn't Barlow a witty groan, chaps?'

'I'm the entertainment here, Oaks,' Millis cried. 'No flipping amateurs need apply. A bit of a song is what we want here. Right, chaps?'

He began singing above the clamour of the sea against the hull.

> 'There was a fool and he went to sea,
> Thus choosing a life of miseree.'

Pretending to be crushed when no one joined him, he stopped singing and assumed a serious expression. 'Here, now, what kind of an audience are you lot? People paid good money to hear me sing. You're lucky to be getting it free. Now, unless you want to walk 'ome let's hear you give it a try.

> 'There was a fool who went to sea . . .'

A handful of the boys joined in raggedly but, except Oaks, without enthusiasm. Clinging to a stanchion, Shirley sang with them and immediately all eyes were on her. Millis faltered only a moment before freeing one hand to wave it like a conductor, at the same time nodding encouragement.

She was a spunky one and no mistake, he thought. It took real courage and devotion to her job to be about in weather like this. And looking prettier than ever, with her cheeks rosy from the wind and cold and a lock of wet hair dangling towards her nose.

There was something in his face, a hint of acceptance or even admiration, that Shirley had not seen before. Despite her opinion of him she could not help being a little flattered by it.

The boys appeared to take it for granted she should be there but seemed little encouraged by her presence. All they cared about was Millis, she thought bleakly. But she was forced to admit he must have qualities which thus far had escaped her.

No one except Millis knew the words to the song he had begun and his attempt to bolster morale appeared doomed to failure until he abruptly switched to an old music-hall song they all seemed to know. Even Shirley had heard it during her months in London. Once they were all at it – even Barlow made the attempt and it seemed to take his mind off his illness – she went from bunk to bunk, maintaining her footing by gripping the iron framing, reassuring even the most frightened.

'The captain says the worst is over,' she said. 'It won't last the night.'

She would have felt better if Penrose had really said it though she did not feel any guilt about deceiving the boys. Her father always said a gentle lie was preferable to truth on occasion. And this certainly seemed such an occasion. Besides which, who knew, perhaps the storm would lessen. Either way, by morning the boys would have learned the *Amindra* could take a lot of buffeting – she was sure it could because Captain Penrose had not seemed at all perturbed – and things were always less fearful by day than at night.

She had been frightened herself making her way along the careening deck and down to the 'tween-deck but now, reassuring the boys, the fear had left her. If that clown Millis could be so utterly imperturbable so could she, although she was sure his attitude stemmed from lack of knowledge rather than outright courage. What he did have in abundance was impudence, which sometimes gave a false impression of courage. Impudence or courage, it was having a good effect on the boys.

She pulled herself hand over hand along the line of bunks to where he sat and said, 'You're doing a good job, Millis. I'll make sure the Board hears about it.'

'Miss Hunt's a bit of all right, isn't she boys?' he proclaimed loudly.

'Yes,' the boys roared.

'Like a mum to you, eh?'

A chorus of voices shouted agreement. When they finally died down, there was a momentary silence. It was finally broken by Barlow who announced quaveringly, 'Not as good a mum as you, though, Mr Millis.'

A roar of approval filled the dormitory.

'You knew that would happen, didn't you?' Shirley said in a low voice. 'Are you trying to humiliate me?'

'No,' he said. It was the first time she had seen him so serious. 'You're the first Yank most of these lads have ever seen. I thought it might help a bit, make them feel more easy with you, so to speak.'

'When I need your help I'll ask for it.'

Did he think she was so naïve she couldn't see he was deliberately trying to undermine her authority over the boys? It was a mistake keeping him down here with them, turning them against her. Frightened as she had been in the Grosvenor House cellar she'd still done her job and they'd respected her for it. And she'd handled things at Euston Station well enough, too, until Millis interfered. Now, even Oaks was trying to emulate Millis, attempting to be funny at the expense of Barlow.

Well, that she could handle. But Millis was another matter. The boys needed an adult with them at night. She

102

couldn't do it. If they were younger, yes. But at thirteen, boys were too old to be sharing sleeping quarters with a woman. She briefly considered asking Mr Rosten to move in with the youngsters. But that was out of the question. He had other duties. And he would be all wrong for it, anyhow, wrapped up as he was in his own misery, and shy at that. Though he hadn't been shy when he lashed out at Donahue. Captain Penrose would probably know how to handle the matter but she didn't want to admit failure by asking him to do her job for her. He had too much on his mind to bother disciplining a few dozen schoolboys. No, the only solution lay in showing the boys that she, not Millis, was in charge.

She knelt down next to Oaks and whispered conspiratorially, 'Will you do something for me?'

He struggled to a sitting position and said, 'Yes, Miss Hunt.'

'Peter Barlow needs a friend,' she said. 'Will you be his friend?'

'But I am,' the boy said. 'That's why I rag him.'

'I don't understand.'

'English chaps always rag their friends.'

'He doesn't seem to understand that.'

'That's not my fault,' Oaks said.

'I know,' Shirley assured him. 'It's probably just that he comes from a different background and doesn't understand. Maybe if you explained?'

'I'll try, Miss Hunt.'

'Good. I'd appreciate that very much,' Shirley said.

She lurched to the door and stood by the light switch.

'That's enough singing, now,' she announced in ringing tones. 'It's long past your bedtime. I want you to all try and get some sleep. Mr Millis.'

He leaped down from his bunk and stumbled across the deck towards his cubicle, reeling like a drunk. Though the

103

movement of the deck was violent, she had the distinct impression that he was only pretending he was going to fall at any moment and, had he wished, could have made his way easily.

She waited patiently until he reached his cubicle before announcing, 'I am going to count to five and then turn off the lights. After that I expect everyone to remain silent. Mr Millis, it will be your responsibility to see they do so.'

Instinctively, Shirley waited for his response and was surprised when it didn't come. It somehow lessened her feeling of having asserted herself, and for once she found herself wishing Millis had come back at her with his customary quip.

She put the lights out and closed the door. The sound of her footsteps had barely disappeared when Oaks called out, 'Miss Hunt wants us to be nice to Barlow. Everybody now, "Good night, Barlow the Witty." '

The boys chorused, 'Good night, Barlow the Witty.'

In his dark bunk, Barlow bit his lip and fought back angry tears. He made a silent vow. They would never see him cry.

'All right, you little buggers,' Millis shouted. 'Next one who makes a sound'll be out of a porthole and can bloody well swim to New York.'

Back on the leaping deck a cruel wind drove the rain in flat, horizontal sheets, soaking Shirley and stinging her face with icy needles. A particularly vicious gust sent her sprawling. She slid on knees and forearms towards the scuppers, filled with bottomless terror. In some places solid plates provided a railing but in others only two lengths of clanking chain, one above the other, offered safety. And above the myriad sounds of the tormented vessel she thought she could hear their ominous rattle. She dug in frantically with toes, knees and elbows but could not halt her progress across the streaming deck. She tried to force her palms down to raise her torso to catch the bottom chain but the wind pinned her to the planking. And smashed her into two rock-steady legs.

'You clumsy idiot!' Barrett bellowed above the shriek of the wind.

His hands reached down and jerked her roughly erect.

'Shirley!' he cried in surprise. 'What the hell are you doing on deck?'

She could not speak. She could only cling to him, legs too weak to bear her weight, not caring that he was the last man aboard to whom she would have wished to be this close.

'You're soaked,' he said less harshly, opening his oilskins and taking her under them.

She could walk now, but he kept her there, supporting her, until they reached the door of her cabin. She did not try to pull away.

'You came damned close to being a goner,' he said, opening the door and guiding her inside.

'I'm very grateful,' she said.

'Is that all I get?'

'What do you . . .'

Before she could complete her sentence he took her face between two clammy gloved palms and, holding her in an inflexible grip, kissed her. She did not try to push him away; it seemed such a schoolgirlish thing to do and anyhow there was little sensation except of cold. Both their mouths were numb with it. But he continued holding her, moving his mouth on hers, their mingled breathing a small source of warmth, until their lips were pliant. She had a barely controllable urge to wind her arms around his neck. It was only gratitude, she told herself, knowing it was not so. Her mouth was open and he took advantage of it. Though she was twenty-six and had been popular, she had been kissed like that only twice before. The first time was by a varsity football star who thought he was God's gift to the coeds, and she had been repelled by it. It had seemed so . . . nasty. She had pulled free in angry confusion. He'd laughed at her and called her 'Miss Kelvinator', a name that had clung to her through the rest of her days in UCLA. The other time was by the man whose deception and persistence, along with her sense of duty, had sent her off to France to help win the war. He had tried to take even greater liberties and she had slapped him. Hard. That was when he had demanded cruelly how she expected him to marry her without knowing what he was getting.

But now the kiss did not feel at all nasty. It was delicious. And stirring. He moved his hands from her face to her hips and pulled her close against him. She felt no body contact – there were too many layers of clothing between them – but it frightened her to be held that way. She hated being handled.

She pulled her mouth free and said, 'Don't!' with strangled urgency.

Barrett released her at once, laughing. It was not the scornful, self-conscious laugh of the surprised football player or the cruel chuckle of her spurious suitor. It was, rather, supremely confident and charged with expectation.

'Not much we could do about it now, anyway,' he said as she slammed and locked the door. And, from outside, 'But there's always tomorrow.'

She threw off her sodden clothes and scrubbed her chilled body with a rough towel. Putting on a heavy night-gown and a pullover she huddled under the blankets, shivering. She was cold everywhere except her face. That was burning.

Captain Freiburg always took dinner in the wardroom with his officers. He was fond of hearty company and what little relaxation there was to be found aboard the *Adler* was among these men, and then only in the informality of the mess when a thousand details did not demand his attention.

Despite the relentless activity of converting the *Adler* to a Norwegian freighter and the brief change of course to avoid the approaching vessel, they had managed a steady sixteen knots since breaking off the rendezvous with the *Nordmark*. He was well pleased with the day's activities.

Dinner was first rate and with it every officer had his choice of a bottle of Foster's Australian beer or two glasses of a dry white wine from Bordeaux. The crew of the *Adler* had been eating well, thanks to good hunting. They'd had fresh pork only a few weeks ago, slaughtering an animal from their own piggery to augment two porkers taken from a British freighter before they sank the vessel with explosive charges.

Freiburg brought along his gramophone and some of his Hans Alber records. It was the duty of the most junior officer to wind the machine and change records.

'Scratch one of them and the Old Man will hang you by your thumbs,' Schramm whispered.

After the last record several officers took up the cry, 'Sperling, Sperling.'

They wanted the Navigation Officer to play his flute. He refused modestly at first, then brought out its case from under his chair. He always had the flute with him at mess. Another officer fetched an accordion and the two played requests for twenty minutes, folk songs, popular tunes and old sentimental favourites. They all joined in most of them and the wardroom rang with a rich mix of voices from basso profundo to tenor. They sounded like a trained chorus, singing parts and harmony. They'd had months of practice at it. Schramm had been forbidden to sing by Freiburg. 'Your voice would curdle milk,' Freiburg said. 'With you aboard we don't need klaxons.' Freiburg himself had a pleasant baritone.

They ended the evening, as usual, with the ship's favourite, a song that had the line, *'Das kann doch einen Seemann nicht erschüttern.'* 'But that can't shake a sailor.' It was the men's favourite, not Freiburg's. His taste ran more to the sentimental. *'Heidenröslein.'* 'Little Heather Rose.'

'Enough,' Freiburg finally called above the din, laughing. 'We'll be alerting every ship within five hundred miles.'

Before going to his quarters he took Schramm with him for a turn around the deck to stretch his legs, check the blackout and have a word with the watch.

The *Adler* continued to knife through the sea at sixteen knots. Freiburg leaned on his elbows at the taffrail and watched the creaming wake, faintly luminous in the darkness. Met reports relayed by the SKL station at Norddeich from its contact in Dublin and the secret German weather station in Greenland indicated the *Amindra* would now be fighting her way through weather so foul she would be obliged to reduce speed. If the storm persisted long enough and was sufficiently violent they might not even require the services of the agent who had been placed aboard her. But it was still comforting to know he was there.

Schramm, standing by his side, by now knew his captain's every mood.

'Let's hope the weather holds for us and the *Amindra* has to fight every metre of the way,' he said. 'It would simplify things for our man, whoever he is.'

'The less he has to do the better, it's true,' Freiburg said, straightening. 'But he'll still have to stop the *Amindra*.'

Chapter Seven

Captain Penrose, wearing foul-weather gear over his dress uniform, watched the storm from the bridge. The *Amindra* pitched and rolled at reduced speed as walls of water appeared to leap out of the ink-black, shrieking night to crash on the deck where they fragmented before streaming back into the darkness.

'Must be about Force 9, sir,' said Second Officer Briscoe, who had the watch.

Penrose made a noncommittal noise in his throat, indicating he was in no mood for idle conversation. He preferred that his officers speak only when spoken to unless they had something pertinent to communicate. He had seen worse storms, but not many. On the *Empress*, even with her gyro-stabilizers, most of the passengers would be queasy or worse in weather like this. He could imagine how it must be for Lady Anne. She'd always been a good sailor aboard the *Empress*, never missing a meal or social event regardless of the ocean's humour. But a ship the size of the *Amindra* was a very different matter. Rosten no doubt had long since lost his dinner. One look at him was enough to see he hadn't the stomach for bad weather. And, after the boorishness he had displayed at dinner, he deserved to suffer.

The children were probably sick, as well. Wouldn't hurt them, though. Children got over such things much more readily than adults, and no one died from being seasick. He allowed himself a smile. They only wished they could.

He hoped Miss Hunt was taking it well. He liked her. She was different from most Americans he had met.

Reminded him a bit of his Alice, though far less mature and, to be honest, quite a bit prettier. Meg was the family beauty. Empty-headed, though. But it didn't matter really, not in a girl. She was sure to marry well. Better than Alice, though he had no complaints on that score. Her husband had gone from subaltern to his captain's pips in very short order. Now he had some sort of staff job he wasn't allowed to talk about. After the war the lad was in for quite a surprise when he learned the enormity of the mission with which his father-in-law had been entrusted.

Curious, he thought, that he should be standing here thinking such ordinary thoughts when he had such extraordinary responsibilities. But why not? Being master of the *Empress* had prepared him for extraordinary responsibilities. And he had not the faintest doubt that he was going to bring this mission off successfully. Yet there was still one thing that nagged at him. He hadn't at all liked the way the secret cargo was stowed. He should have been there during the loading. The DNI should have given him an extra twenty-four hours notice instead of calling him in at the last moment.

'Mr Briscoe,' he said. 'Send a man . . .'

He stopped short. It wouldn't do to have ordinary seamen poking around in the hold. There was nothing to see which might give them a hint of the contents of the crates but in these seas one could never be sure one of the boxes hadn't slipped out of position and burst open. It wouldn't do to have anyone know they were carrying a cargo of gold bullion. If even one man found out, it would soon be all over the ship. That meant Donahue would become privy to the secret shipment and, whatever else he might be, the man was no fool. He'd put two and two together and realize the gamble Churchill was taking. The American was really determined to put the worst possible face on Britain's chances of winning the war. If he were to get any notion that Britain's gold reserves were being sent to Canada for safe-keeping it would be icing on the cake – the last bit of proof he would need to convince President Roosevelt that helping Britain would be foolhardy in the extreme. And Donahue would certainly let it be known to the press. The Prime Minister had been most emphatic about the devastating propaganda effect if even a hint was leaked of the transfer.

Briscoe was waiting patiently for him to complete his order. He had served under Penrose before and knew better than to prompt the captain.

'Never mind,' said Penrose.

He would have a look for himself before he returned to his quarters. A movement on the deck below, hardly perceptible through the streaming glass of the bridge window, caught his eye. None of the watch had business down there in this sort of weather. In all his years at sea he had never lost a man overboard and he was not going to mar his perfect record on this, his most important voyage. He went out on the bridge wing, into the gale, and shouted down at the figure. Such was the roar of wind, rain and sea that he had to call out repeatedly before getting the man's attention. He had struggled to a point just below where Penrose stood and was looking up at him. It was Barrett, his mouth forming words borne away by the wind. Penrose motioned angrily for him to come up to the bridge.

When he arrived, wiping his wet face on a sleeve freed from his oilskins, Barrett said, 'You want me, Captain?'

'I'd like to know what you are doing down there?' Penrose demanded.

'Having a look at Mr Donahue's car, sir. It wouldn't look good if we lost it over the side. He really loves that old bus.'

The Special Envoy's Rolls-Royce had been deck-loaded forward of the superstructure on a pallet bolted to the hatch cover and protected by a double set of well-lashed tarpaulins.

'It seems okay,' Barrett continued.

The word 'okay' grated on Penrose's ears.

'Mr Donahue's car is not your responsibility, Mr Barrett,' he said coldly. 'You seem to value your skin even less than I do but I do not propose to complete this voyage without the services of a First Officer. As long as this weather holds you will keep off the deck unless I issue instructions to the contrary. Is that clear?'

'Aye, aye, sir.'

Penrose sensed veiled insolence in the other man's tone. He looked at Second Officer Briscoe to see his reaction but Briscoe was staring fixedly out through the revolving Kent screen, his face expressionless in the shaded light of the bridge instruments.

Barrett left the bridge with a smart naval salute. A little too smart, Penrose thought. He was tempted to say something, but restrained himself. If it had been any other officer taking the initiative to check the deck load he might well have complimented him. Concern for passengers' property was admirable, particularly at such personal risk. But Barrett's manner was openly offensive. He would not have lasted a single voyage on the *Empress*, even as Third Officer. He no doubt would have spent all his time impressing the female passengers. Penrose had seen enough of that in his time. It was one of the prime reasons he did not like overly handsome officers or cabin stewards.

In fairness to the man, Penrose wondered if that might be his reason for taking such an instant dislike to Barrett. He was, after all, highly qualified. Penrose had checked the other man's papers carefully. Perhaps more restraint was called for. On a trip like this it was more important to have an officer who knew his trade than one who possessed the necessary peace-time graces.

112

The storm, unexpectedly, was easing off a bit. Penrose left Briscoe with instructions to increase speed gradually if the trend continued and made his way down to the hold. He was nearly there when he saw a flashlight beam weaving erratically in the passageway. Hailing the man, he saw it was Millis.

'What do you think you're doing here?' Penrose snapped.

'I got a bit tired of being cooped up in there with the boys,' the other man said. 'Thought I'd stretch my legs a bit.'

'Have you been drinking?' Penrose demanded, leaning forward to smell his breath.

'No, sir.'

'I won't have passengers wandering about my ship unescorted. Please return to the dormitory immediately.'

'Yes, sir.'

Penrose held his light on Millis until he disappeared around a turning. The below-decks entrance to the bullion hold was only a few yards from where he had accosted Millis. Penrose wondered if he had been nosing around in it. It would be just like Millis to be looking for anything he could steal.

The moment Penrose opened the door to the hold, even before he shone his light inside, he heard a sound he did not much like: the soft splash and gurgle of moving water. He stiffened. The hold should have been perfectly dry. He stepped inside and played the light over the deck. It glistened on a faint sheen of wetness which thickened and thinned as the *Amindra* wallowed. Water was getting in somewhere. He quickly shut the door behind him and turned on the hold lights. A rare oath escaped him.

'Bloody hell!'

Improperly stowed crates had broken free of their fastenings and lay burst and spilling out their contents against bulkheads and in the narrow spaces between tiers. Dunnage that had filled the space around the bullion boxes was strewn about like the leavings of a rowdy soccer crowd and, worse still, bullion boxes had shattered, strewing ingots among the cargo. A canvas sack of gold coins had ripped itself open on a nail projecting from a broken crate and bright discs gleamed in the litter. And, worst of all, one of the crates, kindling now, had smashed against the hull, ripping a great rent in the frames and battens of the hold insulation. It was through this rent that the water puddling the deck was pulsing.

Penrose ran for the fire-axe clipped to a bulkhead and hacked away at the remnants of the insulation, dragging away the material until he exposed the naked steel hull. The crate had battered the plate with such force that rivets had popped from a foot-long section. As the *Amindra* thrust forward it was scooping in sea-water through a bulge between its plates two inches wide at its widest point. Even as Penrose watched, a rivet popped with a sharp cracking sound and the opening enlarged.

He knew it was inevitable that if the breach was not repaired, and quickly, the *Amindra* would tear a killing hole in her side.

He must get Perkins, the ship's fitter/machinist, down here at once. But even as he turned to hurry from the hold he knew he could not. It was not that Perkins was not absolutely trustworthy. He knew the man from previous voyages. But Penrose had received instructions from the lips of Winston Churchill himself that only he and Rosten were to know the gold was aboard.

He realized he would have to do the repairs himself. He had done a lot of minor welding jobs aboard numerous ships when he first went to sea. It was one of the many skills he'd been required to learn. And he remembered enough about it to realize that this job was more than one

114

man could do unassisted. There was a heavy acetylene tank to be brought from the locker and a section of plate to be lifted waist high and held in place while it was welded over the gap. Rosten. Inadequate though he would be, he was the only person aboard who could be allowed in the hold without disobeying the Prime Minister's orders.

Penrose turned off the lights, shut the hold door and went quickly topside. His dress uniform was sodden with sweat from his exertions under his foul weather gear, and even in the midst of this grave emergency he was distressed by the clammy feeling. His first instinct was to change his clothes but he decided that would have to wait. There were other, far more important, decisions to be made. Had Millis been inside the hold? Had he seen the scattered ingots? It was not likely. The man would have to have been a far better actor than the second-rate music-hall clown he was, not to betray such shocking knowledge.

He rapped lightly on Rosten's door and called in a low voice, 'Mr Rosten . . .'

When there was no response he knocked harder and spoke louder. Finally, a hesitant voice replied, 'Just a minute, please.'

The door opened and Rosten stood there in the light from the swinging door of the tiny bathroom, dressed in his pyjamas and a striped dressing-gown, his face greenish.

'I didn't hear you,' he said. 'I was in the W.C. throwing up last week's breakfast.'

It surprised Penrose that the man could attempt a joke, however feeble, in his condition.

'Come with me,' he said, without explanation.

'I'll get dressed.'

'There's no time for that.'

Silently Penrose led him down to the hold. At least the man could rise to an emergency, Penrose thought, and did not waste time with questions. Perhaps the DNI had

115

known what he was about after all. Rosten gasped when Penrose turned on the hold lights, revealing the state of the cargo. He ran immediately to where the ingots lay thickest and began stacking them.

'Later,' said Penrose. 'We're taking water.'

Rosten noticed the sprung plate for the first time. To Penrose's eyes, the gap was noticeably wider, the pulse of water more fierce.

'It doesn't look too bad,' Rosten said.

'If we don't seal it immediately it'll get a lot worse.'

'What do you want me to do?' Rosten asked quietly.

Penrose led him to the locker where the acetylene tanks and cutting torch were stored. A spare plate leaned against a bulkhead near where they stood and dark goggles swung from the hook. The hull plate was far too heavy for even the two of them to drag to the opening. A section would have to be cut out that was large enough to cover the hole but still small enough to be manageable.

'It's years since I used one of these things,' Penrose said, reaching for the torch and goggles.

He felt almost friendly towards Rosten. The man was behaving far better than he had any reason to expect. Working together, they slid a tank towards the spare plate. Penrose put on the goggles, lit the torch with a match, and began cutting out a section. Rosten watched as attentively as a surgeon assisting in a delicate operation as sparks flew, and the hold filled with the smell of burning metal. When the section was free he reached for it and burned his hand. He gave one sharp cry but that was all. Without being told he removed his dressing-gown, soaked it in the icy water sluicing over the deck and ran it, steaming, around the cut edge. An ugly weal rose visibly across his palm where he had grasped the section.

'You all right?' Penrose asked.

Rosten nodded.

Slipping and sliding in the soaked waste littering the floor of the hold, staggering under the weight of the section and fighting to maintain their balance against the erratic pitching of the ship, they manhandled the metal piece to the sprung plate. Another rivet had popped out and the opening was half again as wide as it had been when Penrose left to fetch Rosten. They leaned the section against the hull. It was a good yard below the hole.

'You'll never be able to hold it in place,' Penrose said.

Rosten knelt and began piling ingots against the hull. Seeing what the other man intended, Penrose stripped off his goggles and began manhandling more of the bars to add to the pile. Each weighed twenty-seven pounds. The work made both men stream with sweat. Penrose stripped off his foul-weather gear and his dress jacket and unfastened his tie and collar. He should have done that before he got to work with the torch, he thought, heaving breathlessly at a trapped ingot.

Together they fashioned a ramp of ingots to within inches of the hole, still streaming water, and laid boards from broken crates against it at an angle to provide a smooth incline.

'I wonder what the Old Lady would make of us using her bullion for building blocks?' Rosten said.

Penrose smiled, not needing to be told that Rosten meant the Bank of England, 'The Old Lady of Threadneedle Street'. He felt exhilarated. It was the first time in years he'd done anything with his hands other than work among his roses. It made him think nostalgically of the days when he first went to sea. Even then he had dreamed of one day being the master of a passenger liner but never in his most fevered imaginings had he ever thought he might one day have Britain's future, literally, in his two hands.

They brought tank and torch from the locker,

then worked the rough metal sheet up their improvised ramp. Penrose left Rosten holding it balanced over the hole and fetched an armful of welding rods from the locker. Warning Rosten to turn away from the sparks, he set to work. In less than an hour the hull was sealed, the patch ragged-edged and skewed, but solid and seaworthy.

Despite the damp icy cold of the hold they were both soaked with sweat and streaked with grime. Once done, however, they felt the rawness of the air. Penrose put on his clammy jacket and insisted that Rosten cover himself with his foul-weather gear. Rummaging in the locker, Penrose found what he was after, a heavy padlock. Two keys were attached to it with a bit of twisted wire. He untwisted the wire and gave Rosten one of the keys.

'Extra protection,' he said grimly.

As he started to leave, Rosten waved a hand at the tumbled ingots and said, 'Shouldn't we do something about those?'

'Later,' Penrose said. 'First we'd better both get some rest.'

The hold door was fitted with a hasp. Penrose locked it with the padlock. Then he led the way topside, trying to ignore his aching muscles.

'Do you have anything to drink in your cabin?' he asked.

Rosten shook his head. 'I'm not much of a drinker.' His teeth were chattering.

'Come with me,' said Penrose. He took him to his own quarters and poured them both a double measure of brandy.

'Get that down you,' he ordered. 'Then take a hot shower and go to bed. Understood?'

Rosten nodded. He suddenly felt weak. Sitting down, he sipped his brandy and began to relax, looking around the captain's quarters with curiosity, noting the fancy desk, the photographs, the needlepoint motto. When he looked at the photograph of Penrose's wife he felt a quick stab of pain. Yet somehow he was more at peace now than at any other time since his wife's death. Down in the hold was the first time that every waking moment had not been filled with grief and memories. He had been too busy. Grief had been banished by violent physical activity.

He looked at Penrose who, chin on chest, was staring down into his drink. Despite fatigue, the captain's face emanated strength and assurance. A strange person, this Captain Penrose. When he had first met him at the Hole-in-the-Ground he'd thought him vain and cold. But now, and down in the hold, he had been so different. Nothing like a sheen of sweat to emphasize a man's humanity, he thought, wryly.

Penrose looked up and caught Rosten studying him.

'You've been a great help,' he said quietly. 'Thank you.'

Rosten flushed with pleasure and finished his brandy. Feeling stronger and warmer, he rose to leave. 'If it's awkward for you to have Mr Donahue and me together at your table I can take my meals with the crew,' he said.

'That won't be necessary. You're entitled to your opinions. Though it might be better if you kept them to yourself.'

'Of course.'

'And first chance you get, have Dr Grimes take a look at that hand.'

Rosten nodded, surprised. He'd forgotten all about his injury. 'Good night, then,' he said. 'Or should I say morning?'

He paused at the door, aching, tired and mind-benumbed. There was something he had intended asking Penrose ever since dinner but the turn of events had knocked it quite out of his head. With his hand on the door handle he recalled it. Miss Hunt. Something about the

119

boys' food.

Penrose was looking at him quizzically but not unkindly.

'At dinner last night Miss Hunt asked if we couldn't do something about the evacuees' food. She says it's below the standard of the other passengers'.'

'She asked *you*?'

'I'm a member of the executive board, you know,' Rosten explained with a rare, wry smile. 'Actually, she wanted me to ask *you* to do something about it.'

'Nothing I can do, I'm afraid. The passenger stores are limited. They should have no complaint. They're getting the same as the crew.'

'She'll understand, I'm sure. Sensible young woman.'

'And distinctly an ornament at dinner.'

Rosten, almost reeling with fatigue, closed the door quietly behind him. As soon as he was alone Penrose took the advice he had given the other man, warming himself in the shower and getting quickly into bed. The ship's motion seemed noticeably easier. He tried to concentrate on all that remained to be done, thankful that the storm was abating, but in minutes was fast asleep.

It seemed he had scarcely shut his eyes when a discreet rapping at his door awakened him.

'Captain Penrose, sir!'

'Who is it?' Penrose called.

'Nutley, sir,' replied a diffident voice. 'We have an Asdic contact.'

Penrose was on his feet at once, reaching for the fresh uniform Dutton laid out for him every night.

'How close?' he asked.

'Thirteen thousand yards, sir.'

No immediate danger then, Penrose thought, unless the U-boat managed to close or surfaced to pursue the *Amindra*. To be on the safe side he'd better call the bridge and order full speed ahead and standard evasive action. But even as he picked up the phone he felt the ship tremble and alter course. That was for the ship's master to decide, he thought angrily.

Barrett answered the bridge phone. The First Officer had the watch. I might have known, Penrose thought.

'Captain Penrose here,' he said, speaking into the bridge phone. 'What's the situation?'

'Asdic reports echoes at thirteen thousand yards, sir,' Barrett's voice replied. 'Off the port bow.'

'On a closing course?'

'Too soon to tell, sir. But we can outrun her in any case unless she surfaces. I've altered course . . .'

'That's my decision to make, not yours, Mr Barrett. Is that clear?'

There was a momentary hesitation. 'Aye, aye, sir,' Barrett said finally.

Penrose shaved before putting on his shirt and tunic. When he was fully dressed he opened his safe and got out his sealed orders. As he expected, the pouch held instructions for Halifax, but he was looking for something else: the location of the arming device for the scuttling charge. He doubted if a U-boat would attempt taking the *Amindra* as a prize instead of sinking her but he had to be prepared for any possibility.

The information he sought was in a folder, with a schematic drawing showing the location of the charges and an envelope containing two keys and instructions that one of them was to be given to Benjamin Rosten.

When Penrose reached the bridge, he found Barrett holding the hand transmitter to the Asdic room to his mouth with one hand and a pair of binoculars to his eyes with the other, scanning the sea off the port bow. The loudspeaker above the Asdic cabinet said, 'Echoes off the port bow, fourteen thousand yards, fading.'

121

At the bow, a seaman was also searching the horizon with binoculars. At least Barrett knew his job, Penrose thought.

Seeing Penrose had arrived, Barrett handed him the binoculars and said, 'We seem to be losing him, sir. I don't think we've been detected.'

'We'll continue as if we had,' the captain said.

'Aye, aye, sir.'

'And perhaps you'd like to tell me who authorized you to change course?'

'Under the circumstances I believed . . .'

'Never mind what you believed,' Penrose snapped. 'I make such decisions. Is that understood?'

'Perfectly.'

Penrose looked the other man in the eye for a moment, before saying, 'Carry on.' He turned away.

'If the U-boat has detected us he'll be surfacing to give chase,' the First Officer said. 'Do I have your permission to sound Emergency Stations?'

Penrose did not think it necessary just yet and did not like honouring Barrett's suggestion with approval, but it occurred to him that this might be as good a time as any for a drill. Yesterday's lifeboat stations drill had been disgraceful.

'Very well. And lifeboat stations drill as well.'

Barrett hit the emergency stations switch. The siren and klaxons sounded. Passengers and crew began streaming on deck.

'This is your captain speaking,' Penrose announced over the loudspeaker. 'This is a drill. Repeat. This is a drill. But conduct yourselves as if it were the real thing.'

He turned to Barrett and said, 'Is this your lifeboat station, Mr Barrett?'

'No, sir. I'm on my way.'

Barrett left the bridge at a trot.

122

The Asdic speaker said, 'Echoes off the port bow, fourteen thousand yards, fading.'

At the *Amindra*'s present seventeen knots it would be minutes before Penrose could be sure they were continuing to increase the distance.

Shirley had her boys in two rows at their station. Barlow was the only one not wearing his life-jacket. He was carrying it.

'Barlow,' she said, 'put on your life-jacket.'

'The straps are all in knots,' he said, worrying at them and shooting an angry glance at Oaks.

'Help him, Oaks,' Shirley said. 'Like a good boy.'

Barrett stood with a hand on a boat stanchion grinning at her. She looked away and in a moment he was at her elbow, whispering.

'Sleep well last night, Miss Hunt?'

'Yes, thank you.'

'I didn't. Couldn't. Thinking about what fun we could have had if you weren't so timid.'

Millis drifted over and was standing near them.

'What do you want?' Barrett demanded.

Millis cupped his ear as if deaf and said, 'Eh? Wot's that you said?'

'You're supposed to be looking after the boys,' Shirley said, wanting to head off trouble. Millis was obviously too thick to realize Barrett was not the sort of man to antagonize.

On the bridge, Asdic reported echoes at sixteen thousand yards and fading. Penrose ended the lifeboat stations drill but kept the gun crew and all watches at emergency stations. In another fifteen minutes Asdic reported no further echoes. Puzzled, he ordered the *Amindra* back on course at cruising speed. Under ideal conditions, their new, top secret Asdic could pick up echoes as far distant as twenty miles. These were hardly

123

ideal conditions, seas choppy and a stiff wind left over from the night's storm, but they shouldn't have lost the U-boat this quickly.

The bow lookout, who was still scanning the horizon, took the binoculars from his eyes and shouted something towards the bridge. Penrose quickly raised his binoculars. There was something out there, perhaps twenty thousand yards off to port. Twelve miles. A surfaced U-boat! So that was why there had been no echoes. Asdic was useless against surface sounds. The sides of the dummy crate dropped and the *Amindra*'s stern gun swivelled and lifted, tracking the U-boat without waiting for orders from the bridge. The gun crew would not fire until ordered. Barrett hurried to the bridge.

'We should open fire before he does,' he said breathlessly. 'We have him outgunned at this range and he'll dive. He'll never catch us submerged.'

'I am perfectly aware of the situation,' Penrose said acidly.

His instinct had been to alter course and increase speed again, hoping the *Amindra* had not been sighted. He had never been in action against a submarine before. He knew from Barrett's records that the other man had.

The cabin passengers, hearing the excited calls on deck, had come out and stood at the rail peering into the distance. Lady Anne was without her life-jacket. Donahue stood with his feet planted and cigar going. Rosten had a bandage on his hand.

'All passengers will please return to their quarters,' Penrose said over the loudspeaker. 'And please wear your life-jackets.'

'Well, sir?' Barrett persisted.

'I'm going to play a waiting game,' the captain said. 'No point in attracting any more attention than we must.'

The U-boat continued to maintain its distance, its course

paralleling the *Amindra*'s.

'He's seen us, all right,' Barrett said. 'He'll stay out there until dark and then close.'

Penrose ordered the stern gun to open fire. The *Amindra* shuddered with each shell that went hurtling out over the water and the thunder of the discharge echoed throughout the ship. The first round splashed short. Penrose waited for a responding flash from the U-boat's deck gun. It did not come. The second shell was long. The U-boat started to submerge and was already two-thirds beneath the choppy waves by the time the third shell hit the sea. It was closer than either of the others but still short of the target.

In the dormitory, Shirley was assuring the boys there was nothing to fear.

'Captain Penrose won't let anything happen to us,' she said. 'He knows exactly what he's doing.'

'I dare say,' said Oaks. 'Barlow, the little chaps are frightened. Say something witty to cheer them up.'

'That's quite enough, Oaks,' Shirley said.

'Let's have a song,' Millis cried. 'My old mum always gave me a song when I was scared. Helped, too. Her voice was like a cow giving birth. Terrible. I used to laugh so hard I'd forget what I'd been frightened about in the first place.' He cleared his throat and started singing: 'I don't want to join the army, I don't want to go to war, I want to hang around Piccadilly Underground, living off the earnings of . . .'

' "England and America," ' Shirley interrupted quickly. ' "Two empires by the sea, two peoples great and free, one anthem raise . . ." '

The boys knew the words. All evacuee children being sent to America were taught them. They were sung to the tune of 'America'.

One by one they joined her, even Millis, who did not

125

know the words but improvised amusing lyrics of his own. They were clever, Shirley thought grudgingly.

By early afternoon on Tuesday the *Amindra* had logged 430 miles since departing Greenock, despite having been obliged to reduce speed during the storm.

Aboard the *Adler* it was two hours earlier, the merchant raider being still considerably west of the *Amindra*. Since her Sunday morning rendezvous with the *Nordmark* she had steamed 768 miles and was now north of the Tropic of Cancer at roughly the same latitude as Miami, Florida, but some 2,000 miles east of it. Despite her head start and somewhat greater speed, she was still behind schedule if she meant to intercept the *Amindra* in the planned area.

At the moment the *Adler* was steaming at half speed. Captain Freiburg had had his launch lowered and was now circling the ship examining her disguise. He missed nothing: height and position of masts and cranes; length of spars; angle of braces; deck configuration and new paint. From time to time he took photographs from different angles, to be developed and printed immediately for further study at his leisure. Remembering the British officer's ruse aboard the *Nordmark*, he smiled. The Britisher had had a Leica just like his own.

Schramm shouted at him from the poop and waved at him to draw closer. Freiburg ordered the launch alongside and looked up at Schramm.

'We've just had a signal, sir,' Schramm called down to the bobbing launch. 'One of our U-boats has found the *Amindra*.'

Chapter Eight

The Asdic room began reporting echoes again. The U-boat was falling behind steadily. When, at last, contact was lost, Penrose was not sure whether it was because they were out of Asdic range or the U-boat had surfaced again to resume the pursuit. He ordered extra lookouts.

He left the bridge for a look at the concealed arming switch for the scuttling charges. It was in a passageway between his quarters and the bridge in a locked cabinet fixed to the bulkhead and marked 'Spares'. Looking about to be sure he was alone in the passageway, Penrose unlocked the cabinet. At first glance it appeared to contain only small cardboard boxes of the sort containing wireless valves and electrical fuses. He removed some of the boxes and found they concealed a small knife switch protected by an easily removed metal cover.

He looked at it, fascinated. By moving this strip of copper, no longer than his finger, a matter of inches, he could kill his ship and send 250 million pounds sterling to the bottom of the Atlantic. It was difficult for him to absorb the thought of a ship under his command dying by his own hand. Yet he knew if it ever became necessary he could pull the switch without flinching.

Except for the extra lookouts, the crew had returned to normal watches. Rosten slipped down to the bullion hold without being seen and began trying to restore a semblance of order. It was an impossible task for one man alone with only his bare hands, but he thought that if he worked steadily throughout the balance of the voyage he would be

127

able to gather and conceal the spilled coins and ingots. There was nothing he could do about the sodden waste littering the deck and he did not try. He was surprised to find himself whistling under his breath as he lugged the heavy gold bricks to the crates he thought repairable. He'd need Penrose to get him hammer and nails. He'd never been very handy with tools but he had built a bird-feeding station for the back garden to please Marjorie. It hadn't attracted too many birds at first. Marjorie's cat considered the back garden its private preserve and the bird-feeding station a cat-feeding station. It had brought a sparrow into the house once and reduced Marjorie to tears. After that he had moved the feeder from its post and hung it from the projecting roof of the small shed where they stored things. The memory triggered images in his mind: blazing buildings, houses collapsing in a gush of plaster, the incongruity of death among the rubble. He blotted them out by focusing his attention on the ingots.

Donahue and Lady Anne walked the blustery deck continuing the debate they had begun at the captain's table the previous night. It was less bitter than it had been. Lady Anne discovered the American was a witty man and quite intelligent despite his appalling blind spot about the ability of the British to win the war.

'If you'd lived at the time America was a British colony I'm sure you would have been a Tory,' she said. 'And argued that a handful of poorly armed revolutionaries didn't stand a chance against the forces of the world's greatest sea power.'

'Maybe,' he admitted. 'Experience has taught me to go where the power is.'

'And the dollar?'

He nodded. 'And the dollar. And I never let sentiment interfere with my judgement.'

'It's not just your judgement,' Lady Anne said. 'I suspect you're simply not too fond of us British under any circumstances, are you?'

'I'm only one generation removed from Ireland, ma'am.'

The conversation was taking an uncomfortable turn. In unspoken agreement they turned to less controversial matters: the relative merits of the Dorchester and the Waldorf-Astoria; where the best dinner was to be found in London before the war and now in New York.

'I'm sorry you won't be staying over in New York,' Donahue said. 'There's a little restaurant on West 57th Street I'd like to show you personally.'

'That's kind of you,' Lady Anne said, abruptly subdued. 'But I'm afraid you'd find me gloomy company.'

She had visited New York several times with her husband and once, the last time, just after his death in 1934. Tony was sixteen then and had come home from boarding school for the end. He had been quite brave about it, as he was about everything. Her husband's illness had been almost as draining on her as on her husband and her doctor had suggested an ocean voyage and a change of scene. With Tony back in school there had been no reason not to go. She had found New York a melancholy place without her husband despite its undeniable, though overwrought, attractions. Even before her solitary visit she'd had mixed feelings about the city. It was vibrant and varied, with some excellent theatre, marvellous shops, quite decent restaurants and that vast, magnificent park in the midst of the city, but it was also noisy, dirty and vulgar. Unfinished, in a way. And crowded. Without her husband the bad had far outweighed the good. Yet, had she had any heart for seeing New York again, which she most certainly did not at the moment, it might have proved amusing to do so with such a knowing guide as Andrew

Donahue. One day, when the war was won and the pain of her loss less acute . . .

Donahue knew she was thinking about her reason for being aboard the *Amindra* and regretted triggering the thought.

'Hey,' he said quickly, 'there's my car. Let's see how it made out in the storm.'

He led her to the tarpaulin-covered mound and the two of them pretended to be absorbed in examining the lashings.

After the ship had returned to normal routine Shirley took the boys on deck for fresh air and recreation. It was too windy for any sort of deck game and several of the boys, despite specific instructions, did not have suitable clothing for such cold weather. Barlow was among them. He shivered but did not complain.

'Poor Barlow,' Oaks said, shaking his head sadly, 'his dad wouldn't buy him a proper coat. You may have one of mine, if you say something witty.'

'Keep it,' Barlow said, clenching his fists. 'He'd have bought me one if I wanted it.'

'That's not witty enough. My, aren't you a hothead? Let's cool you off.'

He snatched off Barlow's cap and held it high above his head, too high for Barlow to reach, and jerked it away when Barlow jumped for it. The boys near them gathered in a circle to enjoy the fun. Neither Shirley nor Millis saw what was going on. Millis was on the deck under a pile of yelling eight-year-olds playing a game he had just invented. 'Gulliver and the Lilliputians'. Shirley was holding the head of a boy being sick over the rail.

Third Officer Nutley, who had stepped on deck for a look around, saw the knot of boys and went to investigate.

By the time he arrived, the frustrated Barlow had seized Oaks's arm and tried to pull it down. Oaks put a leg behind him, gave him a push and fell to the deck on top of him, both boys clumsy in their life-jackets.

'Say something witty and I'll let you up, you little bastard,' Oaks said.

Nutley reached down and dragged him up by the back of his life-jacket.

'What's going on here?' he demanded.

'They were just having a bit of fun,' one of the boys said.

The boys had grown noisy enough to attract Shirley's attention.

'We'll have no fighting,' she said severely.

'We weren't fighting, Miss Hunt,' Oaks said. 'Just having a bit of fun.'

Shirley looked at Barlow.

'Are you all right?' she asked.

Barlow glared at Oaks but said nothing. Don't you never say anything about my dad again or I'll say something with my boots, you sodding bully, he thought.

'No one's been hurt,' Nutley said. 'They were just being boys.' Noting the question in her eyes he added, 'Nutley. Third Officer Nutley.'

'Thank you for helping,' she said, thinking he looked terribly young for a ship's officer and why couldn't Millis have been there to stop it as he should have.

'Everyone!' she called. 'We're going down now. It's too cold and windy on deck. Find your buddies.'

The boys assembled in twos with much shoving and shouting. Millis brought one under each arm and another clinging to his leg like a monkey.

'I'm off watch,' Nutley said. 'If you'd like me to help . . .'

'Thank you,' she began, 'but . . .'

He looked so pathetically eager and, well, lonesome. She

could well imagine he found little in common with the other officers. They were all so much older.

'Why not?' she said. 'Do you know any games?'

There was another reason for letting him come down with her boys. They'd not be giving Millis all their attention. She was being objective about that, she told herself. This young man would set a better example for the youngsters.

'I'm pretty good at knots,' he said. 'I'll fetch some line and show them how.'

'That would be very nice,' Shirley said. 'Come on, children. Everybody downstairs.'

'Below,' said Barlow. 'Not downstairs.'

'That was very witty, Barlow,' Oaks said.

'Thank you, Barlow,' said Shirley. 'Everybody below.'

After a while Nutley came down with cut lengths of light rope draped over an arm. Shirley had him sit at the middle of a long table with the boys crowded around on all sides. She passed out lengths of rope to those who wanted to learn knots.

Oaks and Barlow were not among them. Barlow went to his bunk and lay facing the bulkhead. Oaks said tying knots was childish. Immediately some of the boys put their ropes down and started to get up from the benches on which they sat.

Nutley looked terribly hurt.

'Anyone who doesn't tie knots gets them on his head,' Millis said. 'Barlow, get over here. You'd be good at knots. I can tell by your hands. Sensitive, like mine.' He held up his broad hands with thick, strong fingers. 'My old mum always said I had the hands for a musician. If only I'd kept up my violin I'd have made her ever so proud.'

He sighed piteously and squeezed out two real tears.

Shirley laughed despite herself.

Nutley was very serious with his knots, and an excellent

teacher. The boys were quickly intent on what they were doing. Oaks watched for a while, an amused smile on his face and, when no one took notice of him, went to his bunk and began leafing idly through his copy of *This Token of Freedom*, a book given to all evacuees by the American Outpost in Britain. It was the first time he had displayed interest in it.

Millis's joke about Barlow's hands proved surprisingly prescient. He had to be shown even the most complicated knot just once before being able to duplicate it.

'You're quick,' Nutley said. 'As quick as my brother.'

Oaks looked up from his book and scowled.

'He's off to Gravesend Sea School next year, my little brother,' Nutley said to Shirley.

She had been thinking his expression was exactly like that of the boys he had been teaching. Not much more than a child himself and he was an officer on a merchant ship. What marvellous people the British were. He was probably frightened of Captain Penrose. The crew all seemed so in awe of him. She could understand that, of course. But what they didn't seem to know was how gentle and understanding he could be. She was thinking about Captain Penrose when Nutley spoke. She flushed, as if he could read her thoughts.

'Where's your home?' she asked, to cover her confusion. 'I don't know your accent.'

'Cornwall.'

'Where in Cornwall?'

He seemed not to want to tell her, pretending not to hear and giving all his attention to the knot he was demonstrating.

Her curiosity piqued, she repeated, 'Where in Cornwall?'

'Muzzle, actually,' he mumbled.

'Muzzle?'

'M-o-u-s-e-h-o-l-e.'

'Mousehole?' she said with a delighted laugh. 'Is there really a place called that?'

'I knew you'd laugh,' he said defensively. 'Most people do.'

'I'm not making fun. Honestly. I think it's a marvellous name.'

'It's just by Penzance,' he said, brightening. 'Everyone knows Penzance, I expect.'

' "The Pirates of Penzance",' one of the boys cried.

'That's right, lad,' Millis said. 'I've done a fair bit of Gilbert and Sullivan myself. Not that either of 'em cared much for the way I did it. Should have stuck to my violin, like my mum always wanted.'

He began whistling a tune from the comic opera. He was good, very good. It was difficult for her to reconcile the melodious tones with the clownish face and manner.

'You're full of surprises,' she said.

'That's what the pickpocket said when he reached in my coat and came away with a hot meat pie and a bottle of stout. "Stout with meat pie?" he says. "Stout's with roast beef. Half and half's with meat pie." '

'Do you know "I'm called Little Buttercup"?'

'Just toss a shilling in me cap and I'll oblige,' he said.

He took off an imaginary cap and she pretended to drop a coin in it, feeling less silly than she expected.

The boys got after him to whistle their favourites and even Nutley had a request. After fifteen minutes Millis came to attention with his hand over his heart and whistled 'God Save the King'.

'Concert's over,' he said. 'Nothing permitted after the anthem. Though I wouldn't object to a bit of applause.'

Shirley applauded as vigorously as any of the boys.

'That was wizard,' Nutley said. 'You should go on the stage, Mr . . .'

Shirley expected Millis to say something to ridicule Nutley but he said, 'Call me Joe. I had a go at it, actually, but a chap has to try to improve himself, doesn't he?'

He said it as if making fun of himself, not the earnest young Third Officer. Millis might play the fool with Captain Penrose, Shirley thought, but at least he didn't pick on helpless innocents like Nutley. He could be really nice when he wanted to.

'Mr Millis is a professional entertainer,' she explained, by way of reward for Millis's restraint. 'He's along to help keep the boys amused.'

'Isn't that wizard! Mr Millis, I wonder . . . I wonder if you mightn't put on a show for the crew?'

Shirley was on the verge of scotching the idea. It would only bind the boys more strongly to him. But on the other hand, why deprive the crew of a little entertainment because of petty jealousy? And it was petty. And, if Millis did a show, the arrangements would be up to her, which naturally would call for conferences with Captain Penrose.

'Your Captain Penrose doesn't think I'm too amusing,' Millis said.

'I think it's a perfectly swell idea,' Shirley said quickly. 'I'll ask the captain. Would you like that, boys?'

They all shouted approval except Oaks.

'I bow to the intelligence and good taste of my constituency,' Millis said. 'If Barlow promises to help with the lemon aid bit.'

Barlow grinned shyly and nodded, pleased to note Oaks looked pained.

She really shouldn't be jealous of Millis over Barlow, Shirley thought. He'd done wonders for the boy's morale. And he certainly had a way with children. He was as good with them as Captain Penrose was with adults. Her father always said a man who was kind to children had a good heart. Her father might even *like* Millis, she thought wryly.

135

Some of his jokes were as lame as Millis's. But never as rude.

Three bells sounded.

'Oh,' Nutley cried, scrambling to his feet. 'I've got to run.'

He dashed for the door, paused just before going out and said, 'May I come again?'

'Any time,' Shirley said. 'Right, Mr Millis?'

Millis looked at her as if he weren't sure he'd heard her correctly, then smiled at her and said, 'Right.'

She went to her stateroom to rest before dressing for dinner. She wanted Captain Penrose to see her at her best.

Penrose had called a meeting in the officers' mess for all the officers at three bells, seventeen-thirty. He had instructions for them to pass on to the crew that he did not wish to reach the ears of the passengers. He had already begun when Nutley reached the door. Nutley hesitated, wondering if he would be missed if he remained outside. He dreaded coming in late and having to face the captain. Second Officer Briscoe and Chief Engineer Richardson had told him, with great relish, what an absolute stickler Penrose was and Nutley had seen enough examples of it already to be terrified of him. He decided to listen from outside.

The appearance of the U-boat had made concrete for Penrose the dangers facing the *Amindra*. He had known them well enough in the abstract but today had been his first actual encounter despite his three previous round trips across the Atlantic. They had all been in convoys, large ones and heavily escorted. Though all the convoys had lost ships, the *Amindra* herself had never come under attack. Now the vessel was on its own and it was doubly important that every member of the crew be on his toes. He could not share his secret with them but he could stress the need for unceasing vigilance.

'I am pleased with the way you all conducted yourselves during today's attack,' he began.

Although the U-boat had launched no torpedoes – at least no telltale wakes had been seen – nor fired on the *Amindra*, in his mind the vessel had come under attack. And the consequences could have been very different if his manoeuvring of the ship and employment of the stern gun hadn't driven it off.

'However,' he continued, 'future attacks may well be more persistent. Now the enemy knows we're here we must expect him to try again at any time. As you all know, we have a grave responsibility in the form of young British children. Their lives, along with those of our distinguished passengers, are in your hands. I want you to impress the need for extreme vigilance on every member of the crew.'

Idiot, Barrett thought. When the U-boat surfaced he hadn't a clue what to do. Dumb bastard didn't know which end was up.

'Thank you,' Penrose concluded, after listening to reports from each of his senior officers. 'You may all return to your duties.'

Nutley quickly disappeared before Penrose emerged from the mess.

Shirley had hoped she might be placed next to Captain Penrose at dinner, but the seating was the same as Monday night and she understood regretfully that it would remain so. Unlike the night before, Penrose spoke seldom, just enough to be the gracious host. He seemed preoccupied to Shirley. So quiet and dignified. And so attractive for a man old enough to be her father. Despite his preoccupation and the distance between them, he seemed to go out of his way to show her at least as much attention as he did Lady Anne. She took great comfort from that.

137

Rosten, on the contrary, was a far more interesting dinner companion than before. Though looking physically tired, he seemed remarkably content for a man who had just lost his wife. His left hand was bandaged, which made eating awkward for him because the English fed themselves with that hand. When Shirley asked him how he had hurt it he studied the bandage for a moment, as if only now reminded of it by her question, before saying he had managed to cut it changing the blade in his safety razor.

'I'm rather awkward, you see,' he said. Marjorie had claimed that wasn't true. He only seemed so because his mind was usually occupied with important matters. 'It's actually nothing, but Dr Grimes insisted on dressing it.' He didn't like lying but under the circumstances there was nothing else for it.

'Did you tell Captain Penrose about the boys' food?'

'Indeed I did. He regrets there's not a great deal to be done about it. Because they're so many they're having crew rations. I'm sure he's doing the best for them he possibly can.'

'I should have realized that,' Shirley said apologetically. 'He's such a dear, isn't he?'

That seemed to startle Rosten. He gave her a sidelong glance and said, 'He certainly knows what he's about, I'll say that.' Concentrating on a morsel on his fork he said, 'You know, Miss Hunt, he thinks quite highly of you, if I may say so.' It was Marjorie's opinion that if you knew something unpleasant about a person you should keep quiet about it but if you knew something they might like to hear you should pass it on.

'Really?' Shirley said.

Of course she knew Captain Penrose liked her but it was nice hearing someone else say so.

'Indeed he does. Only this morning . . .' how early in

the morning he dare not tell her '. . . Captain Penrose said you were an ornament to his dinner table.'

Flushing, Shirley could not resist stealing a glance at the head of the table, where Penrose was looking thoughtfully into his coffee cup. Just at that moment he looked up. Catching her eye on him he smiled and, so it seemed to her, sighed.

Seeing the effect of his comment on Shirley, Rosten wondered if he had been indiscreet. In his preoccupation with his own problems he had been unaware that the young woman was so taken with the captain. But what harm could it possibly do? The captain was the soul of propriety and Miss Hunt was a sensible young woman. It no doubt was not at all uncommon for a young woman to admire the ship's captain on a voyage. Though in this instance the young woman was young enough to be the captain's daughter.

Shirley had hoped to speak with Captain Penrose more tonight than she'd been able to before but his mood prevented it. She was doubly disappointed now that Mr Rosten had confirmed his interest in her.

Donahue, however, saw to it that she was not ignored. He kept trying to include her in his conversation with Lady Anne and once, when making a point, leaned towards her and put his hand on her leg under the table. Nodding agreement to what he said, she smiled with deliberate brightness, plucked his hand off her leg and put it back where it belonged. Donahue did not miss a syllable.

Captain Penrose excused himself early, saying he had pressing duties and urging the others to enjoy the comfort and fellowship of his dining-room as long as they wished. Lady Anne had been engaged in an animated conversation with Donahue when the captain rose to leave. Her voice faltered and her eyes lost their sparkle for the merest instant. Surely not another early evening, she thought, and another interminable night in her cabin. She regained her festive mood when Penrose asked them all not to allow his departure to change anything.

'The evening's just begun,' she said with determined gaiety. 'We must all do exactly as Captain Penrose asks.'

As soon as Penrose left she said, 'What you say may possibly be true in America, Mr Donahue, but not in Britain. True, Mr Rosten?'

'Indeed it is, Lady Anne,' Rosten said, though he had not been listening to their conversation. He had been thinking about the work still to be done below decks. 'But if you'll excuse me, I must be leaving, too. I'm rather tired.' And would be more so before this night was over.

Dr Grimes and the Chief Engineer appeared to be hesitating over the last of the saloon's good port and the glowing ends of Donahue's Havana cigars.

'Dutton,' said Lady Anne, 'isn't there another bottle of that delicious port? Dr Grimes and Chief Engineer Richardson's glasses are empty.'

Dutton brought another bottle and the two men settled back comfortably.

Impatience grew in Shirley the moment Penrose was out the door. She'd hardly had a chance to exchange half a dozen words with him, not even about the proposed show. She excused herself despite Lady Anne's effusive (for Lady Anne) invitation for her to remain, and went looking for him. She hoped he had not gone to the bridge. She knew passengers were not allowed there except by invitation. He might have gone to his cabin to change out of his dress uniform, she thought. He might still be there.

He was in the passageway to his cabin getting something out of a cabinet. When he heard her coming he put it back quickly and locked the cabinet with a key. 'Spares' was lettered on the cabinet in block letters.

'Captain Penrose,' she said, 'I know you're busy, but if

you have a minute . . .'

'Of course.'

'Mr Millis has volunteered to put on a show for the crew.'

'Millis?' Penrose said with an expression of distaste.

'I know he behaved terribly at Euston Station but really he can be funny.'

She never imagined she would be defending Joe Millis to Captain Penrose but somehow she found it less distasteful than she might have done before the storm. Not only was Millis proving himself helpful but also she was finding herself more comfortable with him.

'I'm afraid the crew have rather a lot to keep them busy,' he said.

Just how much, he would rather she did not know. No point in alarming the child.

'He had one of my boys in one of his turns,' she said almost desperately. 'Poor Barlow will be so disappointed.'

'Very well,' he said, relenting. 'See what you can work out with Mr Bar . . . Second Officer Briscoe. If it fits in with the watch schedules I'll have no objection.'

She knew he was impatient to get on with whatever he had to do but was too much the gentleman to let it show. That was no reason he could not *notice* her. She knew he liked her. He had shown it in any number of ways. And even said so to others, if not in so many words. Yet now that they were alone and he could be more open about his feelings – oh, she didn't expect him to *kiss* her or anything, he wasn't like that and this was not the time or the place – he was being more distant than ever. It couldn't be that he was shy, not Captain Penrose? He was afraid she might think he was too old for her. Maybe if she just gave him the tiniest bit of encouragement . . .

She laid a hand on his braided sleeve and looked into his face. It only seemed to make him uncomfortable. Of course. Someone might come along and see them any minute. She dropped her hand and looked away.

'I thought we might plan it,' she said lamely. 'You and I.'

'That's most thoughtful of you but I'm rather . . . busy.'

His polite words seemed as cold to her as a scornful rejection. She was just another passenger to him. Oh, sure, he thought she was brave and doing a good job with the boys and was an ornament to his dinner table but she meant nothing to him. She'd made a real fool of herself, mooning at him at dinner in front of everyone and just now putting her hand on his arm and looking soulfully into his face. Her own face felt hot and her insides chilly.

'Are you all right, Miss Hunt?' he asked solicitously.

The words repeated themselves mockingly in her head. 'Are you all right, silly Miss Hunt?'

'I'm fine,' she said quickly, searching for ordinary words to hide her misery. 'Really fine. Instead of Mr Briscoe could I have Mr Nutley? The boys like him and I know he'd like to help.'

Nutley. The most dispensable officer he had.

'Excellent choice, my dear. Now if you'll excuse me . . .'

She went to her stateroom feeling humiliated and rejected. As she was unlocking her door Barrett materialized out of the shadows so abruptly he startled her.

'Oh,' she said, surprised she could still feel an emotion, even fear. 'You scared me.'

'I'm harmless, really. Did our captain give you a good dinner?'

'What are you doing here?'

'Just a social call. Aren't you going to invite me in?'

'Look, Mr Barrett. Robbie. I'm very tired. If you don't mind . . .'

142

She opened the door and slipped inside. When she tried to close it his foot was in the way.

'But I do mind,' he said. 'This is no way to treat a friend. What are you afraid of?'

'I'm not afraid of anything. It's just that I'm tired.'

He pushed his way in. She tried to bar the door but he was much too strong. She was angered by his presumption and a little frightened. But also, in a strange way, pleased with herself. Without even trying she had brought him hanging around her door like a schoolboy. Maybe Captain Penrose had not noticed her but Barrett certainly had.

She put her palms against his chest when he tried to pull her into his arms in the dark cabin. He was not wearing his life-jacket. She had let hers drop to the floor when he grabbed her. He bent towards her in the darkness and his lips explored her face for her mouth.

She turned her face away and said in a low, fierce voice, 'Let me go!'

'You'd be disappointed as hell if I did,' he murmured into her ear.

He kissed her neck, not roughly as she expected, but expertly. Involuntarily she arched her neck to the kiss for a moment before struggling to get free. He held her fast.

'I mean it. If you leave now I won't tell Captain Penrose.'

'That old bastard. He wouldn't know what you're talking about.'

She could never mention this to Captain Penrose, she realized. It would be too embarrassing. And he would think somehow it was her own fault for leading Barrett on, think she had thrown herself at Barrett as she had at him. But Penrose wasn't even aware she had thrown herself at him. Why couldn't he want to hold her like this? Kiss her like this?

143

But it was not Captain Penrose kissing her. It was Robbie Barrett. And her arms were around his neck. What would Captain Penrose think? What would her father think?

'See?' he whispered. 'It's not too bad once you try it, is it?'

'That's enough,' she said firmly.

The few times she had been stirred by men before she had always been able to bring herself under control quickly, and them as well, with tones of cool command.

'Not nearly,' he said.

She felt the cardigan slipping from her shoulders and then the neck of her dress being pushed aside. He was kissing her bare shoulder, then her chest above her tight brassière and then that was pushed free, too, and he was kissing her breast. And she did not want him to stop.

It was the first time she had ever been kissed there, or even fondled, except briefly before she had been able to extricate herself when taken by surprise by a date and the man who had crystallized her decision to go to France. What was she doing? She was not this kind of girl. What made him think she was?

'What do you think you're *doing*?' she cried. 'Who do you think you *are*?'

'A very lucky man. And you're a very lucky girl.'

The dress was down to her waist now and her brassière was gone. She was glad it was dark. It would be worse if there was light and she was witness to her own shame and weakness.

He picked her up and stumbled towards her bed in the dark, cursing when something caught his shin. Was this really happening to her? Was she really letting it happen? She felt revulsion and feverish anticipation. Would it be awful? Would it be wonderful? What would she think of herself after? What would he think of her? Would Captain

Penrose know? Would Lady Anne? Would everyone?

He found the bunk and laid her down in it. She lay there supine and heard him fumbling in the dark. He was taking his clothes off. Now. She must cover herself and escape. But she lay still. It was not her fault. Captain Penrose should have been warmer. The strangeness and excitement of this voyage. Her concern about the boys. Robbie's cunning and physical strength. They had all conspired to bring her to this state. No one could blame her. Not Captain Penrose nor her father.

The door to the next stateroom clicked open and Donahue's voice sounded clearly in the darkness of her cabin.

'Good night, Lady Anne. We'll continue the debate in the morning.'

The spell was broken. Just as she could hear everything in Lady Anne's room, Lady Anne could hear everything in hers. Shirley sat up and adjusted her dress, relieved and disappointed.

'Robbie,' she whispered. 'You'll have to go.'

'Are you crazy?' he whispered back.

He crawled in beside her. She felt cloth against her bare arm. Lady Anne had returned before he had managed to get everything off. Shirley rapped on the bulkhead with her knuckles.

'Lady Anne?' she called, with great effort keeping the tremor from her voice. 'Did you have a nice evening?'

'What?' came Lady Anne's voice from beyond the bulkhead. 'Oh, it's you, Shirley. Yes, delightful. You should have stayed.'

'Bitch!' Barrett's voice grated in her ear. 'But I'm not leaving.'

'She'll hear us,' Shirley whispered.

'Let her.'

'It'll be all over the ship.'

145

He chuckled in her ear.

'They'll think it was Millis,' he said.

That did it. She was fully in command of herself now.

'That's not funny. Get out.'

'Would you like to pop over for a chat?' Lady Anne called. 'It's early yet.' It wasn't really, but she was not yet prepared to face the night. And it did lift her spirits to be with the young American woman even though it sometimes evoked memories . . .

There was silence for a moment, then Barrett laughed silently again, as if in conspiracy with Shirley against Lady Anne.

'You would, too, wouldn't you?' he whispered. 'To put off doing something you'd rather. I'm going.'

'Thank you, but I'm very tired,' Shirley called.

'Good night, then,' Lady Anne said, disappointed.

'Good night, Lady Anne,' Barrett whispered.

Shirley wanted to laugh. He was absolutely impossible. But manageable, thank goodness.

He kissed her, open-mouthed and probing, and his callous but deft hand explored her body for a long moment. Then he was out of the bunk, whispering, 'Until next time. I'll find a better place.'

The door shut quietly behind him.

She lay in her bunk until she could breathe naturally again before getting into her nightgown and trying to sleep. She was grateful to Lady Anne for her narrow escape but she could not help wondering what it would have been like had Lady Anne returned a few minutes later.

Manfred Freiburg was writing a letter to his wife. He wrote faithfully three times a week, keeping the letters in a teakwood box until they could be sent home on a prize or put aboard a supply ship. He had entrusted two dozen to

146

the captain of the *Nordmark*. This, and another he would write later in the week, with God's help might reach her before any of them.

There was little he could tell her of his activities except the ordinary things of day-to-day life, that he was keeping well, a sow in the piggery had given birth, Schramm was still as solemn as ever, so mostly he filled his letters with questions about her and the children and plans for the future. He finished, signed, sealed and addressed the letter and put it in its box. He filled his pipe and went on deck for a final look around before turning in.

It was a pleasant night, not too cold, with the sea not overly aggressive. A figure was striding the deck ahead of him. That would be Schramm, taking his constitutional. Every night he circled the deck at a rapid clip for precisely twenty minutes. He counted the number of circuits, converted that to metres and kept a running total of the number of kilometres walked with nightly entries in the log he kept in his cabin for that purpose. It was not only his way of keeping fit but was also the pragmatic lieutenant's only flight of fancy. He was not circling the deck of the *Adler*. He was on a walking tour along the Rhine from Strasbourg to Cologne. He kept a weekly record of his progress on a touring map in the chartroom.

'Where are you now?' Freiburg asked, falling in step with him.

'Mainz, by the end of the week,' said Schramm.

'Don't be surprised if you find the *Amindra* waiting there for you.'

'I don't like it,' Schramm said. 'She's outrunning us. If she's not slowed she'll be off Newfoundland before we can catch her.'

'Don't be such a worrier. Our man still has three days.'

Chapter Nine

Rosten waited until he was sure everyone aboard the *Amindra* except the watch was asleep. He had changed into seaman's clothes that Captain Penrose had found for him, including heavy work gloves to protect his hands. His burned palm gave him discomfort but was protected by a vaseline-smeared bandage. He could just fit the hand into a large glove.

He had the key to the hold in his pocket and another key on a cord around his neck under his shirt. The latter was the key to the 'Spares' cabinet outside Captain Penrose's quarters. Penrose had shown him the arming switch as well as the schematic drawing showing the locations of the scuttling charges, noting that they were in not only the predictable places, at the bulkheads between the engine room and the adjacent holds, but also in less likely spots along the hull under the cargo. Rosten had been flattered by the confidence thus shown in him. Penrose had not been required to show him that, only where the switch was and what was to be done with it in the event that it had to be used.

He stole down to the hold, not using his flashlight, and flattened himself against a bulkhead, holding his breath, when he heard someone moving about in the 'tween-deck. Only when he was sure he was alone did he continue to the hold. He fumbled in the dark for the padlock and had to remove a glove to get the key into it.

Inside, he turned on the hold lights and set to work. When he paused to rest from the task of gathering the heavy ingots, he spent the time usefully, searching for spilled coins among the sodden dunnage. The coins had a more tangible appearance of value than the ingots. They were the last of over 50,000 sacks which had been shipped to Canada – French napoleons; British gold sovereigns ranging from George V and Queen Victoria back to George III's rare 'spade guineas'; Maria Theresa gold thalers; and thousands of Scandinavian and other European gold pieces. They had a voluptuous aura of romance and history about them which the ingots, yellow blocks gleaming softly in the light, did not. And he knew that the value of most of them far exceeded their gold content. He longed to have one of them, not for its intrinsic worth but as a memento of the undertaking. How nice it would be one day when the war was over and there was no longer any need for secrecy to show it to Marjorie and explain what it meant. But that was a fantasy. He would never see his wife again. Abruptly, he stopped whistling and went about his search with sombre doggedness.

Barlow lay shivering in his bunk. He could tell by the sounds, and the lack of them, that everyone else was sleeping. He would like to creep to Oaks's bunk and smash him in the face. He thought he was so clever, always ragging him and making those snide comments about his mum and dad. Mr Millis saw through him, though. But not that Yank woman. She thought Oaks was a perfect little gentleman. The bastard. If gentlemen were like Oaks he never wanted to be one. Oaks had known what it would be like when he tricked him into taking the bunk under the ventilator.

That ventilator. Where did it go? When he was still a little chap he'd liked to explore dark narrow places. He remembered the time he'd crawled into a drain on Mile End Road and fallen asleep there. Hadn't his mum and dad been crazy with worry when he didn't show up for supper? And when he'd come home all dirt from top to bottom they'd not known whether to hug or thrash him. He wished he was home with mum and dad now.

Where did the bloody ventilator go? He'd wager even Mr Millis didn't know that and he certainly was not going to ask him. Things like that you found out for yourself. None of the chaps knew, he was sure of that. Not even Oaks, who pretended to know everything.

Draping a blanket over his shoulders he climbed down from his bunk, not making a sound, and crept across the deck on hands and knees to Millis's cubicle. He listened outside the curtain for any indication that he was awake. There was no sound at all inside. Cautiously he pushed aside the curtain and, not daring to breathe, stole close to Millis's bunk. There was just enough light from the single weak bulk left on all night for Barlow to see the bunk was empty.

Had he gone to the bog? His dad did that at night. He couldn't very well go messing about with the ventilator if Mr Millis was going to come back and catch him. He went out to look. There was no one in the wash-rooms.

Barlow hurried back to the dormitory and ran on tiptoe to the tier below the ventilator. Oaks was talking in his sleep. Barlow bent close to hear what he was saying. Wouldn't it be grand to learn something to tell the chaps? But Oaks's words made no sense.

From the top bunk he could just reach the grille covering the ventilator. He tried it tentatively. It moved. He tugged at it with both hands and it came free with a scraping sound. He looked around quickly to see if he had awakened Oaks or any of the others but they slept soundly. He pulled himself up to the ventilator and, hooking his elbows over the lip, got his head and shoulders inside. It was cold and dark, smelling of metal and wet sacks that had been left to lie a long time in a cellar. But the darkness drew him on. It was a place no one but he had ever been. Oaks had never been there. Oaks wouldn't dare.

He was not afraid. It was no different from the drain in Mile End Road except that mum and dad were not waiting supper for him. He crawled through the darkness, gritting his teeth against the cold. He was a Red Indian creeping to attack his enemies, a tiger stalking its prey. The tunnel ended. No, it had not ended, just divided, with one duct slanting up, the other down. He followed the one going down, because it was a bit wider.

His hands and knees smarted from scraping on the chill metal of the tunnel but he ignored the discomfort, urged on by a yearning to see where it led. He had been crawling for miles, it seemed, when he saw a glow up ahead, just a suggestion of light in the pitch black. He crawled faster. The glow intensified as he neared the source. The light came through a grille of the sort he had removed back at the dormitory. He pressed his face against the grille and looked down into a cavern filled with crate after huge crate, the narrow aisles between them strewn with litter. It was odd, he thought, all that litter when the captain kept the rest of the ship so smart. He remembered the captain giving that officer who looked like a cinema star, the one Miss Hunt was keen on, the rough side of his tongue just for dropping a fag-end on the deck. There was someone down there. He could hear him moving about, and the dull clank of metal and hammering.

Some of the crates had been smashed and lay broken and empty between the stacks. There was a pile of bricks in one aisle looking oddly smooth and yellow. As he watched, a man as old as the captain came from between the stacks and plucked a brick from the pile. He was not very strong. He took only one brick and carried it with both hands.

Barlow knew who he was. Not his name, but that he was a passenger, one of those going to America. Barlow

151

wondered if he was American. He looked rather foreign. Darkish. But what was he doing working down here if he was a passenger? Perhaps he was working for his passage. Passage to America was dear. He'd heard his mum and dad talking about it when they thought he was sleeping, and hadn't they been pleased when they learned he could go to America after all even if they didn't have the cash? His stomach started hurting again as it had when he saw how happy they were he was going, as if they couldn't wait to be rid of him. Of course they'd tried to explain it was because they wanted him away from the bombing and they would miss him more than he missed them, and his mum had cried when they left the hotel that afternoon, but there it was, they'd behaved as if they'd won the pools when they got the news about the passage money, hadn't they?

The memory took the excitement out of his explorations and perversely enhanced the homesickness he had felt since his first night on the *Amindra*. His dad had said he was a lucky lad to be going to America and think of all the new friends he'd make on the way. He'd only made one friend, Mr Millis, but lots of enemies. And the worst of them was Oaks. He thought he was so brave and clever. But not brave and clever enough to crawl through the dark with cold metal scraping his hands and knees, not knowing or caring where the dark led, as he had. Oaks would get that silly pleased-with-himself look off his face if he knew Barlow the Witty hadn't been afraid. But Oaks wasn't going to know. This was his secret place and his alone.

Feeling better, he squirmed and wriggled to turn around in the confines of the duct and crept back to the dormitory. He looked out cautiously to be certain no one was awake before getting himself turned around again and letting himself down on to the top bunk and replacing the grille. Mr Millis's curtain was still drawn and he did not know if he'd come back from wherever he'd been. He wondered where Mr Millis had gone off to in the night. Perhaps to see Miss Hunt to talk about the show they were giving. Perhap he could be a music-hall star himself one day, like Mr Millis.

'I can't hear you,' he whispered to himself as he stole to his bunk. 'I've a lemon in my ear.'

In the hold, Rosten heard someone fumbling at the door. There was a latch inside and thank heavens he'd remembered to fasten it. He hurried to the door and whispered, 'Captain Penrose?'

He was answered by silence and after a moment the sound of retreating steps. It wasn't Captain Penrose, then. Who could it have been, trying to get into the hold at this time of night? Had he given anything away by revealing his own presence in the locked hold? Perhaps it was someone's duty to make a regular check of the holds. In any case he'd have to report the incident to Penrose.

He was suddenly aware of his fatigue and the pain in his hand. And he was too put off by the unexpected visitor to be in any mood to continue. He'd made good progress and should have all the spilled ingots safely out of sight in salvaged crates well before they reached Halifax. There were not enough of the crates to distribute the bullion among them in the original small numbers. Instead of forty ingots there would be more than a hundred to each repacked crate. They would be considerably heavier than the other crates. He hoped he could put them together strongly enough that they would not burst from their own weight when unloaded. Captain Penrose had provided him with a quantity of nails.

He had no way of knowing if he had found all the coins. There still might be the odd sovereign or napoleon down in the waste. He'd not know that until the final inventory in Ottawa. The contents of each numbered sack were listed

153

down to the last coin. He wondered if he would be docked for anything missing, smiling wanly at the absurd notion.

He took a last look around the hold. Even with the bullion hidden again it was not a reassuring sight, with wet shredded paper, rags and cotton wool everywhere and stacks of broken boards. Not to mention the ugly gap in the insulation and the makeshift patch covering the sprung plate. However, he was sure there was nothing Captain Penrose could not explain his way out of as long as no outsider actually saw any gold. He must ask Captain Penrose to find him a heavy needle and waxed thread, he thought, as he let himself out, to sew up the torn canvas, coin sack. How it would have amused Marjorie to see him sewing, he thought with a pang.

Feeling for the hasp in the dark, he snapped the padlock shut. As he turned he was dazzled by a sudden burst of light. It transfixed him for a moment and all he could do was shout in surprise. The light went off as abruptly as it had come on and steps fled along the passageway. He turned on his flashlight and ran in pursuit, wondering what he would do if he overtook the man but determined to apprehend him if he could and learn what he was doing here.

Heavy steps pounded up the companionway ahead of him but by the time he reached it it was empty. The 'tween-deck, too, was empty when he reached it. Rosten hurried to Captain Penrose's cabin and rapped on the door, whispering urgently, 'It's Rosten.'

Penrose swung his legs over his bunk immediately. He had not been sleeping. He had been lying awake thinking about U-boats and his precious cargo and his heavy responsibility, going over in his mind every possible contingency and realizing how truly helpless the *Amindra* was in the face of a skilled and determined attack. He could imagine a U-boat stalking her now in silent menace, making a surface approach under cover of darkness, perhaps, to attack with her deck-gun at first light. He had the DEMS crew sleeping on deck at their gun, keeping their own twenty-four-hour watch, which was some comfort. And the Asdic room and the bridge had orders to inform him immediately any echo was detected, no matter how distant.

He turned on a light and opened the door. The light went off the instant the door came away from the jamb. It was rigged to do that, as were all doors opening on to the deck or any place from which a stray light might be visible from the sea. The light came on again when he shut the door behind Rosten.

The man was plainly agitated, breathing heavily, his face lined with fatigue. Rosten had the wind up, that was evident. He'd come not to expect that sort of thing from him, which made it all the more clear that he should not take anyone or anything for granted until they were safely berthed in Halifax.

'What is it, man?' he demanded.

'Someone,' Rosten panted, 'someone tried to come in the hold. And when I left he was waiting outside and shone a light on me.'

'Did you get a look at him?'

Rosten shook his head.

'I ran after him but he was too quick,' he said.

So Rosten was panting from effort, not from fear, Penrose thought, relieved.

'Did he get a look inside?' he asked less sternly.

'No. He couldn't have. I'd locked the hold from inside, and had shut it when I came out before he caught me in the light. Is anyone meant to make a check of the holds?'

'Not that one. You didn't get a glimpse of the man at all, then?'

'I'm sorry. No.'

155

'Millis,' Penrose said, more to himself than Rosten.

'The escort chap?' Rosten said, puzzled, breathing more easily now. 'What would he be doing down there?'

'Looking for something to steal, probably. I've already caught him down there myself.'

'Could have been,' Rosten said thoughtfully. 'A large man, I expect, from the noise he made getting away.'

'You must be more careful in the future,' Penrose said.

'I've been very careful. When I heard him at the door I thought it was you or I'd not have called out to him.'

'You should have kept silent. If I'd wanted you I'd have identified myself.'

'But I didn't know that, did I?' Rosten said with a trace of heat.

'You do now. I'll have word passed among the crew to keep an eye on Millis.'

'You might tell Miss Hunt as well.'

'Miss Hunt?' She'd seemed rather confused last night. Perhaps the boys were proving a bit much for her. Well, if things really got out of hand he imagined she'd be sensible enough to tell him and he'd see to it Millis pitched in more.

'He works for her. It shouldn't be necessary to tell her why, should it?'

'No. Now suppose we both get some sleep. You look as if you could use it.'

Penrose lay awake after Rosten left. Suppose it had not been Millis skulking about below? Who, then? And why? No one but he and Rosten knew about the secret cargo. It might have been the officer of the watch having a look around, but if that was the case why had he run off without identifying himself? No, everything pointed to Millis.

Barlow was still awake when Millis came in. The youngster pretended to be sleeping but opened his eyes a crack and watched Millis as he surveyed the tiers of bunks before parting the curtain around his cubicle and disappearing inside. If Mr Millis had been seeing Miss Hunt about the show they'd certainly kept at it long enough, he thought. It must be very late. He had heard two bells while he was crawling back along the ventilator shaft. That would be one o'clock. He knew because Mr Nutley had explained the bells while he was showing the other boys how to tie knots.

Mr Millis was breathing fast and deep through his mouth, as if he'd been running. It was hard for Barlow to picture Mr Millis running. He never did anything quickly except make jokes. But he was glad Mr Millis was back. He was the only thing Barlow liked about this trip. Except the ventilators. Tomorrow night when they were all asleep he would go farther and see more.

Penrose took breakfast with his passengers on Wednesday morning instead of having it, standing, on the bridge as was his custom. Donahue had his breakfast brought to his cabin by Dutton, which pleased Penrose because he wanted to speak with Miss Hunt as casually as possible and he knew that would be difficult across the talkative Special Envoy.

Shirley felt uncomfortable in his presence and was still angry with him for having been so imperceptive the night before and leaving her so vulnerable to Barrett. She was angry with herself, as well, for having so misunderstood his feelings towards her. She thought she had learned her lesson before running off to France. She did not know which would be worse, for Captain Penrose to guess what schoolgirl thoughts she had entertained about him or for him to learn how she had behaved with Robbie.

When he invited her to take Donahue's vacant place she was relieved and grateful. He had no idea that anything had changed. Perhaps now she could accept his civility for what it was and make the best of it.

'Everything all right with the boys?' Penrose asked.

'So far,' she said.

'You're doing an excellent job with them. I know how restless boys that age can get. I'd expected them to be into everything.'

'They're a good bunch of kids,' Shirley replied, feeling more confident. 'And they're not allowed off on their own.'

'I wish that were true of Mr Millis.'

'Millis?' She sounded surprised. 'What's he done now?'

'It isn't what he's done so much as where he's been,' the captain said. 'Various members of the crew have reported seeing him wandering around below decks.'

'He's not supposed to leave the boys alone.'

'Well, he does,' Penrose said. 'I'd better have a word with him.'

'Thank you,' she said grimly. 'But I'll do it.'

Penrose nodded. It was exactly the response he had anticipated. He looked at the clock and pushed away his half-eaten breakfast.

'Time for me to go on duty,' he said, getting up.

Shirley rose as he did.

'About the show . . .' she said.

'The show?'

'The one Millis is doing for the crew. You said Mr Nutley could help with the arrangements.'

'Oh, yes. Of course.'

'I'd like to get started as soon as possible, if it's all right with you.'

She needed something to keep her occupied. Anything that would put Barrett out of her mind. When she came to breakfast she had been nervous about seeing Lady Anne, wondering if she had heard him in her stateroom. But Lady Anne had given no indication of it.

'Start right away, if you like,' Penrose said.

Nutley had had the late watch and would just be getting to sleep. Being routed from his warm blankets would serve as punishment for failing to attend the officers' briefing.

'I'll have somebody go and get him,' he said.

'Tell him to come directly to the dormitory,' Shirley said. 'But not for a few minutes. I want to talk to Millis first.'

She finished breakfast quickly and hurried below. The boys were just clearing away their dishes. Millis was nowhere to be seen.

'Oaks,' she said, 'have you seen Mr Millis?'

'In the bog, I expect. He rushed off with that look on his face, Miss Hunt.'

All the boys except Barlow laughed, as if Oaks had said something very funny.

'I'll fetch him if you like,' Oaks said.

'That won't be necessary.'

The boys laughed again at Millis's entrance. His surprise was evident only for an instant.

'What a smashing audience,' he said. 'Haven't said a word and we're already rolling in the aisles, aren't we? Good morning to you, Miss Hunt. To what do we owe the pleasure of a visit so early in the morning?'

'I want to talk to you, Mr Millis.'

'I'll just have my secretary check my appointment book.' He mimed leafing through a notebook. 'Yes, I can spare a moment. Step into my office.' He mimed opening a door and waved her through it.

He had every boy's attention.

'All right, everyone,' Shirley said, 'Get to work. I want to see those tables cleared and your bunks neatly made.'

She led Millis towards his cubicle, away from the boys.

'You've put me in an embarrassing position with Captain Penrose,' she said severely, without preamble.

159

'Just how did I manage that?' He was surprised and disappointed. Here she was, using that tone again, just when he was beginning to think they could be friends.

'You've been wandering around the ship making a nuisance of yourself when your place is with the boys.'

'Oh, I know me place, I do, ma'am,' he said. 'Who's been saying otherwise?'

'Never mind who.' She fixed him with a stern glance, as Captain Penrose might. 'You are not to leave my boys unattended. Is that clear?'

He looked at her quizzically. Just let him try one of his corny jokes on me now, she thought.

'Perfectly,' he said, looking her in the eye.

She was getting straight answers from him at last. It paid to be firm. She must remember that Captain Penrose look and use it again if necessary. She hoped it wouldn't be. When he behaved himself he was good company.

Nutley arrived, looking subdued.

'Captain Penrose said I was to give you any help you needed in organizing the entertainment,' he said. 'And that it must be during daylight hours and not interfere with anyone's duties.'

Penrose had also dressed him down for not attending the officers' meeting and cut him off when he stammered out a lame excuse.

They decided the best place for the show was in the dormitory. There were plenty of seats, using the benches and bunks, and it was out of normal shipboard traffic.

'When can you be ready?' Shirley asked Millis.

'I'll ask my partner. Barlow, we've an engagement. Top of the bill and paid after each and every performance. How soon can you be ready?' Before the startled Barlow could answer he said, 'There's a good lad. Ready at the drop of a hat.' He leaned down as if picking something from the deck and offered it to Nutley, who instinctively

160

reached to take it before jerking his hand back, blushing. 'Not your hat, sir? Oh, I see, it's a boy's hat. Barlow, did you drop this lovely hat?'

Barlow stopped laughing to look at him blankly but was not displeased with the attention.

'As you see, my partner's always ready with a joke or a song,' Millis said. 'Taught him everything he knows, I did. Just give us our cue and we're off, as the lady . . .'

'You're not doing your show now,' Shirley said, cutting him off. 'So save it for the customers.' Now why had she done that? Millis was just having a little harmless fun.

'That's what my mum always said. Don't give nothing away you can sell, she always said to me. Or was it to my sister?'

Nutley blushed again. The boys hooted and Shirley said, 'Don't be crude in front of the children.'

'Sorry, ma'am, my worst got the best of me.'

It was decided, since Millis needed no preparation, the boys were restless and the off-watch crewmen were easily assembled, to have the entertainment that afternoon. Nutley was sent off to pass the word around and Shirley had Millis help her organize a game on deck in which two sets of boys tossed a braided rope ring back and forth. Oaks was very good at both catching and tossing. Barlow was hopeless. Oaks began throwing to him, manoeuvring him closer and closer to the rail and then tossing the ring just out of his reach so that at last it flew over the side into the ocean.

'Now see what you've done,' Oaks cried. 'He's lost our quoit for us, chaps.'

Some of the boys hooted Barlow but one of them, a quiet, red-haired thirteen-year-old, said, 'It was your fault, Oaks, not Barlow's.'

Oaks looked at him scornfully and said, 'I didn't know you were his sort, Graham.'

161

'I'm certainly not yours,' the boy said.

The other children, sensing a punch-up, began egging them on. Shirley put a stop to the clamour and took them on a circuit of the deck, with Millis at the rear barking out commands like a drill sergeant. She saw Captain Penrose looking down at them from the bridge and impulsively waved at him. He acknowledged it with a cordial nod. She felt good about that. He did admire her, in his way, and now that she had learned not to embroider on it she was in no danger of being silly again.

Barrett was on deck watching two seamen doing something with lines stretching down from a crane. When Shirley went by he saluted and said, 'Good morning, Miss Hunt. Fine-looking bunch of lads you have there.'

She wanted to look away, not because she wanted to snub him but because he brought back embarrassing memories, but she forced herself to smile normally and say, 'Thank you.'

Lunch time was less than an hour away. She took the boys back to the dormitory and left them with Millis after taking him aside to repeat her orders that he was not to leave them and wander around the ship.

Barrett was waiting for her in the 'tween-deck passageway when she emerged.

'I want to show you something,' he said.

'I'm on my way to my stateroom,' she said. 'I've got things to do.'

'It'll only be a minute.'

He took her arm and urged her along. Her reluctance was mingled with curiosity. She had no idea what he wanted to show her but did not feel threatened. It was broad daylight and a ship was not a very private place. It was not like being trapped in her room. At a companionway they heard someone descending and he drew her back out of sight until the man had gone on.

'Wouldn't want anyone to get any wrong ideas,' he said.

They went along passageways and up and down companionways until she was hopelessly lost, knowing they must be somewhere in the bowels of the ship but not knowing where. He stopped at a metal door. He opened it and motioned her inside.

'What do you think of it?' he said, closing the door behind him.

The only light came from a rectangular wire grating set high up in the passageway bulkhead. The place smelled of paint and oil. As her eyes adjusted to the dimness she could make out heaps of folded tarpaulins, coils of rope, paint cans. It was a storage locker.

'It's our honeymoon suite,' he said.

'Is this your idea of a joke?'

She wanted to think so but knew it was not. She was as much repelled by the thought of him fondling her in such a place as by that of being touched by him at all. She had quite got over her irresolution of the previous night.

'I was never more serious,' he said.

He blocked the door when she tried to leave.

'You'll learn to like it,' he said. 'Over here. I've brought blankets and a pillow.'

'No. Last night was a mistake. Just forget all about it.'

'I'll help you with your life-jacket.'

He began undoing the straps.

'Didn't you hear what I said?' she demanded, trying to pull away from him. She was beginning to be frightened.

'Yes. But I don't believe it. And neither do you.'

He kissed her then, more roughly than he'd ever done before. She was genuinely frightened now and struck out at him with her fists. He caught them easily in his big hands. She was transfixed by animal fear, feeling isolated and cut off from any hope of rescue. He was a violent man. She sensed that. Capable of anything if she resisted

163

him. But she was going to. As long as she had an ounce of strength left.

'I'm sorry,' he said contritely. 'It's just that I haven't been able to stop thinking about you.'

She was utterly disarmed by relief. This rough seaman was really not so different from the college boys and the proper young men she was accustomed to handling when she really put her foot down.

'Let me go and maybe I'll forgive you.'

'Sure,' he said, releasing her at once. 'I thought you'd be all for it.'

'We all make mistakes, Robbie.'

'Kiss and make up?' he asked humbly.

She did not want to kiss him but he seemed genuinely sorry for having misjudged her so. It would be needlessly cruel to refuse him. She'd kissed men before to spare their feelings.

He put his mouth on hers, gently at first, then, winding his arms around her, as roughly as before. She struggled to turn her head and pull free but his mouth remained locked on hers and his arms were like cables, holding her powerless.

'I know what you really want,' he said, drawing his face back and looking down at her.

Holding her with one strong arm, he began fumbling with her sweater, saying coaxingly, 'Remember last night? We'll just finish what we started.'

She seized his hand in both of hers and dug her nails into it. He released her with a surprised oath and before she knew what he intended cuffed her in the stomach with the back of his hand. She bent double with the surprise and pain of it, gasping for breath.

'Just be a good girl and you won't get hurt,' he said quietly. 'And you'll thank me for it later.'

He pulled the sweater over her head and began dragging

the sleeves from her arms. She clutched the rough material and for a moment there was an unequal tug-of-war. He stumbled backward when the sweater pulled free. Gaining strength from fear and fury she hurled herself against him, shoving and kicking. He fell over a roll of canvas and landed heavily on a shoulder. She ran to the door, flung it open and fled down the passageway without looking back. She did not stop running until she reached a companionway to the top deck, where she waited long enough to catch her breath and compose herself before emerging, relieved to find only an indifferent deckhand in view.

She reached her cabin without being seen by anyone she knew, and huddled on her bunk without moving. Her fear subsided but not her anger. How dare he? He was not going to get away with mauling her like that. But who could she tell? Certainly not Captain Penrose, the only person who could be expected to give him the punishment he deserved. Millis was big, and strong enough to hold his own with Barrett. The absurdity of the notion made her wince. She really must be overwrought.

What had happened to her was too humiliating to tell anyone. And was she entirely blameless? Could she honestly say she had not given Barrett reason to expect an easy conquest when just last night in this very bunk . . .? Reluctantly she admitted to herself she could not. Last night she had allowed Barrett to expect something and today he had tried to take it. They were quits. But if he ever again so much as tried to touch her . . .

A knock on the door startled her.

'Who . . . who is it?' she called.

The only sound was swiftly retreating footsteps. She opened her door cautiously. Her sweater lay crumpled on the deck just outside. Barrett had had second thoughts too, she realized. She was relieved and, strangely, triumphant.

When she undressed to shower she found a bruise on her stomach where Barrett had struck her. She hoped he had some bruises of his own to show for their encounter. Now she would scrub herself clean of his touch and go to her boys. They were having a show in their dormitory and she owed it to Captain Penrose to see they behaved themselves.

By midday on Wednesday the *Amindra* had come a bit more than 800 miles. If she continued at her normal fourteen knots, some time on Thursday night she would reach the point in mid-Atlantic where the *Adler* had been ordered to intercept her. The *Adler*, having had an earlier start and with a two-knot edge in speed, had logged more than 1,100 miles, and was between Casablanca and Charleston, South Carolina, but still had more than two full days' steaming at a steady sixteen knots if she was to cut off the *Amindra*.

Captain Freiburg was in the chart room with Lieutenant Sperling studying the coloured pins Sperling had pressed into the converging routes of the two vessels. A black pin for the *Adler*, advanced every change of watch; a white one for the *Amindra*'s last reported position; a yellow one at the point where she would be now if she had continued to steam unhampered, and a red one where she must be if there were any hope of catching her before she came under the protective umbrella of routine air patrols out of Newfoundland.

Where was she now, Freiburg wondered, though his expression betrayed no uncertainty. Yellow or red? Had their man aboard done his work yet, and if he had not would he bring it off in time? Norddeich had full confidence in the agent, but the British were no fools and surely had an agent of their own aboard. He would have the answer within the next sixty hours, sooner if he received another position report.

166

The boys sat on the top bunks, buddy with buddy. Barlow being a participant rather than a spectator, Oaks sat with the boy who was usually odd man out, there being thirty-seven of them. Captain Penrose, Lady Anne and Donahue had chairs, the seats of honour closest to the little area between the tables and benches where Millis was scheduled to perform. A crew, fewer than fifty of them because Penrose had decided that not more than half the ship's complement could attend, occupied the benches, with the officers at the front. Rosten and Dr Grimes sat with the officers.

Rosten was in no mood to be entertained. He itched to be down in the cargo hold where so much remained to be done. But Penrose had insisted he be there, 'for the sake of appearances'.

Nutley, whose watch it should have been, was there to help Shirley with the boys. Second Officer Briscoe was taking his watch. Penrose had not wanted both himself and Briscoe away from the bridge at the same time when the ship was in such dangerous waters.

Shirley made work for herself by going from boy to boy, quieting the noisy ones, commending the well-behaved, calling each by name. Being occupied helped blot out the memory of what had happened in the stores locker. She had seen Barrett come into the dormitory among the first arrivals, filling her with rage and shame.

'Afternoon, ma'am,' he said, as if nothing had happened between them. If he expected her to forget how he had behaved he was in for a large surprise the next time he tried anything.

The seamen began stamping their feet and the boys whistled. Millis, behind the curtain of his cubicle putting make-up on Barlow from a small supply he'd brought with him, stopped to thrust his head out. He looked around owlishly and said, 'Could have sworn I heard something out here. Must be the mice.'

The boys cheered loudly.

He finished making-up Barlow, who was trembling with stage fright, and patted his head.

'Chin up, lad. You're going to be a star. I can see you ten years from now with the world at your feet and I'll bet you'll have forgotten who taught you.'

'No, I won't, Mr Millis, honest,' Barlow said earnestly.

'All right, then. Now you just stay here calm and quiet while I warm up the audience a bit. Remember, come out when I say, "You, there, eating the toffee apple . . ." '

'Oh, excuse me, sir, it's your nose,' Barlow said, completing the sentence for Millis.

'You're a quick learner, right enough,' Millis said. 'Got your lemon?'

Barlow held it up, smiling tentatively.

'Good lad. Let's get on with it, then, eh?'

Millis flailed the curtain as if unable to find the opening and his audience was already laughing when he darted out, tripped and fell flat on his face. He reached back, got a handful of his trousers seat and appeared to pull himself up bodily until he was poised on toes and palm.

He must be even stronger than he looks, Shirley thought. What Millis had just done required powerful arms and stomach muscles.

Instead of acknowledging the applause and laughter, Millis crawled around on hands and knees as if looking for something, found it and pretended to be studying it as he got to his feet.

'A bloody needle,' he complained. 'Criminal what they leave lying about for a body to trip over, ain't it?'

He eyed his audience as if seeing them for the first time, his bewilderment turning to a slow, ecstatic smile which changed to a look of apprehension as he pretended to be dodging missiles.

'If you must throw money let it be notes,' he said. 'Coins can do a man a real mischief, they can.'

He sidled over to Captain Penrose and leaned down until his face was only a few inches from the captain's.

'Enjoying ourselves, are we, sailor?'

Penrose forced a smile, while behind him the crewmen and boys laughed and nudged each other.

Millis turned to Donahue and Lady Anne.

'Nice little lad you've got 'ere,' he said, inclining his head towards Penrose. 'Not too, bright looking, mind. Wouldn't let 'im roam around the ship too much. Captain wouldn't like it. A proper stickler, he is . . .'

He winked at Lady Anne, who smiled and whispered something to Penrose, who was sitting rigidly upright in his chair. Donahue, choking with laughter, took out his wallet, selected a note and slipped it in Millis's shirt.

'Generous lot, you Yanks,' Millis said. He took out the note and examined it. 'Here, what's this? Two vests, three drawers, one shirt and mind the starch.'

He stared out at his delighted audience, thinking, it's easy to please them when there's nothing better for thousands of miles around.

He shaded his eyes and squinted at Dr Grimes.

'You, there, eating the toffee apple. Oh, excuse me. It's your nose, is it?'

He turned towards his cubicle. Nothing happened.

'It's your nose, is it?' he said, louder.

Barlow emerged at last holding the lemon to his ear, his face half-turned from the audience.

'I say, do you know you've a lemon in your ear?' Millis demanded.

Barlow got his line right and, gaining confidence from the laughter, did his others with more assurance. The volume of applause startled him. Millis surreptitiously thrust Donahue's banknote into his pocket and sent him to join the other boys.

Millis was well into one of his standard routines when a seaman hurried into the dormitory and, bending low to avoid blocking the audience's view, went quickly to Captain Penrose and whispered in his ear. Penrose turned to Lady Anne, murmured something and left.

'Down the hall, first door to your left,' Millis called after him. 'And don't forget to leave tuppence in the dish for the attendant, mind you. He's got a wife and kids to support, hasn't he? Now where was I before I was so rudely interrupted?'

He continued with the routine and had his listeners clutching their sides when the clamour of klaxons and whistles stilled the laughter. The benches emptied quickly as crewmen ran to emergency stations.

'This is Captain Penrose,' the bulkhead loudspeaker said. 'There is no immediate cause for concern but all passengers will return to their quarters at once, and stay there until further notice. Repeat. There is no immediate cause for concern but all passengers will return to their quarters until further notice.'

Shirley decided to disobey and remain with her boys. If the *Amindra* were in any danger her place was with them. Nor did she want to be alone.

'There's nothing to be afraid of, children,' she said. 'We all heard Captain Penrose. Mr Millis, why don't you do the lemon aid thing again?'

Millis called Barlow to him and repeated the lemon aid routine. Barlow, who had had time to look at the note

Millis gave him, said, 'Did you know it was five pounds?'

'Only five? It was worth a tenner.'

'I never had five pounds before. The most was ten bob. My dad gave it to me for Christmas.'

'Been drinking, had he?' Millis said.

'How'd you know?' Barlow said incredulously.

'Mums know everything, and don't you forget it.'

Barlow wondered if he knew about the ventilator and the passenger messing about in the hold. Even if Mr Millis knew he'd been in the ventilator he wouldn't tell Miss Hunt. He wouldn't sneak on a friend. Mr Millis was his friend, the best friend he had ever had. He wished Mr Millis was in charge of things instead of that bloody Yank lady. She'd gone off that Mr Barrett she'd liked. Wouldn't even look at him all during the performance.

Captain Penrose scanned the horizon through his binoculars. There was nothing to see but endless billows. The Asdic echo report that had brought him from the boys' dormitory to the bridge had been picked up first at more than 22,000 yards off the starboard bow – so it could not have been the U-boat he'd driven off the day before – and closed to under 18,000 before a sharp change of course to port by the *Amindra* started it fading again. The echo had grown faint too abruptly for the *Amindra* to have put that much distance between her and its source even if they had been on opposite headings, and he could only assume that if it actually was a sub it had surfaced or shut down its engines. In any case there was no sign of anything now, either from the Asdic or the lookout. If it had been a U-boat they had lost it. But just to be on the safe side he would keep the crew at emergency stations and the *Amindra* on its altered course for another hour.

Captain Freiburg was napping in his quarters when a rating from the wireless room rapped on his door and gave

171

him a signal that had just been received and decoded. He looked at it, frowning, and went to the chart room. Sperling was not there; there was no reason for him to be at this time, so Freiburg took a pair of dividers and stepped off the co-ordinates of the new position himself. It fell a trifle beyond the yellow pin representing the *Amindra*. His quarry was still proceeding steadily towards its destination. SKL's boasted agent was certainly taking his own time doing his job. Or had he been detected and neutralized? Freiburg did not like even to consider such a possibility.

Shirley did not go to dinner in the saloon. She had no appetite for food or table talk. During the performance Millis's antics had put the ugly encounter with Barrett quite out of her mind – Joe Millis could be terribly funny at times and even the awful things he said to Captain Penrose were intended in fun – but now the humiliating incident was vivid in her mind again. The reek of the locker, Barrett's insulting assurance, his brutal mouth stopping her breath, her momentary but utter helplessness. She would never again let anyone make her feel that helpless.

Dutton came to inquire about her for Captain Penrose and she made an excuse about not feeling well. Minutes later Dr Grimes was knocking at her door.

'Thank you for coming, but it's only a headache,' she said, not inviting him inside.

'Captain Penrose said I should have a look at you,' the doctor said. 'I though you looked a bit peeky at the entertainment. Millis puts on an amusing show, doesn't he?'

She was obliged to admit him and submit to a superficial examination. She stiffened at his touch. She did not want any man touching her, not so soon after Barrett.

He seemed not to notice.

'A bit pale,' he said. 'But otherwise . . . Do you often have headaches?'

172

'No,' she said. 'It's nothing, really.'

And it wasn't. She was making too much of it. She wished she had gone to dinner instead of going through this charade.

He left her two aspirin and told her to get a good night's sleep. She wished they were sleeping pills. Instead of reliving the frightening, demeaning encounter with Barrett she'd have got a good night's sleep and tomorrow it would be as if it had never happened.

Lady Anne tapped lightly on the bulkhead separating her stateroom from Shirley's when she returned from dinner.

'Miss Hunt. Shirley. Are you all right?'

'Yes, thank you. Dr Grimes gave me a couple of aspirin.'

'Don't worry, dear. You'll be as good as new in the morning.'

And I will, Shirley thought. Also wiser.

Barlow waited impatiently for the others to fall asleep. He had been thinking about the ventilator since dinner, when he was not thinking about the five-pound note under his pillow. He was rich. As soon as he thought it was safe he wrapped himself in his blanket and climbed up to the ventilator. His own private world lay behind the grille, his own secret place that only he knew about, that he didn't have to share with anyone.

He was removing the grille when fingers grasped his ankle and a voice whispered. 'What do you think you're doing?'

It was Oaks.

'Nothing,' Barlow said.

It would be Oaks. Oaks ruined everything. He would have ruined the performance if he could have. He hadn't laughed or applauded the lemon aid bit and the looks he'd given the boys nearest him stopped them, too.

'Come down then and get back to bed,' Oaks ordered.

Barlow stopped on the verge of complying. Oaks wasn't going to order him about, even if it meant revealing he was exploring the ventilator duct. What did he care if Oaks knew, anyhow? Oaks wouldn't tell because then everyone would know Barlow the Witty was brave enough to go crawling about in the dark where no one else would dare. Barlow the Brave, not Barlow the Witty.

He finished taking out the grille, put it on the top bunk and reached for the ventilator lip. He looked challengingly under his arm at Oaks.

'*You* go back to bed,' he said. 'I'm going exploring.'

'Think I believe that?' Oaks demanded, his smile sceptical.

Barlow scrambled into the ventilator.

'It's no good, Barlow the Witty,' Oaks said. 'You'll just stay in there until I've gone to bed, and then expect me to believe you went on.'

Barlow got himself turned around so he could look down at Oaks, who was staring at him scornfully in the dim, reddish light.

'Come along, then,' he said.

'And ruin my clothes?'

'It's not your clothes you're worried about,' Barlow taunted. 'It's your guts.'

Secrecy was no longer as important to him as shaming Oaks.

'Not so loud,' Oaks said. 'You'll wake Millis.'

'So what? Him and me're friends. Gave me five pounds for helping him, didn't he? Oaks the Windy. I'd rather be Witty than Windy.'

'You're looking for a bloody lip!'

'Why don't you have mum tuck you in while I go exploring, Oaks the Windy?'

'I'll do anything you will, you little sod.'

'Follow me, then.'

Barlow squirmed around and began crawling along the duct. He heard Oaks squeezing himself into the ventilator behind him. Barlow smiled in the darkness. It would be much harder for Oaks the Windy than for Barlow the Brave in the duct. Oaks was bigger. In the duct it was better to be small. Ruin his clothes, indeed. The bastard was in for a lot worse than that.

Barlow crawled as fast as he could, not minding the metal scraping at his hands and knees.

'Wait for me!' Oaks ordered, trying to overlay his fear with bluster.

Barlow forgot about tormenting Oaks for a moment. He was in his own world now, a world that was a tube stretching in smooth, endless loops through the darkest bowels of the ship, a world known only to Barlow the Brave. The swearing, panting outsider scrambling behind him could follow or not. It didn't matter a farthing to the world of the tube or to Barlow the Brave.

He came to the turning and paused for a moment. He could hear Oaks blundering after him. He wanted to laugh aloud but he did not. He kept perfectly still and silent, holding his breath.

'Barlow!' Oaks cried. 'Where are you? Don't leave me!'

'Go back, then,' Barlow called.

'I can't turn around. It's too tight.'

'It divides back here, Oaks the Windy. One up, one down. Guess which one I'm taking?'

'No! Don't! Wait for me.'

'Say, "Please, Barlow the Brave." '

'Get stuffed.'

'Goodbye, Oaks.'

He made sounds as if he were going on but remained in place. He could hear Oaks scraping along frantically back in the duct.

'Please, Barlow the Brave.'

It was almost a whisper.

'I can't hear you. I've a lemon in my ear.'

Louder. 'Please, Barlow the Brave.'

'That's better. I'm taking the down tube.'

'Wait for me.'

'Say, "Wait for Oaks the Windy, Barlow the Brave." '

'Wait for Oaks the Windy, Barlow the Brave.'

Barlow waited until Oaks touched his leg before crawling on down the duct. He wanted to see if Mr Rosten – he'd found out the passenger's name at the performance – was working again. Oaks kept wanting to go back but Barlow had him hopelessly lost now, and even if he managed to get turned around he would never find his way. Barlow stopped talking to him even to taunt him but tormented the older boy by crawling faster from time to time so that he had to labour to maintain contact.

Oaks was gasping for breath when Barlow reached the grille overlooking the hold.

'There's a light!' Oaks cried, relieved. 'Can we get out there?'

'Sssh,' said Barlow. 'Someone's there. Oh, it's Captain Penrose. He wouldn't half be angry if he found us here.'

It was not Penrose, though, it was Mr Rosten. Barlow thought it would frighten Oaks more if it were the captain. All the boys were frightened of him. All the boys except Barlow the Brave. He was not frightened of anyone or anything.

Rosten was working away as he had last night, carrying the yellow bricks, knocking nails into crates.

'Where are we?' Oaks whispered.

'In the hold.'

'May I have a look? Please?'

Barlow felt generous. He made himself as small as

176

possible and Oaks squeezed to the grille beside him. Like sausages in a tin, Barlow thought. Oaks had gone all sweaty.

'That isn't Captain Penrose,' he said.

'Of course it is,' Barlow said. 'Can't you see proper?'

'It's the Jew.'

'Captain Penrose wouldn't like you calling him a Jew. Do you want to find your own way back?'

'No.'

'Who is it, then?'

'Captain Penrose,' Oaks muttered.

They watched until Rosten turned off the lights and left.

'Can we go back now?' Oaks said.

'Do what you like. I'm going in.'

The top row of crates was only five or six feet below the vent. No distance at all for Barlow the Brave.

'Please,' Oaks begged.

Ignoring him, Barlow pushed at the grille until it came loose and fell to the crates with a ringing sound that echoed in the hold.

'What was that?' Oaks cried.

'Dropped my false teeth,' Barlow said.

It was the sort of thing Mr Millis would say, he thought. Perhaps Mr Millis was right. He did have a clever way with words. Barlow the Brave was best, but Barlow the Witty had a ring to it, too, said the right way.

He made Oaks back up enough to give him room to turn around, then inched his way backwards until he was hanging from the ventilator opening. His toes encountered only empty darkness. He was frightened for just a moment, dangling over nothingness, but he reminded himself there was solid wood not far below him and he was Barlow the Brave. He took a breath and let go. The drop was only a few inches.

He got to his hands and knees and crawled, feeling

ahead cautiously. To the left, crates had been stacked unevenly, like giant stairs. If he was very careful he could climb down to the bottom where Mr Rosten had been working.

'Barlow,' Oaks called. 'Peter. Where are you?'

'Down here. Coming?'

'It's dark.'

'Afraid of the dark? Only babies are afraid of the dark.'

He felt his way to the end of a tier of crates and let himself down to the one below. Then another and another. This should be the last. He tried to remember how far above the floor it rose. Was it one or two tiers? If two, it was a long drop. He could break his leg. But he didn't care. He wasn't like Oaks the Windy up there wetting his pants. Hanging by his fingers, he let go and dropped into the darkness. Before he could be truly frightened his feet plunged into the soggy softness of the waste he had seen in the aisles among the tiers.

'Are you all right?' Oaks called anxiously.

Barlow knew Oaks was frightened for himself, not for Barlow the Brave. Instead of answering he stood for a while with one hand against the reassuring rough wood of a crate, orienting himself. The light switch he'd seen Mr Rosten at was straight along the aisle, then a bit to the left on the wall about the same height as his head.

'Barlow,' Oaks called again, as Barlow felt his way along the crates, the waste squelching like wet leaves under his feet.

At the end of the tier he groped towards the bulkhead with hands outstretched. His foot kicked something that rolled across a bare place with a metallic sound and struck the bulkhead. Guided by the sound, he moved more confidently until he touched smooth wood. He felt along it to the metal box where the switch should be, found the lever and pulled it down. The hold became a dimly lit cavern. Oaks was looking down at him from the ventilator, his eyes round as pennies with fear and wonder.

Barlow looked along the deck for whatever it was he had kicked. There it was, a few inches from the wall, round and dully gleaming. He picked it up. A coin, but unlike any he'd ever seen before. Bigger, heavier, and foreign. Perhaps Mr Rosten had dropped it. He put it in his pocket. Finders keepers.

'Are you going to stay up there and gawk, then?' he demanded, looking up at Oaks.

'Is there a door?'

'Why don't you have a look for yourself?'

'I can't get down.'

'What a pity.'

He watched while Oaks tried to turn his overgrown body around in the narrow duct. Oaks got stuck, with his feet thrust out of the ventilator and his buttocks pressed against his heels.

'Help me, Barlow,' he begged. 'Please.'

He would have to, Barlow thought, if he was going to get back to the dormitory the way he had come. The top of the lowest tier was out of reach. He dragged over some of the boards Mr Rosten had stacked so neatly and made a pile tall enough for him to reach the first tier. He had to jump as high as he could at the last tier and clutch the edge to pull himself up. He still could not reach Oaks. The vent was set too high.

'Push, Oaks,' he said. 'Get your back into it.'

Oaks worked himself free at last and dropped heavily to the crate. They went down together, Barlow nimbly leading the way. He showed Oaks the bricks with the air of a proprietor.

'This is gold!' Oaks exclaimed, hefting one.

'What would gold be doing down here?' Barlow demanded, angered that Oaks should presume to know

179

something he did not.

'See the markings. And the weight. Only lead would be this heavy and lead's not yellow.'

'I know what colour lead is. And gold, too. I know it's gold. I wanted to see if you did.'

He took out the coin he'd found and said, 'Here's something else gold.'

He showed Oaks both sides of the coin without letting the older boy take it into his own hand.

'It's a napoleon,' Oaks said. 'My father has one in his collection. They're worth tons.'

'Don't put on airs with me, Oaks the Windy.'

Now that he was out of the tunnel Oaks had regained much of his courage and it showed in his changed attitude towards Barlow.

'Where'd you find it?' he demanded.

'In that lot,' Barlow said, jerking a thumb at the litter on the floor.

'Perhaps there's more.'

'If there is, they're mine.'

Oaks began prowling around the hold. He saw the door. He did not need Barlow now.

'Get stuffed, Barlow.'

'Watch how you talk or I'll leave you down here, Oaks the Windy.'

'Call me that once more and I'll bloody your nose, you little bastard. And I'll have that napoleon.'

'I won't show you the way!'

Oaks advanced on Barlow threateningly, holding out his hand. Barlow backed away from him until his back was against a crate. He clutched one fist around the gold piece in his pocket and lifted the other. When Oaks kept coming he lashed out and hit him on the cheek. Oaks hit him in the chest, bending him over, gasping. He jerked the fist with the coin in it out of Barlow's pocket, tearing his trousers, and pulled at his fingers. The pain was excruciating but Barlow would not give him the pleasure of crying out. The coin in his own hand now, Oaks sent him sprawling with a shove and ran to the door. It would not budge. It was locked on the outside.

Oaks looked back at Barlow, who was on his feet now rubbing his chest and smiling ominously. Silently, Barlow held his hand out, palm up. Oaks came back and put the napoleon in it.

'What do you mean to do?' Oaks asked meekly. 'You'll show me the way back, won't you?'

'If you apologize nice. "Oaks the Windy is a stupid sod and evermore will be Barlow the Brave's slave. Even after we're back." '

'Right,' Oaks said quickly. Too quickly. 'Oaks the Windy is a stupid sod and will be Barlow the Brave's slave.'

'Come on, then.'

They climbed back to the ventilator. Barlow was too short to reach it, even jumping as high as he could.

'Let me,' said Oaks. 'I'll pull you up.'

'No.'

He made Oaks form a stirrup with his hands and lift him high enough to reach the ventilator. He pulled himself in and turned around. He looked down into Oaks's bulging-eyed, upturned face and reaching hands. They were a foot short of the lip.

'Come on, Barlow,' he said. 'Give us a hand.'

'You've two of your own,' Barlow said, laughing. 'What do you want with one of mine?'

He *was* witty, he thought. Mr Millis would be proud.

'Help me up. Please.'

'A lad like you should be able to manage. I mean, if you're strong enough to bend a chap's fingers and take his money I wouldn't think you'd need any help.'

Oaks jumped and hooked his fingers over the edge of the ventilator. Barlow pushed them away. Oaks dropped heavily, lost his balance when he hit and sprawled on his back.

'Goodbye, Oaks the Windy,' Barlow said. 'Find your own way back. If you can.'

Just as he started to turn around, the *Amindra* reared and tilted, sending Oaks sliding backwards across the stacked crates and forcing Barlow to clutch desperately at the sides of the ventilator with both hands to keep from being ejected. As he watched in horror, Oaks disappeared over the edge with a cry. Oaks cried out again when he struck the deck below with a soggy thump and a moment later the *Amindra* heeled the other way and a crate slid across the other side of the aisle and fell betwen the tiers. One more dreadful cry and a bloodcurdling sound of expelled breath, like a bellows quickly pumped, and then there was silence except for the creaking of the ship. Barlow clung to the ventilator as his world, all dim yellow and dark shadows, seemed to turn slowly in a lazy circle until he no longer knew if he were looking up or down. The ship righted itself. Now he could see the crate blocking the aisle where Oaks had fallen. In his mind's eye he saw Oaks crushed under it like a bug, oozing blood, guts and brains. He vomited, and plunged into paralysing darkness.

Chapter Eleven

The steering-gear compartment of the *Amindra* was separated from the massive rudder beneath it by the aft peak tank and a storeroom in which a man could not easily stand erect. Above it were the crew's quarters and lavatories. The only access was through a door that was always kept locked. The heavy rudder responded to the wheel on the bridge by means of a servo motor controlling two hydraulically powered pistons operating the steering rams. Should this hydraulically operated steering system fail, the rudder could be operated manually, though with great difficulty, by a mechanism the circumference of a bicycle wheel that meshed with a series of gears.

The Number 6 'tween-deck, below the greasers' mess and carpenter shop, gave access to the compartment. Shortly after one o'clock on Thursday morning a husky man felt his way stealthily along the Number 6 'tween-deck bulkhead without benefit of the overhead lights or even a hand torch. When he reached the door to the steering-gear compartment he put the heavy maul he was carrying on the deck between his feet, took a ring of keys from his pocket and felt for the lock. He tried several keys before the bolt slid back. He put the key ring back in his coat, picked up the maul and entered the compartment, shutting the door behind him. He found the light switch and turned on the bulb, which was protected by a wire basket in the overhead.

It was almost three hours before Third Officer Nutley went on watch but he was already up and dressed, trying to read Agatha Christie's *Peril at End House*. Dr Grimes had lent it to him with the highest recommendation, but he had a hard time keeping his mind on it. He did not understand the sort of people Miss Christie wrote about and did not much care for them. His mind kept straying to the harsh lecture Captain Penrose had given him about missing the meeting and to how much he had liked teaching the boys knots and ship lore. The hour or so he spent with them was the first time he had felt really comfortable aboard the *Amindra*. To them he was a proper ship's officer, not the youngest one aboard, and none of them had made bad jokes about his inexperience or sent him off on fool's errands. He wished there were some way he could show the boys how much he appreciated being accepted by them.

Perhaps there was a way. He'd overheard two seamen talking about some cases of tinned pineapple and condensed milk they'd managed to make off with on the wharf at Greenock. They'd hidden the cases among the stores below the crew accommodation. Boys fancied tinned pineapples topped with condensed milk. He had when he was a boy. He still did, for that matter. It would be a simple piece of work to nip down there and bring away a dozen tins of each. The seamen would never miss them and if they did they wouldn't dare say anything about it.

He put away the book without regret and got his pea-jacket and his seabag. The bag would do nicely to hold the tins.

Down in the steering-gear compartment the intruder had taken off his coat and was unwrapping the tools he had hung inside it. The wrappings were to keep them from clanking together when he came below and passed through the 'tween-deck. It didn't matter how much noise he made now, with the screw churning away below. With a heavy wrench he undid the bolt fixing one of the reduction gears in the manual steering apparatus and pulled the gear free.

Letting it fall, he jumped clear so it would not hit his feet. He picked up the maul and began pounding a cylinder head. The hydraulic seal ruptured and beet-red fluid leaked out and ran down the smooth metal of the cylinder to form a growing pool beneath it.

Below, Nutley stopped moving stores around in his search for the stolen tins when he heard the banging just above his head. He jerked erect and hit his skull on the low overhead. He was aware the sounds came from the steering-gear compartment. Something must have come loose up there and the gear was knocking itself to bits. He hurried up the ladder to the steering-gear compartment door and tried the handle. To his relief, the door swung open. A broad-shouldered man was battering one of the cylinders with a maul and hydraulic fluid was streaming out of the other.

'What the hell are you doing?' he cried.

They were the last words he ever spoke. In a single motion the man whirled and swung the maul against his head. Nutley fell to the deck without a sound. The man looked down at him briefly and returned to his attack on the cylinder. It was soon ruptured.

He pulled the pea-jacket from Nutley's inert form and worried a sleeve between the almost meshing cogs of two gears in the manual steering apparatus until it was caught fast. He pulled at the jacket until the material tore a bit, as if someone had tried to pull it free and failed. He slid the gear he had removed out the door with his foot and took it down to the storeroom, where he concealed it behind a stack of boxes. He raced back up the ladder, stowed his tools in his coat and put it on. With the maul in one hand he turned off the light with the other, holding the door open with his foot. He reached down, groped for Nutley's collar, wound his hand in it and dragged the body out.

He relocked the door with his key and, stooping, heaved

185

up Nutley's body and slung it over his shoulder. Walking rapidly despite his burden, he passed through the 'tween-deck and went up the companionway to deck level. He put the body down, opened the door and went out to have a look around. Satisfied there was no one to observe him, he went back for Nutley and dropped him over the rail. He did not watch the body fall. He threw the maul and his tools overboard and disappeared into the darkness.

At 2.10 A.M. the wind picked up and began to veer. The helmsman eased the wheel around to maintain the heading but the compass needle in the binnacle continued to drift as the wind moved the *Amindra* off course. He spun the wheel to correct for the drift, but to no effect.

'Watch your heading,' Second Officer Briscoe warned.

'No response, sir! I've lost steering control!'

Briscoe spun the wheel himself. The *Amindra* continued its leisurely drift off course. He blew in the windpipe to wake Captain Penrose and picked up the telephone.

'Bridge, sir,' he said. 'We've lost steering control.'

'What happened?' Penrose asked.

'Don't know yet, sir.'

'Go to manual. I'll be up at once.'

Penrose arrived unshaven and without a necktie, a telling indication of his concern.

'Still not responding, sir,' the helmsman said with a nervous, apologetic look.

'Where's Mr Briscoe?' the captain demanded.

'Gone aft, sir.'

Penrose looked at the phosphorescent glow of the compass. The *Amindra* was ten degrees off course and drifting badly.

Briscoe had rushed to the crew's quarters and woken two men to accompany him to the steering-gear compartment. It took two to operate the manual override. He unlocked the compartment door and sensed a major

186

breakdown even before he found the light switch. The air was pungent with the odour of leaking hydraulic fluid. The light went on to reveal the battered cylinders and puddled floor.

'Bloody hell!' murmured one of the seamen crowding into the compartment behind Briscoe.

'The hydraulic steering's done for,' Briscoe muttered grimly. 'Get on that override!'

It was only then, so hypnotized had they been by the smashed cylinder heads, that they saw a gear was missing from the manual override mechanism and a pea-jacket was caught between two gears. They watched helplessly as the turning of the helm on the bridge signalled corrections they could not make.

'What's this?' Briscoe asked, jerking at the pea-jacket until it came free, ripping the sleeve and pulling out a seam at the shoulder.

He went through the pockets quickly, finding only a soiled handkerchief and a packet of Maltesers. He opened the coat. There was a name tag sewn into the collar.

Arthur G. Nutley.

'Whose is it?' one of the seamen asked.

'Someone smashed this lot on purpose,' said the other.

'Never you mind,' snapped Briscoe. 'Look for that bloody missing gear. And not a word to anyone until we get this mess sorted out. Understood?'

'Aye, aye, sir,' the men answered in unison.

Briscoe hurried out with the pea-jacket under his arm, ran along the passageway and scrambled up ladders to reach the bridge. He was gasping. He was sixty-three years old and not accustomed to such exertions.

'Well, Number Two,' Penrose asked. 'Why aren't we on manual override?'

'It's done for, sir,' Briscoe replied between gasps. 'The whole bloody lot's been sabotaged!'

Penrose clamped his jaws tight and drew Briscoe to the side of the bridge, as far from the helmsman as he could get.

'What,' he asked in a low, controlled voice, 'is all this about sabotage?'

Briscoe thrust the pea-jacket at the other man.

'Nutley's, sir,' he said. 'It was caught in the manual override. The hydraulics are all smashed. Looks like he did it.'

Penrose crossed quickly to the binnacle. They were off course another couple of degrees.

'Engines stop,' he told the helmsman calmly.

The helmsman yanked the bridge telegraph as Penrose picked up the phone.

'Bridge here,' he said. 'I want all engines stopped.'

Less than a minute later the sound of the huge diesels, muffled by distance, ceased, as did the steady vibration of the vessel, so minor and constant as to become unnoticed until it was no longer there. The ship creaked and sighed and the slap of the tossing sea against the steel hull suddenly seemed louder.

The *Amindra*'s forward motion gradually slowed until it stopped completely. The ship lay dead in the water.

'I left two men in the steering-gear compartment, sir,' Briscoe said, 'with orders to keep their mouths shut.'

Penrose nodded. 'Get Perkins back there quick as you can. And tell Mr Barrett I want him on the bridge.'

'Aye, aye, sir.'

'Then get some men and find Nutley.'

Penrose waited until Briscoe had left the bridge before returning to his quarters to shave and dress himself properly. It promised to be a long night and, in such U-boat-infested seas, an even longer day. The situation was grave but he knew he must not reveal his concern to either the passengers or crew. Why had Nutley done such a thing? Possible reasons gnawed at Penrose as he made his way aft to the steering-gear compartment. Could Nutley have been working for the Germans? It seemed so improbable he dismissed the idea. Nutley was far too young and callow to be an Intelligence agent for either side. Could it be so simple a thing as retaliation for the dressing-down he had given the Third Officer?

The situation in the steering-gear compartment was as bad as Briscoe had described it. The two seamen saw him enter and stiffened to attention. Penrose kept his face expressionless as he surveyed the damage. As for the ruptured seals and gaskets, there would be spares. But the cylinders themselves were damaged and that called for major repairs. It must be done as quickly as possible. The longer the *Amindra* lay dead in the water the greater the possibility of her becoming a target for prowling U-boats.

He had improved the odds in his favour by stopping the engines. With them running, the sound of the *Amindra*'s screws could be picked up at a considerable distance by a U-boat's listening gear. With them off, only a visual sighting would detect her.

The sound of voices and movement floated through the overhead. Men were awake and milling about in the crew accommodation. That, Penrose knew, was not necessarily an indication that news of the *Amindra*'s plight had spread through the ship. The stopping of the engines was enough in itself to bring experienced seamen awake.

Perkins came in with another seaman and looked glumly at the broken steering gear.

'Rum,' he said, scratching his chin. 'Bloody rum.'

'How long will repairs take?' Penrose asked.

Perkins took off his knitted cap and ran the palm of his hand over his thick dark hair.

'Hard to say, sir.'

'Can you have it finished before first light?'

'The way that lot is?' Perkins shook his head. 'Not a chance. See this?' His stubby fingers moved from cylinder head to cylinder head and traced the fracture along a casing. 'Needs new seals, gaskets and a fair number of other bits and pieces. Don't know if a weld will hold.'

'How long?' Penrose repeated, his face still expressionless.

'Four, maybe five hours if we're lucky,' Perkins replied.

'Very well,' the captain said. 'Let me know when it's finished.'

He left. There was nothing to be gained by staying. Perkins knew his job and the quicker he got on with it the better. The captain returned to his cabin expecting to confront Nutley, but the young Third Officer was not there. He called the bridge and spoke with Barrett.

'What's happening, sir?' the First Officer asked. 'When will we have engines?'

'It's not the engines, Number One,' Penrose replied. 'It's the steering gear. And it looks like sabotage.'

There was a moment of stunned silence.

'Are you sure, sir?' Barrett asked finally.

'Cylinders on both rams smashed.'

'Why aren't we on manual, then?'

No 'sir', Penrose noted. He decided to ignore the other man's question.

'Finish Briscoe's watch. And take the late watch.'

'Nutley's too, sir? Would you mind telling me why?'

'I would.'

Penrose was on the point of sending Dutton to see what was keeping Briscoe and Nutley when the Second Officer knocked on the door.

'No sign of him yet,' Briscoe said. 'I've got both off watches combing the ship. Couldn't get into Number 2 hold. Mr Donahue's bloody car's got the hatch blocked and the passageway door's locked. None of my keys fit.

190

Shall I break it in, sir?'

'Would you mind telling me how Nutley could have got into Number 2 hold and left the door padlocked behind him?'

'Right, sir,' Briscoe said sheepishly.

Penrose decided some explanation was required.

'We had some damage down there Monday night,' he said. 'A few burst crates. With all those boys running wild . . . well, I didn't want them playing around the cargo. It could shift again in these seas.'

'Right, sir.' The Second Officer sounded satisfied with the explanation.

'Keep after Nutley,' Penrose said. 'I want him rooted out before the passengers are up. And they're to know nothing. Understood?'

'Sir.'

Briscoe stiffened to attention and left the cabin. Penrose partially undressed and went back to bed. There was nothing he could do now and a couple of hours' sleep before dawn would stand him in good stead. It seemed he had barely closed his eyes when the first light of day invaded his cabin. Still tired, he dressed and went below to the steering-gear compartment.

The hydraulic fluid had been mopped up and the dismantled hydraulic steering apparatus lay in neat rows on the deck, but the gear to the manual override was still missing. Only one seaman was present.

'Where are the others?' Penrose demanded.

'The machinist's gone to fetch the welding stuff, sir.'

Penrose nodded.

'Been 'ere since mid watch, I 'ave sir,' the seaman added tentatively.

'You'll be relieved.'

Briscoe should have taken care of that but there was no point in taking him to task about it. The Second Officer had had enough on his plate the past few hours and had handled it well for a man his age. It was past time for Briscoe, too, to be relieved. Still looking for Nutley, he supposed. Where could that young maniac be hiding?

Penrose went up to the bridge and found Barrett and the late watch helmsman lounging with their hands in their pockets. The helmsman removed his immediately and snapped to attention but Barrett made no effort to move from the bulkhead.

'I want you shaved and back on watch in ten minutes,' Penrose snapped. 'And find Mr Briscoe and tell him he's relieved until his regular watch.'

He waited for Barrett to say something, anything, but the other man only said, 'Aye, aye, sir,' and left the bridge at a pace not much more than a saunter.

Below, Donahue came out on deck obviously bewildered. He hurried to the rail and looked down at the water. Then he turned to the bridge and held his hands out palm up in an interrogatory gesture. Penrose motioned him to stay where he was and went to join him. He would tell the Special Envoy and the other passengers no more than was absolutely necessary to explain the *Amindra*'s loss of way.

In the boys' dormitory, Millis sat on the edge of a bunk yawning and scratching himself. He slipped his stockinged feet into his unlaced shoes – like the boys, he slept with heavy socks on – and left his cubicle. As was his habit, he checked the tiers of bunks. The boys were still sleeping. Oaks's bunk was empty. In the bog, no doubt. Barlow wasn't sleeping, though. He lay on his back, uncovered, legs straight out, arms along his sides and fists clenched, staring up at the overhead with his eyes unnaturally wide. Millis hurried to him. Barlow did not turn his head or move his eyes or indicate in any way he was aware of Millis's presence.

192

'What is it, lad?' Millis asked.

Barlow continued to stare blankly at the overhead. Millis touched his shoulder, then shook it. The boy was cold and rigid as a board. Were it not for the slow rise and fall of his chest as he breathed Millis would have thought the boy dead.

'Barlow,' he said. 'This is no time for games. Want to give your old mum a seizure, is that it?'

Barlow did not respond. Millis felt the boy's forehead. It was cool. More than cool. Cold. He put his ear to Barlow's chest. He could hear the slow, muffled thump of his heart. He covered the lad with both blankets and with two more he took from his own bunk before hurrying out of the dormitory.

On deck he was aware of what he had only sensed earlier. The engines had stopped and the *Amindra* was not moving except with the motion of the sea. As nearly as he could see no one seemed to be doing anything about it. He knocked on Shirley Hunt's door.

'Go away and leave me alone!' she called out fiercely, to his surprise.

'It's me. Millis. Barlow's in a bad way.'

There were sounds of hasty movement and the door was flung open. Shirley, her hair in disarray and her face flushed, stood there wearing a heavy robe and thick socks. She motioned him inside.

'Is he ill?' she demanded. 'Did he have an accident? Don't look while I get dressed.'

'I don't know,' he said, turning his back. 'He's just lying there in a daze, like.'

'I'm sorry I yelled at you,' she said, pulling on skirt and sweater. 'I thought it was – someone else.'

His eyes showed a flicker of comprehension.

'I don't mind being yelled at,' he said. 'It makes me feel right at home.'

193

She knew he meant it as a kindness, not as an automatic joke. Strange, but it was beginning to appear as if he was the only man aboard she could understand and depend on.

'The ship's not moving!' she exclaimed, suddenly aware of the silence. 'Has it anything to do with Barlow?'

He shook his head.

'I'm going down to him. You bring Dr Grimes. You know which cabin?'

'I'll find it.'

She hurried below, thinking, I hope it's nothing serious, it would be Peter Barlow, that poor, forlorn child.

The children were all awake and staring across the dormitory at Barlow. Only his face was showing above the blankets Millis had tucked about his rigid form. His eyes had a glazed look, fixed and frightening. Shirley rushed to him.

'Is he dead?' one of the boys asked curiously.

'Don't say that!' Shirley cried, whirling to face him.

Someone tittered.

'It isn't funny,' she shouted – she must not shout and let them see how upset she was. 'Everyone wash and get dressed.'

'Peter,' she said, kneeling beside him. 'Can you hear me?'

He did not move. Was he paralysed? Where were Millis and Dr Grimes? She should have gone for the doctor herself.

'Oaks,' she called. 'Run up and see if you can find Mr Millis and the doctor.'

'He ain't here,' one of the boys said. 'Oaks.'

'Where is he? Someone go and look in the wash room.'

She turned back to Barlow as two of the older boys went off to find Oaks. Dr Grimes arrived, hustled along by Millis. He needed a shave and was wearing carpet slippers and carrying a black bag. He shone a penlight in Barlow's eyes to no effect, peered into them, pulled back the blankets, unbuttoned Barlow's shirt and listened to his heart with a stethoscope. He pursed his lips.

'What is it, Doctor?' Shirley said. 'What's wrong with him?'

Instead of answering, Dr Grimes took out a large, plain pocket watch, flipped open the cover and took Barlow's pulse.

'You say you found him like this?' he asked Millis.

Millis nodded.

'Do you know if this episode was preceded by convulsions?'

'No, I don't.'

'Doesn't seem like an epileptic seizure,' the doctor mused.

His fingers explored Barlow's skull with an expert, gentle touch.

'No contusions,' he said. 'And he's not concussed.'

'What is it, then?' Shirley asked.

Before the doctor could answer the boys who had gone looking for Oaks returned.

'He's not in the W.C.,' one of them said.

'I'm not sure,' Dr Grimes said.

'But you must have some idea,' Shirley persisted.

'He's obviously had a severe shock of some sort,' the doctor said. 'I want him moved to my cabin so I can keep him under close observation.'

'No,' Shirley said. 'I'll stay with him. Here. I'll send for you if there is any change.'

'As you wish,' Dr Grimes said, shrugging. He put his stethoscope back in the black bag. 'But the responsibility is yours.'

Shirley knew from the way he stalked out she had made him angry but she did not care. She was not going to leave Barlow. And the doctor was right. He was her responsibility. All the boys were.

'Where's Oaks gone off to, I wonder?' Millis said when the doctor had gone. 'Do you suppose he had something to do with this and is hiding somewhere?'

'He wouldn't do anything like that,' Shirley said. 'Oaks teases him a lot but he's really very protective of him.'

'Like a wolf protects the sheep,' Millis said.

'Help me make him more comfortable, will you, please?'

They tried to rearrange Barlow's limbs, but his arms and legs would not bend. There was no flicker in his eyes when they touched him.

'We can at least cover him up and see he's kept warm,' Shirley said.

'Hold on a mo',' Millis said. 'He's got something in his hand.'

He pried Barlow's fist open, being careful not to exert too much force.

'What's this?' he said.

Something shone in Barlow's palm, round as his eyes but larger. A gold napoleon.

Chapter Twelve

'That's a gold coin,' said Shirley after an astonished silence. 'Where would he get a coin like that?'

He would hardly have brought it aboard with him, she thought. It wasn't the sort of thing even a boy with wealthy parents would have, let alone one whose folks couldn't afford the price of their child's fare to America. It was something Oaks's parents might have given him as a parting gift. Where was he, anyhow? He knew they weren't supposed to be wandering around the ship. She would have to find him and bring him back before Captain Penrose learned of it. She would not want him to think she could not control the boys. Had Barlow stolen the coin from one of them? He did not seem like a thief. What could have given him such a shock? Dr Grimes said it did not appear to be anything physical. Maybe he would come out of it naturally. If not, what could she do until the ship got to New York? And when would that be? The ship was still not moving. What was wrong? Why hadn't Captain Penrose made an announcement? But she was more concerned about Barlow than the ship right now. And where was Oaks?

She sent Millis looking for him.

'And don't let Captain Penrose see you,' she said. 'He doesn't want you chasing all over the ship.'

It was a friendly admonition. She did not want Captain Penrose making trouble for Millis any more than she wanted Millis making trouble for the captain.

After he left, Shirley called the boys to the benches and had them pair off and sit down.

'What went on here last night?' she said.

She was answered by shrugs and blank looks.

'Does anyone know where Oaks is?'

No one knew. Or if they did, no one admitted it. Boys had a way of sticking together.

She held up the coin for all to see.

'Has anyone seen this before? Is it Barlow's?'

They all said, 'No,' or 'What is it?'

The stewards started bringing in breakfast and she released the boys. If Millis did not return soon with Oaks she would have to go to Captain Penrose. He could be somewhere with a broken leg or – she did not even like to think about it – fallen overboard. She was responsible for the boy and all the others. She did not like going to the captain with her problems.

Mr Rosten. She'd go to Mr Rosten. He was an executive of the Board. Let him take it up with Captain Penrose. No, she couldn't do that. That would be hiding behind him. Nutley would help her look for Oaks. He knew his way around the ship far better than Millis. She shouldn't have sent him looking for Oaks. There would be real trouble if the captain caught him wandering around.

'Why have we stopped?' she asked the steward.

'I'm not too sure, ma'am,' he replied. 'Lads below say it's something to do with the steering.'

'Is it serious?'

'I wouldn't know, ma'am.'

'Where can I find Mr Nutley?'

'There isn't a man aboard who wouldn't like to know that,' the steward said. 'Most of the crew are looking for him.'

A chilling thought occurred to Shirley. If such an intensive search was underway for Nutley, why hadn't they found Oaks? Suddenly filled with apprehension, she sat beside Barlow's bunk stroking his cold, clammy brow, whispering words of encouragement and watching the door for Millis.

The bulkhead loudspeaker crackled to life.

'We are experiencing temporary difficulties,' the captain's voice announced calmly. 'There is no cause for alarm. We should be underway shortly. Until then I ask all passengers to continue their normal activities. Thank you.'

Lady Anne already knew there was a problem with the steering gear but not its cause or extent. At breakfast Donahue had told her as much as Penrose had told him.

'I don't like it,' he said. 'He's holding something back. There's more going on than he wants us to know. I saw men chasing around all over the ship like chickens with their heads cut off.'

'British seamen do not do that, Mr Donahue.'

Donahue grinned and said, 'I do tend to let my prejudices run away with me. But there's a lot more activity than usual.'

'And so there should be, with the ship helpless.'

'I suppose. I must say you don't seem too concerned.'

'I'm British,' she said with a smile.

'How could I forget?'

Lady Anne excused herself and went looking for Captain Penrose. She was confident he would tell her a good deal more than he had Donahue. He was not on the bridge or anywhere on deck and none of the crew she asked seemed to know, or was willing to admit, where he was.

Millis returned to the dormitory at last, his clothes and hands streaked with grease.

'I've poked about in every nook and cranny a boy could hide,' he told Shirley.

'And?' she asked.

Millis spread his hands in a gesture of hopelessness.

'Nutley's missing, too,' he said.

'I know,' she replied. 'You stay with Barlow. I'm going

199

to see the captain. Do what you can to cheer the boys up, will you? This whole business has got them pretty frightened.'

He nodded and when she had gone, asked, 'Who knows how to swim?'

Most of the boys raised their hands.

'Get in the water and give us a push, then.'

Their laughter broke up the tension pervading the dormitory.

'The rest of you can find something else to do,' he added. 'But stay where I can keep an eye on you.'

He sat down next to Barlow. 'Hello, lad,' he said, putting his mouth close to the boy's ear. 'It's me. Mum. Can you hear me?'

Barlow's eyes were open but did not flicker. As Millis watched, the lids slowly closed and the youngster's body relaxed in sleep.

'That's the ticket,' Millis murmured. 'A bit of shut-eye'll do you a world of good. Wake up right as rain, you will.'

Millis went to Oaks's bunk and pulled back the blankets, looking without hope of success for a clue to his disappearance. The bunk had been slept in but told him nothing. Straightening, he caught sight of the ventilator grille on the top bunk and the open mouth of the duct. He vaulted to the top bunk, surprisingly agile for a man of his physique, and thrust his head into the opening. It was not nearly wide enough to admit the rest of his body. But Barlow could have got in, and Oaks as well, though not as easily. The boys were all watching him.

'You lot,' he said. 'Haven't you got anything better to do than look up your old mum's skirts?'

The boys laughed as he climbed down, thinking Millis's actions were a prelude to another of his comedy routines. But when he spoke his tone was serious.

'Did any of you see Oaks or Barlow go into the

200

ventilator?' he asked.

When no one answered he said, 'Telling me won't be sneaking. Oaks might be stuck in there, hurt. I promise you no one will be punished.'

Still none of them volunteered any information. Finally, the red-haired boy who had defended Barlow about the quoit said, 'I'll go in there and have a look, if you like Mr Millis.'

'Too risky,' Millis said. 'But I won't forget that you offered. Graham, isn't it?'

'Yes, sir.'

Millis went back to Barlow. He was sleeping peacefully. It seemed a pity to wake him but there was no choice. He shook the boy's shoulder.

'Come on,' he said. 'Wakey, wakey!'

Barlow's eyes opened. They were no longer fixed, but his expression was blank.

'Were you in the ventilator?' Millis asked.

Barlow appeared not to hear.

'Was Oaks?' Millis persisted, more loudly this time. 'Did you go in together?'

When Barlow did not respond, Millis examined the boy's hands. The knuckles were scraped. He threw back the blankets. Barlow's trousers had holes worn in them at the knees. It was obvious he'd been crawling on his hands and knees. Where but in the ventilator? And with Oaks, no doubt, though Millis couldn't fathom why they should have gone larking off together. They weren't exactly chums. He looked at Barlow. He was sleeping again.

Millis drew the blankets up over him and turned to Graham.

'I'm off for a bit,' he said. 'And I'm leaving you in charge.' He turned to the others. 'Did you lot hear that?'

A few were visibly unnerved by his serious tone.

'Actually, I'm just nipping off to the pub. Even a mum needs to wet her whistle once in a while.'

Reassured, the boys smiled tentatively.

Walking to the door he tripped and fell headlong, as he had at the beginning of his show for the crew. He pulled himself up by the seat of his pants. The boys were all laughing now.

Shirley had looked first on the bridge when she reached the deck. Penrose was not there but Barrett was. He looked at her quizzically, then smiled, as if he thought she'd come looking for him. She turned away quickly, her face composed, feeling nothing. Not even distaste. First Officer Barrett was now ancient history to her, she thought.

Donahue was forward, leaning on his arms on the rail. She hurried to him and said, 'Have you seen Captain Penrose?'

'Not recently.' He looked at her, concerned. 'Is there anything I can do?'

She hesitated, then shook her head.

'I've got to find him, Andy. It's one of my boys. He's missing.'

'I heard.'

She looked surprised.

'Millis told me,' Donahue said. 'But you mustn't worry. There are so many places for a boy to get lost on a ship. What about Barlow? Dr Grimes says . . .'

But she had already left him to accost a seaman who was tightening a line dangling slackly from a crane. He had not seen the captain, either.

She hurried to Lady Anne's cabin. Lady Anne opened the door and invited her in but Shirley said she had to find Captain Penrose at once. Through the open door of the stateroom she glimpsed a photograph of a young man in RAF uniform. Lady Anne's son, she thought. He seemed real to her for the first time. What sad times for England, she thought. Lady Anne's son, Rosten's wife: the war touched everyone.

'Is it about the child?' Lady Anne asked.

'Yes.'

'I hope he hasn't taken a turn for the worse. If there's anything I can do, anything at all . . .' Perhaps she should have been helping Miss Hunt with her charges from the outset. It would have been something to occupy her time and thoughts. But she knew neither she nor the boys would have enjoyed that. She had never considered herself a motherly type. She'd always got along well with Tony, of course, but he hadn't needed much minding. Independent. Not that he hadn't been full of mischief. But in a way that made one laugh, not lecture.

Shirley realized Lady Anne was talking about Barlow and, rather than explain, said, 'We're managing, thank you. He's the same. I need the captain for . . . something else.'

A cabin door opened and Rosten appeared in the passageway carrying a pair of heavy gloves. When he saw Shirley he hurriedly stuffed them into a pocket of his coat. His rough seaman's clothes were incongruous, she thought, before remembering he'd lost everything when his house was bombed. Maybe she could talk to him about Oaks. He was, after all, a member of the CORB.

'Mr Rosten,' she said. 'I need your help.'

'Of course.'

'One of my boys is missing,' she said without preamble.

'I thought he was ill.'

'That's Barlow,' she said. 'The missing boy is Oaks.'

It was obvious neither name meant anything to him.

'How can I help?' he asked.

'I've got to find Captain Penrose and get him to organize a search.'

'Of course. But I'm afraid I've no idea where the captain is.'

'Would you ask Mr Barrett?' Though she felt nothing for the man, she did not wish to speak with him. 'I think

203

he's on the bridge,' she continued, fingering the gold coin in her pocket. On impulse she took it out and showed it to Rosten. 'This was in Peter Barlow's hand. I've no idea where he might have found it.'

Rosten's lips parted soundlessly and his sallow face grew paler. There was only one place the boy could have found it. How had he got in there? He must tell Penrose at once.

'What's wrong?' she asked solicitously. 'Are you all right?'

'Did he tell you where he found it?' Rosten asked harshly.

She shook her head.

'He can't talk,' she said. 'Or won't.'

'It's mine,' Rosten said. He didn't like saying that but there was nothing else for it.

'I don't think Barlow's a thief,' she said coldly.

Executive of the Board or not, no one was going to accuse one of her boys of stealing.

'Oh, dear. I'm not suggesting that. I . . . I lost it. The lad must have found it. May I have it back, please?'

She gave him the napoleon, pleased to be rid of it. At least one part of the riddle was solved.

'You must want to get back to him,' Rosten said. 'I'll find Captain Penrose for you. I'm sure he'll do whatever needs doing.'

'That's so kind of you,' she said, relieved.

It made him feel such a hypocrite. He comforted himself with the knowledge that even without the napoleon he'd have done whatever he could to assist Miss Hunt.

'If he should regain his speech . . . I think it would be best if you don't question him about this. He might think he's being accused of something.'

'That's terribly thoughtful of you. I won't.'

Rosten left her and hurried up to the bridge. Barrett, after angrily informing him passengers were not allowed on the bridge, told him Captain Penrose was in the steering-gear compartment.

'But that's no place for passengers, either,' he warned.

Rosten did not press him, unwilling to reveal the urgency of his need to speak with Penrose. He hurried to the deck and asked a seaman the way.

Going down the companionway, Shirley met Millis coming up.

'I asked you to stay with Barlow,' she said, disappointed that he had neglected his duty when she had come to rely on him so.

'I think I know where Oaks is.'

'Thank God! Where?' She was almost as happy to learn her trust had not been misplaced as by Millis's news.

'Barlow's been in the ventilators . . .'

'He's conscious, then, and told you Oaks was with him,' she interrupted, enormously relieved.

Millis shook his head.

'He's still sleeping it off. But you can tell Penrose to call off the search and try the ventilators.'

'I couldn't find Captain Penrose. Mr Rosten's looking for him now.'

'Rosten?'

'He wanted to help. The coin was his, by the way.'

'What?'

'The coin Barlow had. Mr Rosten lost it.'

'He said that, did he?'

She ignored him. 'What makes you think they were in the ventilators?'

Millis told her as they hurried to the dormitory. When Rosten located Captain Penrose and didn't see her on deck he would know she was there.

Graham was sitting by Barlow's bunk when they came in.

'He's still sleeping, Mr Millis,' he said.

He was tall for his age, and slender, with green eyes and

205

freckles to go with his ruff of wavy red hair.

'Good lad,' said Millis. 'I knew I could depend on you.'

The boys watched as Shirley studied the open ventilator. She wanted to climb up and look inside but did not know how she could without her skirts hiking up. She thought it silly she should still think that way after her experience in the paint locker but it was something ingrained. Sensing her dilemma, Millis picked her up and deposited her on the top bunk. He did so effortlessly and the arms she had imagined were plump were hard with muscle.

'Just ring for the lift when you want down,' he said.

She could just see in by standing on tiptoe. The air inside was cold and smelly. She shivered involuntarily, thinking of Oaks being trapped somewhere in there.

She let herself down to the bunk and said, 'Somebody's got to go in and find him.'

'It's too close for a grown man,' Millis said. 'We'll have to find where it leads and tap along the bulkheads until he answers.'

'I could get in,' Shirley said.

'But could you get out? Captain Penrose will have the schematic somewhere.'

'I'll ask him.'

Millis reached up and lifted her down. She found his strength reassuring even though his hands were gripping her waist and their bodies were only inches apart. After what happened with Barrett she'd thought she'd shrink from a man's touch.

'Thanks,' she said, dropping her hands from his shoulders and stepping back.

'Tell the management, won't you? I'm new on this job, operating the lift. On probation, as it were.'

She wished he hadn't tried to be funny. It had been sort of a nice moment. Then she realized he had felt something, too, and only joked to hide it.

Rosten arrived at the steering-gear compartment in a state of suppressed agitation. Once he reached Number 6 'tween-decks he had no trouble finding the compartment because of the screech of metal on metal coming from the stern. The door stood open and through it he saw Captain Penrose's straight back and the bluish-orange flame of an acetylene torch as a goggled man worked on a complicated-looking piece of machinery.

'Captain,' he called from the door.

Penrose turned with an annoyed expression.

'What are you doing down here?' he demanded.

'I must see you.'

'Later.'

'It's urgent.'

'Nothing can possibly be more urgent than . . .'

'I must insist,' Rosten interrupted with a firmness that surprised Penrose.

'Very well,' Penrose said impatiently. He tapped the man wearing the goggles on the shoulder. 'Keep at it, Perkins. I'll only be a moment.'

He stepped outside to face Rosten, his annoyance clearly evident, leaving the door open. Rosten shut it.

'One of the children got into the hold,' Rosten said, displaying the napoleon.

'Bloody hell! You left the door unlocked, didn't you?'

'He must have got in through the ventilator,' Rosten said stiffly. 'No one knows where he found it.'

'How can that be?'

'He's in a state of shock. Speechless. Something happened down there but we don't know what.'

'How'd you get the coin, then?'

'Miss Hunt gave it to me.'

'Then she must suspect something.'

'I told her it's mine. That I'd lost it.'

'Good,' Penrose said, relaxing for the first time. 'Sorry I lashed out at you. Things have been rather touch and go.'

It was difficult for him to apologize to anyone but he owed it to Rosten.

'What's the state of the hold?' he asked. 'Could the boy have seen the ingots?'

'I'm afraid so. I hadn't got them all put away yet. It's possible he wouldn't know what they were.'

'We can't be certain, can we?'

It was a rhetorical question which Rosten did not bother to answer.

'I'm afraid there's more,' Rosten said apologetically. 'It seems there was another boy with him – who can't be found. Miss Hunt thinks he's lost somewhere in the ventilators.'

Captain Penrose sighed, for him a rare display of resignation. He recovered quickly.

'Don't say anything to Miss Hunt until you've searched the hold,' he said briskly. 'If the boy's there, tell him something to explain the ingots before you bring him out. If not . . . he'll be somewhere in the ventilating system and we'll simply have to find him.'

'I'm off,' said Rosten.

Penrose returned to the steering-gear compartment. The seals had been replaced on the undamaged casing and Perkins was finishing up welding the cracked one.

'We'll have the seals on within the hour,' he said. 'But I can't promise the weld will hold.'

'We'll know soon enough,' Penrose said.

He had scarcely stepped out of the compartment when a seaman came pounding through the 'tween-decks, breathless.

'Sir,' he said, panting, 'you're wanted on the bridge. Asdic's reporting echoes.'

Chapter Thirteen

Rosten wanted to search the hold before having to face Shirley Hunt. She had been so agitated and determined he knew she would be difficult to put off. However, he did not know how to reach the hold from the Number 6 'tween-decks and had to go up on deck. She was waiting there for him.

She rushed to meet him, but before she could ask questions he said with all the sincerity he could muster, 'Captain Penrose is most concerned. He'll have men checking the ventilators immediately they find the system plans. He wants you to remain with the other lad. When he's speaking again Captain Penrose wants to know at once.'

'Thank you. Thank you so much.'

As she turned to leave, Captain Penrose came striding purposefully towards the bridge, his face grim.

'Please hurry, Captain,' she said.

He looked at her as if she were an intrusion. She felt rebuffed. He must know she'd gone below decks with Barrett and drawn the wrong conclusions.

'I was just telling Miss Hunt men will be getting after the boy shortly,' Rosten said quickly.

'Of course,' Penrose said. 'Shortly.'

He continued towards the bridge with hardly a pause.

'He could be hurt or suffering from exposure,' Shirley called after him.

He gave no indication he had heard. He did know, she thought. But that did not give him the right to neglect Oaks. If it were Lady Anne stuck in a ventilator somewhere . . . .

'It's simply that he has so much else on his mind. The

steering . . . a man missing.' He must be careful not to overdo it. None of the passengers knew the nature of the problem with the steering. He would not have known himself had he not seen it with his own eyes, and Penrose had not seen fit to explain the cause even to him. 'Just go back to the other boys and don't worry.' He patted her on the shoulder. 'There's a good girl.' He did not at first know where that had come from. He wasn't good at dealing with distraught young women. Then he realized. It was what Marjorie would have done.

In any case, it seemed to be having the desired effect. Again he felt such a hypocrite. He was not good at lying. But it was not entirely false. Penrose would be seeing to it as soon as he let the captain know the state of affairs in the hold.

As soon as Shirley was out of sight he ran to the companionway.

On the bridge, Barrett was on the phone to the Asdic room. His bloodshot eyes and slack face showed the effects of lack of sleep and prolonged strain. This new breed didn't have the stamina of men who'd spent a lifetime learning the sea, Penrose thought with grim satisfaction.

'Thirty-two thousand yards,' Barrett said.

Penrose took the phone from him without replying.

'Captain here,' he said. 'Report.'

'Echoes at thirty-one thousand yards, sir. Astern.'

Eighteen miles, Penrose thought. With the engines shut down the U-boat, if it was a U-boat, wouldn't be getting any echoes from the *Amindra*. Even if it surfaced to have a look around they couldn't be seen at that distance.

'Seems to be closing,' Barrett said. 'When will we have steering control, sir?'

'You're relieved, Mr Barrett,' said Penrose, ignoring the question. 'Get some sleep. You look half dead.'

He really did not care if Barrett ever got any rest. He

simply wanted the man to know his exhaustion had not gone unnoticed, and that he thought of it as a weakness. As for himself, he felt strong and alert enough for hours more on the bridge.

'If you don't mind, sir . . .'

'I do mind.'

What did Barrett think his continued presence on the bridge could possibly contribute to the well-being of the *Amindra*? Her master was in charge and had the situation well in hand.

The expression on Barrett's face said plainly that he understood why he was being relieved before the end of his watch. Penrose was satisfied that his message had been received loud and clear.

The echoes continued to close slowly. At twenty-eight thousand yards Penrose ordered Emergency Stations.

Then just as he was fighting to suppress a feeling of helplessness, Perkins came to the bridge to report the steering gear functioning again. At once Penrose called the engine room and ordered power. The *Amindra* came alive. She vibrated and moved ahead as he signalled first half speed and then full. The ship responded when he gave the helmsman a heading taking her away from the echoes.

'Well done, Perkins,' he said, trying not to betray the relief he felt.

If only the weld holds, he thought, we'll have got out of a sticky situation better than we had any right to expect. And I'll see Perkins is properly thanked for it.

In the hold, Rosten thought at first that things were exactly as he had left them, but a more careful scrutiny revealed the gaping maw of an uncovered ventilator duct a few feet above the highest tier of crates. If he had needed more proof than the napoleon that the boy had found his way into the hold, the absence of the covering grille provided it. He did not recall actually seeing the grille in place but knew it must have been. The open duct was too jarring a note. The arrangement of the cargo provided a natural though difficult approach to the duct. He climbed to the top tier to find the grille and replace it.

A brutal cry of klaxons, somewhat muted by its passage from the upper areas of the ship but still alarming, echoed in the chilly hold. His first impulse was to scramble down and make his way to the relative safety of the top deck. At this very moment a torpedo could be streaking towards the *Amindra*. He was well below the waterline and would be trapped. If the torpedo struck the hold he would not have to worry about drowning, though. He would die in the explosion.

He had taken only a few steps across the rough wood of the topmost crates when he knew he had no intention of leaving the hold. With Marjorie gone, his life had no great importance except the contribution it could make to the success of the *Amindra*'s mission.

Strangely calmed – was this bravery, he wondered, or merely resignation? – he returned to his task. The grille was nowhere to be seen. It could have slid from the tier with the ship's motion. He went to the edge of the tier and looked down. There was a crate wedged at the bottom between the tiers. He did not recall that aisle being blocked. Looking across to the opposite tier, he saw an empty place which he also could not remember from his last visit to the hold. Obviously the crate had become dislodged and fallen to the deck. Fortunately it did not appear to have been breached.

He had to go almost all the way forward to climb down before making his way back to the crate. From deck level he saw that it had not fallen into the litter in the aisle but appeared to have wedged itself a few inches above it. If the grille were beneath it it might be possible for him to fish it out. It was too dark under the crate for him to see anything. He took his electric torch from inside his coat and, kneeling in sodden litter that soaked his trouser legs, flashed the beam under the crate. There was something beneath it, an unidentifiable mass. By lying flat on his stomach and reaching in as far as his arm would stretch he could just touch it. Whatever it was, it was soaked, just as he was now. He brought back his hand and stood up, shivering as his damp garments chilled his flesh. He wiped his wet hand on the nearest crate. It left a dark stain. He snatched back his hand and stared at it. His skin was smeared with blood. Something hot and bitter rose in his throat and he swallowed to keep from vomiting.

He had found Oaks.

He sought desperately for solutions as he fled from the hold to the bridge to inform Penrose. The boy's body must be brought out but he and the captain could not possibly lift the crate unassisted. No one from the crew must be allowed in the hold until all the ingots had been cleared away and that would take time. Time during which Miss Hunt would be insisting the boy be found.

In the dormitory, Shirley was growing increasingly impatient.

'I don't believe they're doing a thing,' she told Millis. 'You'd think Captain Penrose would be as anxious about Oaks as we are.'

'I think he's more anxious about losing the lot than one boy,' Millis said. 'Or didn't you hear the signal for Emergency Stations?'

'If he doesn't do something soon I'm going to look for him myself.'

On the bridge, Captain Penrose ordered a change in heading. The Asdic echoes had been fading and he thought it safe to put the *Amindra* back on course. The helmsman turned the wheel. The ship continued to plough along on the old heading.

'We've just lost steering control again, sir,' the

213

helmsman said.

Just then Rosten rapped on the glass of the bridge and gestured violently for Penrose's attention.

The weld hadn't held. The *Amindra* was helpless again and worse: the engines had been running, sending out sounds which might well have been detected by the U-boat whose echoes they had been picking up. These waters were infested with German submarines. Should he continue running on an unalterable course and risk being heard by one of them lurking up ahead, which with the steering out he would be unable to avoid? Risk running towards calamity instead of away from it?

Rosten rapped on the glass again. Penrose shook his head at him savagely. He had reached his decision. He ordered the engines shut down again. No need to send for Perkins. He would already be working on the steering gear. Penrose had sent him back to the compartment to stand by until further orders.

He called a seaman from the deck to fetch Briscoe, ignoring Rosten's urgently whispered demands to speak with him. Only when the seaman was on his way did he turn to Rosten, leaving the bridge to confront him out of the helmsman's hearing.

'The boy's in the hold,' Rosten said. 'Crushed under a crate.'

'Alive or dead?' Penrose asked, suppressing a sigh.

'Dead,' Rosten replied.

Or was he? He hadn't considered any other possibility. But the crate had been resting a few inches above the deck. There was the off chance the boy was alive and unconscious though badly injured. If alive, he had to be freed as quickly as possible or he would most certainly die.

'I'm not sure,' he said. 'We'll have to get him out.'

'Out of the question,' Penrose snapped.

He knew how cold-blooded that sounded but there was much more at stake than the life of one boy. The *Amindra*

214

was dead in the water, easy prey for any marauding U-boat. He could not even think about the boy until his ship was safely on its way again. Churchill's words echoed in his mind. 'Do you have children, Captain? . . . The future of the British Empire may well be in your hands.'

'What must I tell Miss Hunt?' Rosten demanded, unable to believe Penrose's callousness.

'Tell her anything you please! Except that the boy's in the hold.'

Briscoe came puffing up to the bridge wing and looked surprised to find Rosten there. Penrose sent him back to the steering-gear compartment to see how Perkins was getting on.

'And send a man back to let me know when I may expect steering control again,' he said.

When Briscoe had left he turned back to Rosten.

'As soon as you've got Miss Hunt quieted down, get back to the hold and get those bars out of sight. Then we can think about getting the boy out.'

In the dormitory, Millis said, 'We've stopped again.'

'That does it,' said Shirley. 'Nobody cares about Oaks. I'm going to look for him myself.'

'Let Graham go,' said Millis. 'He's a strong, willing lad.'

'I won't risk another of my boys. It's my responsibility, not Graham's. I'm going and don't try to stop me.'

'It's your fune . . .' Millis began. Her determined expression stopped him. 'Wait until I fetch something. I'll only be a minute. Will you promise to wait?'

Something in his tone and posture stilled her protests. Reasonable, assured, as if expecting to be obeyed. It could almost have been Captain Penrose speaking, but with more honest concern than the captain. He really cared.

'Don't be long,' she said.

While she waited she resumed her fruitless attempts to

question Barlow. He was awake now and had been for some hours. His eyes were no longer expressionless. They seemed to stare quizzically into space as if searching for explanation of some absorbing mystery.

'Barlow,' she said. 'Peter.'

He continued to stare at the overhead, seeming to ignore her deliberately.

She put her mouth next to his ear and said harshly, 'Say something, damn it!'

She bit her lip, ashamed of her loss of control.

Millis returned with two large coils of light line hanging from his shoulders. He tied the end of one of them around her waist.

'When you find Oaks, give a sharp tug. If you get in trouble, give two. I'll know where you are from the line played out. And I'll come and chop you out.'

'You won't know which way I've gone.'

'I'll get the ventilator schematic from Penrose if I have to wring it out of him. And I'll hack away in every direction until I find the right one.'

Somehow she knew she could depend on him to do just that.

'You lot,' Millis called to the boys gathered in whispering clusters to watch them. 'Haven't you seen my rope trick before?'

He lifted Shirley to the top bunk, handed her an electric torch and vaulted up to join her. Getting on his hands and knees to make a platform of his back he said, 'Climb aboard. But mind your heels.' He was not as confident as he sounded. He didn't like her going in there. She was as brave as she was lovely. He hadn't met many like her.

She stood on his solid back and put her head and shoulders into the vent. Cold, threatening air, smelling of iron and damp, washed over her. Beyond the range of the feeble light streaming past her from the dormitory, the blackness was thick and menacing. She had always been frightened of dark, narrow places. But she steeled herself. If she did not find Oaks nobody would. Penrose's priorities obviously put the safety of his ship far above that of the children. How could she ever have admired him so?

She turned on her torch and squirmed the upper part of her body into the vent. Her shoulders touched the sides, but just barely. She hung in the vent to her hips, legs dangling, unable to insert the rest of her body.

'You can still change your mind,' Millis said quietly. 'You needn't be embarrassed if you do.'

'Help me in,' she said, her voice echoing hollowly in the vent. He was more worried about her than he let on, she realized. Sweet, she thought, wanting to laugh. Joe Millis sweet!

He wound his arms around her legs and lifted. She tensed, remembering Barrett's embrace. Then she was in the vent on her stomach in a space almost too confining for her to get to her hands and knees. Dear God, let Oaks not have gone too far. She crawled forward, feeling a light but reassuring tension in the line around her waist. Millis was letting her know he was there. She wondered if she could have forced herself to move forward were it not for him and the cord at her waist.

It hurt her fingers to put weight on the hand holding the torch. She tucked it into her cardigan with only the lens protruding. She was dismayed to see that just up ahead the duct branched and became two. How would she know which one Oaks had taken? The problem solved itself when she reached the double vent. One branch, that leading upwards, was smaller than the other. She doubted if Oaks could have squeezed into it. He was not that much smaller than she. She shone the light into it on the chance that he had tried, and got himself stuck. The duct was clear as far as she could see.

She started down the other branch. It was easier going down than it had been crawling straight ahead. If she did not find Oaks somewhere that could be reached from outside she did not know how she would manage to crawl backwards up the duct.

The duct seemed to narrow as she made her painstaking way down into the ship, constricting her as if she had been swallowed by a giant snake and was being digested. She knew it was only her imagination because her shoulders still had the same limited play and the rounded top pressed no closer on her back, yet she could not shake off the notion. The continued light tension of the rope at her waist gave her courage to continue. It was a life-line, a link with light and room to stand erect and breathe easily. A link with someone who could be counted on to help.

She wished she had been less curt with Millis. He hadn't been trying to undermine her authority with the boys. He'd only been trying to do what was best for them and he had done a good job of keeping them amused and manageable. It had been petty of her to resent it. She wondered what it was that had kept him out of military service. He seemed strong and healthy. His heart, maybe, or something like asthma, or flat feet. She tried to remember what his feet looked like but couldn't.

Thinking about Millis helped her fight off claustrophobia. He had been a good friend of Barlow's from the very beginning. Her thoughts verged towards Barrett. He wasn't ancient history after all. She shut them out. She would rather be here, filled with primitive fears and muscles aching, than be back with him in that awful little room.

Up ahead the darkness beyond the range of her light seemed less intense. She reached into her cardigan and snapped off the torch. There was light ahead! She crawled towards it with new vigour and courage.

The light came from a round opening, a vent, to which the duct led her. She lay flat on her stomach and rested her chin on the lip, looking down into a dimly-lit subterranean chamber crammed with stacks of wooden crates like exaggerated children's building blocks. There were gaps in the upper layers of the stacks, and in the narrow spaces between them there were scraps and wads and streamers of packing materials, as if someone had been uncrating fragile crystal or china.

She knew as surely as if she had been with him that Oaks had come here. He must have climbed down and been unable to get back up. The vent was at least a man's height above the stacked crates. He was somewhere in that maze, probably curled up and sleeping, or hurt and unconscious from a fall. But there was no way she could get down to look for him. She could not turn around in the duct. If she tried to worm her way out she would only fall head first to the crates below.

She began a meticulous scrutiny of the aisles and tiers visible from the duct, finding nothing to indicate his presence. The only thing at all unusual was a small neat stack of yellow bricks at the end of the aisle and a crudely patched area in the hull at the other end, surrounded by tattered insulating material. One was as odd to her as the other. But neither was any concern of hers. Oaks was what mattered and she must find a way of getting him out of here.

She opened her mouth to shout his name but checked herself as a figure emerged from between towering stacks of crates, its back to her, and went to the bricks.

'Oaks!' she cried, giddy with relief.

The figure whirled and Rosten's startled face stared up at her. For a moment neither spoke, both too dumbfounded by the other's presence to say anything. Rosten was the first to recover. Stepping quickly between her and the bricks he said, 'Miss Hunt! What on earth are you doing up there?'

'Did you find him?' she asked anxiously.

The line tugged sharply at her waist. She had not moved

219

for so long Millis must have feared she was stuck.

'Find him?' Rosten said blankly.

Shirley gave three tugs on the line. Millis had said one tug if she found Oaks, two if she was in trouble. There had been no signal for anything else. She hoped he would understand that three meant she was all right. She did not signal she had found Oaks because she really hadn't, yet.

'Oaks,' she said. 'Gregory Oaks.'

'Oh. No. Not yet.'

She felt a surge of admiration and appreciation for Rosten. He had taken it on himself to go looking for Oaks when no one else would. But how did he know where to look? Captain Penrose, of course. He would know where the duct led. She had been mistaken in thinking him cruel and heartless. Unable to come himself or send any of his crew, he had enlisted Rosten's help. Rosten was, after all, a concerned party, being a member of the Board.

'I'll help you,' she said. 'Come and help me down.'

'I'm afraid I can't get to you,' he said. 'You must go back the way you came. I don't believe he's here but I'll keep looking.'

'I can't turn around. I'll have to come down. Look, you can climb up over there.'

'So I could.'

He took off his coat and spread it over the bricks. It seemed an odd thing to do until he said, 'It's constricting, you know. I don't think I can manage with it on.'

While he was climbing to her she untied the line at her waist and gave three tugs, hoping that when Millis tried to signal back and found it slack he would realize she had reached safety. She knew he was more intelligent than she had assumed at first.

Rosten reached up to her with outstretched arms. She wriggled forward enough to free her shoulders and reached down for his hands. Steadied, she emerged farther, leaning down and sliding her hands along his arms until she was hanging half out of the vent with her hands firmly on his shoulders. He held her under the arms, moving back slowly as she worked her legs free. He braced himself with widely planted feet as he took her weight. Only her feet were still inside the vent. His eyes bulged with strain as he looked up into her face.

'Now for the tricky part,' he said through gritted teeth.

He moved forward until her knees touched the bulkhead below the vent. She pulled her feet free. He staggered under the increased weight and stepped back, still holding her under the arms as she droped feet first to the crate. They clutched each other to keep from falling, their bodies pressed close together, her breasts flattened against his bony chest. Shirley thought of Barrett and felt momentary revulsion. It passed quickly. Poor Mr Rosten was certainly no threat. He freed her hastily. He was actually embarrassed, she thought.

'Are you all right?' he asked awkwardly.

'Thank you, yes. Where have you looked?'

'Everywhere. I'm afraid he's not here.'

She sensed he was lying and that it was not easy for him to do so. Why would he do that?

'A minute ago you said you'd keep looking.'

'I didn't want to dash your hopes. But I assure you he's not in this hold.'

'How can you be sure? It's so big. And there are so many boxes. I want to look.'

'Very well,' he said, resigned. 'I'll help you.'

They climbed down, helping each other to negotiate the difficult places. He stayed at her elbow as she went along each aisle and stood on tiptoe to look into gaps among the higher tiers. He shivered.

'You should put on your coat,' she said. 'You'll catch cold.'

221

'I'm quite comfortable, really.'

But she could see the dank chill of the hold was affecting him.

'I'll get it for you,' she said.

'Please don't trouble,' he said hastily. 'I'll fetch it.'

She followed him when he went after his coat, curious why he was making such an issue of it. He plucked it from the bricks and began heaping the litter in the aisle on them with his feet.

They were not bricks. They were metal. Ingots.

He sensed her nearness and spun around to face her. She read panic in his expression.

'What's going on?' she demanded. 'That's gold, isn't it? And you lied to me about Oaks. Why?'

'It is gold, actually,' he said. 'A small shipment by the Board. To pay for new facilities we're setting up for evacuees in New York.' How dreadful having to lie like this, he thought wretchedly.

He was obviously lying, but gaining confidence in his rush of words, Shirley thought.

'The chest they were in burst open in the storm. I've just been putting things back in order.'

'That doesn't explain why you lied to me about Oaks,' she said.

'Why would I tell you he wasn't here if he was?'

'That's exactly what I intend to find out.'

There was a moment of strained silence.

'Miss Hunt,' Rosten said at last, choosing his words carefully, 'I must ask you to leave here immediately and to tell no one what you've seen.' Pray God she'd obey so he could end this horrid charade.

'Why?'

'I'm not at liberty to say.'

'I'm not going anywhere until I'm convinced Oaks isn't in that hold.'

'Very well,' he said, resigned. 'But you'll find I've told you the truth.'

Shirley resumed her search. Oaks was not in any of the gaps between the crates. One of the aisles was blocked by a huge box wedged between two tiers.

'Did you look on the other side?' she demanded.

'Of course.'

Rosten seemed to have recovered his poise but she still felt he was lying. Climbing on the crate, she peered beyond it. There was nothing in the aisle. Then something protruding from beneath the crate caught her eye. She jumped down for a closer look. The object was partially covered by packing material. She brushed the material away. The object was waxen and looked strangely like a human hand. She reached down and touched it.

It *was* a hand!

Stiff and cold, but a hand. A boy's hand. Oaks's.

She let out a cry, half gasp, half scream.

'What is it?' Rosten cried.

'He's here,' she whispered numbly. 'Under the crate. He's dead.'

'How dreadful!' More dreadful than she could possibly know. Not just that poor lad lying there but his own involvement in a despicable conspiracy with Penrose.

She did not think Rosten was as surprised as he pretended to be.

'We've got to tell Captain Penrose and get him out,' she said.

'Yes,' said Rosten. 'We certainly must.'

Captain Penrose was still on the bridge. Briscoe was with him. He had come up from the steering-gear compartment with disturbing news. Not only had the weld failed to hold but also the cylinder itself had shattered. Perkins would have to improvise a new one and could not even guess how

223

long it might take to do so. Another six to ten hours at least of experimenting and testing. Briscoe was particularly incensed that Nutley, the man responsible for their plight, might never have to answer for it.

'Gone where we'll never lay hands on him,' he said. 'Over the side.'

He was convinced that despite all the places a man might hide himself aboard a ship, the search had been too thorough for Nutley to escape. He had done his foul deed and then, either distraught with remorse or fearing reprisal or simply insane from the outset, had thrown himself overboard. Penrose was inclined to agree with Briscoe. Only a madman would have done what Nutley did.

On deck, Rosten was holding Miss Hunt's elbow with one hand and gesturing towards the bridge with the other. Rosten's urgency was obvious to Penrose, though he was puzzled by Miss Hunt's presence. Leaving Briscoe in charge, he went down to join them.

'Miss Hunt has some dreadful news,' Rosten said before she could speak. 'It's best she tells you privately.'

Penrose knew from Rosten's manner there was a good deal more to his concern than anything Miss Hunt might have to say. Though she did look white as a sheet and was holding on to herself with an obvious effort.

'We'll go to my quarters,' he said, leading the way.

He glanced at the 'Spares' box as he went by. The possibility of having to scuttle the *Amindra* loomed larger now that she was helpless. U-boats had been known to board and search lone ships before sinking them.

As soon as they were inside his cabin Shirley said, 'Gregory Oaks is dead. Crushed under a crate in the hold.'

Penrose gave Rosten a withering look.

'She got in through the ventilating system,' Rosten said.

Captain Penrose wasn't the least surprised by her news, Shirley thought. And Rosten was making excuses for her finding Oaks. They were hiding something from her and it was baffling and infuriating.

'You knew he was there,' she said, her voice shaking with fury. 'Both of you. And you didn't do a damn thing about it. You even lied.'

Rosten looked down, shamefaced, but Penrose regarded her sternly.

'Those are serious charges, Miss Hunt,' he said. 'And I find them offensive.'

She knew he was trying to intimidate her. If she let him it would be as degrading as her experience with Barrett.

'It was meant to be,' she said. 'I want him brought out of that horrible place.'

Penrose looked at Rosten instead of at her.

'Give me another hour,' Rosten said.

'I'll send men down, Miss Hunt,' Penrose said with all his usual formal charm. 'Now, if you'll excuse me . . .'

Shirley positioned herself between Penrose and the door, surprised by her own boldness and feeling greater confidence in herself than she had ever known. If you faced things squarely and asserted yourself you need fear no one.

'What's down there you don't want anyone to know about?' she demanded. 'What's going on?'

Again Penrose turned to Rosten.

'The Overseas Reception Board's bullion,' Rosten said. 'I hadn't finished repacking the spilled ingots.'

'I see,' said Penrose. 'Are you referring to that, Miss Hunt?'

'No. But now that you've mentioned it, why should it be such a big secret?'

'You wouldn't be expected to know about shipboard pilferage,' Penrose said. 'Something that valuable and easily concealed is tempting even to honest men. And with a pick-up, wartime crew . . . I'm sure you understand.'

225

'Not when it means letting that poor boy lie there all those hours. With Mr Millis and me worrying ourselves sick about him.'

'We didn't know he was there until you found him,' Penrose said. 'I assure you, if we had . . .' His tone less apologetic, he continued, 'Miss Hunt, I must ask you not to tell anyone we're carrying a few bars of gold bullion. If it were known, I'd have to post guards and I haven't a man to spare.'

Shirley sensed there was more to it than that but it was no concern of hers, not if they brought out Oaks. She could not stand the thought of his poor crushed body lying down there in that dank, gloomy hold.

'I won't,' she said. 'If you promise to get Gregory out of there into a decent place. I don't know what I'm going to tell his parents.'

'You'll not have to tell them anything,' Penrose said. 'As master of the *Amindra* I'll . . .'

He was interrupted by a whistling sound from his bunk. He went quickly to the telephone and picked it up. He nodded, looking grave, and said, 'I'll be up at once.'

'No,' said Shirley. 'I'll write to them.'

But Captain Penrose was not listening. He was already on his way out of the door.

Briscoe was watching something off the port bow through binoculars. When he heard Penrose arrive he handed the binoculars to him without a word and pointed into the distance. Penrose refocused the binoculars, searched the horizon through a brief arc and fixed on something.

'Yes,' he said at last, without taking the binoculars from his eyes. 'Definitely a periscope.'

Captain Freiburg looked morosely at Lieutenant Sperling's coloured pins. It was mid-afternoon, Thursday. The *Adler* had come another 480 miles closer to the hoped-for interception point and was now squarely between the Lisbon–New York and Gibraltar–New York sea lanes. But the black pin representing the *Adler* was still almost 500 miles from its destination. Thirty-six hours of steady sailing. The white pin marking the *Amindra*'s last known position was meaningless, the *Adler* having received no recent information, but the yellow pin, the one marking the *Amindra*'s estimated position if she continued unchecked, was within twelve hours of the critical area. A full day's advantage over the *Adler*.

If the yellow pin – how he was beginning to resent that damned frustrating bit of paint and metal – represented the *Amindra*'s actual position she would reach the protection of Canadian sea and air forces long before he could intercept her.

Freiburg took no comfort from the knowledge that the failure would not be his but that of the German agent whose mission it was to delay the *Amindra*. Whose failure it might be did not matter. What mattered was that Germany might miss an unprecedented opportunity to bring the war to a speedier and victorious end.

Restless, he looked into the wireless room and waved the operator back down when the man started to spring to attention.

'Have you checked your equipment?' Freiburg asked. 'Could you have missed any signals?'

'Everything's working normally, sir. It's been quiet as a tomb.'

Freiburg lit his pipe and went on deck to walk off his frustration.

Damn it, where *was* the *Amindra*?

Chapter Fourteen

Captain Penrose considered his options. They were precious few. His ship was helpless except for the stern gun, still disguised as a deck load. The gun was useless against a submerged U-boat. If the submarine remained in its present position off the bow it would be of no avail to restart the engines. The rudder was locked in a position which would take the *Amindra* directly into the mouth of the U-boat's torpedo tubes. Moving, she might present a more difficult target than dead in the water but, unable to manoeuvre, the best he could hope for was to cause the U-boat to waste a torpedo or two, hardly a fair exchange for 250 million pounds sterling. Nevertheless, he instructed the engine room to restart the engines and prepare to get under way at his signal. Sudden movement might avoid the first salvo, though the chances for that were slim. A 10,000-ton vessel did not spring away like a racehorse.

But the situation was still not entirely hopeless. Much depended on the character of the U-boat commander. Despite British propaganda to the contrary, he was aware that many of them adhered scrupulously to the rules of sea warfare whenever possible. Unarmed, unescorted vessels were not attacked without warning. Such commanders would surface and permit the crew to take to lifeboats and withdraw to safety before sinking the ship with gunfire. There was a practical as well as humanitarian side to that, of course. Torpedoes were more precious than shells and easier to avoid. And on occasions boarding parties searched chart rooms, masters' quarters and strongrooms for materials which might prove useful to German Intelligence.

If this commander was one of the more decent types it might be possible to lure him into surfacing and to turn the tables on him with a sudden attack from the stern gun before the U-boat could submerge or return fire.

Before ordering the *Amindra* to Emergency Stations Penrose sent word to the gun crew to keep their weapon masked and, while remaining near it, to conduct themselves as ordinary deckhands. They were to be prepared, however, to spring immediately into action at the first blast of the *Amindra*'s foghorn.

He posted extra hands along the port rail to watch for torpedo wakes. If the commander were of another sort and launched an attack without warning, Penrose was prepared to make the probably futile effort of getting under way to avoid the opening salvo.

He addressed the passengers over the loudspeakers, instructing them to remain in their quarters. For the moment it would perhaps be safer for them and at least it would keep them out of the crew's way. There would be time enough to send them to lifeboat stations once he learned the U-boat's intentions. That done, he sent a crewman to bring Rosten to the bridge. Leaving Briscoe in charge, he left the bridge long enough to brief the bank official and instruct him to stand by the 'Spares' box. If the U-boat knocked out the bridge and Penrose with it, Rosten was to activate the scuttling charges.

The periscope moved deliberately towards the *Amindra*, but instead of angling directly at the vessel it maintained a course that would bring the U-boat abreast of it at a distance of some two thousand yards. The U-boat commander definitely was not the sort Penrose had hoped for. He was clearly positioning his submarine for the most advantageous torpedo attack, with the full length of the *Amindra* as his target.

The *Amindra* was doomed.

Should he try to anticipate the U-boat commander and get the *Amindra* moving just before the torpedoes were launched? If the U-boat launched a spread, there was the risk that he might be running into the path of one torpedo while trying to avoid another. But, expecting the ship to remain motionless, there was a chance the German commander might attack with a single torpedo. Or should he unmask the stern gun and hope to knock out the periscope with a lucky shot? The U-boat would be blind but, having already established the position of its victim, it did not require a visual sighting to launch. Or it might submerge, to surface in an unexpected quarter and, warned of the presence of the *Amindra*'s deck gun, open fire immediately with its own.

The periscope continued its deliberate glide through the choppy sea. No tell-tale torpedo wake traced the surface between it and the *Amindra*. After a while the U-boat appeared to be pulling away. What could it be up to, Penrose wondered? Studying the *Amindra* perhaps, preparatory to surfacing? He had driven off one U-boat with his stern gun and might do the same with another. But the *Amindra* had been manoeuvrable then.

The periscope changed course and curved around the stern of the *Amindra* like the fin of a shark seeking its prey. And then it was on a reciprocal course, passing the *Amindra* to starboard, while still maintaining its two-thousand-yard distance. Did the U-boat commander suspect the *Amindra* was armed and was he trying to sniff out the location of its gun?

Suddenly the periscope vanished. Penrose was certain that it was only a matter of moments before the U-boat launched its torpedoes. He barked orders for lifeboat stations. Passengers and crew were still forming at their boats when the speaker from the Asdic room crackled to life.

'Echoes at twenty-five hundred yards,' it said.

The U-boat had increased its distance from the *Amindra*! Penrose was stunned. What kind of game was it playing? Had its commander recognized the deck load for what it was and was he trying to lull the *Amindra*'s crew into relaxing their caution? But there was no need to go to such lengths against a motionless ship. Unless the enemy intended surfacing and launching a boarding party when the stern gun was silenced?

Penrose ordered the gun unmasked and its crew into position to fire. He was determined the U-boat commander would not take him by surprise.

His bafflement mounted as the Asdic room reported increasing distance between the U-boat and the *Amindra*. Was it a trick or was the German vessel actually withdrawing? Either way, it was now well astern. He ordered full speed. Even on his fixed heading he could escape the U-boat now by outrunning it, unless it chose to surface. And if it surfaced the *Amindra* would be a match for it in firepower.

But the echoes continued to fade. The U-boat *was* withdrawing. The thought crossed his mind that the submarine might be British. But if so, why had it not signalled an identification? If it had been unwilling to risk a wireless signal that might be picked up by German monitors it had only to surface and signal visually.

Though the heading of the *Amindra* was taking the ship off course, Penrose continued at full speed in order to put more distance between her and the mysterious submarine. He did not order the engines shut down again until the Asdic room reported no further echoes.

Captain Freiburg, having decided that fretting was not going to halt the *Amindra*, was having an afternoon nap when Schramm knocked on his door carrying a decoded signal.

'I knew you'd want to see this immediately so I brought it myself, sir,' he said.

The *Amindra* had been dead in the water when first sighted and though she had started her engines that could only mean she was having difficulties. It was obvious to Freiburg from the co-ordinates that the British ship had lost time but he could not know how much until her position was carefully plotted.

'Get Sperling to the chart room,' he said, buttoning his tunic.

'He's already there, sir.'

In the chart room, Freiburg gave Sperling the signal and hovered at his bony elbow while the lieutenant plotted the *Amindra*'s position and moved his coloured pins. First the white one representing the *Amindra*'s last known position and then, to Freiburg's immense satisfaction, the yellow one marking the enemy's estimated position at a steady fourteen knots. Earlier in the afternoon, when the *Adler* had been thirty-six hours from the interception point, the *Amindra* had been dead in the water twenty-two hours from intercept instead of the twelve hours indicated by the yellow pin. The *Adler* was now facing at most no more than a fourteen-hour disadvantage.

And, significantly, the white pin showing the *Amindra*'s actual position was well south of her intended course. Either the other vessel was being appallingly navigated, which Freiburg doubted, or her problems involved maintaining a correct heading. That could mean a faulty compass, which Freiburg also doubted. Even in the unlikely event of a compass gone off, routine celestial observations would soon have informed the *Amindra*'s commander he was off course. It was more likely to mean that the other ship had been dead in the water long enough to drift off course. And even more likely that the *Amindra*'s problem had to do with her steering.

To someone wanting to stop a ship for a while without doing irreparable damage, steering control and engines were the most vulnerable areas. The signal from Norddeich said the *Amindra* had started her engines. That meant that they at least were functioning. Which left only a loss of steering. He knew all too well from his years of experience at sea that if a man could get into the steering-gear compartment of a ship it was a simple enough matter to severely damage the mechanism.

If his guess was right, and he felt confident it was, the agent Intelligence had planted aboard the British ship had finally done his job. And none too soon.

When Captain Penrose fled his cabin, or so Shirley regarded his precipitate departure, she wasted no time getting to the dormitory and Millis. He would be worried, wondering what had happened to her.

He had put the boys to work stripping their straw mattresses and hanging their blankets from the bunks to air. He was sitting on a bench with Barlow. A look of immense relief crossed his face when he saw her, but all he said was, 'You might have written.'

'I'm sorry,' she said, motioning for him to join her at the door. She hadn't anticipated the depth of his concern. When there was more time she would tell him how much it had comforted her to know he was at the other end of her life-line.

The boys stopped what they were doing to look at her hopefully. Barlow sat where Millis had left him, looking fixedly at his hands.

'I'll have an announcement to make very soon,' she told them, trying to keep her voice from betraying her sorrow.

'How'd you get out?' Millis asked, once they were in the passageway.

'Oaks is dead,' she said bluntly, ignoring the question.

'Dead?' he cried incredulously. 'How, in God's name . . . ?'

'Crushed under a crate in the hold.'

She wanted to say more but did not because that would have required explaining things she'd promised Penrose she wouldn't discuss.

'Have you told Penrose?' Millis asked.

She nodded. 'He and Mr Rosten . . .' She checked herself, realizing she was saying too much.

'Penrose and Rosten what?' he asked, his eyes fixing on hers, suddenly shrewd and demanding.

This was another side of Joe Millis she had not encountered before. 'I'm not at liberty to say just now.'

'But you were in the hold?'

'Yes.'

She had to tell him that much. How else could she explain how she'd managed to get out of the ventilator and knew what had happened to Oaks?

'What was it like in there?' Millis demanded.

'Just a lot of huge wooden boxes stacked everywhere. Why?'

'Probably full of Scotch and silk stockings,' he said, avoiding her question. 'I told the crew they could use beads to trade with the Indians in America, but they wouldn't listen.'

Shirley smiled wanly, feeling guilty about keeping secrets from him after he'd been so helpful.

'Captain Penrose has promised to get Oaks out as . . .'

The sound of Emergency Stations drowned her words. The siren was like a scream. Someone cried out in the dormitory. Shirley rushed in ahead of Millis. Barlow was on his feet staring at the ventilator duct.

'It wasn't my fault!' he cried.

It was the first sound he had uttered since Millis had found him stretched out on his bunk clutching the gold coin.

Shirley ran to him and folded him in her arms.

'There,' she crooned. 'It's all right.'

He sobbed into her breast. For a moment he thought he was with his mum. His mum held him like this. But it wasn't his mum. It was Miss Hunt. Being so good to him when he hadn't been nice to her at all. He put his arms around her and clung.

Tears filled her eyes. Holding him tighter, she turned to the other boys, who were more frightened by Barlow's sudden outburst than by the Emergency Stations alarm, and said, 'He's going to be fine.'

'He wanted to go,' Barlow whispered.

'Sssh,' said Shirley.

'Then he fell.'

'I know.'

'The box . . .' His voice cracked.

'Come and lie down.'

She led him to his bunk, the only one still spread with blankets. She folded them back while Millis picked him up and deposited him in it.

'Just lie there and rest,' she said, tucking him in. 'You can talk about it later. If you want to.'

He hadn't asked for Millis, she thought, but she did not feel the triumph she might have a day ago. She understood now that Millis had not been competing with her for the boys' favour. He was only doing the job he had signed on for. No, not just doing a job. He cared about these boys as much as she did. She'd let pride and insecurity colour her judgement.

The alarm for lifeboat stations sounded and the boys, wearing their life-jackets, began forming up in twos.

'Step lively, now,' Millis shouted. 'Stragglers will be keel-hauled.' More quietly, he said to Shirley, 'We can't leave Barlow down here. It may be the real thing.'

She did not feel as frightened by the prospect as she thought she might. In five days she had come a long way from the apprehensive girl in the Grosvenor House basement.

'. . . carry him,' Millis was saying.

'No,' she said. 'He'll go up on his own two feet with the others. Graham,' she called to the red-headed boy, 'from now on you're Barlow's buddy.' To the two boys left unpaired she said, 'Kenrick. Nye. You two are buddies now. Mr Millis, start the boys out. Come on, Barlow, we're going up on deck now.'

Barlow got up without protest and helped her get his life-jacket on. He and Graham, followed by Shirley, were the last out of the dormitory. Barlow kept looking back at her, as if to reassure himself she was there.

Barrett was standing at the boys' forward lifeboat station. She was glad she had sent Millis ahead with the first boys. If they had to take to the boats perhaps she wouldn't be in Barrett's. She was acutely aware of the absurdity of that notion. When she should be concerned about the ship being sunk beneath her she was more worried about sharing a lifeboat with a man who had tried to force her and failed. She moved away without looking at him.

'Miss Hunt,' Barrett called. 'You're at the wrong station.'

On the verge of calling back that she was happy where she was, she changed her mind. She was not going to run from him. She was not going to run from anyone ever again.

'Mr Millis,' she called. 'Will you take over back here, now?'

'Gawd,' Millis grumbled. 'Never a quiet moment.'

When she took her assigned place, Barrett said in a low voice, 'Still browned off at me, are you? I went at it wrong, I'll admit it. I'll be nicer next time.'

'If you ever try to touch me again you won't know what hit you,' she said evenly.

'You *are* browned off with me,' he said, grinning. 'You'll change your mind.'

Millis came strolling up from his station.

'Barlow's doing splendid,' he said. 'A proper little trouper.'

'Bugger off,' said Barrett.

'Thank you, Mr Millis,' Shirley said, sensing that he was trying to help her and wondering how much he knew, or guessed, about her and Barrett.

'If we have to do a bit of rowing we've a nice day for it,' Millis said, ignoring Barrett.

'I said bugger off,' Barrett growled, gripping Millis's coat front.

'If you don't want that arm broken,' Millis said amiably, 'I'd remove it quick if I was you.'

Barrett looked quickly up at the bridge, then at Millis, and dropped his hand.

'I'll see to you later,' he said.

'Lovely,' said Millis, grinning. But his eyes were stony.

'Joe,' Shirley said, 'you'd better get back with Barlow.'

She'd never before called him by his first name, she realized. Had she done it now for Barrett's benefit or because she'd begun feeling close enough to him these past hours to call him that? A little of both, perhaps. She was not sure.

At their forward lifeboat station, Lady Anne asked Donahue. 'Have you any notion what's going on? I've never seen Captain Penrose so preoccupied. Or uncom-municative.'

'If he hasn't told you he hasn't told anyone. Whatever it is, I don't like it. All this starting and stopping. You'd think he'd have the courtesy to explain.'

'I'm sure he has his reasons.'

'I'll say one thing for you British. You stick together.'

He looked around the deck and said, 'I don't see Rosten. Penrose won't like him missing lifeboat drill. If this is a drill.'

'He might be ill in his cabin. The poor man looks as if he hasn't been sleeping well. Shouldn't we tell someone to have a look?'

The drill ended before they could do anything about it.

'I may get my Rolls home in one piece after all,' Donahue said as the groups dispersed. 'If Penrose ever gets us moving again. I can understand what you mean by "muddling through" now.'

'Yes,' Lady Anne said, deliberately misunderstanding his remark. 'We do always manage to make do, one way or another, don't we?'

The latest threat avoided, Penrose left the bridge and sent Rosten down to the hold to stow the last of the ingots out of sight.

'Immediately you've done that I'll send men down to bring out the poor lad.'

He knew Miss Hunt had thought him heartless and he deeply regretted the necessity for appearing so. He felt Oaks's death keenly, both because of the boy's youth and the fact that he was a passenger whose life had been entrusted to him. As master of the ship it would be his duty to inform Oaks's parents. It was a task he did not relish. He put the thought out of his mind and focused on his most pressing problems. It would require at least half a dozen men to lift the crate. Even if they didn't see the gold it would be impossible to hide the condition of the hold and the makeshift patch from them. It was bound to encourage gossip. But as none of the crew had been in the hold before it was loaded, when its state was reported to him he could blame it on the poor quality of Greenock stevedores and welders.

Leaving Dutton in the cabin with instructions that when Rosten came looking for him he was to be sent to the steering-gear compartment, Penrose hurried aft. He found Perkins hard at work welding a metal sleeve around the full length of the damaged cylinder.

'Couldn't fabricate a new one, sir,' Perkins said. 'So I put together the bits of the old one. Next I'll put some stout metal bands around the sleeve to reinforce it. Won't be much for looks but it should see us to New York.'

'When will you be done?' Penrose asked.

'Another hour. Two at the most,' the other man replied.

'Let me know the minute you're finished.'

If Perkins's estimate was on the mark, the *Amindra* would have lost sixteen hours at the most, which meant they would be arriving at Halifax that much later than expected. He could imagine the flap there would be at the Admiralty until the ship was sighted. He considered breaking radio silence to report the delay, but quickly dismissed the idea. In another two days, well before they were expected in Halifax, the *Amindra* would be 150 miles off the coast of Newfoundland. Air patrols would sight her before there would be any real cause for alarm either in Halifax or at the Admiralty.

As he mounted the companionway to the deck, Penrose met Rosten on his way down to find him. Rosten smelled of the hold and his shirt was stained with sweat. He wearily informed the captain that the last of the ingots was safely stowed and the left-over boards from the broken crates well concealed.

'Well done,' Penrose said. 'Your efforts won't go unnoticed in my reports to the Admiralty, I assure you. Now, why don't you go and tidy up for dinner?'

Tonight Penrose intended joining his first-class passengers at dinner and restoring to the *Amindra* at least the illusion of normality.

'Oughtn't I to tell Miss Hunt we're ready to get the boy out?'

'I'll see to it.'

He knew it wouldn't hurt to mend his fences with her. He needed her co-operation about those blasted ingots she'd seen in the hold and he didn't like her thinking he was utterly heartless about the boy's death. Going to talk to her personally would demonstrate his concern.

Penrose sent for the ship's carpenter and the bosun. He ordered the latter to take six men to Number 2 hold to free Oaks's body and to send another group to the cold-storage locker to arrange a dignified place to stow it. He instructed the carpenter to build a coffin and find a flag in which to drape it.

Now for Miss Hunt. He knew she would be with the boys. She spent most of her waking hours with them. No question, she was a very conscientious young woman. He'd take Dr Grimes along to have a look at the other one, what was his name, Barstow? Barlow. He must remember that. It would be tactless to get the wrong name.

Some of the boys rose deferentially when he entered the dormitory with Dr Grimes but their interest in the newcomers did not last long. Within minutes they had returned to their various amusements. Miss Hunt was sitting on a bunk with her arms around the shoulders of a pale-looking lad. That would be Barlow, Penrose thought. Except for his pallor he appeared fit enough. Miss Hunt had probably been overly alarmed.

'I thought you'd want to know that I've arranged for Oaks to be removed from the hold,' he said. 'And the carpenter is making a coffin. We'll put it in a refrigerated place. Not quite what . . .' He hesitated, momentarily at a loss for words. 'It's the best I can do, I'm afraid.'

'Thank you,' Shirley said. 'I'm sorry I made such a scene.'

'Not at all,' he said. 'I'm the one who must apologize. I'm afraid I was rather short with you. But with one thing and another . . .'

'I understand.'

'I brought Dr Grimes to have a look at young Barlow. He seems to have come out of it quite well.'

'Yes. He saw it happen. That's what sent him into shock.'

'Indeed? I'd be most interested in what he had to say about it.'

Had the boy seen the ingots, too? If he had, did he know what they were?

'Only that he was there. I don't think we should question him. It upsets him to talk about it.'

'Very wise of you,' Penrose said, relieved.

Dr Grimes opened his black bag and began examining Barlow for the second time.

'I'd like to see where you're putting him,' Shirley said to Penrose. 'Gregory, I mean.'

'Of course. Why don't we go and take a look now. Millis can keep an eye on things here.'

Millis was not in the dormitory. He had asked Shirley if she minded if he went off to visit a seaman who'd invited him to have dinner in the crew's mess. Knowing the way Penrose felt about Millis she was reluctant to tell the captain where he had really gone.

'He's taking a shower,' she said. 'The boys can look

241

after themselves for a few minutes.'

Penrose accepted the explanation and led her to the cold-storage locker where a space had been cleared, a canvas spread on the deck and the surrounding perishables draped in sheets. It was eerie, she thought, but as much as could be expected under the circumstances.

'Best we could do, I'm afraid,' Penrose said again. 'But we do have a British flag to drape the coffin. A melancholy business.'

Outside he said, 'I haven't told Lady Anne or Mr Donahue yet. But I will at dinner. You'll be joining us, I hope?'

'I'll be there.'

She was ravenously hungry. She had missed lunch and had been constantly on the go for hours. A good dinner was exactly what she needed. She was growing callous, she thought, anticipating food so greedily when a boy for whom she was responsible lay dead. But one thing really had nothing to do with the other. Life went on. She'd seen enough evidence of that in London. Despite the threat of invasion and the bombings people had gone cheerfully about their daily lives, coping with each disaster as it came. Hitler would never conquer people like that. Their spirit was unbreakable. Andy Donahue would do well to understand that, too.

She had just reached her cabin when the *Amindra* began throbbing with the pulse of her engines and the thrust of her propeller.

They were moving again.

She dressed for dinner as carefully as she had the first night Captain Penrose dined with the passengers. But this time it was for herself, not to impress the captain. She no longer felt a need for that. Yet, looking approvingly at herself in the mirror, she found herself regretting that Joe Millis would not be there to see how she looked when she was all dressed up.

Lady Anne wore her evening dress and Donahue his tuxedo. Everyone seemed in a good mood to celebrate the *Amindra*'s return to life. Even Dr Grimes, who like the Chief Engineer rarely had anything to say, unbent enough to welcome Shirley before she was seated and tell her Barlow was doing splendidly.

'You'd hardly know what he'd been through,' he said. 'We sometimes forget how resilient young minds and bodies are. He's very fond of you, you know, Miss Hunt.'

'He is?'

It was an accolade she had not expected.

'You are marvellous with the boy, I must say,' the doctor continued. 'Your training, I suppose.'

Her training, she thought wryly. Fighting off Barrett in a dismal corner, competing with Millis for the boys' loyalty, crawling through ventilators, insulting Captain Penrose and Mr Rosten – she was ashamed now of the way she had behaved with them, and Joe Millis, too – that was her 'training'.

'I couldn't have managed without Mr Millis,' she said.

Penrose tapped lightly on a water tumbler with his butter knife to get everyone's attention.

'I know some of you are puzzled by today's unusual events,' he announced. 'And I think you deserve an explanation.'

'About time,' Donahue murmured softly to Shirley.

'Firstly,' the captain said, 'I have some very sad news. Some of you are already aware of it. Two of the boys Miss Hunt is escorting to America somehow got into the ventilating system and I'm afraid one of them suffered a tragic accident. I'm terribly sorry to inform you he did not survive.'

Lady Anne gave a little cry. Shirley knew she was thinking about her son.

243

'The other lad has quite recovered from his ordeal,' Penrose continued.

'Thank God,' Donahue exclaimed.

'Secondly, you must all be aware the *Amindra* has been experiencing difficulties. I can tell you now that our Third Officer, Mr Nutley, for reasons we shall never know, damaged our steering apparatus and then apparently took his own life by drowning.'

Shirley joined in the shocked murmur that ran around the table.

'The damage, I am pleased to report, has been repaired and we are now on our way again with every expectation of a safe, though somewhat delayed, arrival at our destination.'

Despite the delay, the *Amindra* was still eight hours ahead of the *Adler*. By the time the German raider arrived at the point of intended interception, the British ship would be more than a hundred miles west of it. With only a two-knot advantage, the *Adler* could not possibly overtake her before she reached protected waters.

Chapter Fifteen

Captain Freiburg almost always fell asleep quickly. Tonight he could not do so. His thoughts were roiled with coloured pins, white, yellow, black and red. Particularly white. He could see the chart in which they were fixed as if it were spread out before him. The white pin marked the last known position of the *Amindra*. Despite reports that the British ship had been dead in the water for some hours and almost certainly had lost steering control, the white pin was uncomfortably close to the place he intended intercepting her.

Assuming the *Amindra*'s problem was indeed steering, he had no way of knowing when control might be restored. Even now, as he lay in his bunk, the other ship could be under way again. If that were so, the *Amindra* could have an advantage of a dozen hours or more. And that meant one thing: she would escape.

He sprang out of bed, threw on his outer clothing and went to wake Lieutenant Sperling. He led the sleepy Navigation Officer to the chart room and with a thumbnail marked a crease across the *Amindra*'s route. The mark crossed it roughly 200 miles west of the interception point. Fourteen hours steaming from the enemy ship. 'Give me a heading for here,' he said.

He would risk getting that much closer to Newfoundland and then turn back along the *Amindra*'s intended course. Then it would not matter how quickly she made her repairs. Somewhere along that route he was certain to intercept her.

And it might work to his advantage to approach the

Amindra from the direction of Halifax. It would add conviction to the *Adler*'s disguise. The master of the enemy ship would assume she was a Norwegian vessel out of a Canadian port.

Friday's sparkling dawn found the *Adler* within fourteen hours of intersecting the *Amindra*'s route west of the original interception area. Captain Freiburg and half the crew slept in their bunks. Half the *Adler*'s complement was always at Action Stations.

A mote appeared just above the southern horizon, a black speck on a background of rose-tinted pearl. The lookout who saw it first wiped his binocular lenses to be sure it was not merely a salt fleck before alerting the officer of the watch. By the time the officer of the watch fixed his own glasses on it the object was identifiable as an aircraft, though still too distant for its type to be recognized. It was heading directly for the *Adler*, slowly, as if in no rush to get there.

The officer of the watch blew into the windpipe and informed Captain Freiburg. Freiburg got into the Norwegian master's tunic and cap, without which he never went on deck, and hurried to the bridge. By now it was obvious why the aircraft was closing so deliberately. It was a British Walrus seaplane, a single-engined patrol craft notorious for its lumbering slowness.

'Shall we prepare for action, sir?' the officer of the watch asked.

Freiburg shook his head. He would not take any belligerent action unless absolutely necessary, and in any case the Walrus would have already signalled to the warship that had launched it that it had encountered a Norwegian freighter. Even if they shot the Walrus down before it could signal that it was being attacked, not too difficult because it moved so slowly, the warship would only launch another patrol craft to come looking for the first one.

'Get thirty or forty men on deck,' he ordered. 'Tell them to wave and cheer and throw their caps in the air.'

Freighter crews were an apprehensive and bored lot. When a friendly aircraft flew over at low altitude it was as entertaining as it was reassuring to them. Every member of the *Adler*'s crew was dressed in clothing appropriate for a Norwegian freighter.

The Walrus was close enough now for the tricolour roundel of the Fleet Air Arm to be clearly visible. The plane descended to within 200 feet of the surface, putt-putting like a donkey engine and yawing from side to side like a huge, awkward bird. The face of its pilot was visible now, white below a close fitting helmet. Sunlight reflected from the observer's binoculars.

Three dozen crewmen had boiled out on the *Adler*'s deck. They waved and shouted and jumped up and down. A few threw their caps in the air.

An Aldis lamp blinked from the Walrus.

'What ship? Port of destination? Cargo?'

Freiburg scribbled some messages and sent them down to a signalman who knew Norwegian. They were to be sent by flag, not lamp. Flag signals were slower and quite possibly more difficult for a flyer to interpret than the Morse code dots and dashes of a lamp.

'Do you understand Norwegian?' the flags man signalled. 'Greetings from the *Ole Lavrans*.'

The answering signal from the Walrus's Aldis lamp indicated doubt and confusion.

'Does anyone aboard speak English, *Ole Lavrans*? Do you require assistance?'

Freiburg took his camera and went down to the deck. He waved at the pilot, held up his camera and gestured that he wanted to take a snapshot. The Walrus responded by dropping almost to sea level and slowly circling the *Adler*. The well-rehearsed crew responded with increased enthusiasm and more seamen ran out on deck to join them. The pilot thrust his head out of the window as the seaplane passed slowly along the length of the *Adler*, close enough to be struck by a stone flung from the deck. Freiburg pretended to take a picture and waved his thanks. The pilot waved back.

The Walrus lifted, ponderous as a pelican, and putted off, dipping its wings in a farewell salute. The crewmen massed at the port rail and waved.

Schramm stepped out of the companionway where he had been standing and said, 'Do you think he really swallowed it?'

'We'll know soon enough,' Freiburg replied. 'We'll see which way he goes and keep a sharp lookout.'

The Walrus dwindled to nothingness astern, two points off the port side. The *Adler* continued on course. Two uneventful hours passed before a lookout called, 'Smoke in sight astern! Two points to port.'

The warship that had launched the Walrus was coming to investigate.

'Have the ladies stand by,' Freiburg ordered.

Schramm sent a man below with the message.

The column of smoke became visible to the naked eye, thin, low down on the horizon and feathering out higher up like a plume. Forty-five minutes after the first sighting came a cry from the stern lookout, 'Mastheads in sight! Two points to port astern.'

'Bring up the ladies,' Freiburg said, lifting his binoculars.

There were two masts, thin and close together. Freiburg knew without having to consult his silhouettes that it was a cruiser of the Berwick class. Top speed of 31.5 knots to the *Adler*'s 18. There was no hope of outrunning her. Eight 8-inch guns, eight 4-inchers, four 2-inchers and eight heavy machine-guns. And no hope of outgunning her, either.

Freiburg ordered the wireless room to send the standard

British Merchant Navy signal, 'RRRR', 'Being attacked by German warship'. The signal would certainly be monitored by the *Adler*'s pursuer and would add to the deception.

Two seamen dressed in women's clothes and another in a suit, tie and wide-brimmed felt hat came on deck. One of the 'women' was pushing a perambulator. The man in the suit took her arm and, side by side, they followed the pram sedately along the deck. The other 'woman' followed a few paces behind, a large drawstring cloth purse dangling from her wrist.

'*Feindlicher Kreuzer in Sicht!*' came the call. 'Enemy cruiser in sight!'

Freiburg estimated the British cruiser was closing at a rate of only ten or twelve knots, which meant she was making something less than her top speed. It indicated to him that she was suspicious but not convinced the *Ole Lavrans* was anything but an innocent Norwegian freighter. The cruiser's master might, however, be intending to order the *Adler* to heave to and receive boarders. If it came to that, he would quickly order the camouflage dropped and his guns to fire. At close range, and with the element of surprise on his side, he might deal the cruiser a death blow before he himself was sunk.

And the *Amindra* would then sail triumphantly to Halifax.

The cruiser continued to overtake them. Freiburg could see her 8-inch turret guns trained on the *Adler*. Her captain was taking no chances. Any instant now Freiburg expected to see the 'K' signal, 'Stop at once', followed by the 'XL', 'Stop or I fire'.

A seaman's voice called off the ranges to the *Adler*'s hidden guns.

'Six thousand yards.'

'Fifty-five hundred yards.'

The couple on deck pushed their pram to the rail and looked across the sparkling sea towards the approaching warship, the woman shading her eyes with a white-gloved hand. The other woman took a handkerchief from her purse and waved it. Freiburg left Schramm in charge and went down to join them.

The cruiser drew abreast of the *Adler* at less than four thousand yards. Through his binoculars Freiburg could make out sailors clustered at the starboard rail and the mouths of 8-inch turret guns trained on his ship. He knew he and the *Adler* were under close scrutiny from the enemy bridge. Deliberately, he fixed his glasses on the British ensign snapping at the cruiser's bow and held them there. At that distance, off course, it would not be obvious to the British what he was looking at but they could not fail to see he was inspecting them closely. He let the binoculars dangle on their strap and ordered a signal run up.

He came to attention and saluted, saying to the seaman in the civilian suit, 'Your hat! Take off your hat!'

The seaman whipped off his hat and stood at attention, holding the hat over his left breast. The blue-bordered P, the red and yellow diagonally striped Y and the red and white checkerboard U flags blossomed from the *Adler*'s foremast.

PYU.

The international signal code for 'Good voyage!'

Freiburg broke his salute and put the binoculars on his eyes again. A cluster of three signal flags ran up a line aboard the cruiser and fluttered in the breeze.

PYU.

'Wave,' Freiburg ordered.

The man in the suit waved his hat, one of the women her handkerchief and the other her gloved hand. The cruiser wheeled and, with a burst of smoke from her stack, sped off in the direction from which she had come. Freiburg could hear the cheers rising from every quarter of the *Adler*.

'Congratulations,' he said to the two masqueraders

250

dressed in women's clothes at his side. 'When the war is over you should have successful careers as female impersonators.'

Though the *Amindra* was logging only her normal fourteen knots, because she had been helpless for so long and because the morning was bright and clear she seemed to race through the sunlit seas. From the bridge, Captain Penrose looked aft, where Shirley was leading the boys in callisthenics. Except for the outrageous antics of Joe Millis, it was a sight that added to his sense of well-being.

Millis was clowning, pretending to be unable to do the simplest exercises, and even from the bridge Penrose could see he was distracting the boys' attention. He wondered why Miss Hunt put up with it. She was, though he had not suspected it when the voyage started, a woman of spirit and determination. Perhaps, he thought, her forbearance was a way of showing gratitude for the way Millis had responded during the stressful period when Oaks was missing and Barlow was in such a bad way.

Despite her unexpected display of tenacity, she still seemed unable to control the man. He had told her Millis was not to roam the ship freely, yet the bosun had informed him that only last night Millis had been visiting the crew accommodation and had eaten in the crew mess.

'And asking a lot of questions, too,' the bosun added. 'Mostly about Mr Nutley.'

Penrose could not think why a man like Millis should be interested in the Third Officer's disappearance. Perhaps Miss Hunt had asked him to make some inquiries. She had liked Nutley for his way with the boys and she obviously wasn't satisfied that everything possible had been done to find him. Just as she hadn't been satisfied with the search for Oaks. While she was justified in the boy's case, she was quite wrong about Nutley and must be told that Millis could not be allowed to wander about the ship making a

251

nuisance of himself asking totally unnecessary questions.

He turned to see Briscoe, who had the watch, looking quizzically at the compass. Penrose had put the *Amindra* on the course which would take her to Halifax and soon his Second Officer would realize they were not bound for New York. This afternoon he would announce to passengers and crew that the ship was putting into a Canadian port for repairs to the steering gear instead of chancing New York with a makeshift hydraulic cylinder. In that way there would be much less speculation and he could explain the off-loading of part of the cargo by saying that shipping it by rail from Canada would make up for time lost at sea.

Shirley was demonstrating an exercise called the side-straddle hop when she was suddenly aware that she had an audience. The exercise involved jumping up and down and raising her arms. Her breasts bounced when she jumped. She would not have given the boys that particular exercise had she realized beforehand how it was, but once begun she thought it would only call even more attention if she stopped abruptly. She had always been somewhat more conscious of her body than most women of her age and her encounters with Barrett in her cabin and the paint locker had made her more so.

And Barrett was now part of her audience. Though she did not look directly at him she was still aware of his gaze. She knew his bold, brutal eyes were stripping her as he had been unable to do in the locker. To hell with him, she thought. Let him look. Looks could not harm her.

She jumped higher and more rapidly than before, counting, 'One. Two. Three. Four.'

Millis was aping her movements, pretending to be clumsy as a bear. The boys were laughing at him and the bird-like flapping of the exercise they were doing. Barlow laughed with the others. He was changed now not only from the boy who had lain transfixed in his bunk but also from the timid child who had fought to protect his comic books in the basement of the Grosvenor House Hotel.

Lady Anne and Donahue were also watching the boys' exercise. Lady Anne's smile was tempered by a sadness in her eyes. She was recalling the days when her son was no older than these laughing youngsters. Donahue, however, did not give the children his undivided attention. He, too, was aware of the intriguing lift and fall of Shirley Hunt's breasts, though he hid his interest much better than Barrett. Not well enough, though, to escape Lady Anne's attention.

'She's quite attractive, isn't she?' she asked dryly.

'I've always appreciated the better things in life,' he replied, unabashed.

Only Rosten was not taking advantage of the fine weather. Physically and mentally weary from the strain of the past days, he was resting in his cabin. He felt sad and empty. Now that he had nothing to occupy his mind and body he thought almost constantly of Marjorie. His only relief, and that was temporary, lay in contemplating the role he had played in one of the most momentous undertakings of the war. Despite the perils of the journey he was not anxious to reach Halifax. Once the gold was delivered he would return to being a glorified bank clerk in a reserved occupation. He had found that a hard role even when Marjorie was alive to offer him solace. Now she was gone there was nothing to which he could look foward.

His burned palm throbbed. Strange, while he was lifting the ingots and it should have troubled him most, he had been scarcely aware of it. He got up and changed the bandage, smearing on some of the ointment Dr Grimes had given him. Now that he was up, he thought, he might as well go on deck. At least he could be among people there.

Captain Penrose made his announcement after lunch. The reaction to it was less dramatic than he'd expected. Donahue wanted to know which port they were going to land at in Canada. If Montreal, he would arrange to have his Rolls-Royce unloaded and would drive it to New York himself. That way he would arrive ahead of the *Amindra*. He knew there would be a lot of red tape about taking the car off in Canada and getting it over the border but he had every confidence that his high-level connections in both governments would enable him to do so. He'd ask Shirley to make the trip with him, though he doubted if she would leave her boys. Between now and making port, wherever it might be, he would try to persuade her to stay over in New York a few days. What he had seen when she was bouncing around on deck was very tempting indeed. And she might be less elusive now than when he had made his first play for her. She'd changed during the last day or two. He had no idea why but she seemed somehow more self-assured. He knew the ship's First Officer, Barrett, had had his eye on her out there, too. His intentions were obvious. A handsome man. He wondered if Shirley was the type to be impressed by good looks, or whether she'd be more impressed by money and power. On the surface, she did not seem much impressed by either, which was a challenge in itself. He liked challenges. They were half the fun.

Penrose had refused to tell Donahue which port they were heading for. Wartime security, the captain said. But Donahue considered it more likely Penrose was just demonstrating his authority. Damned stiff-necked snob. Typically British. None of them seemed even remotely to understand that Britain was losing the war.

Before evening mess, Captain Freiburg went to the chart room for the shifting of Lieutenant Sperling's coloured pins. It had become a ritual in which he was joined by Schramm. The white pin still marked the spot where the *Amindra* had been sighted dead in the water. Freiburg had instructed Sperling to assume the British ship had overcome its difficulties soon after the sighting, and accordingly the yellow pin was advanced to within a few miles of the point where Freiburg had originally intended to take her. The black pin of the *Adler* was still eight hours from the *Amindra*'s route west of that point. However, it would be at least eighteen hours before the enemy ship could arrive at the place where Freiburg intended turning east to meet her.

Splendid, Freiburg thought. He would intersect her route with at least ten hours to spare and be certain she was still to the east of the *Adler*. It would not matter now how long she had been delayed. He had only to steer eastward along her route until he found her, rushing unwittingly towards her fate at the combined speed of the two vessels.

The red pin, which had marked the position beyond which the *Amindra* must not be allowed if the *Adler* was to intercept her, was no longer relevant. Instead of removing it, Freiburg had Sperling move it alongside the yellow. The yellow pin was no longer a source of irritation. In fact, he thought, with the red pin nestling alongside it, it formed part of a pleasing colour combination.

Freiburg ordered an officers' call after mess. It was time to reveal to the crew as much as was necessary of the operation and put the men to work preparing for it. He intended telling only Schramm and Sperling the entire operation, Schramm because he was his second in command and Sperling because the Navigation Officer must calculate the required new routes and headings.

'Gentlemen,' said Freiburg. 'Tomorrow, God willing, we will take the most important prize of the war.'

He waited until the excited babble died away.

'Because of its importance,' he continued, 'tomorrow's operation will differ from any we have previously attempted. You will be given further orders as the operation requires. Preparations will begin at once.'

He continued in greater detail, releasing each man charged with a specific part of the preparation immediately after he had received his instructions. Certain stores were to be assembled for quick transfer. Fuel transfer gear was to be readied. English- and Norwegian-speaking officers needed briefing. The Gunnery Officer must quietly prepare a detail of picked men to do what was necessary with the *Adler*'s guns at a moment's notice.

'I know you have many questions,' Freiburg said. 'But I assure you by this time tomorrow they'll have all been answered.'

Or most of them, he thought. There was one he would be unable to answer to anyone's satisfaction. He was not entirely satisfied with that one himself. He could see the political value of it, of course, but to him the *Adler* was more important than politics. Still, a sailor did as he was ordered.

He told Schramm and Sperling to stay when he dismissed the few remaining officers. When the others had gone he turned to Sperling and said, 'Bring your Denmark Strait, Norwegian Sea and North Sea charts to my quarters.' He took Schramm to his quarters to wait for the Navigation Officer and sat him down in a chair without answering the questions he knew lay behind Schramm's stolid expression.

Sperling returned with the charts.

'Put them on the desk,' Freiburg said.

Sperling let down the desk and deposited the rolled charts on it, not trying to conceal his bursting curiosity. He was emotional for a mathematician, Freiburg thought.

'Schramm, old man,' Freiburg said, poker-faced. 'What do you think of continuing your walk to Cologne on a different deck?'

'Sir?'

Schramm's unusually impassive face was as startled as Sperling's.

'We're changing ships with the British,' Freiburg said quietly.

Chapter Sixteen

For propaganda reasons the Reich desired that the American Special Envoy and the British children should reach North America safely rather than be taken to Germany with the *Amindra* and its priceless cargo. The only way to do that was aboard the *Adler*.

Freiburg understood this with his mind but found it hard to accept with his heart. Had he been able to think of an alternative he would have suggested it to OKM, the Oberkommando der Marine, even at the risk of jeopardizing his career, but he had been unable to think of any. He could not take them aboard the *Adler* and transfer them to a less valuable ship. There was no such ship available. Nor could he take them to a neutral port. The moment they got ashore the *Adler*'s presence in those waters would be revealed to the enemy and she would almost certainly be hunted down.

No, the *Adler* must be sacrificed. The OKM thought it a more than fair exchange. One merchant raider for a massive share of Britain's wealth and a stupendous propaganda coup. By considering the safety of the Special Envoy and the British children, Germany would reveal to the world and especially the United States, now wavering on the verge of assisting the enemy, that the Reich was humane and responsible, notwithstanding British lies to the contrary. And, by inviting neutral observers to view the cargo in the *Amindra*'s hold, Germany would also reveal to the world Churchill's hypocrisy in publicly trumpeting Britain's inflexible determination to resist invasion while secretly sending her wealth to safety in Canada. The effect on the British people's vaunted morale would be devastating.

The *Adler* would be exchanged for the *Amindra* only after her armaments and wireless had been rendered inoperative, the *Amindra*'s fuel tanks topped up from her own, and the *Adler*'s engines made incapable of propelling her at a speed of more than four or five knots. By the time she was sighted by the air patrol which would undoubtedly be launched from Newfoundland when the *Amindra* was reported overdue, the British ship with the *Adler*'s crew aboard would be well away.

To further mislead the British, Freiburg had received instructions to reveal inadvertently that the *Amindra* was bound for Dakar. His orders were, in fact, to deliver her to Kiel. He was to take her there by the same route along which the *Adler* had evaded the British to ravage shipping in the South Atlantic: north through the Denmark Strait between Iceland and Greenland; then a wide swing through the Norwegian Sea into the Neck, the narrowest part of the North Sea between Norway and the British Isles; and finally through the Gap, the heavily mined waters north of the Frisian Islands, to the broad mouth of the Elbe River and the Kiel Canal.

British auxiliary cruisers and aircraft from the Shetland Islands patrolled the Denmark Strait, their cruisers patrolled the Neck and their submarines lurked outside the Gap, but Freiburg was confident that he could outwit them just as he had done outward bound with the *Adler*.

The moment the captured *Amindra* passed out of sight of the relinquished *Adler* on a heading for Dakar, the *Adler*'s crew would immediately set about a task at which they were well-seasoned experts. Disguising their ship with the stores they had brought from the *Adler*, paint, brushes, spars and sections of wood, canvas and sheet metal, they would convert the *Amindra* to a Swedish ship.

She would continue in that disguise well into the Norwegian Sea, where she would be transformed again, this time into a Russian freighter. The *Adler* had already run the Gap as just such a freighter.

Schramm and Sperling did not like the notion of giving up the *Adler* any more than Freiburg had and, unaware of the nature of the prize for which they were exchanging their ship, complained bitterly. As bitterly as was prudent to one's commanding officer.

'I understand your feelings,' Freiburg said. 'But our orders are specific. And who knows, maybe when you discover what we're traded for you won't think it such a bad bargain.'

He refused to say more. He knew he could trust both officers with such vital information but Freiburg was just a trifle superstitious. He knocked on wood, he did not like spilling salt and he preferred that good news arrive in its own time.

Freiburg slept soundly until one o'clock in the morning, an hour or so before the *Adler* was to make her turn to the east to meet the oncoming *Amindra*. He joined Sperling on the deck and both men took celestial observations with the sextant for a position check. Sperling's last observations had been routine dusk sightings. There was actually no need for the early-morning star shots because Sperling's navigation was first rate and between celestial observations the *Adler*'s position could always be determined by dead reckoning. However, Freiburg thought it wise to be doubly sure the *Adler* made her turn at the proper time and place.

Not that a sea lane was like a highway, he thought, along which a ship travelled a narrow path. The *Amindra* could be to one side or another of the route on the *Adler*'s chart, far enough off it for the *Adler* to miss her if he depended only on visual sighting from his vessel.

It was shortly after 1 A.M. that the *Adler* reached

Sperling's dead-reckoning position for the turn. Freiburg was on the bridge for it, though he let the Officer of the Watch give the orders to the helmsman. It was not his custom to take over during routine manoeuvres.

At 2 A.M. the *Amindra* was some 230 miles from the *Adler*. After the *Adler*'s turn they would be closing at thirty knots, the sum of the *Adler*'s sixteen and the *Amindra*'s fourteen. Under eight hours sailing time. She was twenty-six miles south of the route along which the *Adler* would be steaming in minutes, beyond the twenty-mile radius of visibility from the *Adler*'s mast periscope. Except for the mid watch and Lady Anne, everyone aboard the *Amindra* was sleeping. For years Lady Anne had wakened at least once during the night. Before her son's death, a few pages of a novel or a glass of warm milk had put her to sleep again. Since then, however, sleep did not come nearly so easily. She was thinking of him now not as he was in the photograph on her dressing-table, a young man in uniform, but as he had been at the age of the boys she had watched doing exercises with Shirley Hunt, flushed and laughing, his life still ahead of him. How soon that life had been ended. And not even in battle.

Shirley's sleep was deep but troubled. She was crawling through confining darkness pursued by some nameless terror. The darkness wound tighter and tighter around her until she could scarcely move and the threatening sounds grew closer. It was Barrett coming after her and she was naked. His rough hand was on her ankle, dragging her back. His bruising grip moved to her calf and then her thigh and now the darkness no longer held her in a vice-like grasp but he lay heavy on her, mauling her with both hands. She was unable to move or breathe until all at once outrage gave her savage strength. She fought with nails and teeth, elbows, knees and feet, and he was gone and she felt ecstatically free. Turning on her side, she slept peacefully.

Aboard the *Adler* half the crew was at Action Stations or assembling stores in lifeboat-sized lots for the coming operation. The older men of the off watch slept as if nothing extraordinary were in the offing but the younger ones tossed restlessly or visited each other's bunks, speaking in whispers.

Freiburg was one of those who slept soundly, but he woke at a quarter to four as if an alarm clock had gone off inside his head. He dressed and went to the officers' mess, where Schramm and the pilot of the *Adler*'s Arado seaplane were to meet him at four. Over coffee from a captured Australian tramp steamer, cold sausages, fresh-baked bread and cheese, he gave the pilot precise instructions.

The Arado was to make a broad sweep to the north for 150 miles and if it did not sight the *Amindra* on its outbound leg was to make an S-search back, returning to the *Adler* in a series of curves crossing and recrossing the imaginary line along which the two ships should be approaching each other.

'Under no circumstances should she see you first,' Freiburg warned. 'If you sight a ship, let down at once and fly no closer than is absolutely necessary to identify her.'

He'd had a silhouette of the *Amindra* drawn up for the pilot to take along. It was unlikely that another vessel of the *Amindra*'s exact conformation would be in the same waters.

'Don't get close enough to be seen,' he continued. 'And, of course, observe strict radio silence. When you've found her, return immediately. No communications until you're close enough to the *Adler* to use the signal lamp. When I have her position, speed and heading I'll signal further instructions.'

While Freiburg was briefing the pilot, the Arado was being hoisted from Number 2 hold where, with folded wings, it was securely tied down to a wooden pallet. It was on the deck, surrounded by its launching crew, when Freiburg, Schramm and the pilot came from the officers' mess. The pilot carried a thermos of hot coffee and a packet of sandwiches.

'One would think you're going on a picnic,' Freiburg said with a smile.

'Flying's hungry work, sir,' the pilot said.

'You shouldn't be out more than an hour or two,' said Schramm.

'If everything functions,' the pilot said, gloomily.

On more than one patrol the Arado's engine had failed and the pilot had been obliged to set down on the sea and wait until the *Adler* found him. On one occasion it had been over seven hours getting to him.

Freiburg reached out to a mast and knocked on wood. The pilot did the same.

'*I* knock on wood,' Freiburg said. '*You* see that damned gnat of yours stays in the air.'

The pilot gave his sandwiches and thermos to a crewman to hold while he climbed into the cockpit. Only after he had them aboard did he start the engine. He ran it up for fifteen minutes, by which time there was light enough to see the undulating surface of the sea. He signalled with a thumb and the lines from the aircraft to the electric winch slowly tautened. Other lines connected the Arado to the launching crew. Not all the crewmen held lines. Several bore long bamboo poles with padded ends.

The winch hoisted the seaplane gingerly upwards until it was free of the deck, then swung it carefully over the side. The launching crew steadied the plane with their lines and poles as it was lowered. The critical moment would come when it touched the surface. It must nestle on the sea between swells. If disengaged too soon it could drop like a stone and damage the floats; if too late it might swamp.

Freiburg watched intently from the rail, Schramm at his side. If he lost the Arado he might lose the *Amindra*. It was agonizing to think that the success or failure of the war's single most important operation depended on that frail craft and the skill of its launching crew.

The Arado touched down. The lines fell away and the crewmen shipped their bamboo poles. The plane rose on an erratic swell and tilted awkwardly. A crewman swore. Freiburg held his breath. The Arado righted itself. The pilot grinned and showed a thumb again. Freiburg answered with the same gesture and heaved a sigh of relief.

The plane trundled along the surface, gathering speed, climbing swells and dipping alarmingly between them. Finally it lifted, hung and climbed. Freiburg watched until it vanished in the morning brilliance. He felt strangely superfluous. There was nothing he could do now. Everyone else had his job to do, however trivial. As at the launching of the Arado, there was nothing he could do or say to make the crew perform any better. He and his officers and petty officers had already drilled them to as close to perfection as they would ever be.

An orchestra leader, that's what he was. He rehearsed his musicians until they were letter perfect and when it was time to perform he stood before them with his baton and pretended to be leading them when all the while they knew exactly what they were doing.

The strange notion did not persist for long. What transpired between now and the return of the Arado was not the performance. It was only preparation. The real thing was still to come.

Captain Penrose was up well before seven in the morning. After Dutton brought him his tea he shaved, dressed and went to the bridge. It looked as if it was going to be another fine day, though far off in the distance to starboard the horizon vanished where the grey of the sea merged with towering clouds. Fog, perhaps, or seas rough enough to keep U-boats below periscope level. There had been no Asdic echoes during the night – he would have been wakened had there been – but it was too much to hope there were no enemy submarines prowling these waters. The *Amindra* was as visible as a new shilling on black velvet. He ordered a correction to starboard to take her towards the clouds. If they extended down to the surface they would provide a sheltering fog.

A ship's officer was at the bow rail looking out to sea. When he turned his back to lean on his elbows, Penrose saw that it was Barrett. The First Officer's watch did not begin until eight. Whatever the other man's faults, Penrose was obliged to admit he took his duties seriously and didn't watch the clock. However, Penrose did not much care for the way he was slouching against the rail. That sort of lax behaviour set a poor example for the rest of the crew.

Shirley had breakfast with the boys. Not, she realized with some surprise, merely from a sense of duty. She was beginning to enjoy Millis's company. She was also aware of his change in attitude towards her. He was more sensitive, more understanding. Even his jokes seemed to have improved, although that might be because she was no longer so prejudiced.

The Arado reached the outer limit of its patrol without sighting the *Amindra*. The pilot had seen a ship and grown briefly excited but soon observed it was a tanker and on an easterly heading. He believed he had been far enough from it not to be seen. He made an 180-degree turn and began searching along the route in a series of huge esses which took him twenty miles to either side of the centre line. He saw the wake first, a mere wisp of white foam spread fan-like on the surface of the sea. Minutes later the fan had a minuscule handle, a dark fleck at its point. He estimated it was a good twenty-five miles south of the track he had been briefed to follow but it was worth investigating. He turned towards the fan, letting down to approach out of the sun at low level. He flew only close enough to observe the ship's silhouette without being seen himself. He compared the silhouette with the diagram fastened to his left thigh with an elastic band.

No doubt at all, it was definitely the *Amindra*.

He noted his time and airspeed, made some calculations on his navigation disc reckoner and marked the ship's position on the folded chart fastened to his right thigh. He gave the Arado full throttle and sped towards the *Adler*.

It was now 6.45 A.M. The *Amindra* and the *Adler* were 110 miles apart. In less than four hours they would be abreast. If they continued on their present courses, they would miss each other by twenty-five or thirty miles. However, within half an hour Captain Penrose would be putting his ship on a heading taking him directly towards the *Adler* as he steered for the protection of the distant clouds. Even had he not done so, in less than an hour from the time the Arado made positive identification of the *Amindra*, Captain Freiburg would know her position.

After half an hour, the Arado climbed to gain a broader view of the sweep of ocean beneath it. The pilot had made many changes in heading in his search and he did not trust his dead reckoning enough to expect to find the *Adler* exactly where he calculated it would be. He was not even certain of the Arado's own position.

The *Adler* was only fifteen miles or so from the position he had aimed for. He dived towards her.

Freiburg saw the Arado from the bridge, and then the wink of its signal lamp. Schramm and Sperling were on the bridge with him, Sperling clutching a chart. Freiburg clattered down the companionway to the deck, the two officers at his heels. The petty officer flicking the shutter of a signal lamp did not turn at the sound of pounding footsteps behind him.

Sperling unfurled the chart on the deck and the three officers knelt around it, Freiburg and Schramm holding down the corners. The signals man called off the grid co-ordinates flashed from the Arado. Sperling marked the position on the chart.

'Signal "Well done," ' Freiburg said, still kneeling and looking up at the petty officer's back.

'He's still sending, sir,' the petty officer said, not turning. 'Heading, two hundred sixty three degrees. Speed, twelve to sixteen knots.'

'Got that, Sperling?' Freiburg asked.

'Yes, sir.'

'Pilot Officer Glimwitz signals, "Thank you," sir, and asks your permission to finish his breakfast now,' the petty officer said, turning at last.

'Granted,' Freiburg said. He got up with a groan. The steel deck was hard on his middle-aged knees. 'And ask if he has another couple of hours' fuel.'

The petty officer resumed signalling.

'Yes, sir,' he said at last.

'Tell him to orbit us and watch for further orders. Sperling, when will we be within twenty miles?'

Sperling got to his feet. Freiburg was pleased to note that the younger officer also groaned. Sperling's face showed concentration. Freiburg enjoyed watching him do calculations in his head. At the beginning of the voyage he hadn't trusted Sperling's figures and had made him do his calculations on the slide rule which was always at the

Navigation Officer's belt in a leather case. He had long ago begun to accept Sperling's mental calculations as accurate, however.

'Two hours and seventeen minutes, sir,' said Sperling.

'He'll have to top up,' Freiburg said. 'Bauer, signal Pilot Officer Glimwitz to set down for refuelling. Schramm, get up to the bridge and order full stop.'

It was better to lose a few minutes than risk jeopardizing the trickiest manoeuvre yet. The Arado had to be in precisely the right place at the right time and must succeed on the first attempt.

At 9.40 A.M. Penrose was strolling the deck with Lady Anne and Donahue.

'I wonder if he'll tell us where we're going,' Donahue said to Lady Anne. 'If it's Montreal I'd get that car of mine out of his way.'

He looked at the captain with a challenging half smile. Penrose didn't rise to the bait, thinking, you'll get it out of the way at Halifax when we offload a thousand crates or so of American office supplies.

'I wouldn't dream of asking,' Lady Anne replied with mock seriousness. 'Loose Lips Sink Ships, you know.'

Astern, between the hidden gun and the ship's aft mast, Shirley and Millis were playing a spirited though confused nineteen-a-side game of deck quoits. Though it might appear callous, she thought it was far better for the boys to be playing on deck than sitting in their dormitory thinking about Oaks in his flag-draped coffin among sides of mutton in the cold-storage locker.

Shirley was captain of one team, Millis of the other. When they chose sides, she had been stirred to see Barlow leaping from one foot to the other for attention, wanting to be on her team. She had picked him first.

It was Barrett's watch. For some time now he had been

scanning the horizon ahead of the *Amindra* through the bridge binoculars.

'See something, sir?' the helmsman asked.

'No,' said Barrett, continuing to scan the horizon. 'Looks like our captain's taking us into some weather.'

On the *Adler*'s bridge, Freiburg looked at his watch at 9.55 and then, pointedly, at Sperling, who was standing by with the unrolled chart in his hand.

'We lost time in the refuelling,' Sperling said calmly. 'Thirteen and one half minutes. We should sight the *Amindra* at ten ten and one half. If Glimwitz was correct in his position report.' He added charitably, 'Of course, it's difficult for him to be exact with so much to do. And aerial navigation isn't particularly precise.'

'I didn't even ask a question,' Freiburg complained with a smile, 'and I got a lecture for an answer.'

Overhead, the Arado was orbiting the *Adler* in lazy circles. When it wheeled past the bow, Freiburg could see Glimwitz's face looking out. It reminded him of the British pilot looking out of the Walrus. More than twenty-four hours had passed since the encounter with the British cruiser. Since it had gone back the way it had come, the warship almost certainly had not been heading for this part of the North Atlantic. The *Adler*'s crew would be well on its way towards the Denmark Strait aboard the *Amindra* before the British Admiralty learned from the treasure ship's master that it was being taken to Dakar. Even should the cruiser then be sent in pursuit, Freiburg would have nothing to fear from it.

Sperling was only three minutes and a few seconds off. At 10.14 the mast periscope lookout called, 'Masthead in sight! A point off the port bow.'

Almost simultaneously the Arado, coming around on a lazy turn off the stern, blinked a signal. Glimwitz had spotted the vessel, too.

His position report had been accurate. Had the *Amindra* not turned towards the cloud bank, the sighting would have been dead ahead of the *Adler*.

The petty officer had been standing on the deck keeping his eyes on the bridge.

'Go!' Freiburg called down to him.

The petty officer signalled with his lamp. The Arado had already wheeled sharply out of its orbit and was streaking towards the *Amindra*.

The British ship was heading for the cloud bank nestling on the horizon off the *Adler*'s forward port quarter, Freiburg thought. He ordered a correction to port. He would cut off the *Amindra* long before she could slip into the fog.

No one aboard the *Amindra* saw the Arado diving out of the sun in a silent slide until Glimwitz restarted the engine and pushed the throttle full forward. Shirley, Millis and the boys were still on deck, though no longer playing quoits. The boys and Shirley were sitting in a circle around Millis, who was doing his stout-woman-getting-out-of-a-girdle act. Captain Penrose, Lady Anne and Donahue had paused at the tarpaulin-shrouded Rolls-Royce in their promenade. The Special Envoy was insisting that the car be taken off if the *Amindra* put into Montreal. All of them, and the deckhands performing routine duties, jerked their heads towards the sudden burst of sound, startled and transfixed.

The Arado swooped towards the wireless antenna, dangling a six-pronged grapnel from a thin, strong cable. It was a manoeuvre in which Glimwitz was well drilled and which he had used successfully before on two occasions. The grapnel caught the antenna with a nerve-grating metallic scrape clearly audible above the roar of the

Arado's engine. The antenna tore free at both ends and the *Amindra*'s wireless was silenced before its operator could tap out 'AAAA', the signal for 'Air Attack.'

Without a word to Lady Anne or Donahue, Penrose whirled and ran for the bridge, forgetting both courtesy and dignity in his flight.

'Shirley! Boys!' Millis cried, his voice ringing with authority. 'Get below!'

It was only when she was leading the boys to a companionway that Shirley realized how quickly and unquestioningly both she and the boys had sprung to obey.

Donahue stared at the departing seaplane.

'What the hell was that?' he demanded of no one in particular.

'A German plane,' Lady Anne said quietly. 'Didn't you see the crosses?'

There must be a German warship not too far distant, she thought. Were the Nazis going to deny her even a last goodbye to her son?

'Some stunt, wasn't it?' he said admiringly. 'Those German pilots know their stuff.'

'When the ship that launched it attacks us I shouldn't be surprised if you lose some of your enthusiasm.'

'It wouldn't attack without warning. Penrose'll let 'em know we're carrying non-military cargo for the US and a bunch of children. Not to mention an American with diplomatic status. And we'll be on our merry way again.'

'I've always known you were misguided, Andrew. But I hadn't thought you a fool. Mr Rosten was right.'

'You'll see,' said Donahue, not taking offence.

On his way to the bridge, Penrose encountered Barrett coming down.

'Who relieved you?' Penrose snapped.

'I'm on my way to the wireless room, sir,' the First Officer said with surprising civility. 'To see if we can rig a

270

jury antenna.'

'Get on with it, then. But never leave the bridge again without permission. Is that understood?'

'Aye, aye, sir.'

From the bridge, Penrose ordered Emergency Stations, with the gun crew, as before, not revealing their presence. If the ship that launched the patrol plane found the *Amindra* it might be lured close enough for the stern gun to take it by surprise. The patrol plane had flown off to the east. Unless the German ship had greater speed than any he'd heard about, the *Amindra* would reach the fog bank she was driving towards before Jerry could reach her. He ordered full speed and kept his binoculars fixed aft on the area into which the aircraft had disappeared.

He looked down briefly to the wireless room and saw no activity. No one was climbing the mast to rig an antenna. Where the hell was Barrett?

The bow lookout shouted.

'Ship dead ahead! Hull down on the horizon.'

Penrose whirled without taking the glasses from his eyes. More and more of the approaching ship grew visible, as if it were rising from the sea.

A freighter! But still too distant to make out its flag.

Penrose's relief was short-lived. It might be a merchant raider. A number of them had slipped through the blockade. All the more reason for keeping the stern gun hidden. Raiders had no armour plate. They could be easily damaged. He ordered a hard turn to starboard. The stern gun would be of little use if the two vessels closed dead on.

Now he could see the ensign. Norwegian. Or so it appeared. Briscoe came up to the bridge for instructions and Penrose sent him down to have a signals man ask the Norwegian for identification with the Aldis lamp.

'And tell the DEMS lot to stay alert,' he said.

The approaching vessel was winking signals. It had been

271

too long since Penrose had been obliged to take down lamp signals for him to decipher Morse code sent so fast. A seaman came running up to the bridge with the Norwegian's signal scribbled on a message form.

'Antenna taken by German aircraft. Wireless useless. Enemy raider in area. Signal for assistance.'

Penrose crumpled the message form in a ball and thrust it in his pocket.

'Tell her to heave to and identify,' he said.

The seaman raced down to the signalman. The Norwegian vessel slowed but kept coming. Through his glasses Penrose could see two ship's officers and the helmsman on the bridge. The caps the ship's officers were wearing looked Norwegian. Two women and a man in a suit were on deck. One of the women was holding a bundle in her arms. Something wrapped in a pink blanket. A baby! He could make out the name on the bow. *Ole Lavrans*. If only the *Amindra*'s wireless was working he could signal Trade Plot and learn if such a ship was in the area.

The runner came with another message.

'*Ole Lavrans*. Bound for Cardiff with mixed cargo out of Halifax. Have you signalled for assistance?'

The Norwegian was less than two thousand yards away from the *Amindra* and still closing. Penrose thought the deck load at its stern looked suspiciously like that of his own ship. It was certainly large enough to conceal a gun. He did not know of any Norwegian merchantmen so equipped. Through his glasses he could see other deck loads, these small and covered with tarpaulins. Thirty or forty of the Norwegian's crew were at the rail, waving and shouting inaudibly. A dozen or more of the *Amindra*'s crew were waving back. Lady Anne and Donahue were close by, passing binoculars back and forth. Donahue waved his hat.

Penrose shouted down to his crewmen to get back to

272

their stations. Barrett still had not returned but Briscoe was back on the bridge now. Where was the damned Canadian? He'd had more than enough time to find a spare antenna and set a gang to rigging it. Leaving his Second Officer on the bridge, Penrose rushed down to the deck. On his way aft he collected the signalman and took him along.

Hurrying past Lady Anne and Donahue, Penrose said, 'Please leave the deck!' It was an order, not a request.

'That's a Norwegian flag,' Donahue protested.

'I think we'd better do as the captain asks,' Lady Anne said.

Rosten overtook Penrose as he neared the masked stern gun. He looked as if he had been sleeping.

'What's wrong?' he asked breathlessly.

'Get back!' Penrose snapped.

He ordered the stern gun unmasked.

'Prepare for action!' he ordered.

As the wooden sides dropped away and the gun crew slid a shell into the breech he barked a command to the signalman.

'XL!' 'Stop or I fire!'

The *Ole Lavrans* slowed, imperceptibly except to a practised eye. Had the Norwegian obeyed the signal or only reduced speed? Penrose wondered. He would give it another half minute. Signal flags ran up aboard the Norwegian. 'Engines stopped.' And an Aldis lamp blinked peevishly from its deck.

'Your government will be informed of this, *Amindra*,' the message read.

He would apologize later, Penrose thought. If apologies were in order.

Captain Freiburg's intention had been to close to within a few hundred yards of the *Amindra* before running up the battle flag and unmasking his guns. Then the enemy ship would unquestionably have no alternative but to obey his orders to heave to and receive boarders. At such point-blank range a single broadside would blow her out of the water. He had no intention of sinking the *Amindra* but her master could not know that.

That changed when the *Amindra* displayed her stern gun. He studied it through his glasses. A 6-incher. Trust SKL to overlook that bit of information. He would be obliged to open fire on the *Amindra* now. But not a broadside into her tempting hull. He must take out that stern gun, and before it could fire more than once. One shell from the enemy ship could damage the *Adler* and inflict casualties but unless it was extraordinarily lucky a single hit would not prevent him from carrying out his instructions. He ordered full stop. While the enemy was pondering the next move he would tell his gunners exactly what was expected of them.

Satisfied that the Norwegian had obeyed his command to heave to, Penrose instructed the gun crew commander to keep his weapon trained and turned to go back to the bridge. He intended putting the *Amindra* back on her course for the fog bank, which was now within less than thirty minutes' steaming time at full speed. There he would find concealment from the German warship which, signalled by the scout plane that had taken the *Amindra*'s antenna, even now must be racing to overtake her.

Barrett stepped from a sheltering doorway. He held a Sten gun loosely in steady hands, its muzzle tracing a lazy arc covering Penrose and the gun crew.

'Everyone over there,' he ordered. 'Quick-time!'

Chapter Seventeen

The gun crew froze.

'What the hell!' Penrose cried. He started to move, but was brought to an abrupt halt by a menacing gesture from the Sten.

'Over there,' Barrett ordered. His tone was humourless and deadly.

'Are you out of your mind?' Penrose demanded incredulously. His mind racing frantically, he tried to think of a plan. Any plan.

'You're relieved of your command, *Captain* Penrose.'

Penrose went cold. Suddenly the situation became crystal clear. Barrett was one of *them*. He meant to hold the *Amindra* defenceless until his fellow Germans could board her. Involuntarily he glanced towards the *Ole Lavrans*. If they were not already here in the guise of that Norwegian freighter, he thought. It was Barrett, not Nutley, who had wrecked the steering gear. How could he have been such a fool as to believe the young Third Officer capable of so insane an act?

'Rush him!' he ordered, taking a step towards Barrett.

The muzzle of the Sten lifted again and pointed into his face. He stopped in his tracks. No one moved. He would willingly give his life to save his ship's cargo but he knew it would be foolish to pit himself against the Sten. He would be dead before any of the gun crew could take adantage of the diversion even if they were rash enough to try, and at the moment they were still immobile with surprise. And he himself must live to activate the scuttling charges. Somehow he would find a way to get to the 'Spares' box before his ship could be taken.

'I will make sure you pay for this,' he said icily.

'It's already been paid for,' Barrett said. He smiled glacially. 'And very well.'

From the moment the *Amindra*'s stern gun was unmasked, Lieutenant Schramm held his glasses on it from a place of concealment. When the *Adler* made its approach only Freiburg, the Officer of the Watch and the helmsman were visible on the bridge. Everyone else except the decoys on deck remained hidden, even the Gunnery Officer, who was issuing a steady stream of corrections for range and elevation.

Schramm could see that something strange was happening aboard their quarry. The gun crew, hands raised, was moving back from its weapon. The ship's master, or so Schramm assumed he must be from the gold braid on his cap and uniform, made a hasty movement towards a lone man standing apart from the others, then stopped abruptly. The lone man had something in his hands, a weapon. He was obviously the agent SKL had planted aboard the *Amindra*. Concealment was no longer necessary. Schramm ran across the deck to the foot of the bridge. Freiburg was not looking across at the British vessel but was speaking into the tube.

'Captain!' Schramm shouted. 'Our man's taken their gun!'

'*Fallen Tarnung*!' Freiburg cried. 'Drop camouflage!'

Metal clanged on metal. The Norwegian ensign went down, to be replaced immediately by the Nazi battle flag. Aldis lamp and flags signalled 'K', 'Stop at once!' as the raider began to speed up again.

At the sight of the *Adler*'s broadside of guns and the unfurled German ensign Briscoe looked towards the stern for instructions from Captain Penrose. But he saw the captain and the gun crew lined up along the rail, hands raised. What the hell was going on? With all those guns aimed point blank at the *Amindra* there was nothing for it but obey the 'K' signal. He ordered Stop.

After Penrose's order to get back, Rosten had withdrawn only to the shelter of the deckhouse forward of the stern gun. He had heard the exchange between Barrett and the captain but could not see the First Officer. He stole a glance around the corner of the deckhouse. That was a Sten gun in Barrett's hands. Rosten was familiar with the Sten, as well as with other weapons. He had learned to use them in his two nights a week with the Auxiliary Military Pioneer Corps. If he could take Barrett by surprise and wrest the gun from him . . . but there was little chance of that. Barrett was far too powerful. But, Rosten thought, perhaps if he went around the deckhouse he could steal up behind Barrett and pinion his arms long enough for Penrose and the gun crew to come to his assistance.

A metallic clang rolling across the water distracted him from his purpose. He looked towards the sound. The Norwegian freighter was now close enough for him to discern that it had a new ensign, though he could not make out what it was. He did not need to recognize the flag in order to appreciate that the freighter was a disguised German raider. The guns where before there had been only hull plates revealed the bitter truth.

Bloody Nazis, he thought. They intended to destroy the *Amindra* with its vital cargo or, worse still, they would capture it. He was consumed with a cold rage that made him indifferent to the threat to his own life. He felt strangely exhilarated. His anger had left his mind as keenly logical as if he was at his desk in the Bank of England, totting up the market value of gilt-edged securities.

The Nazis were on no account to capture the treasure in the *Amindra*'s hold, or even to learn of its presence. Captain Penrose was obviously helpless. Rosten knew that it was up to him now. If death had to come, he was pleased it would come this way. A Jew, a single unarmed Jew, would render hollow what could have been Nazi Germany's single greatest triumph of the war. There was no way they could be made to pay fully for killing his wife but at least this would be partial compensation.

Keeping the deckhouse between himself and Barrett, he moved quickly and silently towards the bridge housing, walking, not running, to avoid an appearance of haste. Barrett might have allies among the crew. His hand did not tremble when he inserted his key in the 'Spares' box lock, removed rows of cardboard boxes and threw the copper arming switch without an instant's hesitation. He felt an insane urge to laugh. He suppressed it. How proud Marjorie would be, he thought.

He took out his silver pocket watch and noted the time. Except when the watch was being cleaned or adjusted he had carried it constantly for twenty-one years. Marjorie had given it to him when they exchanged engagement presents. In later years, when he reached a higher position with the Bank of England, she had urged him to give it up for a more modern and expensive wrist watch but he had refused. Now it would go down with him and the *Amindra*.

It was 11.19. In precisely 120 minutes explosions would wreck the *Amindra* and its hull would be breached in a dozen places below the water line.

He felt the greatest inner peace he had known since his wife's death. He felt no qualms at the prospect of dying with the *Amindra*. And if he could take a Nazi or two with him, so much the better.

Rosten replaced the cardboard boxes meticulously, relocked the cabinet and went on deck to join Captain Penrose. He feared nothing that Barrett might do but he wanted to tell the captain what he had done. Penrose

278

would no doubt be beside himself with anxiety. He must put his mind at ease.

In the dormitory, Shirley, totally ignorant of what was going on, was telling the boys about California. Although they were joining families in the eastern or mid-western United States, they were all curious about Hollywood. Had she visited a film studio? Had she seen Errol Flynn, John Wayne, Rita Hayworth or Betty Grable in person? She was obliged to admit that she had never been inside a studio, but she told them she had once seen Flynn's yacht off Santa Monica through a telescope on the pier. She'd also had a glimpse of Rita Hayworth leaving a première at Grauman's Chinese Theater. As a child she had shaken Charlie Chaplin's hand at a charity affair and once got the autograph of Claudette Colbert. The boys were impressed.

'Could have been in the films herself, if she'd wanted,' Millis said.

'She's pretty enough,' said Barlow. And blushed.

The other boys laughed, but with none of the malice they had shown when Oaks was among them.

The feel and sound of the engines stopped.

'Damn!' Shirley groaned. 'Sounds like the steering's broken down again.'

'I'll have a look,' Millis said. 'You keep the lads entertained and no pinching my jokes. All right?'

Then he did something Shirley found extraordinarily curious. He went to his cubicle and from where she was sitting she could see past the curtain as he opened his suitcase and took out a large black pistol. He thrust it into his waistband under his sweater at the small of his back. She looked around quickly to see if any of the boys had observed what she had but none of them was in a position to do so. Joe Millis was certainly full of surprises. This was one that would call for an explanation.

On deck, Millis found more of the crew than he'd seen together at one time since his show in the dormitory. They were standing in small, tense knots looking forward. Lady Anne and Donahue were on deck as well, a little apart from the others. Another vessel was approaching the *Amindra* just off the port bow. It was already close enough to see the German ensign snapping at its bow and the guns trained on the *Amindra* from its deck. A merchant raider with Norwegian markings. It was obvious from its wake that it had just turned to approach head on, allowing the *Amindra*'s stern gun the narrowest possible field of fire.

Millis looked quickly aft. A mast, cranes and the deckhouse hid the gun and its crew from view. He made his way sternwards, slipping from cover to cover until he reached the deckhouse. Lying flat on the deck, he peered around the corner. Barrett was sitting on the barrel of the stern gun, a Sten across his lap, finger ready on the trigger. Penrose and the gun crew were lined up along the taffrail facing him.

Millis reached back for the pistol in his waistband. One shot would knock the First Officer off his perch and they would have the Sten as well as his own Webley. He looked towards the bow. The raider was only a few hundred yards away now and blinking a signal. With dismay he recognized its message.

'Stand by to receive boarders.'

It would be worse than useless to kill Barrett and free Penrose and the gun crew. That would only reveal to the Germans that someone aboard the *Amindra* was armed. They might kill a few of the boarding party but they would be quickly overcome with an unnecessary loss of life. And a pistol the Germans didn't know about might prove invaluable at a more opportune time.

Still flat on his stomach, he eased back along the side of the deckhouse before getting to his feet and running on tiptoe, as noiselessly as possible, to Captain Penrose's quarters. The door was locked. He stepped back, drew his knee to his chest and kicked it open with his heel, trusting to luck that no one would notice the noise. The drawers of Penrose's ornate desk were locked. He ran out into the passageway and found a fire axe on a bulkhead rack. Heedless now of the consequences he smashed the drawers open and went through them. As he searched, he heard the raider approaching, its engine sounds throttling back to a low throb. A loud-hailer call came in heavily accented English, 'Passengers and crew of the *Amindra*. Remain calm and do not attempt to interfere with boarding operations. No one will be harmed.'

Millis found the two padlocked green canvas pouches Penrose had brought aboard at Greenock. Their weight and the brassbound holes in them indicated clearly that they were meant to be jettisoned rather than allowed to be taken. He paused on his way out, the pouches in one hand, the fire axe in the other, to look at the family pictures over Penrose's bunk. Somehow, he had never thought of a man like Penrose being a parent. And there was a needlepoint motto, 'Keep then the Sea, which is the Wall of England, And then is England kept in God's own hands.'

He put the axe back in its rack and tossed the pouches over the rail on the side of the *Amindra* away from the raider. They sank immediately. He thrust his hands into his pockets and with studied nonchalance, whistled under his breath, joined a cluster of silent crewmen watching the raider lower a launch and two lifeboats only a hundred yards away. The German ship was armed just below deck level with 5.9-inchers, astern with another 5.9-inch deck gun, concealed like the *Amindra*'s, and light anti-aircraft guns and heavy machine-guns mounted strategically along its length. Seen close up, it was obvious the raider's stack had been altered and some of its rigging was only for show.

Except for that and the guns, and the black and white German ensign, Millis thought ruefully, the *Ole Lavrans* was a harmless Norwegian freighter. Penrose apparently had not been completely taken in, though, he thought. He'd been ready to do something with the *Amindra*'s gun and obviously Barrett had stopped him. Barrett. That probably wasn't his real name. How had he managed to get aboard as First Officer? Whatever his methods, it was obvious they had succeeded and the Germans clearly knew enough about the *Amindra* to want her.

An Arado seaplane skimmed into view from the east, set down and taxied towards the raider to disappear under its lee. An electric hoist swung over the raider's port side and the Arado's pilot appeared at deck level dangling from the hook in a bosun's chair. In a moment the Arado appeared beyond the raider heading off to sea, propeller whirling. Heavy machine-gun fire from the raider tore splinters visibly from its fuselage. In a moment it was engulfed in flames. Then its floats, riddled with bullet holes, began to fill. Slowly the Arado sank beneath the surface.

Millis was puzzled. Why would the Germans deliberately destroy their own scout plane? Barrett had been placed aboard the *Amindra*. It was mystifying how German Intelligence knew there was a reason for wanting him there. And as mystifying how they had achieved it.

The launch and the lifeboats were approaching now, in V-formation with the launch at the point. Other than the two ratings operating the launch, its only occupant was a squat, thick-chested man wearing a double-breasted reefer jacket and a braid-encrusted peaked cap. He sat on a padded seat in the stern. The lifeboats bore two officers and twenty-six heavily armed sailors with tassels hanging from the back of their *Kriegsmarine* hats.

Penrose, Rosten and the gun crew came amidships, herded by Barrett. Walking close beside Penrose, Rosten whispered that he'd armed the scuttling charges. His grim expression unchanged, Penrose murmured, 'Right.'

'What's bloody goin' on?' a seaman cried.

'Throw down lines and drop the ladders,' Barrett ordered.

No one complied. He fired a burst from his Sten in the air. The sailors in the lifeboats shifted their weapons threateningly. But still no one moved.

Barrett nudged Penrose with the barrel of his gun.

'Order them to do it, Captain,' he said.

Penrose eyed him stonily.

'Stand clear, you men,' Barrett said to the gun crew behind Penrose.

They hesitated, then stepped away.

'It's your choice,' Barrett said, levelling the Sten at Penrose's belly.

Lady Anne ran up and stood beside the captain, Donahue at her heels. He tried to pull her away, crying, 'Don't be foolish!'

When she would not budge, he stepped clear, saying uncertainly, 'He's bluffing.'

Suddenly a seaman broke, and ran to push a rolled Jacob's ladder over the side. It clattered against the hull. The sound seemed to galvanize the others. Silently they dropped another ladder and threw lines to the sailors waiting in the boats to catch them.

A cap with a crusted visor appeared at deck level, then a tanned, weathered face, strong-featured, with dark eyes and heavy brows. Captain Freiburg reached up and, smiling, took hold of the rail and drew himself up the rest of the way. All eyes were on him. Millis took advantage of the moment to edge away without being noticed and quietly head for the dormitory.

Freiburg boarded the *Amindra* first, alone and unarmed, against the advice of Schramm. Normally,

Freiburg did not board a captured vessel at all. That was Schramm's job, accompanied by a specially trained party of men armed with machine-pistols, side-arms and grenades.

'Herr Gannion, isn't it?' Freiburg said to Barrett in English. 'Congratulations.' He indicated the Sten with a tilt of his head. 'That will not be necessary.'

Barrett let the Sten drop loosely to his side.

Turning to Penrose, Freiburg extended his hand and said, 'Freiburg, commanding the *Hilfskreuzer Adler*.'

The effrontery of the Nazi swine, Rosten thought, to offer his hand. Penrose would ignore it, of course.

But Penrose said, 'Edward Penrose, master of the *Amindra*,' with studied formality and briefly shook the extended hand.

Rosten felt betrayed.

Behind Freiburg, German sailors were streaming over the rail from the two ladders and quickly forming ranks. The British seaman eyed them curiously and, to Rosten's disgust, without obvious hostility. At crisp commands the sailors deployed along the deck. Two of them went briskly to the bridge companionway and disappeared inside it. Others ran to the officers' quarters or below to the engine room and crew accommodation.

Freiburg turned to Lady Anne and, putting his heels together and leaning in hint of a bow, said courteously, 'And Madam is . . . ?'

He wished Hilde could see how correct he was with this obviously aristocratic lady. She always maintained he had absolutely no social graces and no more dignity than a donkey.

Lady Anne did not answer. She cut him as if he were an uninvited guest at a party in her home. Donahue stepped forward and put out his hand.

'Lady Anne Saville-Fletcher,' he said. 'And I'm Andrew

284

C. Donahue. I'm American. Special Envoy returning to the United States with a personal report to President Franklin D. Roosevelt.' He continued easily as Freiburg accepted and released his hand. 'The prompt delivery of my report to Mr Roosevelt will be to your government's advantage.'

Freiburg nodded.

Lady Anne was furious, though it was evident only in the frostiness of her pale eyes. How could Donahue possibly believe these creatures were reasonable men? And how dare he embarrass them all by accepting the Nazi's presence aboard a British ship so easily and addressing him as if he were an honourable man? The Hun must be made to understand that this American did not, could not, speak for Englishmen.

'You wretched . . .' she began.

Penrose caught her eye and shook his head. Pray God let Donahue keep on! Donahue might yet get them out of this.

Lady Anne did not complete her sentence. Captain Penrose no doubt had his reasons. And why dignify this German creature by acknowledging he'd made her lose her temper?

'Other than Lady Anne and myself the only passengers are British children, a young American woman escorting them and an official of the Children's Overseas Reception Board,' Donahue went on confidently. 'The cargo is American property being returned to its owners. May I suggest you assure yourself of this and let us continue on our way? I will see to it personally that Mr Roosevelt is informed of your courtesy and co-operation. And the American press, as well.'

'Thank you, Herr Donahue,' Freiburg said. 'Lady Anne, please do not be alarmed. Neither you nor anyone aboard the *Amindra* will be harmed.'

'I am not alarmed,' Lady Anne said icily.

Freiburg smiled and tilted his head in tribute to her spirit and then, all business again, said crisply, 'Captain Penrose, if you will please take me to your quarters?'

Penrose led the way, wondering, in the uncomfortable silence between them, what the German's intentions were. Could he be after the pouches containing the *Amindra*'s secret orders? He doubted it. Such documents would normally be locked in a ship's strongroom. Penrose had kept them in his quarters only so that he could get at them quickly in the event of an emergency. That emergency was now, he thought ruefully, but how was he to reach them? Perhaps the German merely wanted to confirm what Donahue had said, and after inspecting the passenger list and bills of lading would let them go on. It was a thin hope, he knew. The enemy would hardly have gone to the trouble of getting one of their own agents aboard if they did not suspect something unusual. How had they managed to get Barrett, or Gannion, as the German had called him, in the crew? First Officer Campbell's accident had no doubt been arranged, but surely the Admiralty would have taken considerable pains in selecting his replacement? Barrett's papers had all been in perfect order. He had checked them carefully himself.

Perhaps the Germans didn't know what the *Amindra* was carrying, and putting Barrett aboard was only a way of getting an agent to America. Perhaps Barrett was meant to jump ship in New York and . . . That wouldn't explain his appearance at the stern with a Sten gun. Penrose was clutching at straws and knew it. But he hadn't much else left between himself and failure.

Yet, thanks to Rosten, it would not be a total defeat. A Pyrrhic victory, perhaps, but victory nevertheless. Penrose glanced at his watch but could not make out the time without his glasses. No matter. At 1.19 precisely his ship would be torn apart when the scuttling charges exploded.

He had never thought he would welcome that. It was still agonizing to contemplate but far preferable to the alternative. He must find a way of getting his passengers and crew off the *Amindra* before then, and without making the Germans suspect anything.

His cabin door was swinging open, its fastenings shattered. His orders! Oblivious of protocol he rushed in ahead of the German. His desk had been broken into, all its drawers pulled out and their contents dumped on the deck. The pouches were not among them. His stomach knotted. He had not only failed Britain and Churchill, he had failed them utterly. And it did not mitigate his failure that the Germans would be unable to capitalize fully on their success. With the evidence at the bottom of the sea, Churchill could claim the documents were forgeries. And the Prime Minister would sound convincing. But he, master of the *Amindra*, would know it was not Captain Edward Penrose who had denied the Germans their triumph. It was Benjamin Rosten. The bank clerk had triggered the scuttling charges. Had it not been for his prompt action all would have been lost.

He sat heavily on his bunk. He did not like displaying weakness to the German but his legs would not support him.

'Do you have whisky?' Freiburg asked solicitously. 'Would you like a drink?'

'Certainly not! Now, would you tell me why we have come here?'

Freiburg looked at the desk chair and said, 'May I?' before sitting in it.

'Captain Penrose,' he said, his elbows on the chair arms and his fingers laced together, 'I know there are explosive charges in position aboard this ship.'

Penrose stiffened. Pray God his face did not reveal his consternation.

'Nonsense,' he said, his voice steady. 'Why should I be carrying munitions to America? That traffic comes the other way.'

'Explosives for scuttling the *Amindra*,' Freiburg said patiently, as if he had not heard the denial. 'Have they been triggered? What is the delay? One hour? Two . . . ?'

There was a clock on the bulkhead behind the German, its hands and numerals large enough for Penrose to read the time from his bunk. He resisted an almost over-powering impulse to look at it.

'There are no such charges,' he said evenly.

If Barrett had the pouches the Germans would soon know he was lying. Not only that, but also where the charges were placed. But if Barrett had the pouches, he would have opened them by now and given the contents to the German captain once he realized the importance of what they contained. And in that event the German would not be questioning him so persistently.

Rosten. Had he got rid of the pouches too? How would he have known where to find them? And he had made no mention of the pouches when he whispered that he'd triggered the charges.

'I understand your feelings,' Freiburg said, breaking the silence. 'But we will find those charges even if you refuse to co-operate. It will simply save time for us all if you tell me what I must know. And if they have been triggered, time is important. Many lives are in your hands.'

'Lives?' Penrose demanded. 'Am I to understand you intend killing people to force me to tell you the location of these non-existent charges?'

What *would* he do if it came to that? Penrose wondered. But even as he asked himself the question he knew the answer. Under no circumstances would he reveal any information about the charges to the German. His fate and that of everyone aboard the *Amindra* weighed too lightly

288

in the balance compared with Britain's future.

'We are not savages,' the German said, unlacing his fingers, his eyes narrowing in anger.

Good, Penrose thought, he'd touched a nerve.

'I assume you intend taking my ship as a prize,' he said in the most reasonable tone he could muster.

The German studied him but did not answer.

'Some prize,' Penrose continued. 'The office equipment of a neutral country.' He forced a laugh. 'But that's your affair. I believe the practice is to take a ship's complement prisoner and sail your victim back to one of your ports with a prize crew?'

'Occasionally,' the German said.

Penrose stole a glance at the clock. It said 11.48. In one hour and thirty-one minutes the charges would explode. The *Amindra* would not go down immediately, of course, but there would not be a great deal of time to get passengers and crew into lifeboats and safely away from the sinking ship.

'The American . . .'

'Donahue?'

Freiburg nodded. 'He said there are children aboard.'

'Refugees from your Luftwaffe attacks on . . .'

'Where are they now?' Freiburg interrupted.

'In their dormitory.'

'You will take me to them,' the German said, standing.

Why not? Penrose thought. Particularly if it meant the German intended to take them off if he actually believed the *Amindra* was in danger of going to the bottom.

'Have you children?' he asked casually as he led the German out on deck. If the German had, all the more reason why he would want to get the evacuees to safety.

'Yes,' said Freiburg. 'And you?'

'Two. And a grandchild.'

It was the first time he had volunteered the information

289

to anyone that he was a grandfather. Why had he done so to this German? Certainly not to ingratiate himself with the man. Was it perhaps because he was so painfully aware that the fate of future generations might well hang on the fate of the *Amindra*?

There were a dozen or so of the *Amindra*'s crew on deck and half that number of German sailors. Aboard the raider, lying abreast of the *Amindra*, sixty or seventy yards to port, a gang was loading paint buckets and less identifiable material into boats and another group was heaving at what looked like a fuel hose. The morning's fog was still banked to starboard, an abrupt wall of thick, swirling grey mist.

Lady Anne, Donahue and Rosten stood together a little distance from the crewmen, watching the activity aboard the raider. Penrose went to them and said, 'Perhaps you should pack a few belongings. I expect they'll be taking you off soon.'

'Where to?' Donahue demanded.

'Aboard that ship,' Penrose replied, nodding towards the raider.

'You can't seriously be thinking of taking neutrals prisoners?' Donahue said to Freiburg.

'Certainly not,' the German said.

It surprised Penrose that the other man would lie.

'Where are you taking Captain Penrose?' Lady Anne asked Freiburg, as if addressing an impudent waiter.

'To see the children,' Penrose said.

'In that case,' Lady Anne said, 'I'll come along.'

'It is better you do not,' Freiburg said.

Ignoring the German, she linked her arm in Penrose's. It took him by surprise. She had never done that before. He understood she was deliberately trying to bait the German.

'I might as well come along, too,' Donahue said.

He didn't relish not knowing exactly what was going on.

Usually it was he who had all the answers. Now Penrose and Freiburg had them and he might learn something. He would not let Freiburg forget he was Roosevelt's Special Envoy. Perhaps he could convince him that he could do his country a service by seeing that the President's envoy was sped on his way home.

'Do you mind if I . . . Lady Anne?' Rosten asked.

Watching the Nazis, and seeing their hateful flag flaunting itself, he had entertained fantasies of taking Barrett's Sten gun and killing Freiburg and as many of his men as he could before falling himself. He knew it was impossible but the mere thought of positive action, of seeing Nazis bleeding on the deck, gave him a small measure of comfort. Marjorie would have been astonished to find him capable of such thoughts. He had never been able to bring himself to kill anything except bothersome insects. Now he relished the thought of killing human beings. If you could call Nazis that.

'The more the merrier,' Lady Anne said.

Freiburg paused at the dormitory door and reached out to touch its stout hasp, as if gauging its durability.

Inside, Millis was walking on his hands, a ludicrous spectacle for a man of his bulk, to the obvious delight of Shirley and the boys. When he first came below he had taken her aside and told her quietly that the *Amindra* had been taken over by a German raider but that she and the boys were in no immediate danger.

'What will they do with us?' she asked quietly, her face pale.

'Prison camp for the crew,' he said. 'I'm not sure what they do with children. You'll be repatriated, of course.'

'What about you?'

'Don't worry about me,' he said, falling easily into his clown's posture. 'My mum always said they could drop me in a midden heap and I'd come up smelling like a rose.'

291

'And if they find you've got a pistol?'

'What pistol?'

'I saw you, Joe.'

'Oh, that pistol! Just something I use in my act.'

'Be careful!' she said, gently touching his arm with her hand. He covered her hand with his so briefly she would hardly have been aware of the contact were it not for the lingering warmth.

The boys were restless and apprehensive. Barlow and Graham showed it the least. Millis enlisted Barlow for the lemon aid bit, substituting a biscuit for a lemon, and when he had their attention began walking on his hands. Coins fell from his pockets and rolled across the deck. The boys made a game of pursuing them.

When Penrose entered, followed by Lady Anne and the others, Millis snapped to his feet, his face still flushed from his exertions.

'Visitors, boys,' he announced loudly. 'Mind your manners.'

'Who are you?' Freiburg asked, visibly puzzled by the other man's appearance.

'Millis, your honour. Civilian and devout coward. War's not in my blood, you might say. So, if it's all right with you, I'll just pack my things and get out of your way.'

Freiburg looked quizzically at Penrose, eyebrows lifted.

'Not a member of my crew,' the captain said, making no effort to hide his distaste. 'He's a professional entertainer hired to help with the boys.'

Freiburg studied Millis closely. It was impossible to tell from the German's expression what opinion he formed of the other man.

'What is above?' he asked finally, looking up.

'Only the top deck,' Penrose replied.

'Have the charges been triggered?'

'I've told you repeatedly, there are no charges.'

But Rosten stiffened at Freiburg's question. Lady Anne and Donahue looked from Freiburg to Penrose, baffled by the exchange. Shirley, who was searching in her suitcase for a handkerchief for one of the boys, had not heard.

'You leave me no choice,' Freiburg said quietly. 'The children and yourself will remain locked in here until you are willing to tell me what I must know.'

'What's he talking about?' Donahue asked.

'Captain Freiburg has the quaint notion that the ship is infested with timed explosive charges,' Penrose replied lightly.

Lady Anne gave him a quick, hooded glance. She knew Edward Penrose. It was not in his nature to speak lightly. Even his rare pleasantries fell heavily. He was lying. She realized now that deep down she had felt from the second day out that he was concealing something. He had so often seemed strained. And there was his closeness with Rosten, who was not his sort at all.

'Are there?' Donahue asked. 'I demand to know!'

'Of course not,' Penrose said without emphasis.

Shirley, seeing the strained faces, returned to the group.

'What's going on?' she asked.

'I'm not sure myself,' Lady Anne replied.

'I leave you now,' Freiburg said. 'You others will come with me.'

Donahue took a step after him. Rosten hesitated.

'Come, children,' Shirley said.

'The children remain,' Freiburg said, turning. 'Until the captain is willing to tell me what I wish to know.'

'What's he talking about?' Shirley asked.

'He thinks Captain Penrose has explosive charges hidden to blow up the ship,' Lady Anne said.

'Do you?' Shirley demanded, confronting Penrose.

'Certainly not.'

Something faintly uneasy in his manner reminded her of

293

their confrontation about Oaks. He may have been lying then and he might be lying now. She turned to Freiburg.

'And you intend using the children as hostages?' she cried angrily. 'How dare you! I insist they be taken to safety.'

Freiburg looked embarrassed.

'It is your captain's decision, not mine,' he said.

'Then tell him to let them leave, Captain Penrose.'

'I'm sorry,' Penrose said. 'He wants me to tell him something I simply do not know.'

She looked to Rosten for help but he was studying his shoes as if suddenly aware that he had feet.

'Very well, then,' Shirley said defiantly. 'I'm staying with the boys.'

Penrose wanted to urge her to leave but he could not. Freiburg would know why.

'I'll remain also,' Lady Anne said. 'There are too many Huns out there for my taste.' If there actually was danger here she intended sharing it.

'Coming, Rosten?' Donahue said.

Rosten shook his head. He was not going to run off and leave the others. It was he who had triggered the charges and if the Nazi actually intended to keep them here he would share their fate.

Donahue hesitated.

'What the hell,' he said. 'If nobody else is going . . .'

'If that is your decision,' Freiburg said regretfully.

He turned towards the door again.

'Wait for me, your honour,' Millis said. 'I've got this terrible fear of being locked up. Got it from my dad, I did. Always in and out of the nick, wasn't he?'

Shirley was stunned. She felt betrayed and cheated. Just when she had begun to admire, and even care for him. He was abandoning the children who loved and looked up to him and whom he was duty bound to protect.

'Just let me say goodbye to my girl,' Millis said, taking her hand to draw her aside.

She tried to pull free but he gripped her upper arm so fiercely she clenched her teeth against the pain.

'Be quick,' Freiburg said. 'Captain Penrose, I am posting a man on deck above. When you decide to be sensible, give a knock on the overhead and he will fetch me.'

He went out without looking back, as if unwilling to face his captives any longer.

Shirley saw everyone was looking at them, even the boys. Millis was still gripping her arm. It was better to do as the coward wished and get it over with than endure the stares any longer. Sniffing contemptuously, she let him lead her to the bulkhead beside his cubicle.

'How dare . . .' she began furiously, keeping her voice down.

'Shut up and listen,' he said in a low voice, holding her eyes with his compellingly. 'There *are* charges in the holds. I don't know where or if they've been triggered. Don't look so startled, for God's sake. Pretend I'm whispering sweet nothings.'

Shirley forced a smile.

'That's better. I can't help if I'm locked up here. I'll see what I can find out.'

'What if the charges have been triggered?' Shirley whispered.

'I'll be back to get you and the lads out.' The note of confidence in his voice was convincing. Only he knew what the effort cost him.

For a moment she did not care if there were charges and they exploded. Her joy at learning that Millis was what she had come to believe was too overpowering.

'What are you?' she whispered.

'No time for that. Now kiss me. As if you enjoy it.'

295

She kissed him, and she did enjoy it.

'I've been wanting to do that since you gave me that dressing-down at Euston Station,' he said, releasing her. 'Ta ta, luv,' he went on in a louder voice. 'I'll send a postcard.' He struck an attitude.

Then he was gone.

The door clanged shut. Outside there were sounds of shuffling feet, of things being done to the door. The feet went off and then there was only silence.

Shirley went to sit with Barlow. Donahue's knowing smile, Lady Anne's disappointment and Penrose's disgust did not disturb her. She was sure of Millis now.

'Well,' said Lady Anne, 'we might as well make ourselves comfortable.'

She took a blanket from a bunk, folded it and sat on one of the long benches, using it as a cushion.

'Captain Penrose . . .' Rosten said hesitantly.

Penrose stopped him with a single stern look.

He looked at his gold wrist watch. Its face was a blur. He took out his spectacles, wiped them and put them on.

Two minutes past twelve. There was a powerful charge on the aft deep tank in the Number 4 hold immediately below the dormitory. In an hour and seventeen minutes it would explode.

Chapter Eighteen

Penrose was at first dismayed that Lady Anne had elected to remain with the boys. There was no reason why she should not be spared. On considering it, however, he realized it might well work to his advantage. Had she gone with the German, Donahue most certainly would have gone as well. If the German were not bluffing, and Penrose believed he still might be, it was possible he would think twice before permitting the cold-blooded murder of an American Presidential Envoy. The Germans might try to gloss over the deaths of British children. The outcry over the *Athenia* had been furious but in the end had meant nothing. But an American on a diplomatic mission was something else again. It was America Hitler wanted to impress favourably more than all the other nations of the world combined. If Donahue as well as the children went down with the *Amindra*, Britain would have lost a fortune but gained a huge propaganda victory. Half a loaf was better than none.

He was surprised at how calmly he was contemplating the deaths of thirty-six children and the others in the dormitory. Even his own. He had always known he was a cold man, despite the charm he could muster when necessary for passengers, but he was not inhumane. Not under normal circumstances. But these were not normal circumstances. He had a solemn duty to perform. Should he be tempted to weaken in his resolve he had only to remember what Churchill had said to him in the Cabinet War Room and consider the consequences to the whole nation should the Germans break his will and succeed in getting away with the immense wealth entrusted to him.

Yet he still could not bear to look at the children. All those bright young faces unaware that they had but an hour to live. Though he sat with his back to them he could not escape the sound of their voices. Miss Hunt had sat them side by side on bunks along the far bulkhead and was teaching them the words to a popular American song. He could not fathom how she had permitted herself to form an attachment to that wretched clown, Millis. It was a pity that she, too, must die, when her country had no part in this war.

Millis trailed behind Freiburg, and the sailor who had secured the dormitory door, hoping the Germans would ignore him. However, when Freiburg reached the companionway he turned and motioned for Millis to come along.

The entire crew of the *Amindra*, as nearly as Millis could judge, was sitting in rows on the deck, guarded by four sailors with machine-pistols. The raider had withdrawn another fifty yards. A fuel hose, buoyed by floats, extended less than half way from it to the *Amindra*. Men not manning the raider's guns or on lookout duty were elbow-to-elbow along its starboard rail watching the British vessel. The bridge of the *Amindra* was occupied by a German officer and a tassel-hatted sailor. The wall of fog to starboard seemed thicker. Either it or the *Amindra* had drifted. Millis took this all in quickly before edging towards a nearby companionway.

One of the sailors guarding the crew saw him and gestured with his machine-pistol for Millis to sit down with the others. He did so, loudly complaining, 'I paid for the best seat in the house and look what I get. A bloody outrage. Complain to the management, I will.'

Those close enough to hear laughed. The reaction was strained but genuine. It puzzled the German sailors for a moment, then one of them smiled.

Millis let a few minutes go by before holding up his hand to catch a guard's eye.

'The bog,' Millis said. 'Got to go to the W.C. . . .'

The German scowled at him.

'Anyone here know German?' Millis asked. 'I'm ready to mess my bloody drawers.'

Dr Grimes, who was sitting four men away, spoke to the sailor in German.

'You can go,' Dr Grimes said. 'But be quick about it. They're a nervous lot.'

'Tell him nature can't be rushed,' Millis replied, getting quickly to his feet and trotting to the nearest companion-way.

Immediately on returning topside, Freiburg had sent for his petty officers and set them to organizing search parties. He knew from experience the strategic points in which to place scuttling charges, having done so himself on several occasions to sink captured vessels. The bulkheads between the engine room and the adjacent holds: the British would certainly have placed charges there. But they would have set them elsewhere, too, having unlimited time in which to do the job. Even a single undiscovered charge would be enough to prevent him from carrying out his mission to take the *Amindra* back to Germany. He must find them all.

After he dismissed the petty officers he went at once to the captain's saloon. One of his officers had told him Gannion was there. Barrett was sitting at the head of the table with his feet up, a glass in his hand and an opened bottle of whisky by one foot, his Sten gun lying carelessly askew by the other. He reached quickly for the Sten at the sound of the opening door but, seeing it was Freiburg, sat back again.

'Join me, Captain?' he asked, raising his glass.

His attitude, both mental and physical, confirmed Freiburg's first impression of the man. Though he had done an exceptional job, Freiburg did not like him. He was one of those tall, handsome men who, blessed with good looks, expected success to be handed to them on a plate. Hilde would say he was prejudiced because he was squat and ugly. That was not the reason at all. It was just that such men considered advancement their indisputable right when others had to work hard for what they got. There were exceptions, of course. Captain Penrose, for example. Despite his stubbornness, or perhaps even partially because of it, Freiburg admired him. He had proved himself a capable adversary and one who was clearly willing to sacrifice his life in the performance of his duty. It was less certain, however, that he would be willing to sacrifice the lives of so many others as well.

'No time for that!' Freiburg said curtly. 'Have you any information on the charges?'

'What charges?'

'The scuttling charges. This ship is equipped with them.'

'Nobody told me. All I was told was to stop her and neutralize the gun.'

'Which you did splendidly.' *Einem das Seine einräumen.* Give the Devil his due. 'Did you find anything of importance in the captain's quarters?'

'I haven't been in the captain's quarters. I found the whisky in the pantry.'

'You weren't there at all?'

'It wasn't part of my instructions. What the hell do you expect one man to do, anyhow?'

It had been a member of the crew, then, Freiburg thought, someone who knew where the *Amindra*'s secret orders were to be found. And they definitely had been in the master's quarters. There had been nothing of significance in the strongroom. A party had broken into it and searched it thoroughly immediately on boarding. And another had gone to the master's cabin. It had been broken into before they boarded.

300

His respect for Captain Penrose increased. Though he had been surprised at the stern gun and prevented from returning to his quarters, he had had contingency plans for disposing of his orders.

'You cannot remain here,' Freiburg said. 'And stay away from the crew. Their anger might encourage them to rash actions. Go to your quarters until further orders.'

'Two of a kind,' Barrett said flippantly, getting up. 'You and Penrose.'

He picked up the whisky bottle with the thumb and forefinger of the hand holding the glass, the Sten in the other.

'What about those charges?' he asked.

Freiburg looked at him distastefully for a moment and left without answering.

'Two of a kind,' Barrett said again, shrugging.

As soon as Millis was out of sight of the Germans guarding the crew he stole down to the engine room. He did not enter it but instead peered around the edge of the bulkhead. There was only one German sailor there, a rifle under his arm and two potato-masher hand grenades dangling at his belt from metal rings.

Counting the four on deck and the two on the bridge that was seven, Millis thought. No, eight. Freiburg had posted another man on deck above the boys' dormitory. That left nineteen of them searching the ship. He needed to know where they all were before he could plan any effective action.

Cautiously he returned to the deck, keeping out of sight of the guards and the bridge. Before he could reach it, Barrett came round a corner, bottle and glass in one hand and the Sten in the other. He grinned evilly at the sight of Millis.

'What have we here?' he demanded. 'Get back with the rest of your crowd.'

'Can't stand crowds,' Millis said, slipping immediately behind his clown façade. 'Comes from being pelted when . . .'

'You heard me,' Barrett said, taking a step towards him. 'Shove off!'

'A skinful of whisky and a Sten gun do give a chap courage, don't it, now?' Millis said, deliberately taunting him. He wanted that Sten. He tried to convince himself that the gleam in Barrett's eye was over-reckless.

'You can come off that,' Barrett said, disappointingly controlled. 'You haven't got the Yank piece to impress now. Not worth the trouble, anyhow. Worst I've ever had.' He smirked.

'That's exactly what she said about you,' Millis replied, maintaining his smile with an effort. 'You promised to come after me once. Were you trying to impress her, too?'

Barrett looked at him, narrow-eyed. 'Come along then,' he said, turning away. Millis's heart leapt.

His back was tempting but Millis was unwilling to do anything to attract attention on deck. He fell in beside Barrett and said conversationally, 'Jerry was damn clever getting you aboard, wasn't he? However did they have you in the right place at the right time to get posted as a replacement? Bit of luck, wasn't it?'

'Luck had nothing to do with it.'

'You must be cleverer than you look, then.'

'And don't you forget it. I finished the original Barrett and took his place.' Barrett's tone was gloating.

'It *was* luck then, them picking a man that looked like you.' Somehow Millis had to break through the man's self-control.

'He was as ugly as you. But who on board knew Barrett? You Limeys are so stupid anybody could say he was him.'

'You're a clever one, ain't you?' Millis said, forcing grudging admiration into his tone.

'Won't help trying to get on my good side, you sodding

bastard.'

'Didn't know you had one.'

'Here we are,' Barrett said, stopping at a door. He stepped back, motioning with the Sten. 'Open it.'

When Millis did so, a shove between the shoulder blades sent him sprawling inside. Barrett kicked the door shut behind him and deposited bottle, glass and Sten tenderly on his bunk.

He turned towards Millis and said, 'I'm going to enjoy this.'

With practised music-hall skill, Millis grabbed himself by the seat of his trousers and pulled himself to his feet.

'Just an old trick I used to do for me . . .' He hurled himself to one side, his right foot scything towards Barrett at knee height, his hands outstretched to fend himself off the wall of the cabin. Barrett, taken totally by surprise, went down with a grunt of pain and anger. His head caught the side of the bunk with an audible thud. Senses reeling, he groped for the Sten. But Millis was in motion again, bouncing off the wall and stamping savagely on Barrett's outstretched left hand. Barrett hissed with agony as his fingers ground against the deck. Before he could recover, a foot smashed into his right arm, and Millis's body was launched across his chest to land anyhow on the bunk, covering the Sten. For a moment the whole small cabin seemed full of panting bodies. Then Millis's groping hand found the Scotch bottle. Gripping it round the neck he flailed backhanded at Barrett who was struggling to his knees. It caught him high on the side of the head with a splintering thud that sounded ominously loud in the confined space. Barrett's eyes glazed and he slumped sideways to the floor, blood and whisky starting to flow stickily down the angle of his jaw.

'Too bad about the Scotch,' Millis said breathlessly to his unconscious form. He sat heavily on the tumbled bunk and tried to recover his breath. A hard shape beneath his buttock brought him startled to his feet. In the stress of action he'd forgotten the Sten. It was digging into him painfully. Thank God the safety-catch was reliable, he thought to himself, remembering horror stories he had heard.

Barrett groaned, semi-conscious.

'No permanent damage to your looks, you'll be pleased to know,' Millis said.

He tore strips from a sheet, folded them for increased strength and bound Barrett securely hand and foot. He wiped away the blood on his face and gagged him.

'There,' he said, still slightly out of breath. 'Are we all comfy now?'

He bundled Barrett under the bunk and hung a blanket down over the side to conceal him, though he doubted that anyone would be looking in the First Officer's quarters, at least for the moment. He took the Sten gun out into the passageway and stowed it behind a folded firehose from where it could quickly be retrieved. Then he dusted his hands together, took a deep breath, and slipped off to count Germans again.

In the boys' dormitory, Penrose, Lady Anne and Donahue were playing three-handed bridge at one end of a mess table. Lady Anne had suggested a rubber or two to while away the time after discovering that one of the boys possessed a pack of playing cards. Knowing what he did, Penrose was not sure he could concentrate but knew it was essential for him to maintain an appearance that all was well. Shirley declined to make a fourth, saying the boys required all her attention. Rosten did not know the game and refused Lady Anne's offer of instruction as they played.

'It would only spoil the game for everyone,' he said apologetically.

In any case, he was far too nervous to sit still. How long

was Penrose going to hold out? he wondered. He, too, had heard Churchill's instructions, but Draconian orders issued in the Cabinet War Room did not seem nearly so simple to carry out in the presence of three dozen innocent youngsters. He loved children and envied those who had them. He and Marjorie hadn't had any. Doctors had told them there was no physical reason for it, but somehow it had never happened. It made him feel doubly guilty to be party to condemning other men's children when he had none of his own.

He paced the dormitory, looking frequently at his silver watch. There were times when he took it out of his pocket immediately after putting it there, as if he could not believe what he had just read.

'What's the matter with him?' Donahue asked, looking up from the cards.

'A bit windy, I imagine,' Penrose said.

It distressed him to speak so of Rosten, who had been such a great help in so many ways, and when the pinch came had triggered the charges. But it was essential to account for the other man's overt nervousness and that was what popped out. It seemed to satisfy Donahue's curiosity.

Penrose kept his spectacles on to see his cards. They also enabled him to keep abreast of the time, but not as noticeably as Rosten. It was 12.23. In fifty-fix minutes the charges would go. There was still a chance the German captain would relent before then and let the boys out. Clinging to that thought made the waiting more bearable. Thank God the boys had stopped singing and Miss Hunt had them doing quieter things. If he kept his eyes fixed on his cards and his mind on the play he was hardly aware they were there.

At 12.31 someone rapped sharply on the door and Freiburg's voice called, 'Captain Penrose.'

All eyes turned towards the sound. Rosten stopped his

305

pacing and stood transfixed. Penrose suspended the card he was playing in mid air and said loudly, 'Are you opening the door?'

'Not until you agree to my conditions,' Freiburg replied. 'But I thought you would be interested to know that we have found four of your charges: two each fixed to the engine room bulkheads, fore and aft. They have been deactivated.'

So, Lady Anne thought. There *were* charges. And Captain Penrose would not give in. She expected no less of him. She did not regret remaining with him. Were it not for the children and Miss Hunt she would welcome this opportunity to show the Hun what English men and women were made of. Perhaps then they would understand that if they could not break the will of one ship's captain they could not possibly hope to break the will of a nation. But it was ironic. Tony had died without facing the enemy. Now she might die resisting them, and with purpose.

Donahue sprang to his feet, his face livid.

'You son of a bitch,' he cried. 'You lied!'

'It's a ploy,' Penrose said soothingly. 'Don't believe . . .'

'It's no good, Captain.' Freiburg called. 'We have proof now. Where are the other charges? And how many?'

'Tell him, damn it!' Donahue cried.

'I know of no charges,' Penrose said calmly, loud enough for Freiburg to hear.

Donahue did not believe him. He hurried to the door and shouted, 'This is Andrew Donahue. I've got nothing to do with any of this. I'm an American.'

'I understand,' Freiburg replied. 'It was your choice to remain, however. You are free to leave at any time.'

'I'm ready now.'

'It will require a moment. The door is secured.'

Donahue looked back across the dormitory. They were all watching him. The boys looked at him fascinated, as if

306

he were some alien creature. Shirley seemed embarrassed by his behaviour. Lady Anne regarded him with amused contempt. None of them had asked the German commander to let them out. He'd been accused of many things in his life, Donahue thought, but never of being a coward. Yet it wasn't cowardly to want out of here – just simple common sense. They all thought it was, though, which added up to the same thing. He knew if he left he would never forget the expression on those faces.

'Forget it,' he called. 'I'm staying.' He stamped angrily back to his chair.

Shirley went to Penrose.

'Are the boys in danger?' she asked quietly.

'No,' he said.

Now she was certain he was lying.

'I insist the boys be allowed to go up on deck,' she said, her voice rising.

Millis had promised to get them out if there was any real danger, but how could she be sure he could do it? And he hadn't known about the charges. If he had she was certain he would have told the German captain. He cared for the boys as much as she did.

Rosten approached. He seemed on the verge of saying something but at the last moment he turned away.

'I am going now,' Freiburg called from outside. 'You have only to knock on the overhead to fetch me back.'

Penrose looked at his watch. Twelve thirty-five. Forty-four more minutes.

'Why are we all sitting around like a bunch of sheep?' Donahue demanded. 'Let's do something!'

Getting up he shooed boys off one of the benches and tugged at it. It held firm.

'Tell them to help me,' he said to Shirley.

She sensed what he intended.

'Boys,' she announced. 'Give Mr Donahue a hand.'

They attacked the bench in a mass and soon pulled it

loose. Eight to a side and with Donahue among them, they picked it up and ran at the door. The door rang with the impact but did not budge, and the sudden stop caused the bench to tear loose from the boys' grasp, sending them banging into one another. A heel kicked threateningly on the overhead and minutes later Freiburg was at the door again.

'If you attempt that again I will have the door welded closed,' he called. 'Then even I cannot save you.'

Penrose stole a glance at his watch. Twelve forty-three. Only thirty-six more minutes and all would be over.

Millis had located nine more Germans before he himself was discovered and escorted back to the deck to join the crew. Looking at the guards, who were paying special attention to him now, he wondered how he could possibly make good on his promise to get the boys out before the *Amindra* sank. If he could have found all the boarders he might have worked out some plan. With Barrett's Sten he could have surprised the Germans on the bridge and then these guards and, with the captured weapons in British hands, he could have taken the other Germans before they knew what was happening. If he could yet do all this before the charges went off he might still be able to get Shirley and the boys out. That was as much as he could hope for at best. Even if he managed to retake the *Amindra* there were still the charges to be reckoned with, and the raider, lying only a few hundred yards away. Once everyone was out of the dormitory and the charges detonated they could surrender. They would be prisoners but live ones and the *Amindra* would not become a prize. He should not have considered anything so elaborate. With the Sten for protection he should have gone directly to the dormitory and got everyone out. But Freiburg might still have had time to lock them up again and nothing would have been gained. Now, at least, he knew where to lay his hands on a Sten when he needed it.

The pistol in his waistband was still digging into his back. It occurred to him to be thankful he'd fallen forward only, during his fight with Barrett. But a Sten was much more intimidating. The Germans would be far less likely to try rushing him. The air on deck had grown perceptibly colder. The fog bank to starboard, closer now, had lowered the air temperature. He shivered.

Meanwhile, the search for the other charges went on. Far from reassuring them, the discovery of the four in the engine room had greatly added to the tension the Germans were suffering. It was noticeable that as they prowled 'tween decks the search parties were increasingly silent, occasionally surly. Even their iron discipline was beginning to break down under the threat of imminent death. More than one longing glance was sent towards the *Adler*, and brows were mopped ever more often, though the air temperature was dropping. As the obvious sites were exhausted, the areas searched were becoming more and more unlikely – and more cramped and airless. Physical distress began to supplement psychological.

Freiburg was relieved when a search party found a fifth charge, this one in the aft peak tank just over the screw. He had thought it a possible place. He knew he was risking the lives of his men, keeping them down below, searching, but he did not even consider bringing them topside. He would have preferred to stay below with them himself, to share their peril, but that would have been worse than foolhardy. A commander's responsibilities were not to be idly sacrificed to romantic notions of courage. Captain Penrose had elected to remain below, of course, but he had no choice. He was duty bound not to let the *Amindra* fall into enemy hands. But what about the children? Freiburg wondered what he might do if the roles were reversed. He was glad he did not have to make such a decision. Yet, in a way, he thought, as he paced restlessly, he had contributed to it. It was he who was keeping the children locked up. He could tell himself it was only because of Penrose's stupid stubbornness, that the British captain could free them with a word any time he wanted, but looking at the situation honestly, Freiburg realized the final responsibility for the children's lives rested on his own shoulders.

Back in the dormitory, Penrose, Lady Anne and Donahue had abandoned the pretence of playing cards. Penrose sat quietly, answering Donahue's angry questions with patient lies. Lady Anne joined Shirley and the boys. It had finally dawned on them that this was not just a game and they were in grave danger. They fell into frightened silence, looking to Shirley for comfort and assurance. She did her best to provide both.

'If there was any real danger Captain Penrose would say so and have us out of here in double-quick time,' she said, knowing it was not so. 'And Mr Millis will come for us at the first sign of trouble.'

She wished she could believe that. She knew he would try but what chance would he have? He might even be killed in the attempt. She found herself almost hoping he would not try. Wistfully she wondered where he was and what he was doing. Was he perhaps thinking of her?

Barlow and Graham were helpful. Though they were frightened, too, they did their best to conceal it. Graham was better at it than Barlow. They tried to distract the younger boys with stories from Barlow's collection of comic books and he offered to do the lemon aid bit for them. No one expressed any interest.

Rosten was bursting with a mixture of conflicting emotions. On the one hand, hatred for the Nazis, the thirst for revenge for the death of his wife, a yearning for an atrocity which would confirm German barbarism beyond doubt and provide the incident needed to bring America into the war on Britain's side, made him welcome the thought of the bloody death of everyone in the dormitory. But on the other hand, he was filled with guilt because their lives were in his hands as surely as they were in Penrose's. He was in anguish for all those poor lads sitting over there in huddled silence, torn with regret for Lady Anne and Miss Hunt, even for Donahue, whom he did not like at all. The man was no friend of Britain but he could have left and hadn't.

He had felt cheated when it appeared that Donahue might escape. Donahue's death would stir up public opinion in America as much as if not more than that of the children.

He looked, wincing mentally, into the faces of the children. That dark-eyed one next to Miss Hunt, his fingers wound in hers, his face pressed against her upper arm, might have been his and Marjorie's if they'd had children. The boy *was* his child, in a way. They were all his children. To a man with none of his own, all children are his. How could he deliberately sacrifice their lives on the altar of duty? Doing so would make him as barbaric as the Nazis. He should be thinking of saving them. But he could not do that if it meant allowing the *Amindra*'s cargo to fall into German hands. He agreed with Penrose there. If only somehow the Germans could be denied the gold and the children still go unscathed . . .

He stopped pacing and went to Penrose, his mind made up, feeling calmer than he had since being locked in.

'May I have a word with you?' he asked, his voice almost normal.

'Concerning?' Penrose asked.

Donahue was leaning towards them, intent and suspicious.

'Something personal.'

That should satisfy both men, Rosten thought.

Penrose hesitated, then permitted Rosten to lead him aside.

311

'If the Nazis knew where the charges were placed,' Rosten asked, 'how long would it take them to winkle them out?'

Penrose did not answer immediately. He studied Rosten's face, trying to determine what the other man was thinking. He put on his glasses and looked at his watch. Twelve forty-four. Thirty-five minutes left. Some of the charges were easily got at but four were behind cargo, two of them in Number 2 hold with the gold. It was a pity the charge on the Number 4 hold aft deep tank wasn't on a longer delay than the others, he thought. Once any of those other four charges went, the *Amindra* was doomed. The German commander would know that, and realize there was no point in holding them captive any longer. But it wasn't. It was on the same delay and when the others went, it went. And everyone in the dormitory with it.

'It may already be too late,' he said. 'Why do you ask?'

'I want to be sure,' Rosten replied.

'Sure of what?'

'That our secret's safe.'

'Jerry already knows,' Penrose said. 'But a precious lot of good it'll do him now. He's had it.'

That was what Rosten had wanted to hear. If it was too late for the Nazis to capture the gold he could save the children without breaking trust.

'Quite,' he said.

He went straight from Penrose to the bunks. Pulling himself on to a top one, he took off a shoe and, reaching up, began pounding the overhead with it. Everyone looked at him as if he had gone mad.

Penrose shouted, 'What the devil are you . . .' and ran to stop him.

He seized Rosten's leg and pulled. Rosten tottered.

Lady Anne could not believe what she was witnessing. That quiet, withdrawn Overseas Board official was behaving like a madman and Captain Penrose, *Captain*

Penrose, was attacking him as if he, too, were mad.

For a moment Shirley was too startled by Rosten's and Penrose's bizarre behaviour to realize its significance. Then she remembered Freiburg's parting words when he locked them in. 'When you decide to be sensible, knock on the overhead.' Rosten knew where the explosives were and wanted to tell. Penrose was trying to stop him.

She sprang from her seat between two small boys and went around the tables to Rosten's aid. He was holding desperately to a piece of piping on the bulkhead, with Penrose pulling savagely at his leg. She seized Penrose's arm with both hands.

'Stop this!' Lady Anne cried. 'Stop it at once! Is everyone mad?'

Penrose tried to jerk his arm away and, failing, flung Shirley from him. She fell to the deck. Lady Anne rushed to her.

'Are you all right, dear?' she asked.

She hadn't the faintest idea what had got into everyone but, whatever it might be, there was no excuse for Captain Penrose's shocking behaviour. Unless, as it appeared, the poor man had broken under the strain. She found that most difficult to believe.

Before Lady Anne could help Shirley to her feet one of the boys shot from the cluster and hurled himself on Penrose's back. Barlow. Graham followed, then all the others. Penrose went down snarling, and was engulfed by small bodies, all yelling at once.

'You boys!' Lady Anne cried. 'Come away from Captain Penrose. Miss Hunt, give me a hand.'

She seized a boy by the back of his sweater and the seat of his pants and lifted him from the mass. When she put him down he hurled himself back into the fray.

'Keep out of this, Lady Anne,' Shirley ordered.

Lady Anne regarded her coldly. She was not accustomed to being addressed so peremptorily. A sharp reply died on

313

her lips. She was not intimidated by Shirley, Lady Anne was not intimidated by anything, but she was deeply impressed by what she saw in Shirley's face. Resolution. Certainty. Rosten and Captain Penrose might be mad but this young woman certainly was not. She knew exactly what she was doing. Lady Anne sat down on a bench, a composed spectator, looking on at a scene of astonishing chaos.

Rosten pounded on the overhead again. He was answered by a banging from above. He climbed down awkwardly over Penrose's struggling form and said, 'I'm sorry, Captain. But you said the Nazis had had it. So there's no reason for . . . no reason at all.'

'You don't know what you're doing!' Penrose cried, muffled beneath the boys' bodies.

'Does anyone?' Donahue said, mystified.

He had kept his seat throughout the turmoil, rising only once when it seemed Lady Anne might need assistance and sitting back down when he saw it was unnecessary.

'Mr Rosten is trying to help us,' Shirley said. 'Lady Anne, I'm sorry I was rude.'

'You were, rather,' Lady Anne said with a smile. 'But I deserved it. Forgive me for being so obtuse.'

Penrose struggled to get up but he could not shake off the hands clutching his arms and legs and the bodies piled on him. Poor man, Lady Anne thought. It must be acutely embarrassing for him. Later, when he had quite recovered, which he surely must, she would assure him that it was all forgotten and done with.

Boots pounded in the passageway.

'Captain Penrose,' Freiburg called. 'You have made a wise decision.'

'It's not Captain Penrose,' Rosten called back, his gorge rising at being obliged to speak civilly to a Nazi. 'My name is Rosten. Benjamin Rosten. I can tell you where the charges are placed. But only if you bring the children out.'

Chapter Nineteen

The door opened and Freiburg entered, followed by an armed sailor. His eyes widened with astonishment at the spectacle of Penrose struggling on the deck under a pile of children.

'What is this?' he demanded.

'The man knows nothing!' Penrose cried. 'Absolutely nothing! Don't listen to him, Freiburg!'

'He wanted to stop Mr Rosten from calling you,' Shirley explained.

'How am I to know you are telling me the truth?' Freiburg asked Rosten, fixing him with dark, penetrating eyes.

'You'll have to take my word for it, won't you?' Rosten said coolly.

'No,' Freiburg said. 'First tell me where the charges are placed. Then I will release the children when all are found.'

Rosten shook his head. You don't frighten me, you Nazi bastard, he thought.

'The children first,' he insisted. 'When they're safe I'll tell you.'

'How can I be sure?' Freiburg demanded.

'I give you my word.'

Freiburg hesitated. Rosten wondered if a Jew's word meant anything to a Nazi, and if this one knew he was a Jew. He would not mind at all breaking his word to a Nazi but there was no need to further endanger the children by doing so. He could tell the Nazi everything, almost everything, and they'd still be too late to stop at least some of the explosions.

'It is not enough,' Freiburg said at last.

'Very well,' Rosten said. 'Miss Hunt, may I have pencil and paper?'

She tore a sheet from one of the children's notebooks and found a pencil.

Rosten sat down at a table and sketched a rough outline of the *Amindra*'s hull. He knew where the charges were located but not what the parts of the ship were called. Freiburg, Shirley and Donahue looked on avidly. Rosten marked each charge with an X. There were twelve in all.

Shirley sucked in a breath. There was one immediately below the dormitory. And Penrose had been willing for them to stay.

Penrose cried out in despair and momentarily dislodged some of the boys holding him down. They swarmed back immediately, like parasites on a host. The sounds that came from deep within Penrose's chest seemed almost sobs.

Freiburg studied the diagram thoughtfully. The engine room bulkhead charges were marked, but the Englishman was aware that those had already been found. However, he had also put in the one on the aft peak tank, which he could not have known was found. But how could he be sure the Englishman was not leaving one or more off the diagram? He wanted to believe the man and not risk the lives of the children.

'When will they detonate?' he asked.

Rosten got out his watch. Twelve fifty-six. The charges would explode at 1.19. Twenty-three minutes.

'Thirty-five minutes,' he said.

It was already too late for the Nazis to deactivate the charges but it wouldn't hurt to let them think they had more time than they did.

'In that case,' Freiburg said, 'you will all remain here for thirty minutes. We will easily have you out in less than five minutes.'

316

Rosten sighed. 'The charges are set to explode at one nineteen,' he said. 'And that's God's own truth. Now, will you let the children go? I'll stay here, if that's what you want.'

Freiburg ran for the door. As he raced along the passageway he called to the guard to take the prisoners topside.

'Thank you, Mr Rosten,' Shirley said. 'We'd have all been killed.'

'My government'll hear about this, Penrose,' Donahue said.

'Andrew,' said Lady Anne, 'don't be tiresome.'

When the children left him, Penrose lay back, numb with dismay. He wanted to remain in the dormitory but did not resist when finally Barlow and Graham each took an arm and led him after the others.

Freiburg pounded heavily to the top deck and called his men together. The search parties clattered up from below, relieved to be in the open.

Facing them and the captives, he said, 'Gentlemen, the *Amindra* has been fitted with explosive charges set to detonate in twenty minutes. It will mean the death of many, if not all.'

He did not believe that was entirely true, but if the Englishmen were to be persuaded to co-operate they must believe it. Four charges were obviously blocked by cargo and he did not have enough of his own men aboard to move it. And he had brought no crane operators. He would need English seamen for that.

'If we work together we can prevent this,' he went on.

Millis jumped to his feet.

'He's right, lads. Let's hop to it.'

'Bloody Nazis,' someone said. 'They'll get no help from me.' There was a murmur of agreement from among *Amindra*'s crew.

317

'Sit down, Millis,' another stated. 'This ain't no sodding music hall.'

'We don't mind Jerry going up in a blaze of glory but we don't want to go up with him, do we?' Millis shouted back.

The prisoners from the dormitory came streaming on deck, blinking in the light. Shirley wanted to hurry to Millis, but contented herself with a smile and a wave of her hand. Her place was with the boys. Rosten joined her. Lady Anne assumed a defiant stance near the crew, while Donahue stood a little apart, as if proclaiming his neutrality. Lady Anne had at first remained at Captain Penrose's side, assuring him it had been but a temporary aberration, that no one thought the less of him for it and that he must now carry on as if none of it had happened. The Huns must not see him like this. Penrose had only looked at her with tormented eyes, muttered, 'You don't understand. It's finished. Done for,' and closed his eyes wearily. Now he was sitting alone on the deck, his head between his hands, deliberately ignoring events he could not control. Despite the fact that he had been willing to let them die, Shirley was sorry for him. He was a travesty of the assured man he had been.

There was a long silence. Then, 'Only nineteen minutes now,' Freiburg announced.

Millis went to Penrose and dropped to his knees beside him, his back to the watching Germans. He shook him.

'Listen to me,' he said in a low voice. 'I'm Naval Intelligence.'

Penrose chuckled in bitter, amused disbelief without lifting his head.

'The night before you left London for Greenock you attended a meeting,' Millis said quickly, hoping desperately Freiburg would not interfere. 'In the Cabinet War Room. Rosten was there, too. You met Winston Churchill and the DNI.'

318

Penrose was looking at him now, his eyes narrowed.

'You had two green pouches in your desk,' Millis murmured. 'I dropped them over the side.'

'Then you know what we're carrying,' Penrose said, his voice barely audible.

Millis nodded.

'Then why do you want to help the Germans?'

'Because I think we can retake the ship.' He glanced over his shoulder at the guards and winked theatrically. He was sweating.

'Eighteen minutes,' Freiburg announced.

'You're mad,' Penrose whispered.

'Freiburg's only got twenty-six men,' Millis said urgently. 'If your whole crew pitches in Jerry'll be dispersed among them and not expecting anything. If we act together it'll be over before they know what hit them.' Ostentatiously he shook Penrose again.

'And the raider looking down our throats across the way?'

'We'll start up the engines and nip into that fog bank before they know who's in charge.'

Penrose stole a glance forward. Wind and current had moved the *Amindra* around until she was pointing towards the bleak wall of grey mist. The fog looked thick enough to carve and close enough to touch, though he knew it was at least a couple of ship's lengths away. But the *Amindra* was much closer to the fog than she was to the *Adler*, which now lay astern and broadside to her. When the *Amindra* started up, the *Adler* would have to make a wide turn to come after her. If its guns did not get her first. But as Millis said, the *Adler* wouldn't know at once who was in control of the British ship. And they might hesitate before firing on a vessel with their own captain aboard.

'I've a pistol,' Millis said, 'and Barrett's Sten.'

Penrose looked at him, startled. Barrett. Penrose

319

wondered if Millis had killed him. But there was no time to ask about that now. He was sorely tempted. It was an opportunity to snatch victory from the jaws of certain defeat. But what if it failed? The most dangerous gamble was not, as the Prime Minister had said, risking Britain's gold on a lone, unescorted vessel, but risking all on the slender chance of retaking the ship.

'Sixteen minutes.' Freiburg's voice sounded like a death-knell.

'Just get the crew going and leave the rest to me,' Millis urged, under his breath.

I'll do it, by God, Penrose thought. If the raider wakes up over there and wants a fight I'll give her all she wants. All I'm showing is my stern and they're broadside. If the *Amindra* must go down she'll do it fighting, like the merchant cruiser *Rawalpindi* less than a year ago against the *Scharnhorst* and *Gneisenau*, and not by ignominious scuttling. Yes, if the *Amindra* went down it would be with the Old Red Duster proudly flying.

Millis saw the change in Penrose before the captain spoke. His shoulders squared, his eyes gleamed and he looked younger than he was. Only moments ago he had seemed an old man.

'Right,' said Penrose.

He rose stiffly and strode across the deck to face his crew. Freiburg watched him quizzically.

'You men,' Penrose said. 'You will take your orders from Captain Freiburg until I tell you otherwise.'

Puzzled though she was, Lady Anne felt a great quickening of spirits. Captain Penrose was himself again. Even though he appeared to have capitulated to the Hun, something in his manner whispered to her that he was doing it with good reason, just as he obviously must have had good reason to risk the lives of his passengers.

The men muttered among themselves, not knowing what

320

to make of this, and Freiburg's quizzical expression turned suspicious.

'Why are you doing this?' he demanded of Penrose as the men began getting to their feet.

'I simply can't kill my ship,' Penrose said, and knew it was at least halfway to the truth.

Freiburg understood that and accepted it. He gave brisk orders to his own search parties.

There were seven charges to be deactivated in thirteen minutes. That on the aft deep tank was easily got at, as were two others, but the four behind cargo were another matter entirely. Freiburg sent men to fore and aft cranes to lift hatches before dispatching parties to the three accessible charges, one of his sailors with each gang. The others, including the rating on the bridge with the officer, went to the holds to assist in moving cargo. Out of the corner of his eye, Freiburg saw Millis moving off.

'Where are you going?' he demanded.

'Back to my little lads. They've missed me something terrible, they have. Maybe they could help too?' He smiled ingratiatingly.

Millis's behaviour in the dormitory had already convinced Freiburg that he was a harmless, co-operative clown. With an impatient nod he dismissed the Englishman from his thoughts and returned to more important matters.

Shirley had the boys sitting in orderly rows and was talking to Rosten. He had saved the boys and she no longer held a vestige of a grudge against him for his conduct when she found Oaks.

'Shirley,' Millis said quickly, 'something's up and I need your help. Yours and the boys'. There isn't much time.'

He explained quickly. He needed four boys to go below where the charges were being hunted. They were quietly to tell an *Amindra* crewman in each party that the ship was being retaken and to pass the word to his shipmates. Immediately a party located and deactivated its charge the *Amindra* men were to overpower any Germans with them and wait for the signal indicating the ship was back in British hands, one short blast of the horn. As the charges were deactivated and Germans disarmed, the boys were to report at once to Millis, who would be on the bridge. But there was to be no noise. He repeated that urgently.

'They could be hurt,' Shirley protested.

'Beats dying,' Millis said. 'We've only ten minutes. Eight minutes from now I want you to do something, anything, to get Freiburg's attention and hold it until you hear from me. All right?'

Shirley nodded. Already she was trying to think of some suitable and effective distraction.

Lady Anne joined them while Millis was explaining to Barlow, Graham and the two other thirteen-year-olds exactly what was expected of them. They would need watches to know to leave before 1.19 if the charges had not been found. Only Graham had one. Shirley borrowed a watch from another boy and Rosten gave Barlow his. It was a wrench, parting with the watch Marjorie had given him, but he did so willingly. Shirley had to retain her own watch because she needed to engage Freiburg's attention at exactly the right time.

'What on earth's going on?' Lady Anne asked.

'We're retaking the ship,' Millis said.

He expected a reaction of shock or surprise but all she said was, 'There must be something I can do.'

'Let me have your watch.'

She gave it to him, seeming to find nothing strange about his request. How utterly marvellous, she was thinking. In London the Hun was bombing helpless women and children. Now women and children were fighting back.

'Anything you can do to distract our friends across the water will be helpful,' Millis said, giving her watch to the fourth boy. 'Now we'll all set our watches by Mr Rosten's.'

'What about me?' asked Donahue, who, unable to bear being left out, had joined them. 'What can I do?'

'Just what you've been doing,' Millis said. 'Nothing. You're a neutral, remember?'

'But they would have let me die,' Donahue said indignantly.

'Now you're beginning to understand the Hun,' Lady Anne said.

Disgruntled, Donahue went forward, where crewmen had attached a hoist to his deck-loaded Rolls-Royce.

'What do you think you're doing?' he demanded.

'Got to clear the hatch, sir,' one of the seamen replied.

'Be careful. You can't get cars like that any more.'

He hovered anxiously over them as the crane lifted the car and pallet, swung them over the side and let them go. The Rolls hit the water with a splash. Donahue was struck speechless. When he could talk again he let out a string of obscenities, and leant over the rail, looking after his vanishing car.

The seamen were already removing the hatch cover.

'Where would a toff learn language like that?' one of them asked with detached admiration.

'He's no toff. He's a Yank,' another answered.

Lady Anne had gone to Penrose, who was alone again on the deck, and offered her arm.

'Shall we promenade?' she said.

'My dear Lady Anne, this is hardly the time . . .'

'It's just the time, my dear Captain Penrose. We're being watched from across the way. What could be more innocent?'

323

They strolled the deck as if on a pleasure cruise, Penrose lending an attentive ear as Lady Anne chatted. He even contrived a laugh. Lady Anne patted his arm.

After watches were synchronized Millis went below to where he had hidden the Sten. He took the opportunity to look in on Barrett, who made thumping noises at the sound of the opening door.

'Patience, mate,' Millis said. 'We'll have you out soon. One way or another.'

He put the barrel of the Sten down his trouser leg and the stock under his sweater. He went to the bridge companionway and waited.

When the four boys had gone, Rosten went forward to watch the activity at the forward hold where the gold was. Barlow was on his way down to that hold now. When he learned it was one of the places the charges were fixed he had insisted on going there. Shirley tried briefly to dissuade him, thinking that when he saw the place where Oaks had died he might be upset, but the youngster was not to be denied.

Donahue left the rail and rushed to Penrose, his face flushed.

'Did you see what your men did?' he cried, stuttering with rage. 'Did you order that? You'll damn well replace it.'

'Jerry's responsibility, not mine, I'm afraid.'

'It'll be after the war before I can get another car like that.'

'How awful for you,' Lady Anne said maliciously. 'If the war goes as you seem to think it will, there may never be another made.'

Below, gangs of seamen, each accompanied by a handful of Germans, were going after the scuttling charges. Now that they were working as one and with the

Adler standing off less than two hundred yards away, the Germans appeared to feel no threat from the British sailors. Millis had anticipated that.

When the youngster sent to the hold below the dormitory reached it, the charge had just been found. The British seamen and their guard watched tensely as the deactivating lever was turned. They all relaxed then, even the armed German, in a moment of relief very close to camaraderie. The British seamen began to talk and laugh boisterously. When the boy whispered Millis's instructions to the handiest *Amindra* seaman it was a simple matter for him to tip off his friends. Ostentatiously friendly, he offered the German a cigarette. Unsuspicious, the man bent towards the proffered light. A piece of two-by-four wielded by a brawny stoker smashed across the back of his neck. As he slumped to the deck an engineer caught up his machine-pistol. One down!

In each of the holds where access to the charges was blocked by cargo, twenty British seamen and half the remaining German sailors worked furiously side by side to clear the bulkheads to which the explosives were attached. One gang heaved crates from a tier and others slid them back to where they could be reached by hoists let down through the open hatches. To expedite clearing the area around the charges, the cranes picked up the crates, swung them over the side and dropped them into the sea, making room for those being slid back from the bulkhead.

On the deck above Number 2 hold, Rosten watched in relief as the crates he had so carefully repacked were shunted about the deck. Number 2 was not so crowded as the rest, and the crates did not have to go overboard. It was quicker and simpler just to shift them. Such was his new-found confidence in himself and Millis that he had no doubt he would be turning over the gold to the Canadian authorities before many more days went by. He was glad he would not have to account for a discrepancy. In the midst of it all, Rosten took a certain small satisfaction in the knowledge that he had concealed the spilled gold well and rebuilt the crates so solidly that they did not burst under the rude manhandling they were receiving.

In the aft hold, Graham approached a seaman snatching a respite from his exertions and whispered Millis's scheme. The word passed quickly from man to man with none of the Germans being the wiser. The way to the two charges was cleared at 1.17. Everyone, Germans and British alike, gathered to watch them being deactivated. Unobtrusively, the British seamen mingled with their captors. As the switch was pulled, the seamen fell on the outnumbered Germans. The struggle was quick and murderous. The startled Germans fought back, but were disposed of in hard-breathing silence.

'Raise a cheer, chaps,' a seaman murmured. The sounds of celebration covered the moans of the injured.

In Number 2 hold, where the gold was, the shifting of the cargo in the storm had made some of the crates difficult to get at, and the men worked frantically. When Barlow reached the hold with its vivid memories he did not immediately carry out his instructions. The hatch stood open and through it poured a luminous square of sunlight. Germans and British together cursed and sweated as they heaved at unwieldy crates. Though this was where he had seen Oaks fall to his death he could not associate the busy well-lit place full of frantic activity with the dim, lonely cavern where it happened.

'What the hell are you doing here?' a panting seaman demanded, wiping the sweat from his brow with the back of his hand.

'Sir,' Barlow whispered, coming close, 'Mr Millis is retaking the ship.'

'Millis?' the seaman said incredulously; glancing hastily

round.

'Please, sir, not so loud. When you find the charges and stop them from going off you're to knock down all the Germans. Everyone else is doing it, too. Tell the others.'

Briscoe noticed the pause in the frenzied activity, and called to the seaman, 'Stop skiving, Newcomb! And you, boy, get out of here!'

'You'll know they're all done for when you hear the signal,' Barlow said hurriedly. 'One blast of the horn.'

The seaman nodded hastily and said, 'Now off with you.'

Instead of leaving, Barlow retreated only far enough to hide behind a tier of crates. Mr Millis had told him to come to the bridge after the charge was deactivated and the Germans taken. The seamen reached one charge and deactivated it. Barlow looked at Mr Rosten's silver watch. It was ever so much nicer than his dad's tin-plated one. Some day he meant to have one like Mr Rosten's. One sixteen. Mr Millis had said to leave before 1.19. But he was not going to leave until he'd done his job. Barlow the Brave did not run.

In the hold around him, the tension increased. A German sailor back by the bulkhead cried out something he could not understand and a British seaman at the German's side shouted, 'There it is! Christ, I can't reach! Everybody out!'

It was 1.17.

Barlow scrambled up the crates like a monkey, shouting, 'No! Wait!'

The men paused in their retreat as the small boy ran across the crates towards the bulkhead.

Newcomb, the seaman Barlow had accosted, ran after him.

'Down there!' Newcomb cried as the others, British and German, resumed their rush to the far side of the hold.

327

Taking Barlow by the ankles, he let him down head first into the narrow space between bulkhead and cargo, shouting, 'The handle at the left! Near the top! Turn it!'

The German guarding the work gang put his machine-pistol between his feet and took Newcomb by the back of the belt to steady him.

Mr Rosten's watch slipped from Barlow's pocket. He reached for it frantically, only to hear it shatter on the deck below. He groped in the darkness behind the crates. His hand encountered smooth, cold roundness, slid along it and touched a flat, protruding bit of metal. He grasped it. It would not turn! The other way, Barlow the Brave. Hurry.

The handle turned.

Mr Rosten was going to be angry about his watch. But he had done it! Barlow the Brave had saved the ship.

'I did it!' he shouted. 'I did it!'

Newcomb pulled him from the darkness and dropped him shoulders first to the crate on which he stood.

'Now!' Newcomb cried, snatching at the machine-pistol between the German's feet.

Though startled, the German's well-trained reactions were quick as a cat's. He laid hands on the pistol at the same time as Newcomb, and opened his mouth to yell. As he did so, Newcomb's knee smashed into his face. Barlow heard the crunch as his nose broke and flattened against his face. He fell to his knees, dazed, spitting blood and teeth. Without hesitation Newcomb swung the butt of the machine-pistol which the German had relinquished at the unprotected head. The German was raising his hands to his face when the raw metal caught the side of his skull. The sound was obscenely soft. The man fell back without even a groan. An ooze of grey seeped from the deeply depressed puncture above his ear. He was dead.

Before the other Germans in the hold could recover

from their surprise, Newcomb had swung the pistol in their direction. The snarl on his face, no less than the spatter of bright blood across the knee of his trousers, shocked them into immobility. Before they could recover their wits, each was seized and overpowered.

One unwary Nazi put up a struggle. He might have broken free had not Briscoe, with a speed that was pure reflex, hurled at him one of Captain Penrose's discarded welding rods. The point took him in the very centre of his unguarded throat and sank through to the spine. The impact tore his body from the hands of the two seamen who held him. They looked down at the corpse with horror. Then one bent sideways and was noisily sick. There was no further resistance in Number 2 hold, and Newcomb could put down the pistol on a nearby crate and sink to the floor, his knees, trembling with reaction, too weak to hold him.

Barlow had picked himself up and had run across the crates towards the door. He paused only long enough to be sure all the Germans were subdued before dashing for the companionway to the deck. Just wait until Mr Millis heard what he had done! If only, he thought, he had not broken Mr Rosten's watch.

After Millis left her, Shirley divided her attention between her watch and Captain Freiburg. The German was prowling the deck, going from one open hatch to the other and back again. It was less than eight minutes after Millis's hurried departure when Freiburg approached on his way to the forward hatch. She must stop him now or it might be too late. She reached out and plucked at his sleeve as he picked his way past the sitting boys. She had been thinking how well behaved they were. American boys this age could not be made to sit still for a minute.

Freiburg stopped but stood poised to continue on his way, regarding her impatiently but politely.

'Captain Freiburg,' she said firmly. 'How long are these children to be left sitting here?'

It was difficult to show indignation about the boys being required to remain on deck, she thought, considering the fact that only a few minutes before this same man had ordered them locked in to face death.

'Only as long as necessary,' Freiburg said. 'Now, if you please will . . .'

Clutching his arm with both hands when he turned away as he spoke, she said, 'I do not please. And I'm not pleased by anything you've done. You were willing to sacrifice these children and the lives of civilians and neutrals. For what reason I don't know. And I don't care because there can't be sufficient reason.'

She did not sound like herself talking. So stuffy and pedantic. But it seemed to be effective. He was obviously anxious to go but he was listening.

'These youngsters have already had a terrible shock. One of their little friends was killed in an accident . . .'

'I am sorry to learn this, madam, but . . .'

'. . . and then you had them locked in their dormitory.'

'Most regrettable, I agree. But necessary. And now I must leave you.'

He had stolen a glance at his watch. Shirley looked at hers, as well. One eighteen. She must keep him another minute.

'Boys,' she said. 'Stand up and let the captain have a look at you.'

The boys got to their feet.

'Can you look them in the face?' Shirley demanded theatrically. 'All these innocent young lives you were willing to sacrifice?'

Freiburg looked at them involuntarily, then at his watch.

Half a minute past 1.19. Unless the Englishman had lied or the timing devices were faulty, the *Amindra* was out of danger. He relaxed.

Shirley saw it. She looked at her own watch. The danger of explosion apparently was over but she was not sure how long Millis wanted Freiburg occupied. She would keep him here as long as she could to be on the safe side.

'I suppose in wartime you have to do things you'd rather not,' she said, less belligerently, not meaning it, trying to be consciously charming.

'I am happy you understand,' Freiburg said. 'I hope you will say the same to Herr Donahue. I would not want him to take a bad opinion of us to America.'

'America? We're not going to Germany?'

'It will all be explained very soon,' Freiburg said. 'And now I really must . . .'

A brief horn blast interrupted him.

The first two boys had come to Millis at the foot of the bridge companionway soon after he took up his vigil there. When the hand of his watch moved towards the nineteen minute mark and neither Graham nor Barlow had arrived, Millis began to fear the charges had not been reached. He braced himself for the explosions, hoping the boys and the crewmen had taken themselves out of danger. But one nineteen passed quietly. The charges had been found and deactivated. But what had happened below? Now he had a greater fear than for the safety of the boys and the crew. If they had not recaptured the ship he would have made a catastrophic blunder in persuading Penrose to co-operate with the Germans.

Graham arrived breathless to report the aft hold charges had been deactivated and the Germans disarmed.

'Slip down to Number 2 hold and see what's going on,' Millis said. 'Don't attract any attention.'

Graham met an excited Barlow coming up from below. Together they made for the bridge. On the way Barlow told him what had happened.

'Mr Millis will be pleased but I wouldn't say as much for Mr Rosten,' Graham said.

Millis had the Sten in his hand when Barlow reached him.

'Our lot beat their lot,' Barlow said laconically, 'and I did one of the bombs myself.' He eyed the Sten admiringly. 'And would you explain to Mr Rosten? I broke his watch, I'm afraid.'

'Don't worry, he'll understand,' Millis said, smiling. 'Now nip down like a good lad and fetch Captain Penrose.'

Millis crept up the companionway steps and, when he reached the bridge, crouched and looked in cautiously. The German officer stood with his back to him, looking down at the deck.

'Don't move,' Millis said in German. 'There's a Sten at your back. And don't raise your hands. Be natural.'

The officer stiffened and began to turn.

'Don't look at me,' Millis ordered, letting the German see his finger tighten on the trigger.

The German looked hastily away.

'One short blast of the horn,' Millis said. 'If it's any more than that, I'll kill you.'

The German reached slowly for the lanyard, grasped it, held it for a moment as if deciding whether to obey, and gave it one quick pull. The blast was so short and abrupt that it seemed almost as if there had been no sound.

It was sufficient, however, to reach the ears of the crewmen waiting anxiously below and to attract the attention of everyone on deck. Millis knew it must have been heard aboard the raider, as well, but felt that little significance would be attached to it if the sound was followed by no unusual activity aboard the *Amindra*.

'Now move away from it,' he ordered.

Steps sounded on the companionway. Keeping the Sten trained on the German, Millis shot a glance down the steps. It was Penrose, looking dishevelled.

'Congratulations, Millis,' he said. 'You've brought it off.'

'There's still Freiburg,' Millis said. He gave Penrose the pistol from his waistband. 'If you'll just stay here and look after this gentleman I'll see to him.'

With the others on deck, Freiburg had looked up at the bridge at the sound of the horn. The officer he had left on the bridge was standing quietly, looking into the distance. He had sounded the horn inadvertently, Freiburg supposed. But wasn't that Captain Penrose who had just stepped into the bridge companionway? And where were his men and the English? They had finished their work and should be coming back on deck now.

Undoing his holster and taking out his pistol, he started towards the bridge. He had taken only half a dozen steps when Millis appeared in the companionway. He had the Sten flat against his leg, not wanting anyone on the raider to see it if the *Amindra* was under observation through binoculars.

Shirley saw him at the same instant Freiburg did. As Freiburg raised his pistol to fire, she flung herself forward and lunged at his arm. Such was the surprise and vigour of her attack that the pistol clattered to the deck before Freiburg could pull the trigger.

Millis tilted the Sten just enough to cover Freiburg. There were children behind the German. Spreading her arms wide, Shirley herded them out of the line of fire.

'If you'll just come along, Captain Freiburg,' Millis said, casting an anxious look at the *Adler*. Nothing seemed to have changed. Shirley's attack on Freiburg seemed to have gone unnoticed.

'What do you hope to gain?' Freiburg said calmly. 'You cannot escape the *Adler*.'

'But we have a bargaining position now, don't we?' Millis said.

'No bargaining.'

'That's for you and Penrose to decide, isn't it? I'm only along to entertain the children. Barlow, you and Graham nip below and tell some of ours to change clothes with their Jerries and get up where they can be seen. They can put the Jerries in your dormitory for now.'

The boys trotted off. Millis motioned Freiburg towards the bridge, taking care to keep the Sten between his body and the raider.

On the bridge, Freiburg said immediately, 'There will be no bargaining, Captain Penrose. What you have done is brave but useless. You cannot escape the *Adler*. You are hopelessly outgunned and she is faster.'

'But we have you, Captain Freiburg,' said Penrose.

'That will not prevent my men from opening fire if you attempt to escape.'

'That remains to be seen, doesn't it? Millis, find Briscoe and tell him to get some of my crew topside in German uniforms immediately. Things are much too quiet on deck.'

'It's already been done, sir,' Millis said.

'Has it, by God? Do you suppose you could carry on here until I send someone to relieve you?'

'Yes, sir. You might send someone to collect Barrett, though. He's under his bunk, and he'll be uncomfortable by this time!'

By now, crewmen dressed as German sailors were coming on deck, Briscoe among them. He posted them around the ship as if on guard and sent one up to the bridge with a message that the other crewmen were awaiting instructions below.

Penrose went down to speak to them, taking Freiburg with him. It took some doing but he found a man among his crew, an oiler, of roughly Freiburg's build and had him change clothing with the German.

'Sorry, Captain,' Penrose said to Freiburg in genuine apology, 'but I'm afraid there's nothing else for it.'

After Freiburg was locked in the boys' dormitory with his men and Barrett, Penrose sent the engine room crew to their posts with orders to start the engines and await a signal from the bridge. The other crewmen he instructed to remain below until further orders and took with him only the oiler in Freiburg's uniform and a deckhand who looked as if he would fit nicely into the uniform of the German officer on the bridge. The oiler found it difficult not to walk a deferential step behind Penrose until Penrose reminded him, not too gently, that he was supposed to be a captain in the German Navy.

On the bridge, Penrose gave the deckhand Millis's pistol and sent him below with the German officer to change clothes with him before locking him in with the others. That left only himself, Millis and the oiler. He no longer needed Millis but he did need a helmsman, one in a German uniform, to make a proper impression on the eyes watching from the *Adler*.

'Mr Millis,' he said. 'Will you tell Mr Briscoe to send up a helmsman and clear the deck of passengers? Oh, before you go. You needn't apologize for your behaviour to me when under cover. I realize it was necessary to maintain the illusion.'

Millis stared at him, unbelieving. Then he shrugged good-humouredly.

'I enjoyed every minute of it, sir,' he said.

He laid the Sten gun on the deck and left.

Penrose told the grinning oiler, whose face straightened

when he saw Penrose looking at him, to take the glasses and report what was happening aboard the *Adler*.

'Nothing much, sir,' the oiler said. 'They all seem to be standing about with their thumbs up their . . .' He mumbled something to round off the sentence.

Penrose felt the *Amindra* tremble and come alive. He knew the sounds of her engines could be heard across the two hundred yards of open sea separating her from the *Adler*.

'What are they doing?' he asked the oiler as the helmsman, reporting for duty, saluted.

'Salute him, you idiot, not me!' Penrose said savagely. 'And not British fashion.'

'They're moving about now, sir,' the oiler said. 'And signalling.'

'What do they want?'

'I can't read signal, sir. I'm engine room.'

The fog still loomed dead ahead. It was no closer than when Millis had first broached the notion of retaking the ship. Penrose thought it was close enough that the *Amindra* could disappear into it before the *Adler* could make her turn and gather way, though not before the raider's guns could rake his ship.

Penrose pushed the engine room telegraph to Full Ahead. The ship seemed to lurch but its acceleration was agonizingly slow. Then it began creeping towards the fog, gaining way with a ponderous deliberation that was desperately frustrating.

'What now?' Penrose demanded of the oiler, suppressing an impulse to mop his brow.

He longed for a look himself, but it would not do for the master of a captured ship to appear to be in command. Even without binoculars he could see the blinking lamp aboard the raider, sending too fast for him to read, and signal flags running up which he could not make out at

336

that distance.

'Signals all over the place, sir, and they've gone to Action Stations.'

'The flags. Is there a blue cross on a white background and a checkered yellow and black?'

That was XL, 'Stop or I fire!'

'No, sir.'

A wake was slowly building behind the *Adler* as she got under way, turning ponderously towards the *Amindra*. It was clear that the raider's officers were still puzzled and undecided what to do. And why not, Penrose thought. They could see what appeared to be their captain on the bridge of the *Amindra* and boarders wearing German uniforms in apparent control of the deck. Yet their signals were not being answered and the *Amindra* appeared to be running away. Any moment now someone aboard the *Adler* would get his wits about him and fire a warning shot across the *Amindra*'s bow.

The fog was less than two ship's lengths away. In a little over a minute the *Amindra* would be hidden by it. The *Adler* was still on her turn. Any moment now she would blossom with muzzle flashes. The tension aboard *Amindra* was palpable. It seemed that no one dared breathe. Penrose gulped in air. He tried without success to breathe normally.

The *Amindra*'s bow suddenly butted into fog so dense it seemed the ship was driving into a wall. She slid into the clammy greyness. Sunlight vanished abruptly and she was totally enveloped by a chilly gloom so thick that, looking aft, Penrose could no longer see the stern.

They were into the fog unscathed. But still a long way from being safe.

Chapter Twenty

Captain Penrose ordered a hard turn to starboard. When the *Adler* blindly opened fire, which now she most certainly would, it would be into the fog where the *Amindra* had last been visible. And if a turn were anticipated, it would most likely be to port, towards Newfoundland.

Astern the greyness was lit by expanding billows of red and orange. The roar of heavy explosions rolled over the *Amindra*. The *Adler* was close enough for the muzzle blasts of its guns as well as the rattle of smaller armaments on its deck to be heard amid the din of its exploding shells.

Penrose ordered Emergency Stations and sent the oiler down to find Briscoe and have his men get back into their own clothing. There was no longer any need or purpose for disguise.

The sounds from the *Adler* and her crashing shells fell farther astern. From the rate at which they diminished Penrose knew the *Adler* had turned to port in pursuit of her fleeing quarry. His manoeuvre had succeeded. For the moment. He was glad that Freiburg's astute tactical brain was lost to the *Adler*. With her somewhat greater speed the *Adler* would continue to port only long enough to get between the *Amindra* and the eventual safety of Newfoundland and then turn back to search along the British ship's anticipated route. Penrose ordered a 90 degree turn west. When the *Adler* returned the *Amindra* would be steaming away at right angles to the anticipated route. He would hold the heading for several hours before turning for Newfoundland.

Briscoe came to the bridge to report that the Germans had been given back their uniforms and to ask what was to be done with them.

'Leave the men in the boys' dormitory and find other accommodation for the lads,' Penrose said. 'Freiburg and his officers can be kept in cabins. Tell Dutton to sort it out. And have him tidy up my quarters. But first see to getting a new wireless antenna rigged.'

He had already considered the pros and cons of breaking radio silence once he was away from the *Adler* to report the raider's last known position to the Admiralty. Obviously, he couldn't report his own position. The *Kriegsmarine* and the *Adler* would be monitoring all wireless signals. If the Admiralty had anything already at sea or in Newfoundland to send in search of the *Adler* it would have as much chance of encountering the *Amindra* as the German raider. In a few more hours the *Amindra* would be altering course for St Johns and would be in the same general area as the *Adler*.

Penrose, in fact, no longer knew his ship's exact position. It had been some time since the last sextant observations had been taken and in the confusion of the past few hours navigation had been neglected. Penrose guessed he was some 700 miles west and north of St Johns. That would do to estimate a heading until they broke out of the fog and could take some new observations.

When the passengers were sent from the deck, Shirley had taken the boys below. Millis joined her after leaving the bridge and relaying Penrose's instructions to Briscoe. Shirley took him aside and said, 'You've got some explaining to do. Just who and what are you?'

'Mrs Millis's little . . .' Millis began, assuming his old clownish manner.

'You know how I hate that,' Shirley interrupted. 'So stop it.'

339

'I suppose I owe you that much. You did save my life, if that Freiburg chap was any sort of a shot at all. I'm Joseph Millis, really, but music-hall entertainer isn't my first profession.'

'Anyone could see that,' Shirley said, smiling. 'You weren't very good at it, except with children.'

'I'm Naval Intelligence. Have been since the war started. Working the night spots spreading rumours and running them down. Not too exciting but the drinks were free.'

'Why are you on the *Amindra*? It's the gold, isn't it? Mr Rosten wasn't telling the truth, was he?'

'I can't answer that, Shirley. Not now, anyway. And I'd appreciate your keeping any ideas you might have to yourself.'

'Well,' Shirley said, 'I'm glad you're not what I thought you were at first. I'd hate to feel the way I do about someone like Mrs Millis's favourite and only child.'

They leaned towards each other involuntarily but stopped before they touched. The boys were watching them with interest.

'It's all right, Mr Millis,' Barlow called. 'They do it regular in the cinema.'

'Some other time,' Millis whispered to a blushing Shirley. 'I've work to do.'

He went to Barrett's cabin, which Rosten had not yet occupied, and sent an armed seaman to fetch the First Officer from the boys' dormitory. Barrett's head was a mess.

'Looks nasty,' Millis said. 'You should see Dr Grimes.'

'It'd be you if you hadn't taken me by surprise,' Barrett growled, defiant to the last.

'Don't get your back up. I may be able to help you.'

'Doctor as well as Intelligence, are you?'

'You know what I'm getting at. I don't know if you're German or British but either way espionage, murder and

340

sabotage are all punishable by death. If you'll tell me how your lot got on to the *Amindra*'s mission I'll see what can be done for you.'

'Get stuffed. And I'm not German. Or British.'

'What the hell are you, then?'

'French-Canadian,' Barrett said, 'and proud of it.'

'Canada's British.'

'I said *French*-Canadian. I've no use for the bloody Krauts but even less for you Limeys.'

'You don't sound French-Canadian.'

'I worked at it. In Montreal a French accent gets you a sweeper's job.'

'You'll wish you had that sweeper's job. They'll get it all out of you in a proper interrogation, you know. And you won't have gained anything. But if you'll just give me a clue I'll . . .'

'Guard,' Barrett called, knocking on the closed door of the cabin. 'Get me out of here. I've nothing to say.' He sneered at Millis, who shrugged. Even now the man's arrogance was unimpaired.

Millis went back to Shirley and the boys. He hadn't really expected to learn anything and interrogation wasn't his job, actually. But he had thought it just possible that if he talked to Barrett – Gannion – before the Canadian had prepared himself for a full-scale grilling he might learn something useful. Of course, he had already learned something useful. Somewhere in that small, closed group privy to the *Amindra*'s secret was a German agent. It would be someone else's job to discover whom.

After two hours on its westerly course, the *Amindra* turned a point southward in dense fog, a ghost ship in a ghostly maze. The thump of her engines, the churning of the screw, even the click of boot heels on the deck, seemed

341

amplified to ears straining for the sound of the questing raider.

Penrose sent word to his passengers that he would be pleased if they joined him for dinner in the saloon. He included Millis in the invitation though he still had misgivings about him, despite his role in retaking the *Amindra*. One did not have to like a man to admire his competence, Penrose thought.

The *Amindra* had seven two-passenger cabins, only five of which were occupied, and those by only one person each. Barrett's and Nutley's quarters were also available. Dutton, pleased to have duties employing the skills of his *Empress* days, managed to accommodate everyone, including the boys, though the children were of necessity crowded. He put Captain Freiburg in one of the passenger cabins and the two German officers in another. He knew without asking that Captain Penrose would wish the German captain to have a cabin all to himself. Though he would not have presumed to suggest it, he was pleased when Lady Anne insisted on sharing her cabin with Miss Hunt. Even Mr Donahue wanted to help and agreed to take several of the youngsters in his cabin. Dutton thought him unusually quiet and thoughtful and, strangely enough, almost likeable. Dr Grimes and Rosten he moved to the vacant ship's officers' cabins to make more room topside for the boys and Millis.

By mid-afternoon the new wireless antenna had been rigged. Before dressing for dinner, Penrose composed a signal for the Admiralty. He gave the time and co-ordinates, as nearly as he could estimate them, for the *Adler*'s position when last he saw the raider, as well as its assumed name, *Ole Lavrans*, and details of its disguise. The Admiralty, he knew, would deduce that the *Amindra* was safe for the moment and in the same general area. He went to the wireless room to see it sent and ordered radio silence resumed until further orders.

Despite everyone's awareness that a serious threat still existed, the mood in the saloon was festive. Penrose tempted fate by breaking out the champagne he had intended to open the last night before making port in Halifax. Lady Anne wore her long dress and Millis looked surprisingly presentable in jacket and tie, with his hair neatly brushed and his shoes burnished. Rosten, without being asked, gave up his usual place next to Shirley to Millis. They obviously wanted to sit together.

Only Donahue did not share the pervasive mood. He felt very much the outsider and, if not actually excluded, at best tolerated. He had contributed nothing to the retaking of the ship. Shirley, like himself a neutral, had played no small part in liberating the *Amindra*; and even the children, four of them at any rate, had actively participated, while he had loudly protested his neutrality to the Germans and complained bitterly when his car was jettisoned. How trivial that must have seemed to all of them when so much was at stake.

Everyone here had been willing to risk their lives. Except himself. He knew he would not have lifted a finger to save the *Amindra* from the Germans had he been offered the opportunity to do so. It was not his war. He was an American, a neutral. Yet it had not mattered to the Germans, not really. The fact was, and he could not deny it, neutrality did not matter to them if it interfered with their plans. For the first time he had an inkling of what it must be like to be locked in a life and death struggle with such a powerful and implacable enemy.

God, how he admired these people he had once held so lightly: Captain Penrose, sitting there as if on a peace-time cruise; Lady Anne who had openly shown her scorn of the Germans and never lost her poise; Millis, the music-hall buffoon who had organized their daring escape; Rosten,

343

the dry functionary who had revealed unsuspected depths of courage and initiative. And Shirley Hunt, hardly more than a girl, who knew more than he about the myth of neutrality.

He wished more desperately than he had ever wished for anything that he had been a part of it all.

He had never before been the excluded one. Always he had been the centre of attention, the one being catered to, listened to, sought out, envied or admired. Just as never before had he been helpless in the face of naked authority as he had when locked in the dormitory. Was it just possible these people knew something he did not? None of them thought England would go down. It did not matter to them that Germany had the guns and the generals. The Germans had had the guns and the upper hand this morning, too, but a few Englishmen, four of them children, had outwitted and defeated them. It was something to think about.

'You're very quiet,' said Shirley, who most of the evening had been devoting her attention to Millis.

'For once I've got nothing to say,' Donahue admitted wryly.

The *Amindra* drove on through the night in unremitting fog. Penrose slept in his clothes, having changed out of his dress uniform, and spent part of every watch on the bridge, listening for the ominous sound of an approaching ship. The *Amindra* would be invisible to the *Adler*, and vice versa, in the impenetrable darkness, but not unheard if the raider were close enough. Should he hear the sound of ship's engines, he thought, he would stop the *Amindra*'s and become soundless as well as invisible.

Morning came, and the ebony through which the *Amindra* felt her way changed slowly to the drenched grey into which she had first escaped. The fog appeared to Penrose to be thinning. He wished it would persist in its dense, palpable, enveloping presence all the way to Canada, but knew it was a vain hope. But even were the fog to lift completely he thought their chances now of evading the *Adler* were excellent. They had been following their separate courses for eighteen hours and the ocean was vast. Yet he found himself constantly alert to sounds, speaking in low tones and placing his feet softly when he walked. He must hear the *Adler* before he himself was heard.

All aboard the *Amindra*, even the boys, felt the same tension. They spoke almost in whispers when they spoke at all. Most of the time they listened.

The fog became more a veil than a cloak, and more white than grey. From the bridge Penrose could see a cable's length, two hundred yards, in every direction. He kept the stern gun and its crew ready. If the *Adler* appeared out of the mist, unlikely as that might seem now, he intended to draw first blood.

Lady Anne strolled the deck, alone. Though she would soon be witnessing the final reality of her son's death when she saw his coffin being lowered into Canadian earth, she felt at peace. Tony hadn't got his chance at the Hun but she had stood in for him, and in a small way contributed to the *Amindra*'s victory. It was far more than she had ever expected when she set out on her melancholy voyage.

Rosten was taking the air, too, his hands clasped behind him, walking as if measuring each step. He, too, felt an inner peace he had not anticipated at the beginning of the voyage. The gold was safe and so were the children and he was to a considerable degree responsible for it. Marjorie would have been proud of him.

Donahue, still uncharacteristically withdrawn, had returned to his cabin immediately after breakfast when the boys sharing his quarters had gone, and was nowhere to be seen.

345

Captain Freiburg was in the bows, looking off into the fog. Penrose had ordered him locked up only during the hours of darkness. He felt sorry for the man. To have such a prize as the *Amindra* virtually in his grasp and see it slip away must be heartbreaking. But if Freiburg felt any self-pity it was far from obvious. His back was as straight as when he first came aboard the *Amindra*.

Freiburg's posture did not reflect his inner feelings. He had failed in his duty, outmanoeuvred by a deceptively clownish British agent, a few schoolboys and a handful of unarmed seamen. Though they had been determined and resourceful, he had only himself to blame. Not the Canadian for letting himself be taken by the man Millis, nor Schramm for letting the *Amindra* slip into the fog unscathed. As commander he was responsible for all. He alone had let the war's greatest prize slip through his fingers. He would gladly give his life to change that. He might yet have the opportunity, he thought. If by good fortune and the skill of Schramm the *Adler* found the *Amindra*, he would disrupt the Britisher's gun crew by any means at hand and hope Schramm could retake the ship without seriously damaging it.

Millis and Shirley had the boys out on deck – the cabins were too crowded for them to remain inside – but no shouts or laughter arose from their desultory play.

Then it came.

The distant but unmistakable sound of a ship's engine.

Millis was the first to hear it. He raised his hand for silence.

The fog somehow made it difficult to know from which direction the sound came, except that it was not astern. The others heard then, and stood frozen in the postures in which awareness caught them: Lady Anne in the act of looking up at the bridge; Rosten with one foot falling precisely in front of the other; Shirley with her mouth open to speak to Barlow; Freiburg reaching in his tunic for the pipe that was not there.

Shielded by the glass of the bridge, Penrose saw the reaction of those on deck before hearing the sound himself. He opened the door and listened.

The tableau dissolved, everyone on deck looking in the direction from which their separate instincts told them the sound was coming. Seamen emerged from companionways to stare at the bridge. Freiburg looked back at the bridge quickly and began making his way nonchalantly towards the stern, where the DEMS gun crew had assumed their stations. Penrose ordered the engines stopped and, hurrying down to the deck, sent an armed seaman to collect Freiburg and escort him and the two other German officers to the dormitory with the rest of the prisoners.

So much for that, Freiburg thought. If it was the *Adler* and there was a fight, he was not sure he wanted to survive it. Nonsense, he thought ruefully. Of course he wanted to survive. He had always been prepared to die in battle, he was a sailor of the Reich, but only if such were the fortunes of war. He was not such a coward as to be unable to face the consequences of failure. If, indeed, he had failed, he had been defeated by a worthy opponent.

Penrose had everyone except the gun crew leave the deck and passengers and crew were urged, *sotto voce*, on no account to make any loud noises. Sound carried across water as if amplified.

The engine noise grew louder and more localized. Off the port bow. The stern gun traversed and aimed point-blank into the gossamer which draped all but a few hundred yards of the *Amindra*'s world. The fog was touched with shadow deep within its recesses off the bow as the sounds grew nearer. The shadow darkened and gained substance but not outline. Now the blurred extremities drew in and sharpened. The stern gun was dead on it. Should he order it to commence firing? Penrose wondered. Best not to. Firing blindly might do little damage and would be promptly answered by broadsides. He must wait until the gun crew could see its target. The first round into the rudder area and, if there was time, the next into the bridge.

And now the outline coalesced into the unmistakable silhouette of a ship, and a towering prow emerged as if through layers of translucent gauze, the foremost point clearly visible and all behind it less so until two hundred yards from the *Amindra* stood the armoured sides of a squat cruiser.

And at its bow fluttered the British ensign.

Penrose pulled the lanyard of the ship's horn again and again. Passengers and crew poured out on deck. The cheering was spontaneous, and grew into an orgy of sound and back-slapping. Unregretted the tension of the last few hours dissolved away.

Two and a half days later, Captain Penrose stood beside the gangplank, looking out over Halifax harbour and waiting to say goodbye to the passengers who would soon be disembarking.

The cruiser had hove to within fifty yards of the *Amindra* after emerging from the fog. Its captain had come aboard to hear personally from Penrose a full account of his ship's encounter with the German raider. Before he returned to his own ship, the German prisoners and Barrett were already being transferred to the cruiser. Captain Freiburg had shaken hands with Penrose before climbing down into a waiting boat, remembering with rueful irony how a British captain had done the same aboard the supply ship *Nordmark* when Freiburg was the captor.

The warship had reached the *Amindra* so quickly

348

because only a few days earlier she had encountered the *Ole Lavrans* and let her go, only to learn, after an exchange of signals with the Admiralty, that she had permitted a German raider to escape. She had been searching for the raider ever since and instead had found the *Amindra*.

A day and a half out of Halifax, two Canadian corvettes and a steady cover of land-based aircraft had replaced the cruiser as the *Amindra*'s escort. And now she lay moored with the hatch of Number 2 hold open and a crane lifting its precious cargo to the wharf, where Benjamin Rosten stood with a cluster of Bank of Canada officials watching the crates being deposited gently on wooden pallets. Near by, two old buses, a chauffeured limousine and a Royal Canadian Air Force staff car were parked one behind the other.

Rosten was surprised that he felt no sense of triumph at having assisted in a major accomplishment of the war. Rather he was curiously at peace, and the emptiness left by Marjorie's death was no longer pervasive. He still mourned her but no longer felt that life had no further meaning for him. He had been useful and would be again. Of one thing he was sure. When his job was done he would not return to his position with the Bank of England. If he was not wanted in any branch of the military he would find something else that would help the war effort. Perhaps with the Children's Overseas Reception Board. Marjorie would like that. England's future lay in the hands of boys like Barlow and Graham and the others. He would do all he could to ensure that future was preserved. True, children did not respond warmly to him but it did not matter. With his gift for detail and ability at organization he could serve in a capacity which did not require personal contact.

Lady Anne stopped to say goodbye to Donahue before

349

disembarking. The American was still in his cabin. He had been almost a recluse during the final days of the voyage. He seemed to her to be embarrassed by the cordiality of her farewell, as if he could not believe it was merited.

'After we've won this war,' she told Penrose before she started down the gangplank, 'I hope to sail with you again. But on the *Empress*.'

'I'll look forward to that day with the greatest of pleasure,' he said, and escorted her to the staff car.

An RCAF officer saluted and opened the door while the enlisted driver ran to open the boot for Dutton, who was carrying Lady Anne's luggage. Penrose watched the car out of sight before returning to his place by the gangplank.

The boys came next, escorted by Shirley and Millis. The *Amindra* would not be sailing until the following evening and Shirley had asked for a day and a night ashore for them. She had informed Penrose that she would be returning to England aboard the *Amindra* if it was sailing directly back to the British Isles from New York. If not, she would return to London by whatever means were available. He had wondered if it was because of her obvious attachment to Millis. She must have sensed that because she said, 'I want to do my bit to fight the Germans until the United States gets into the war.'

Millis had his suitcase. He was returning to England by military aircraft. Walking behind the two files of boys, he balanced the suitcase he was carrying on his shoulder and put his free arm around Shirley's waist. The boys filed into the buses. Shirley got into one, Millis into the other. Penrose looked on as the buses drove away, feeling elderly and trying to remember how it had been when first he and Nellie were in love.

Only Donahue's limousine remained on the dock. He was flying to Washington in a plane President Roosevelt had sent for him. Penrose looked impatiently towards the passenger accommodation. There was still much to be done before he himself could go ashore and he resented the delay.

Donahue emerged at last, the briefcase chained to his wrist. It dragged at his arm. In London he had put a few of the choicer pieces of his Georgian silver cutlery in it along with his secret papers. Two seamen followed with his luggage.

He walked slowly towards Penrose, hesitated and stopped. He appeared to Penrose to be in the throes of some inner conflict. He turned suddenly and went to the rail away from the quayside. He unlocked the chain attaching the briefcase to his wrist, raised the case and dropped it over the side. He stood watching the bubbles break the surface of the deep, dark water where it had disappeared. When he returned to Penrose he was smiling and his step was brisk.

'I'll say this for the voyage, Captain,' he said. 'It wasn't dull. And damned educational.'

He looked as if he wanted to add something. Penrose waited. He had seen the Special Envoy jettison the briefcase with its damning conclusions. Now, Penrose supposed, he would apologize for having so badly misjudged British determination and resourcefulness.

'About that car,' Donahue said. 'It served me right. I didn't have permission to bring it.'

Penrose watched the limousine drive away. The dock beside the *Amindra* was empty now except for Rosten, the Bank of Canada officials and the cargo workers. Rosten saw Penrose looking down at them and waved. Penrose responded with a salute.

'Mr Briscoe,' he called. 'Carry on.'

He went to his cabin and sat down in the big, familiar chair. Turning his head, he looked at the photographs over his bunk and the needlepoint motto.

'Keep then the Sea, which is the Wall of England, and then is England kept in God's own hands.'

He leaned back and closed his eyes. For the first time since the war began, he did not miss the *Empress* at all.